Praise for Linda Goodnight and her novels

"[A] warm and wonderful romance."
—*RT Book Reviews* on *Home to Crossroads Ranch*

"Goodnight's emotion-packed story celebrates
accepting life with its laughter, sorrow and love."
—*RT Book Reviews* on *The Baby Bond*

"A truly inspiring story."
—*RT Book Reviews* on *The Last Bridge Home*

"This terrific book is touching
and definitely a keeper."
—*RT Book Reviews* on *Missionary Daddy*

D1550880

LINDA GOODNIGHT

Home to Crossroads Ranch

and

The Baby Bond

H HARLEQUIN® LOVE INSPIRED® CLASSICS

Recycling programs
for this product may
not exist in your area.

ISBN-13: 978-0-373-60603-0

HOME TO CROSSROADS RANCH AND THE BABY BOND
Copyright © 2014 by Harlequin Books S.A.

The publisher acknowledges the copyright holder
of the individual works as follows:

HOME TO CROSSROADS RANCH
Copyright © 2009 by Linda Goodnight

THE BABY BOND
Copyright © 2009 by Linda Goodnight

www.Harlequin.com

Printed in U.S.A.

CONTENTS

Books by Linda Goodnight

Love Inspired

LINDA GOODNIGHT

Winner of a RITA® Award for excellence in inspirational fiction, Linda Goodnight has also won a Booksellers' Best Award, an ACFW Book of the Year Award and a Reviewers' Choice Award from *RT Book Reviews*. Linda has appeared on the Christian bestseller list, and her romance novels have been translated into more than a dozen languages. Active in orphan ministry, this former nurse and teacher enjoys writing fiction that carries a message of hope and light in a sometimes dark world. She and her husband live in Oklahoma. Visit her website at www.lindagoodnight.com. To browse a current listing of Linda Goodnight's titles, please visit www.Harlequin.com.

Home to Crossroads Ranch

For by grace you have been saved through faith;
and that not of yourselves: it is the gift of God;
not of works, lest any man should boast.
—*Ephesians* 2:8–9

In memory of my brother-in-law, Bill, who loved kids better than anyone and who always carried a pocketful of quarters or Tootsie Rolls to "magically" pull from behind their ears. The world is a sadder place without your booming laugh, your boundless love and generosity, and your pure joy in living for Christ.
As you would always say in parting, until we meet again, "Be cheerful."

Chapter One

Nate Del Rio heard screams the minute he stepped out of his Super Crew Cab and started up the flower-lined sidewalk leading to Rainy Jernagen's house. He double-checked the address scribbled on the back of a bill for horse feed. Sure enough, this was the place.

Adjusting his Stetson against a gust of March wind, he rang the doorbell expecting the noise to subside. It didn't.

Somewhere inside the modest, tidy-looking brick house at least two kids were screaming their heads off in what sounded to his experienced ears like fits of temper. A television blasted out Saturday-morning cartoons.

He punched the doorbell again. Instead of the expected *ding-dong,* a raucous alternative Christian rock band added a few more decibels to the noise level.

Nate shifted the toolbox to his opposite hand and considered running for his life while he had the chance.

Too late. The bright red door whipped open. Nate's mouth fell open with it.

When the men's ministry coordinator from Bible Fellowship had called him, he'd somehow gotten the impression that he was coming to help a little old schoolteacher. In his mind, that meant the kind who only drove to school and church and had a big, fat cat.

Not so. The woman standing before him with taffy-blond hair sprouting out from a disheveled ponytail couldn't possibly be any older than his thirty-one years. A big blotch of something purple stained the front of her white sweatshirt, and she was barefoot. Plus, she had a crying baby on each hip and a little red-haired girl hanging on one leg, bawling like a sick calf. And there wasn't a cat in sight.

What had he gotten himself into?

"May I help you?" she asked over the racket. Her blue-gray eyes were a little too unfocused and bewildered for his comfort.

Raising his voice, he asked, "Are you Ms. Jernagen?"

"Yes," she said cautiously. "I'm Rainy Jernagen. And you are…?"

"Nate Del Rio."

She blinked, uncomprehending, all the while jiggling both babies up and down. One grabbed a hunk of her hair. She flinched, her head angling to one side, as she said, still cautiously, "Okaaay."

Nate reached out and untwined the baby's sticky fingers.

A relieved smile rewarded him. "Thanks. Is there something I can help you with?"

He hefted the red toolbox to chest level so she could see it. "From the Handyman Ministry. Jack Martin called. Said you had a washer problem."

Understanding dawned. "Oh my goodness. Yes. I'm so sorry. You aren't what I expected. Please forgive me."

She wasn't what he expected, either. Not in the least. Young and with a houseful of kids. He suppressed a shiver. Kids, even grown ones, could drive a person to distraction. He should know. His adult sister and brother were, at this moment, making his life as miserable as possible. The worst part was they did it all the time. Only this morning his sister Janine had finally packed up and gone back to Sal, giving Nate a few days' reprieve.

"Come in, come in," the woman was saying. "It's been a crazy morning, what with the babies showing up at 3 a.m. and Katie having a sick stomach. Then while I was doing the laundry, the washing machine went crazy. Water everywhere." She jerked her chin toward the inside of the house. "You're truly a godsend."

He wasn't so sure about that, but he'd signed up for his church's ministry to help single women and the elderly with those pesky little handyman chores like oil changes and leaky faucets. Most of his visits had been to older ladies who plied him with sweet tea and jars of homemade jam and talked about the good old days while he replaced a fuse or unstopped the sink. And their houses had been quiet. Real quiet.

Rainy Jernagen stepped back, motioning him in, and Nate very cautiously entered a room that should have had flashing red lights and a Danger Zone sign.

Toys littered the living room like it was Christmas morning. An overturned cereal bowl flowed milk onto a coffee table. Next to a playpen crowding one wall, a green package belched out disposable diapers. Similarly, baby clothes were strewn, along with a couple of kids, on the couch and floor. In a word, the place was a wreck.

"The washer is back this way behind the kitchen. Watch your step. It's slippery."

More than slippery. Nate kicked his way through the living room and the kitchen area. Though the kitchen actually appeared much tidier than the rest, he still caught the slow seepage of water coming from somewhere beyond the wall. The shine of liquid glistening on beige tile led them straight to the utility room.

"I turned the faucets off behind the washer when this first started, but a tubful still managed to pump out onto the floor." She hoisted the babies higher on her hip and spoke to a young boy sitting on the floor. "Joshua, get out of those suds."

"But they're pretty, Miss Rainy." The brown-haired boy with bright blue eyes grinned up at her, extending a handful of bubbles. Light reflected off each droplet. "See the rainbows? There's always a rainbow, like you said. A rainbow behind the rain."

Rainy smiled at the child. "Yes, there is. But right now, Mr. Del Rio needs to get in here to fix the washer. It's a little crowded for all of us." She was right about that. The space was no bigger than a small bathroom. "Can I get you to take the babies to the playpen while I show him around?"

"I'll take them, Miss Rainy." An older boy with a serious face and brown plastic glasses entered the room. Treading carefully, he came forward and took both babies, holding them against his slight chest. Another child appeared behind him, this one a girl with very blond hair and eyes the exact blue of the boy she'd called Joshua. How many children did this woman have, anyway? Six?

A heavy, smothery feeling pressed against his airway. Six kids?

Before he could dwell on that disturbing thought, a scream of sonic proportions rent the soap-fragrant air. He whipped around, ready to protect and defend.

The little blond girl and the redhead were going at it.

"It's mine." Blondie tugged hard on a doll.

"It's mine. Will said so." To add emphasis to her demand, the redhead screamed bloody murder. "Miss Rainy!"

About that time, Joshua decided to skate across the suds, and slammed into the far wall next to a door that probably opened into the garage. He grabbed his big toe and sent up a howl. Water sloshed as Rainy rushed forward and gathered him into her arms.

"Rainy!" Blondie screamed again.

"Rainy!" the redhead yelled.

Nate cast a glance at the garage exit and considered a fast escape.

Lord, I'm here to do a good thing. Can You help me out a little?

Rainy, her clothes now wet, somehow managed to take the doll from the fighting girls while snuggling Joshua against her side. The serious-looking boy stood in the doorway, a baby on each hip, taking in the chaos.

"Come on, Emma," he said to Blondie. "I'll make you some chocolate milk." So they went, slip-sliding out of the flooded room.

Four down, two to go.

Nate clunked his toolbox onto the washer and tried to ignore the chaos. Not an easy task, but one he'd learned to deal with as a boy. As an adult, he did everything possible to avoid this kind of madness. The Lord had a sense of humor sending him to this particular house.

"I apologize, Mr. Del Rio," Rainy said, shoving at the wads of hair that hung around her face like Spanish moss.

"Call me Nate. I'm not that much older than you." Being the longtime patriarch of his family, he might feel seventy, but he wasn't.

"Okay, Nate. And I'm Rainy. Really, it's not usually this bad. I can't thank you enough for coming over. I tried to get a plumber, but today being Saturday…" She shrugged, letting the obvious go unsaid. No one could get a plumber on the weekend.

"No problem." He removed his white Stetson and placed it next to the toolbox. What was he supposed to say? That he loved wading through dirty soapsuds and listening to kids scream and cry? Not likely.

Rainy stood with an arm around each of the remaining children—the rainbow boy and the redhead. Her look of embarrassment had him feeling sorry for her. All these kids and no man around to help. With this many, she'd never find another husband, he was sure of that. Who would willingly take on a boatload of kids?

After a minute, Rainy and the remaining pair left the room and he got to work. Wiggling the machine away from the wall wasn't easy. Even with all the water on the floor, a significant amount remained in the tub. This leftover liquid sloshed and gushed at regular intervals. In minutes, his boots were dark with moisture. No problem there. As a rancher, his boots were often dark with lots of things, the best of which was water.

On his haunches, he surveyed the back of the machine where hoses and cords and metal parts twined together like a nest of water moccasins.

As he investigated each hose in turn, he once more felt a presence in the room. Pivoting on his heels, he discovered the two boys squatting beside him, attention glued to the back of the washer. Blondie hovered in the background.

"A busted hose?" the oldest one asked, pushing up his glasses.

"Most likely."

"I coulda fixed it but Rainy wouldn't let me."

"That so?"

"Yeah. Maybe. If someone would show me."

Nate suppressed a smile. "What's your name?"

"Will. This here's my brother, Joshua." He yanked a thumb at the younger one. "He's nine. I'm eleven. My sister's Emma. She's seven. You go to Miss Rainy's church?"

"I do, but it's a big church. I don't think we've met before."

"She's nice. Most of the time. She never hits us or anything, and we've been here for six months."

It occurred to Nate then that these were not Rainy's children. The kids called her Miss Rainy, not Mom, and according to Will they had not been here forever. But what was a young, single woman doing with all these kids? Foster care? Nah, they didn't let singles do that. Did they?

Rainy frantically tossed toys into a basket in an effort to clear up some of the mess. She never let things get like this. Of all the days to have a stranger come into her home. A young, nice-looking stranger at that.

Pausing with a stuffed bear against her cheek, she chuckled. The poor man looked as bewildered as if he'd walked into the *Twilight Zone.*

She'd had to call upon the Handyman Ministry before but her friendly rescuers had been older fatherly types, not a lanky young cowboy in starched jeans and boots with stubble on his chin and a dangerous set of dimples that split his cheeks like long parentheses. Killer dimples.

She tossed the bear into the basket and went for a sponge to soak up the coffee-table mess.

With dimples like that, Nate Del Rio was probably like every other guy she'd noticed in the last two years—married.

She heaved a heavy sigh and dabbed at the spilled milk. For years, she'd prayed for a godly husband, but the Lord didn't appear interested in her single, lonely status or in the fact that she wanted kids. Lots of kids. The dates she'd had never filled the bill and after a while, she'd given up the dating game entirely. It was too stressful anyway.

If she couldn't have a husband and kids, she'd settle for kids only.

But she wasn't dead, and Nate Del Rio was an attractive man.

She clicked off the blasting television and then handed each of the babies in the playpen a rattle. Precious little lambs. They looked so bewildered by this new, unfamiliar environment. As soon as she had a minute, she needed to hold and rock them, give them the comfort they craved and deserved.

With the TV off, the room had grown a little too quiet. She glanced into the bedroom to find Katie sprawled on the floor, coloring. Good. Maybe her stomachache was gone. Now, where were the others?

With another quick, reassuring glance at the babies, she headed for the laundry room. The sibling trio was naturally nosy, but they also hungered for attention from any obliging adult.

Sure enough, Joshua and Will were squatting in an inch of water, peppering Nate with questions. Seven-year-old Emma, the blond charmer, hung over the man's back, her slender arms looped around his neck like a small, friendly boa constrictor.

"Emma," Rainy said gently. "It's hard for Nate to

work with you hanging on him. Why don't you and the boys come out of here and leave him alone?"

"But, Miss Rainy, he's teaching me how to change a hose so I can do it next time." Will's eyes were dead serious behind his glasses. That was the trouble with Will. He was too serious. He seldom laughed, didn't play like a normal kid and considered his younger siblings to be his responsibility. Even after six months of consistent, loving care, he hadn't loosened up. The boy needed a strong man in his life, one of the reasons Rainy worried about adopting him and his siblings, though she longed to do so. She could love and nurture, but she could never be a male role model. She could, however, expose him to good ones and pray that would be enough.

The cowboy handyman twisted his head in her direction. "He's a quick learner."

Rainy beamed as if the compliment was for her. She saw the flush of pleasure on Will's cheeks and decided she liked Nate Del Rio. "He is. Thanks."

She bent to unwind Emma from the man's neck. "This one is a charmer, but also a pest at times." With a counselor and lots of prayers, they were working on Emma's weak personal boundaries. "Come on, Emma. I need help with the babies."

Emma came, but gazed longingly at the cowboy's back. "He's nice."

Rainy stood in the doorway for a minute, watching and listening to Nate's low voice explaining the great mysteries of washing machines to the two rapt boys.

His patience with them solidified her conclusion that he had kids of his own.

She chided herself for being disappointed. She did not covet another woman's husband. She simply wanted one of her own.

"Is there anything you need before I go on about my business?" she asked.

Without turning, he shook his head. "Got all the help I need right now. Thanks."

She wasn't sure how he meant that, but she let it go and headed back to the disaster area that had once been her home.

By the time she'd set things to right, fed both babies and put them down for a nap, Katie had thrown up again. Wearily, she cleaned up the mess, took the child's temperature and debated calling the doctor. The last thing any of them needed was a virus spreading through the house.

Going to her bedroom to change the now disgusting sweat suit, she happened to glance in the mirror. The Wicked Witch of the West stared back.

Bags the size of carry-on luggage puffed beneath her eyes. Her hair shot out in every direction. She slapped at it. Had she combed it at all this morning?

With a growing sense of chagrin, she knew she hadn't. She had shoved the shoulder-length mass into a scrunchie in the wee hours of the morning when the social worker arrived with the babies. After that she never made it back to bed because Katie had started throwing up. Then the washer had sprung a leak and she'd been too busy to care about how she looked.

Horrid. She looked horrid. Horror-movie horrid.

No wonder the kids were crying. She was tempted to do the same.

Quickly yanking away the scrunchie along with a few hairs, Rainy ran a brush over her head and put the ponytail up again. Better.

She leaned into the mirror and grimaced. Makeup. Fast.

She dabbed a little concealer under each eye, mostly to no avail, stroked some mascara on thick lashes and added a hint of pink lip gloss. She was no beauty, but she normally tried to accent her best features, thick lashes and a tilted, full mouth. Today she'd settle for not frightening small children.

"Miss Rainy!"

This would have to do. Without a backward glance, she rushed toward the sound of Katie's voice.

The child lay on the couch where Rainy had left her, a pink Hello Kitty blanket up to her chin.

"What is it, punkin? Are you feeling sick again?"

"I want a Pop-Tart."

"Are you sure that's such a good idea? How about something gentle on your tummy first and then the Pop-Tart later."

A million russet freckles stood out on the sad, pale face. "Okay."

Rainy entered the kitchen as Nate Del Rio and the boys entered from the opposite end. Nate glanced up at her, surprise registering in his eyes.

"You look—" He seemed to catch himself, for which she would be eternally grateful, and said instead, "We're all finished. If you'll hand us a mop, we'll sop up some of the water for you."

"Oh, goodness no. Don't bother. I'll do the sopping up. You've done enough." She whipped toward the broom closet and took out a sponge mop. "Why don't you have a seat and let me get you some cookies and milk."

Those dimples of his activated. Killer dimples. Goodness.

"Cookies and milk? Sounds great. My breakfast wore off after the stop at Milly Jenkins's."

"Milly?" Rainy propped the mop against the wall, only to have it taken by Will, who disappeared into the laundry room with faithful Joshua by his side. "Doesn't she play the organ at church?"

"Yep. Nice lady. Her old Mercury needed new spark plugs."

Rainy took down two glasses and filled them with cold milk, then added milk to the ongoing grocery list posted on the fridge. "This ministry is a real blessing to people, Nate. I hope you men who volunteer realize that."

"It's a blessing to us, too," he said simply, and she liked him for the sentiment. Nice guy. No wonder some smart woman had snapped him up like the last chocolate truffle.

With a plate of yesterday's homemade double chocolate chip cookies in hand, she joined him at the round glass table. She still questioned her sanity for buying a glass dining table with so many children coming and going, but other than the persistent presence of small fingerprints, the glass had held up well so far.

Nate reached for a cookie, bit, chewed. "Wow. Powerful."

"I hope that means good. I tend to be a little heavy-handed on the chocolate, especially during high-stress days."

"With all these little ones underfoot, those are probably pretty frequent." He sipped at his milk, managing not to create a milk mustache. "What is this anyway? A day care?"

Rainy broke an edge off a moist cookie and held it between thumb and finger. "I'm a foster mom."

"They let singles do that?"

"The Department of Human Services is desperate for foster moms. So, yes. They do."

"That explains it, then."

She laughed. "Explains what? The total chaos?"

He had the grace to look guilty. "Well…"

"Today is unusual. You see, I normally take on only school-age children because I'm a teacher. I have to work. But last night, actually early this morning, I got an emergency call from the social worker about the two babies."

"Does that happen often?"

"Most calls do come at night, unfortunately. Night-time seems to be when families fall apart. Drugs, drinking, and in this case, those eighteen-month-old twins were found alone in a car outside a casino."

She didn't mention the ongoing problem faced by the beleaguered social worker. There were not enough foster homes to care for all the needy children. And Rainy had trouble saying no, regardless of how full her house might be.

"The babies were in the car? While their mother was in the casino?"

"Yes. She'd been there for hours."

His horrified look matched her own reaction. "It's still cold outside."

March might be springtime, but at night the Oklahoma temperature tumbled to freezing.

"I know. Very cold, not to mention dangerous as all get out. Anyone could have stolen those children." She popped the bite of cookie into her mouth and almost sighed at the rich, gooey chocolate flavor. "That's why I agreed to take them until the social worker can find another placement, hopefully today."

"Brutal."

He could say that again. Foster care was not for the faint of heart. She'd heard some hair-raising tales and encountered far too many broken children, the exact reason she persevered. God had planted a mission inside her to make a difference in these forgotten kids' lives. And with God's help, she was succeeding, one child at a time.

"Another cookie?" She pushed the plate toward him. "Or will your wife be upset if you spoil your lunch with sweets?"

She hoped the question was as subtle as she wanted it to be.

As he chewed, Nate shook his head from side to side. "Nope. No problem there."

Okay, so she wanted to know for sure. Still playing innocent, she asked, "She doesn't mind?"

"She doesn't exist."

It took Rainy two beats to comprehend.

Nate Del Rio with the killer dimples was single.

Chapter Two

If there was one thing Rainy never wanted to be, it was a desperate, husband-hunting woman. So she refused to be happy that the handsome cowboy sitting across from her was unmarried. He was what he was. And so was she.

After she'd hung out her shingle to be a foster mother, with the intention of adopting as many kids as the Lord saw fit, she'd put aside her dreams of a husband. Mostly. If God dropped the right guy into her lap, she wouldn't argue. She just wasn't going out looking anymore.

"So how long have you attended Bible Fellowship?" Nate was asking.

"Since I moved here five years ago. It's a great church, lots of outreach to the needy, which I think is paramount, plus I love the small-group Bible studies. And the kids' ministry, of course."

"Of course." One side of his mouth quirked. "So you're not from around here, then?"

"Tulsa."

Both eyebrows joined the quirked lips. "City girl."

"I am not!" She leaned back in her chair, saw he was teasing, and laughed. "Well, not entirely. I like the smaller town life. That's why I took the job at Robert E. Lee."

"Summervale isn't too small anymore."

"No, but a good mix of small town and big city, don't you think?"

"Mostly. Traffic's gotten snarly since they put in the mall."

"Nothing like Tulsa at rush hour."

He shuddered. "Spare me that. Three cars on a country road are enough for me. What grade you teach?"

"Second. Five years, and I can't imagine doing anything else. Kids that age are a hoot—their wiggles, their gap-toothed smiles, their concrete, literal way of looking at the world."

He glanced toward the living room, where the children had adjourned. Mercifully, the house had settled into a quieter rhythm with only a now lower rumble of Cartoon Network and an occasional *shh* or giggle from one of the foursome.

"You like kids." His statement sounded a lot like an accusation.

"Crazy about them." Feeling no need to justify what was as natural as breathing, Rainy took another sip of milk. "What do you do, besides rush to the rescue of stressed-out women and their washing machines?"

"Ranch."

"Really? A real ranch, like with horses and cows?"

"You *are* a city girl."

"Am not," she said mildly. "So *do* you?"

"Have horses and cows? Sure. Mostly cattle since that's how I make my living. Angus beef. But I keep a few horses for fun. I mostly use a Mule for the real work these days."

Rainy leaned an elbow on the table, fascinated. She had no idea cowboys rode mules now instead of horses. The idea of lanky Nate on the back of a stubborn mule conjured up a funny mental picture, but she refused to laugh. The guy had gone above and beyond.

Besides, what she knew about ranches and cowboys would fit on a pencil eraser. But a ranch had animals. She knew that for certain, and animals were good for kids. She'd read any number of articles about their therapeutic value with people who were hurting. Like a tiny seedpod, an idea began to germinate.

She was always on the lookout for opportunities for the children, especially her boys. They needed far more than she could teach them. The only animal she had room or time for was Ralph, the fighting beta fish that only serious Will seemed the least bit interested in. But that was because Will worried about everything and everyone, considering himself the caretaker of the world.

A ranch meant lots of animals, lots of opportunities, maybe even healing of some of the hurts these children had experienced, and of equal importance, a male role model and a little recreation.

"Would you consider letting me bring the kids out to your ranch sometime?"

Nate blinked and the air around him stilled. "Why?"

What an odd question. "To see the animals, to see what you do on a ranch. Broaden their horizons. You know, the kind of experiences they won't get here in this crowded subdivision."

She loved her home and neighborhood with its family-oriented residents and tidy, colorful flowerbeds and walkways, but most of the yards were small, and houses butted up against each other on either side. A ranch meant room to spread out and run and be noisy.

Nate didn't appear to be of the same train of thought. Reluctance hung on him like a wet shirt. He studied the rim of his milk glass, gnawed one corner of his lip and didn't look at her. "A working ranch is no place for kids."

Weak excuse. And she was a teacher. Did he think she'd let him get by with that?

"Then, how does one learn to be a rancher?"

The question seemed to agitate him. He leaned forward, forearms on the table's edge, hazel eyes clouding toward mud-brown. "I grew up in the country. Farm animals were a part of the natural order of things."

Having taken to heart Christ's command to care for the needy and orphaned, Rainy was accustomed to pushing when it came to getting things for foster children. After all, she was on a mission for God. If God approved, she didn't care in the least if people found her pushy. "Are you implying that only those who grow up in the country can be farmers or ranchers?"

"That's not what I meant."

She smiled, feeling victory coming on. One more

little push and he'd tumble like stacked dominos. "I'm so glad. I was positive a man thoughtful enough to join the Handyman Ministry would understand how much this could mean to at-risk town kids."

So it was a cheap shot. Rainy had no remorse.

Nate leaned back in his chair, hands dropping into his lap as he stared at her with exasperation. "You don't give up, do you?"

A tiny smile tickled Rainy's lips. "Never. Not when it comes to my foster kids."

This time, she was the one who leaned forward, pressing, determined as a terrier, her voice dropping low so the children didn't hear. "You met my kids, Nate, but you have no idea what they've lived through. They're survivors, but they carry scars. Will is too serious and considers the other children his responsibility. Joshua is my encourager, but he shivers and shakes at the first sign of conflict. Emma's charm can be manipulative. And Katie, poor little Katie—" She choked, tears filling her throat. She had not intended to go this far.

The cowboy across from her raised both hands in surrender. "Okay. They can come."

Rainy pressed back against the hard, wooden chair and drew in a deep, relaxing breath. Thoughts of what these children had suffered and witnessed always tore her apart.

"Sorry. I didn't mean to get teary on you."

"No big deal."

But she could see it was. Her handyman was ready to cut and run like a wild horse. Better grab the opportunity while it was knocking. Besides, one trip to the ranch would be a nice start, but she really had something more in mind. "How about tomorrow after church?"

He flinched. "So soon?"

"The weather is supposed to be decent tomorrow. And the kids will go wild with excitement. I promise to keep a tight rein on them. They're good kids." When he lifted a doubtful brow, she rushed on, "Really. I promise. Great kids. What do you say?"

Before he could answer, Katie's scream ripped through the air. Rainy pushed back from the table to see what was amiss this time.

"Great kids, huh?" Nate said without a bit of humor. "You could sell that scream to Hollywood."

Rainy chuckled anyway. "I know. Pure, high and bloodcurdling. And most of the time, she's screaming about nothing." The scream, however, was Katie's way to communicate. "Katie has some issues we're working through, but today the scream might indicate another episode of throwing up. I'll have to check."

Nate got that helpless, eager-to-escape expression again. Well, who could blame the poor guy? No one— not even Rainy—liked dealing with a stomach virus.

As she pushed out of the chair, Will came into the kitchen. "Katie's all right. She's mad because I gave one of the babies a stuffed animal."

"No throw up?" she asked.

"No." The boy's serious eyes glanced at the cookies.

"Want one?" Nate offered the plate and then thought

to ask Rainy, "Is it okay if he has one? He helped me out back there with the hose. Good worker."

Will took the cookie before she could reply, although she would have said yes anyway. "Joshy and Emma got scared. They're hiding in the closet again."

"Why?"

"Because there's a cop coming up the sidewalk."

Nate watched as Rainy Jernagen's face alternately paled and then flushed, a hot-pink color flaring on delicate cheekbones.

"Are we in trouble?" Will asked, his face alive with worry.

Rainy placed a hand on the boy's narrow shoulder, and in a soft, calm voice asked, "Have we done anything to be in trouble?"

"No, ma'am."

"Then we have nothing to fear from the police." She dipped her head low, making eye contact. "They're our friends, remember?"

From the way the boy's eyes shifted away, Nate figured he didn't buy that. Negative experience must have left a scar.

"Anything I can do to help?" he heard himself asking, though in reality, he'd had about all of the Jernagen house he wanted for one day. He was baffled as to why he wasn't escaping out through the garage.

On second thought, the police wouldn't look kindly on a male slithering out the back way while they stood on the front porch.

Rainy lifted blue-gray eyes to his, and he knew why he hadn't already cut and run.

A few minutes ago, she'd gotten to him with the mere hint of tears—he was a sucker for a woman's tears, as his sister well knew. And Rainy was kind and gentle and patient with the children, even though she was obviously running on adrenaline and little sleep. She was cute, too, now that her hair was brushed and she didn't look like a troll doll about to explode with stress. If he was truthful, she'd been cute all along, though he'd not wanted to notice.

But he was a man, and admiring a pretty, sweet woman came naturally. He couldn't change biology.

If she didn't have this passel of kids, he might even have asked her out.

A chill tingled his nerve endings.

If was a big, big word. He and kids didn't mix, and Rainy's devotion to the children was obviously more than a do-good activity to make herself feel charitable. She was passionate, with a missionary zeal.

Nate Del Rio simply did not understand the sentiment. Kids were a pain. Trouble. He knew from ugly, tenacious experience.

The doorbell played another round of hideous rock music. Rainy jumped.

She gave Will a reassuring pat on the shoulder and a gentle push. "If you'll check on Emma and Josh, I'll talk to the policeman first and then I'll be right in. Don't worry. Everything is fine."

She started into the living room, knees trembling. The nervous reaction made her almost as angry as the notion of someone intentionally frightening her kids. And she had no doubt this was the case.

Strong fingers caught her by the arm. "Why don't I answer the door?" Nate said. "So you can take care of the little ones."

She blinked her surprise, touched by his concern. "Thanks, but we've done this before. It will only take a minute."

He dropped his hold. "The police come here often?"

"More often than I'd like," she said grimly.

Kathy Underkircher and her hostility were wearing thin, for Rainy was certain that the woman who had decided to hate her for reasons that had nothing to do with these children had once again called the police.

"Why? You don't seem the kind to cause trouble."

"I'm not." She waved him off. "It's too complicated to explain right now."

The doorbell screamed again and, under other circumstances, Nate's flinch would have made Rainy laugh. The awful music had that effect on everyone.

"What is with the musical doorbell?" he asked.

"My brother installed it. His idea of a joke." She pushed a stray lock of hair behind one ear and said a little prayer as she gazed around the living room. The place looked better, if not perfect. But who expected perfect with children?

"Not your kind of music?"

"What?" she asked. "Oh, the bell. Despise it. Don't know how to dismantle it." She reached for the doorknob as the raucous tune restarted. Through gritted teeth, she said, "If that thing wakes the babies, I'll take a hammer to it."

Behind her Nate chuckled. "Sounds like a handyman job to me."

It occurred to her then that he was still here. By now the handsome cowboy—the handsome *single* cowboy—would be convinced he'd fallen into some alternative dimension filled with screaming kids, throw up, overflowing washers, irritating music and a policeman on the doorstep. Could her day get any worse? Might as well find out.

She ripped the door open with a little more force than needed.

A familiar officer in a blue uniform stood in the cool shade of the tulip-bordered porch. Sun glinted off his silver Summervale police badge.

"Miss Jernagen?"

"Hello, Officer Wagner," she said with a sigh. "Kathy Underkircher again?"

The policeman's head dipped slightly. "Anonymous caller. Sorry to disturb you but screaming was reported again. Is there a problem?"

The anonymous caller was Kathy, all right. The woman would never forgive her, no matter how she tried to mend the rift.

"None that needs police," Nate said, stepping up beside Rainy to extend his hand to the officer. "Nate Del Rio. Rainy and I attend the same church. Don't I know you?"

"Del Rio?" the young officer rubbed his chin. "Yeah, yeah. You got that ranch outside of town. Right?"

"That's right. Crossroads Ranch."

"My dad bought a heifer off you a while back for my little brother's agriculture project at school. I came with him to pick her up."

Nate's head bobbed. "I remember. Good breeding stock."

Rainy looked back and forth between the two men. It was considerate of Nate to be cordial but he had no idea she and Officer Wagner were old hands at this. She didn't need anyone to soften up the policeman with chitchat.

"Listen, gentlemen, I have four frightened children in there to attend to. Could we have this little reunion later?"

Chagrined, the officer nodded. "Sorry, ma'am. Do you mind if I come in? Check things out?"

"You know there's nothing wrong in here," she said.

"Yes, ma'am, but I have to check."

"I know. I know." She rolled her eyes heavenward, as much to beseech the Lord's help as for effect. "What a crying shame that Kathy can't get a life of her own and leave mine alone."

To let the officer in, she stepped back…and collided with the cowboy. Strong fingers caught her upper shoulders. "Whoa now."

A few minutes ago, she'd been entertaining the idea of getting to know him better. Now that she was completely humiliated, she wanted him gone before she and her family further debased themselves in his presence.

"Nate, I appreciate your help in fixing the washer.

Thanks so much. I'll call you later about visiting the ranch."

Nate didn't seem the least bit moved by her obvious dismissal. "Someone's crying back there."

Her head swung toward the back of the house and then returned to the officer. "I need to see about the kids."

"This will only take a minute."

"I'll go." Before she could protest, Nate's lanky legs carried him down the hall.

Surprised and more than a little touched, Rainy lifted both hands toward the officer and said, "Come on in and have a look. This morning has been incredibly hectic but all the noise is harmless, as always. Katie had a stomach virus. She screams when she hurts. Or about any other time she wants to communicate."

"Yes, ma'am. I understand." The officer glanced around the now tidy living room. "I see you have a couple of new ones over there."

"Temporaries. They arrived last night." She cast a glance toward the bedrooms. The crying had stopped.

Astonishingly, the twins remained asleep. As if he couldn't resist, the sturdy young cop headed toward the playpen. "I got one about this size. They can be into everything."

"These two have been so exhausted, they've mostly slept and eaten."

"That's not natural," he said with a chuckle. "Just wait till they get rested up."

"Hopefully, social services will find another placement for them by then. I'm not exactly set up for infants." She turned toward the hallway. "The other children are back here. But please be very gentle with them. They're terrified of you."

"I'm sorry about that, but I have to do my job."

"I know. Come on. Let's get this over with."

Officer Wagner was young, fresh-faced and genuinely kind, but that had never mattered to the kids. He wore a uniform and that was enough to set Joshua and Emma back for a week. Didn't Kathy Underkircher understand that the real victims of her animosity were innocent children? Even if she knew, would she care?

Bitterness gathered like acid on Rainy's tongue. She'd prayed about the woman, asking the Lord to deal with Kathy's hard heart. And now this. Again. On the worst day possible. In front of Nate.

Thanks a lot, Lord.

Whipping around, she led Officer Wagner through the house and pushed open the door to her bedroom. Her embarrassment at having two men see her unmade bed and pink pajamas was quickly forgotten. Nate Del Rio perched on the edge of her desk chair with Emma clinging to his knee like a blond wood tick. The boys were huddled next to his sides like baby chicks against a hen. In ordinary circumstances, the comparison of the hunky cowboy with a hen would have been amusing. Today, the sight was endearing.

"Everything okay in here?" she asked, her gaze searching each of the children's faces.

Will nodded solemnly. Joshua, bless his heart, trembled like an earthquake but followed his brother's example. Rainy's heart ached for the little guy. Emma's wide, troubled eyes were glued to the policeman.

"As you can see, Officer," Nate said, dropping a hand onto each of the boys' shoulders, "the kids are fine."

"Is this all of them?"

Katie chose that moment to answer for herself. She screamed.

Chapter Three

Nate didn't sleep a wink that night. Every time he closed his eyes, he saw Rainy Jernagen and her big-eyed foster kids. Worse, he felt the pressing weight of responsibility, worrying about them. None of which made any sense, other than he'd agreed to the foolish request to let Rainy bring the children to the ranch today. What had he been thinking?

Kids made him nervous. Not that he didn't like them, but he sure didn't want them running around the ranch getting into danger. Town kids wouldn't know the first thing about staying safe on a ranch. He'd known the dangers and still hadn't been able to avoid a tragedy.

The memory slapped him a good one, and following hot on its heels was the other memory. The one that kept him humble and praying for forgiveness.

He stalked through the kitchen toward the bubbling silver coffeemaker. His grandpa sat at the worn wooden table, glasses on the end of his nose, sipping stout black coffee and reading the Bible. As always, the sight touched a place deep inside Nate. Ernie Del Rio had come to the Lord after the tragedy that had nearly broken their family, and Grandpop's witness had eventually led his oldest grandson to Christ. Nate would be forever grateful to his grandfather for loving him enough to lead the way. Sadly, neither his brother nor his sister displayed the least bit of interest in changing their ways.

As Nate's boots tapped across the tile, Grandpop peered at him over the top of his half-rims. "Looking rough, boy. You going to church?"

"Lousy night."

The old man poked a thick finger onto the printed page. "Says right here that the Lord gives His beloved sleep."

"Guess I'm not His beloved then." The truth was he'd long suspected he was low on God's list of favorites. But he understood and didn't hold it against the Lord. He had a lot to make up before God could be pleased with him, but he was working at it.

He dumped two spoons of sugar into his coffee, sipped and grimaced. "Pop, you make the worst coffee on earth."

His grandfather didn't take the grumbling to heart. "Don't drink it then."

They'd had this conversation at least once a week since Pop moved in with him three years ago. Grandma's passing had left the older man at a loss, and Nate needed help on the ranch. They'd blended their lives amicably—two old bachelors set in their ways, raising cows.

"Janine called a bit ago. I wrote the number on the pad."

"What now?" His sister was like a leech, sucking the blood out of him, always needy. He was the go-to man in the family, the only functional member of a dysfunctional mess. At least, he considered himself functional. He had a steady job and a permanent home, which was more than he could say for Janine and Blake most of the time.

He reached for the phone number, but Pop's voice stopped him. "Sit down and drink your coffee first. You don't have to jump every time she hollers."

Nate dialed anyway. Pop didn't understand. No one did.

Every time one of his siblings called, he got this sick pull of dread and fear in the pit of his stomach. What if...

"Janine? What's wrong?" There was always something wrong. She didn't call otherwise. "I thought you and Sal worked everything out yesterday."

"We did, Nate. I promise. Sal's being good as gold."

Nate grimaced. Sal was a beer-guzzling lout who came and went at will, leaving Janine and their baby to fend for themselves.

"So what's up?"

"Well, you see." She paused and he heard a shaky influx of breath. "Now don't get mad, Nate."

Nate braced one hand against the kitchen cabinet and stared out the window over the sink. Fat black calves grazed on two hundred acres of quickly green-ing Bermuda grass. His cows, his grass, his hard work, soon to be bigger and better if all went well.

"Just tell me what you want, Janine."

The whining commenced. "See? You're already get-ting mad. I can't help that I'm the unluckiest person in the world. You just don't understand what it's like to be in my shoes. You've got it made out there on your ranch. You've always had it made."

Nate didn't remind her of what they both knew. He'd started this ranch on a loan and a prayer, working six-teen-hour days for a long time. Since then, he'd leased an adjacent eight hundred acres with an option to buy. If he could save enough money before the lease ran out, the land would be his and he'd finally feel solvent as a rancher. But that was a big if, and Janine's constant requests for money didn't help him save any extra.

"My car broke down, and Bailey's out of diapers and milk."

Trying to hold his temper, Nate stalked to the table for his now-cooled coffee, grimacing as he drained the cup.

"Nate?" His name trembled from her lips.

"I gave you money yesterday." The silence told him everything. He flashed a glance at Pop but got no help from that corner. "Sal bought booze with it, didn't he?"

"Don't get mad. We paid the rent like you said, but everyone deserves to have fun sometimes. We went out for a little while to celebrate getting back together. You aren't married. You don't have kids. You can't possibly understand how hard it is." His sister's whine grew persuasive. "Anyway, Sal promised to look for a job tomorrow. They're hiring over at Wilson's Manufacturing."

Right. If Sal sobered up. Nate ground his back teeth together. "How much do you need?"

Pop made a rude noise and shook his head. Nate turned back toward the window. How he dealt with his sister's problems was his business, whether his grandfather approved or not. Times like this he wished for a cordless phone and a little privacy.

"Not much," Janine was saying. "A few hundred until Sal gets his first check."

Considering Sal was not likely to get a job, much less a check, any funds Nate dumped in Janine's pocket were a gift. Extortion, really. She knew he worried about her.

"I'll put a check in the mail in the morning."

Pop slapped his Bible shut. Nate didn't bother to look at the older man, knowing he'd see a glower of disapproval.

"Nate, I need money today. Bailey's whimpering right now because she's wet and I don't have any diapers. She'll be bawling for a bottle soon. And tomorrow I need to take my car in to have it looked at. That takes money. I'll pay you back, I promise. Just bring it here to the apartment this afternoon. Okay? This is the last time, the very last time I'll ask. Okay? For me. Please. I promise."

If he had a nickel for every time she'd made those promises, he'd be a rich man. "Where's Sal?"

"Sleeping."

Nate's mouth twisted. Sleeping it off, more likely.

"You don't want me to walk to the store, do you?"

The question sliced through him like a machete.

Janine knew her brother's every weakness, including his guilt, and Nate resented the thunder out of her manipulation. He also knew he was about to drive fifty miles to once more rescue his sister.

No wonder he never wanted to be a father. He felt as if he'd been one most of his life.

A new thought edged to the front of his mind. He didn't really want Rainy Jernagen's passel of kids hanging around Crossroads Ranch, getting into things, taking chances. Even though he'd agreed to let her bring them out after church, he now had a great excuse to renege without looking like a jerk.

For once, he was almost glad his sister had called.

Rainy exited the sanctuary of Bible Fellowship, gazing around in hopes of spotting Nate Del Rio. After Katie's timely scream yesterday, the police officer had rushed into her room to find the little redhead sitting up on her knees on the bed, retching all over the bedspread. Both he and Nate had made hasty retreats shortly thereafter. She didn't blame them one bit.

This morning, everything had looked much better. Katie's illness had passed. The social worker had found a great place for the twin babies. Rainy had actually slept eight full hours last night and worship service had lifted her spirits to new heights.

She squinted up at the blue March sky, where wispy mare's tails swirled, reminding her of today's outing at Crossroads Ranch. The idea of seeing hunky Nate again was pretty uplifting, too.

She couldn't forget that sweet moment when he had rescued Emma and Joshua from the back of the closet. He didn't even know those kids or her, and yet he'd lured them out of their most secure hiding place, something that had, on occasion, taken her an hour to do. Before the policeman arrived, she'd had the notion that Nate didn't like children. Guess she'd rushed to judgment on that one.

Joshua tugged her hand. Though dressed simply like his brother in a clean Henley shirt, blue jeans and tennis shoes, he was a handsome little boy. "Are we going now, Rainy?"

"To see the cows?" Emma asked. All spiffed up in fluffy church dresses and black patent shoes with white lace socks, Emma and Katie were as pretty as spring flowers. They stood together, the redhead and the blond, holding hands. At six and seven, they were close enough in age to be both best friends and worst enemies.

"Home to change clothes and have lunch first." She gazed around again but didn't see Nate.

"Hey, Rainy, got a minute?" A slender man in a green shirt and gold tie bounded down the steps, his toothy smile sparkling in the sunlight.

"Always have time for a friend."

Guy Bartlett was the youth and children's pastor. Rainy worked with the young minister on any number of projects. He was a nice man in an antiseptic kind of way and had even expressed an interest in her at one time. But all she could feel for him was friendship, which was too bad, considering his love for children. And she'd told the Lord as much.

Guy tweaked Emma under the chin and winked at Katie as he spoke to Rainy. "I was wondering if you would do a puppet presentation next week in Children's Church."

"Love to," Rainy said. One of her favorite ways of relating to kids was through puppets. "I've been working up a new skit about forgiveness."

"It'll be great. Your stuff always is."

"Well, thanks. I try." Since Katie's arrival three months ago, she'd had less time to spend on her hobby, but puppeteering came naturally. She'd be ready.

She expected Guy to take his leave. Instead, he cleared his throat, glanced toward the parking lot where cars were already departing, and said, "I'd like to invite the five of you out for Sunday dinner today if you don't have other plans. To discuss the children's ministry, I mean."

Rainy started to refuse, but then scoffed at the thought running through her head. Guy had clearly stated he wanted to discuss the children's ministry, not start a relationship. Even if she didn't find his company scintillating, they were friends and coworkers for Christ. When had she gotten so full of herself?

"Later this afternoon we're headed out to the country to see Nate Del Rio's ranch," she said, "but we have to eat first anyway. Right, kids?"

While murmurs of excitement rippled from the kids, Guy said, "Del Rio? Do I know him?"

"He attends Bible Fellowship, too. Part of the Handyman Ministry. He came to my rescue yesterday when a washer hose broke. I wrangled a visit for the kids to see the cows and horses."

Guy smiled. "Never miss a chance, do you?"

Rainy smiled in return. Her friends knew about her complete dedication to foster care. "Nope. Not if I can help it."

Joshua tugged on Guy's elbow.

"Can we go to Golden Corral?" the boy asked, hopefully.

Will scowled at his brother. "Shut up, Joshua. Don't be asking for stuff."

Guy squeezed Will's shoulder. "Golden Corral, here we come. A buffet is the best place for growing boys like you and me to get our bellies full. Right, Will?"

The teasing brought a tentative smile from the slight-built Will. As one of the smallest boys in fifth grade, nothing could make him happier than to grow taller.

"My car's parked in the south lot," Guy said, motioning in that direction. "Want to ride with me to the restaurant and I'll drop you back here afterward?"

Rainy was about to refuse, but the boys were already racing across the grass toward Guy's vehicle.

By the time they'd battled the long line at the restaurant, finished their meal and returned to the church, mid afternoon had arrived. Rainy was glad she'd gone, though, because the dinner had settled her mind about Guy's interest. They really had talked only about the ministry and, of course, her foster children.

With the kids anxious to get out to the ranch, they'd rushed back to the house, changed clothes and departed in record time. Rainy thought about giving Nate a quick call but then changed her mind. They'd agreed upon three o'clock. As reluctant as he'd been about letting the kids come, she was taking no chances. She would simply go as planned.

With the kids glowing with excitement, she aimed her minivan toward Crossroads Ranch.

With a sense of relief, an agitated Nate turned his truck beneath the crossbars of Crossroads Ranch. After an afternoon of trying to counsel Janine and Sal and listening to a dozen excuses about why they couldn't get their lives together, home was a much needed refuge of peace. Now more than ever he was glad he'd had the foresight to leave a message on Rainy Jernagen's answering machine, telling her not to come to the ranch.

The thought had no more than formulated when he rounded the curve in the long driveway and saw a green minivan parked next to the fat cedar tree in his front yard. He frowned, not recognizing the vehicle. Oh, well, he wasn't a hermit. He liked company. One of his buddies must have traded vehicles. All of them, it seemed, now had families. Everyone but him.

Finishing off the last slurp of a fountain drink, he parked his Crew Cab next to the green van and hopped out, expecting Yo-Yo, his border collie, to come flying around the house in ecstatic excitement.

The sun had disappeared, and clouds added a nip

to the ever-present March wind. Still, the weather was pleasant and he considered taking the four-wheeler down to the fishing pond before dark. Bible Fellowship no longer had Sunday night service, urging its members, rather, to have family time.

He'd had all the family time he wanted for one day, thank you.

"Yo-Yo?" he called. No answer. Ah well, the dog must be outside somewhere with Pop.

As his boots thudded against the long, ranch-style porch, the sound of voices caught his attention. They came from back toward the barns and outbuildings, so Nate hopped over the end railing and rounded the house.

What he saw stopped him in his tracks. A groan escaped his throat.

Standing on the corral fence feeding carrots to the horses were four kids, his grandpa and Rainy Jernegan. Yo-Yo gazed on with pink-tongued adoration.

Nate looked heavenward, wondered if God was laughing at him or punishing him, and then stalked toward the giggling, wiggling, chattering group.

Backs turned, they didn't notice his approach. He planted his boots, his hands on hips and growled, "I guess you didn't get my message."

Six heads swiveled his direction. Yo-Yo leaped to his feet.

Nate's scowl must have startled everyone except Pop, because he was the only one who spoke. Lowering his foot from the fence rail, his grandpop said, "Nate, boy, you made it back."

Obviously. "What's going on out here?"

"Rainy brought the children for a tour. Said you invited them."

No use explaining to Pop that Rainy had twisted his arm until he'd yelled "uncle."

"She told me what you done to help her yesterday," Pop said. "When the young ones got scared. Mighty nice of you."

Nate recalled squatting in front of a dark closet, assuring a shaking boy and girl that he was big and he could protect them. It was a lie. He couldn't protect anyone, but they'd come crawling out anyway, trusting him, messing with his heart.

"I called," he said, turning his attention to the guilty party. "Didn't you get my message?"

Rainy hopped down from the fence, dusting her fingertips together in a feminine gesture that didn't accomplish a thing but sure looked cute. With her hair pulled back in a ponytail, she looked fresh and pretty in jeans, sneakers and a blue hoodie that matched her eyes.

"What message?" she asked, smiling at him despite his obvious irritation.

"I left a message on your machine. Told you not to come, because I wouldn't be here."

One of her slender shoulders hitched.

"Sorry. I didn't get any message." She didn't look sorry at all. Neither did the kids, who now huddled around her, eyes wide as they stared between Rainy and him.

"Don't matter anyway, Nate boy," Pop said. "I've

had a fine time showing them around. I'd forgot how much I enjoy having kids running around the place." His grandpa winked at Rainy. "Even if they are green-horns."

As if the two were old friends, Rainy made a face at Pop and then said, "Your ranch is really beautiful, Nate. And so big. Your granddad was kind enough to drive us over the fields in the hay truck."

"We seen baby cows, too," Joshua said. "They're real nice. I petted one right on the nose and he licked me."

The boy extended a hand as if the image of a calf's tongue would be there as evidence.

Emma lifted a foot toward him, nose wrinkling. The bottom of her light-up pink sneakers was filthy. "I stepped in some…stuff."

"But she's not mad," Joshua hurried to say. "Are you, Emmie? She liked it. We like everything about your ranch. Crossroads is a real good ranch. The best I ever saw."

Probably the only one he'd ever seen, but at the child's efforts to please, Nate softened. The deed was done. Rainy and the children had had their visit to the country and nothing terrible had happened. He should be thankful, he supposed, that Rainy had come while he was gone. Now he wouldn't have to dread the visit. It was done. Over. Never more to return.

"So, you've had a good time then?" he managed, feeling a little guilty for his original gruffness. In truth, his bad mood had less to do with Rainy than his own family. No use taking his troubles out on her.

Rainy's sweet-as-honey smile was his answer. "The best. A field trip of this kind is beneficial. They've loved it. Thank you so very much for allowing us to come. I can't even express how special the afternoon has been."

Rainy Jernagen was as nice as she was pretty. And he was a certified jerk.

He displayed his teeth, praying the action resembled a real smile.

"Great." His head bobbed. "Glad you enjoyed yourselves." *And when are you leaving?* If she kept staring at him with that sweet smile, he might start having crazy ideas about inviting her again.

And that was not about to happen. No way, Jose.

"So," Pop said, clapping his hands together. "Why don't we all adjourn to the kitchen? I got some banana bread in there somebody needs to eat. Maybe a glass of milk. Whatd'ya say, Will? Could you use a little sustenance?"

Will grinned but didn't say anything. The rest of the group chorused their approval, so Nate had little choice except to fall into step. Yo-Yo, the traitor, didn't even bother to say hello. He was too busy making a fool of himself over the children.

"Katie went all afternoon without screaming," Rainy said to him.

"Good thing. That Hollywood scream might cause a stampede."

Rainy stopped in mid-step, eyes wide. "Really?"

Her reaction tickled him. "No. Not really. You *are* a greenhorn."

"Am not," she said amicably, and Nate wanted to tease her again. He liked teasing her. Liked her gullible reaction. He looked ahead where four children pranced around his grandpa, yapping like pups. He was glad they were up there with Pop and Rainy was back here with him. And no, he wasn't going to examine that thought too closely.

"Bet you wouldn't know a stirrup from a saddle horn," he said, baiting her.

"Guess I'm going to find out, Mr. Smartie."

Something in the way she sparkled with energy gave him pause. "What do you mean?"

"Your grandpa invited us back next weekend."

Nate battled back a cry of protest and more than a little panic. He shot a look at his grandfather's flannel-clad back. "He did?"

"Sure did." Rainy tapped his arm with one finger. "To go horseback riding."

Like a punctured balloon, all the air seeped out of Nate.

Without upsetting everyone—including his grandfather, who would never let him hear the end of it—Nate couldn't refuse. He wasn't that much of a jerk.

Uneasiness crawled over his skin like an invisible spider.

Of all the dangerous ideas, Grandpop would have to come up with this one. Horseback riding. Small children on the backs of very large animals with minds of their own.

A recipe for disaster.

He sneaked a glance at Rainy Jernagen's upturned face. His belly dipped.

From the moment she'd opened that red front door looking like a combination of mother earth and the bride of Frankenstein, he'd known she was trouble.

He should have run while he had the chance.

Chapter Four

Nate faced Saturday afternoon with a mixture of dread and anticipation. Long before Rainy's minivan zoomed down his driveway, he worked the horses on a lunge line, rode every single one of them to get rid of any pent-up energy that might cause an issue with inexperienced riders and checked all the tack for wear. But any cowboy worth his boots knew there was only so much he could do to prepare. The rest was up to the riders and the horses.

He shut the door to the horse barn and leaned there a moment to whisper a prayer that none of the visitors would get hurt. A cool, meadow-scented breeze dried the sheen of sweat from his forehead.

"Quit your frettin', boy, and come on. They're here." Pop came around the end of the barn from the direction of the calving shed.

Spring was calving time, and they'd gathered the expectant heifers into the lot for close observation. The old cows did fine birthing on their own most times, but the first calving heifers sometimes required attention. This crop of calves in particular was important to his expansion plans. He'd spent a fat sum of money on artificial insemination from one of the premiere Angus bulls. Sale of the calf crop would go a long way toward the purchase of the Pierson land next to his.

"We have better things to do today than entertain visitors," he groused.

"You been saying that all week."

"But you haven't been listening."

"Nope. Sure haven't." Pop clapped him on the shoulder. "Little relaxation won't hurt you none. Don't tell me a good-looking feller like you hadn't noticed how pretty Miss Rainy Jernagen is."

Nate kept quiet. Anything he said at this point would be used against him. Of course, he'd noticed. That was the trouble. But he didn't want to be attracted to a woman whose entire life revolved around children.

"I like them," Pop said.

Still Nate remained silent. Pop had decided to befriend Rainy and her pack of foster kids and nothing would stop him.

"Place needs a little noise. Even old Yo-Yo is tickled." Sure enough, Yo-Yo had dashed away, furry tail in high gear, at the approach of a car engine.

"They're your company," Nate grumbled, refusing to be mollified. "Not mine."

"Then I'm a lucky man." Pop rubbed his weathered hands together. "Here they come."

Sure enough, like a mama duck Rainy led her charges across the wide front yard. As soon as the kids spotted him and Pop they broke into a run, leaving Rainy to saunter alone.

Nate tried to remain focused on the children instead of Rainy, but somehow his eyes had a mind of their own. They zoomed straight to her.

Pop was right. She was pretty in a simple, wholesome manner. Not knock-your-hat-in-the-dirt, tie-your-tongue-and-make-you-stupid gorgeous, but pretty in a way that made a man feel comfortable around her. Made him want to know her better. Made his belly lift in happy anticipation.

Today she reminded him of the daffodils sprouting up in the front yard, bright and pretty and happy in a yellow fleece shirt above a pair of snug old jeans and black boots. He did a double take at her footwear and grinned. Rolled-up pant legs brushed the tops of a pair of spikeheel, zippered dress boots that sported a ruffle of fur around the top. Girly. Real girly.

"What you wearing there, Slick?" he asked, moseying out to meet her. He leveled a penetrating gaze at her fancy high heels.

"You said to wear boots if we had them."

"Um-hum. Boots." He angled one of his rugged brown Justin Ropers in her direction. They'd seen better days. "Real boots."

"These *are* real boots."

"Yep, if you're walking down Fifth Avenue in New York." His grin widened. "Or Tulsa. City slicker."

The corners of her full lips tilted upward. "Are you making fun of my choice in stylish footwear?"

"Sure am." In actuality, he thought they were feminine and sassy even if they weren't the best boot for riding horses, but giving her a hard time was easier than a compliment.

She waggled a foot at him. "Laugh if you want, cowboy, but I already had them in the closet. After I shelled out money for four pairs of kid boots this week, I decided these would have to do."

Hands fisted on his hips, Nate tilted back, his mouth twitching in amusement. "You bought the kids new boots for this one day?"

Rainy rolled her eyes. "Of course not. Your grand-dad said we could come out as often as we'd like, so I thought the boots a sound investment."

Suddenly the joke was on him. "Pop said that?"

She grinned. "Why do I get the feeling you're try-ing to get rid of us?"

Because I am. But he didn't say that. He did, how-ever, send a scowl toward his annoying, meddling grandfather. What was the matter with that old coot anyway? He knew Nate's feelings about kids. He also knew the reasons his grandson never planned to have a family. He had one. One messed-up, constantly-in-need family was all he could handle.

"Nate, Nate!" Emma, the blond bombshell, barreled at him as fast as a first grader's legs could run. She didn't slow down until she slammed into his kneecaps.

"Whoa now." Nate caught her little shoulders. Bright blue eyes the color of cornflowers batted up at him. She was a gorgeous little girl, already stealing hearts. Some daddy would have his hands full with this one.

His chest squeezed at the thought. Emma didn't have a loving daddy to protect her.

"I got pink boots. See?" The little charmer twisted her foot this way and that for his perusal.

"Nothing but pink would do for Princess Emma," Rainy said.

"They're gorgeous, darlin'," Nate said.

The child's smile was as bright as Rainy's sweatshirt. "Joshy's got red ones and Will gots brown. He told Rainy he wasn't having no sissy boots. Will wanted man boots like yours."

Nate chuckled and glanced toward the corral, where Will and Joshua had gone. Both boys had their hands sticking through the fence. His smile disappeared. "You boys watch out doing that. If the horse thinks you have something in your hand, he might bite."

Both children yanked their hands inside and turned stunned faces toward Nate.

"They didn't know, Nate," Rainy said softly.

"That's the trouble," he groused. "They don't know anything about a ranch."

His sharp tone brought a puzzled look. "I'll keep a close eye on them."

"See that you do." He started toward the barn, where Pop was hauling saddles and tack out into the corral. Rainy kept stride, rushing a little as her fancy-heeled boots poked perfectly round holes in the soft earth.

"Will you teach us how to saddle the horses?" Hands shoved into her back pockets, yellow shirt as bright as the sunshine overhead, Miss Rainy's face was alive

with interest and enthusiasm. Was she always so…
so…optimistic?

He slid her a sideways glance. "Why?"

"Learning new things is good for the kids."

Yeah, so they could hang out on his ranch and bug
him.

"And it will be fun, too."

He made a huffing noise, but Rainy didn't get the
message that he was in a bad mood. She chattered
right on.

"Where's your donkey?"

Nate tilted his head in question. "All you'll find on
this ranch are cows and horses."

"But you said…" She bit her bottom lip, looking
confused.

"I said what? That we own a donkey?" He remembered no such conversation. Was she losing it?

"Last Saturday at my house. You said you had
horses for fun but you rode a donkey…" She paused,
a small furrow between her pale brown eyebrows.
"…or maybe it was a mule, for the real work. Aren't a
mule and a donkey the same thing?"

Nate couldn't help himself. He laughed. Once he
started he couldn't stop. He looked at his grandfather
and things got worse. Pop leaned on a fence post dou-
bled over, one arm pressed against his belly and a fist
against his mouth. His cheeks flared out, ruddy and
misshapen below his shiny, balding head.

All around his feet riding tack lay scattered, as if
he'd dropped everything the minute he'd heard Rainy's
comment. The strangled, chuffling sounds coming

from his short, round body were a failed attempt to be polite.

Nate's sour attitude vanished faster than tortilla chips at a Mexican restaurant. Hands on his thighs, he bent forward, his whole body shaking with laughter.

Meanwhile, Rainy and her children stared in bewildered curiosity at the two chortling ranchers. Joshua and Will exchanged glances, each lifting his shoulders in a shrug.

When Nate could finally catch his breath, he took Rainy's arm. "Come here. I want to show you something."

Still chuckling, he led the way into a covered area at the side of the barn where all vehicles, tractors, mowers, etc. were parked.

"This," he said, grinning as he approached an ATV with a small pickup bed on the back and a sturdy four-wheeler front. "Is the only Mule you'll find on Cross-roads Ranch."

Emblazed across the vehicle's front were the words *Kawasaki Mule.*

"Oh." A becoming shade of pink neoned from Rainy's pretty cheekbones. She touched three fingers to her lips, lifted blue-gray eyes to his and giggled. "Oops."

Her cute reaction got him started laughing again. She joined him, laughing until she grabbed her side and said, "Stop. You're making me hurt."

By now, they were surrounded by the rest of the gang.

"Can we ride it?" one of the kids asked, awed by

the camouflage green machine. Both boys had crawled inside and were investigating.

"Maybe sometime," Nate said before he could think better of such a promise. "Not today. Today we ride horses. Come on. I'll show you where the rest of the tack is kept."

"Can we pick our own horse?" Joshua asked, pointing. "I like that brown one."

"Champ's a good pony. We'll saddle him up."

"I want the blue one," Emma said, pointing toward a blue roan Appaloosa mare who grazed quietly outside the fence.

"Hold on there. We're only saddling three horses today—Champ, Patches and Bud." They were the oldest and most gentle.

"But there are seven of us," Will protested. "Do we have to share?" He said the last word as though it tasted sour.

Nate nodded. "Today you learn inside the corral. Grandpop and I will stay on the ground and teach. Maybe another time we'll all trail ride on separate horses."

Another dumb comment on his part. If he kept talking, the Brady Bunch would be regulars around here.

The group looked a little despondent, but Nate wouldn't budge on the issue of today's ride. Not one of them knew anything about a horse. Before he'd take them outside the corral, they needed instruction.

Demonstrating the proper method of saddling a horse took a while. Except for Will, the kids were all too small to lift the saddles or tighten cinches on their own. With Pop's help, Nate let the kids think they'd done the work. Saddling was the easy part. It was the riding that worried him.

"Okay, kids, go stand on the fence until I call your name."

All four of the children broke into a run. Emma ran directly behind the horses. One of the animals startled and hopped forward. Katie screamed.

Nate thanked God on the spot that all of his horses were dead broke and unfazed by the racket. The fact that Bud had jumped was proof, though, that even the best trained animal could be unpredictable.

He handed a set of reins to Rainy and one to Pop, taking the last one for himself.

"Ever ridden a horse before?" he asked Rainy as they led the horses forward into the center of the lot.

"Well…"

Nate looked heavenward. "That's a no."

"We can learn," she said, all chipper-like.

"Um-hum. Tell you what, I'll use you to show the kids how this is done. Then Pop and I will lead you around until you get the hang of it."

Which he figured would never happen.

"Sounds good." She dusted her fingertips in that pretty way and approached the horse.

"Other side," Nate said, hiding a smile.

"Does a horse know right from left?"

Was she serious? One look at her dancing eyes and he knew she was joking. "Most horses are trained to the right. Hear that, kids? Always approach a horse from the right. Never walk behind a horse where he can't see you. It scares him. And since he's a lot bigger than you, he might accidentally hurt you, not because he's mad but because he's scared."

Rainy did as he instructed, going to the right side. As he helped her into the saddle, her sweet scent mingled with the more familiar smells of leather and warm horseflesh. Coconut. She smelled like coconut. Keeping one hand on the reins and the other on the back of the saddle, he stepped back. A man didn't go around noticing how good a lady smelled if he wasn't interested in her. Which he wasn't. He couldn't be.

"You okay up there?" he asked.

Leather squeaked and shifted as she adjusted her feet in the stirrups. "Great. This is awesome."

At her delighted expression, Nate's heart bumped and he had trouble looking away. "Be careful of those high heels."

Concern creased her brow. "Will they hurt the horse?"

Nate's nostrils flared with humor but he held in a laugh. "Champ doesn't care what kind of boots you wear. For all I know he might even prefer fancy, furry lady shoes." Actually, Nate was growing rather fond of them. "But heels that thin and long could get stuck in a strap or hung up in the stirrups."

"Am I in danger?"

"You're okay. I've got you covered." He hoped it was true.

The kids set up a howl. "When's our turn? I want to ride."

Nate shook off his unwanted entrancement with the

lady and refocused on the children. There were four of them, all too young and inexperienced to go unsupervised for even a minute. Hadn't past experiences taught him anything about the dangers of kids and ranches?

"Hold on now. Miss Rainy and I are going to show you a few things first."

He ran through the basics, emphasizing safety for both horse and rider. No matter how hard he tried to concentrate on the kids, he was abnormally conscious of Rainy watching him from her horseback perch. He couldn't help wondering what she was thinking as she looked down. Was she watching to learn or because she liked what she saw?

The second notion made him uncomfortable, though he couldn't pinpoint the reasons. Maybe he should have shaved this morning.

Finally, Rainy said, "I think I can do this, Nate. And the kids are anxious to try. Let's give them a chance."

With a degree of anxiety, Nate helped her down and then queried each of the children on the lesson he'd just presented. Satisfied that none of them would do anything crazy, he assigned horses, and the adults each helped a child mount. Nate took responsibility for the little girls, putting them both on Patches, an old mare with the patience of Job. Rainy took Will, the oldest and most responsible, while Pop worked with Joshua.

After a while, the boys were riding on their own around the lot, blissfully unaware that the horses knew what to do without any help from the inexperienced riders. Pop walked along beside the boys, talking and instructing as they rode. With Will plodding around in a circle, Rainy drifted over to help Nate with the girls. At least that's what Nate told himself she was doing.

"Want me to saddle another horse for you?" Nate asked. "You look kind of bored."

Rainy, her hands inside the pouch of her daffodil sweatshirt, shook her head. "Not bored at all. Next time, though, I hope we can all ride together."

Oh yeah, next time. Uh-uh. "Maybe."

"The kids are doing really well, aren't they?" Her gaze slid to the two proud boys, sitting straight and tall in the saddle, listening to Pop as if their lives depended on it. Which, in fact, they might.

Grudgingly, he had to admit the afternoon had gone better than he'd anticipated. At least no one had been trampled underfoot or thrown over a fence. "Not bad for a bunch of tenderfoots."

"So you'll let us come back again?"

Did he have any choice? "I thought Pop already invited you."

"He did, but this is your ranch. I'd like to know you're okay with our visits, too."

Nate twitched under her scrutiny. She was smart. She knew he didn't want them here. She just didn't know why. And Nate was not about to share that little tidbit of guilt. "Why does my opinion matter?"

Rainy studied him with cool appraisal but changed subjects so quickly Nate couldn't help wondering. "Your grandfather told me you have a brother and sister. Do they live nearby?"

"My brother's in OKC." Or he had been last time

Nate had bailed him out of trouble. "My sister lives on the other side of Tulsa. Why?"

"Just curious." She walked along beside him, her boot heels making *phht-phht* sounds as they sucked in and out of the loosely packed soil. "I only have one much younger brother. I envy people with big families."

She didn't know how lucky she was. Tempted to say so, he instead stopped the horse and spoke to the two little girls. "Ready to get off for a while, ladies?"

Two heads nodded, so he lifted Emma from the saddle first. She wound her arms around his neck and surprised him with a hug. "Thank you for the ride. I like your horse."

"Mighty welcome, Princess Emma." He handed the little girl off to Rainy, but her needy embrace lingered in his mind right next to Rainy's sweet coconut fragrance. "Come on, Miss Katie. Down you come."

He swung her up and out, braced for a scream that never came. Instead, she too hugged his neck. Nate swallowed a lump of disquiet.

"Can I lead Patches into the barn?" Katie asked.

"No, I want to," Emma said. Inserting herself between Nate and Katie, she worked those baby blues to good advantage.

"Girls, stop." Rainy went to her haunches in front of the children. "If you fuss, Nate won't want us to come back. Fussing scares the horses."

"Both of you can lead Patches," Nate said, handing a rein to each child, while keeping his hand on Patches' headpiece. The old mare would take herself into the barn, for that matter.

"You're certainly diplomatic," Rainy said, a smile in her voice as she fell into step beside him. "Ever consider a career in politics?"

Him? Diplomatic? Now that was a good one. "Ever consider a career in stand-up comedy?"

She laughed. "Maybe. I put on puppet shows. They can be funny sometimes."

One corner of the barn filled with hay caught the attention of Emma and Katie. They dropped Patches' reins and made a beeline for the bales, which were stacked in stair steps all the way to the open-beamed ceiling. Though prickly and itchy, Nate figured the hay was an otherwise great spot for the girls to play safely. He could keep an eye on them from about anywhere in the barn, and as long as he could see them, they'd couldn't get hurt or do anything dangerous.

He led Patches into a stall for unsaddling. Rainy trailed him, looping both arms backward along the top of the half-stall behind her.

"Seriously," Nate asked. "You do puppet shows?"

"Don't look so stunned, cowboy. Even a city slicker has hobbies." She looked around the boxy, cell-like structure. "Can I help in some way?"

The confines were crowded with the three of them inside, though the wide-rumped mare took up much of the space. Smells of dusty hay and sweaty horse mingled with well-worked leather and sweet coconut. That coconut was going to kill him before the day was over. He was sure of it.

"Grab a brush over there." He motioned toward a wall, where various types of grooming tools hung from hooks. "You can brush her mane. She likes that." He pulled hard on the cinch buckle, loosening the tight belt around the horse's middle. "Got a horse puppet?"

"Might get one now that I'm an expert cowgirl." She came up next to him, brush in hand.

Nate decided he liked her gentle humor, liked teasing her and knowing she would appreciate the effort.

"Well, Slick, being how you're an expert and all, why don't you remove this saddle and brush Patches down?" He stepped back, grinning.

The cute greenhorn took the comment as a challenge.

"You think I can't?" She made a proud little sniffing sound, tossed her head, and then bumped him with one shoulder. "Move over, Cowboy. Let me show you how it's done."

Feeling unusually lighthearted, Nate stepped back and crossed his arms over his chest. "She's all yours."

"Okay, I can do this." Rainy bent low to look under Patches's belly. "All unhooked. Okay. That's a start." She patted Patches's neck and leaned close to the mare's ear. "If it's all right with you, Patches, I'm going to take this big old saddle off your back. You'll feel so much better when I do. Ready now?"

A snort escaped from Nate. Rainy shot a pretend glare in his direction. With slender arms that didn't look strong enough to lift a feather, she grabbed the saddle by the horn and the back and pulled.

"Easy now," Nate said, as much to Rainy as to the horse. He uncrossed his arms, ready to jump in with assistance.

The saddle came all at once, its weight bearing down unexpectedly. Rainy staggered. Nate reached in from behind and added his strength to hers. Together they levered the saddle onto the stall divider. He'd move it to the tack room later.

"I could have managed," Rainy said, her breath puffing softly from exertion as she turned toward him.

Still standing a little too close for comfort, Nate grinned down into eyes sparkling with fun. "I know you could have, Slick. First time's always the hardest."

He expected her to slither away from the close contact. Instead, she grinned back at him and stayed put. His pulse ratcheted up a notch.

When she and her pack of kids had come to the ranch today, he'd expected nothing but trouble. Instead, he had actually enjoyed himself. Nothing bad had happened. No one was injured by a frightened horse. And he hadn't minded getting to know Rainy better.

Maybe this wasn't so bad after all.

The idea drifted through his mind that he wouldn't mind kissing her, either. With one hand propped on the wall above her head, he thought how easily he could lean in and give it a try. Nothing wild and crazy, just a friendly kiss. An end to a pleasant day.

Before he could move, a distant rumbling penetrated his consciousness. And then a shout.

"What was that?" Rainy had barely spoken the words when Nate pivoted away.

Another shout and then the roar of a motor.

Ice cold fingers of fear gripped him. He broke out

of the barn in a dead run in time to see Joshua bouncing across the barnyard on the Mule. Alone.

Nate almost went to his knees.

He'd let his guard down.

Now something terrible was about to happen. Again.

Chapter Five

Rainy's pulse thundered in her ears as she raced out into the sunlight. Her blood ran cold at the sight before her. Joshua, alone on the high-powered Mule, bounced out of control over the rough pasture. White as milk, his eyes bugged out and his thready voice rose in terror above the roaring motor.

"Miss Rainy! Miss Rainy!"

Rainy screamed back, "Push the brake," knowing full well Josh didn't know a brake from a gas pedal. In fact, from all appearances, the terrified child had frozen in fear, inadvertently holding the throttle wide open.

Nate, who'd exited the barn so fast she'd needed a minute to understand what was happening, now ran after the fleeing vehicle. His boots pounded hard and fast against the newly sprouted grass.

At the shouts, Nate's grandfather, accompanied by Will, came out of the tack room. The girls ran crying from the hay barn.

"Joshy, Joshy," Emma yelled. "Miss Rainy, Joshy's going to get hurt."

Her throat drier than chalk dust, Rainy feared Emma was right. There was no way Nate could stop the runaway vehicle.

"Dear God, please help." She said, "Pray, kids. Pray."

With growing fear and a terrible sense of helplessness, she watched the scene play out. As if in slow motion, the Mule headed toward a pond in the distance. With oversized tires and four-wheel drive, the machine bounced up and over terraces, in and out of holes, and wildly careened over jutting rocks and fallen tree limbs. In minutes, Joshua would hit the water…and even if he wasn't injured on impact, he couldn't swim.

Rainy's knees quaked. "Jesus, please. You put these kids in my safekeeping. I'm so sorry I let you down. Help. Please help."

A flurry of "should haves" ran through her head. She should have been watching him better. She should have known a curious boy might tamper with what he considered a fancy riding toy. She should have been out in the lot with him instead of inside the barn drooling over Nate's killer dimples.

Because of her carelessness, Nate was in danger, too. With growing fear, Rainy knew he had every intention of stopping the Mule, even if it meant sacrificing himself. As if he could, by brute strength, stop a fifteen-hundred-pound moving vehicle, he ran toward Joshua at an angle to cut him off.

The runaway machine barreled toward him at full

tilt. Joshua held on, screaming. As Nate and the ATV crossed paths, the cowboy grabbed the side of the front grill. He shoved his boot heels into the ground. The overpowering machine wrenched him sideways like a rag doll. Nate's body flopped wildly. He held on, his muscles straining beneath sweat-drenched chambray.

Like a stunt man in an action movie, he threw himself over the hood and clung to the front roll bar. Slowly, slowly, he edged forward until, at last, he leaned inside and killed the switch.

The sudden silence pulsed across the green grass. Shaking so hard she needed to sit down, Rainy sagged with relief. She slid onto the ground and sat for a full minute, hugging Emma and Katie to her side.

"Thank you, Jesus," she whispered.

The Mule's motor kicked on again, this time with Nate at the controls. Still trembling, Rainy waited near the gate. As the ATV passed her, Rainy's heart sank. Judging by Nate's cold-as-January expression, they were in big trouble.

Along with the remaining children, who hovered around her like baby birds, she followed the Mule into the shady vehicle shed.

Nate killed the ATV and stepped out.

"How did this happen?" he demanded to no one in particular.

Rainy reached for the terrified Joshua, pulling him off the ATV and into her arms. When he fell against her and burst into tears, she dropped to her knees and held him close. Barn dust and a little boy's terrified sweat assailed her nostrils.

"I'm sorry, Miss Rainy, I'm sorry. Don't be mad." His body quaked as his tears drenched her neck.

Other than soothing noises, Rainy didn't know what to say or do. The anger radiating from Nate Del Rio was enough to make anyone cry. This was all her fault. Joshua was only a little boy. She should have been watching him instead of flirting with Nate.

The other three children hovered in the entrance, stunned to silence. From the looks of them, they all expected to be deported to Siberia on the next train.

Rainy's protective mama gene kicked in. Joshua had made a mistake, but she wasn't about to let Nate Del Rio or anyone else scare him any worse than he already was. "It's all right, kids. Don't be scared. Joshua isn't hurt."

Three pairs of eyes darted to Nate's grim face. His arms crossed, the cowboy leaned against the fender of a red tractor, ominously quiet.

About that time, the elder Del Rio appeared from the other side of the tractor and headed straight for Joshua. "Now, boy, quit your crying. Nobody's mad at you. You scared us, that's all."

He gave the boy a reassuring thump on the back.

Rainy's focus moved from the children to Nate. Was his grandfather right? Was Nate frightened instead of angry? Over Joshua's trembling shoulder, she studied the ring of white around Nate's lips and the sheen of sweat on his forehead.

"Me and Will went in the tack room," the elder Del Rio said. "I figured Joshua would tag along. Figured wrong. Figure I'm the one who left the key under the seat, too. So if anyone's to blame here, I reckon it's me."

Some of Rainy's defensiveness fled. Ernie Del Rio was a kind man. Gently, she urged Joshua to his feet and swiped a sleeve over his teary face.

"Blame isn't what's important. What matters is that Joshua is safe and he's learned a lesson. Nate," she said, forcing her gaze up to his, "thank you for what you did. You may have saved Joshy's life."

Stiffly, Nate pushed off the tractor. With a shaky inhalation, he went to one knee beside her and the boy.

"Do you understand why we're upset, Joshua? The machines on this ranch are not toys. You can get seriously hurt pulling a stunt like that."

Joshua's brown head nodded, his body still trembling in a way that made Rainy want to shoo Nate away. But as a teacher, she knew Joshua should not be protected from the consequences of his actions. Otherwise, he'd do something foolish again. Next time the outcome might not be so positive.

"You need to apologize, Joshua." To ease her demand, Rainy stroked Joshua's back over and over again. "Tell Nate and Mr. Del Rio that you will never, ever do anything like this again."

The nine-year-old's reddened eyes filled. In a broken whisper, he said, "I won't."

Straightening his little spine, he stepped toward Nate to extend a trembling hand. His brown hair was sweat-stuck to a still pale forehead. "Thank you for saving my life. I won't make you have to do it again."

Rainy pressed her lips together to keep from smiling and crying at the same time.

"I believe you're a man of your word, Joshua," Nate said, taking the small offered hand into his much larger one.

The fact that Nate used his left hand and kept the right one crooked against his belly caught Rainy's attention. She studied his slow, careful movements. In all the commotion, no one had considered that Nate's heroics could have caused him injury. Indeed, his right shoulder seemed to hang at an odd angle.

"Nate, are you hurt? Your arm—"

He shot her a silencing look. "No big deal."

"I think it is." She touched his shoulder. He winced.

"I said I'm fine, Rainy. Let it go."

She pulled back, stung by his sharp retort.

"All right, then," she said stiffly. "Guess it's time for us to head home. Come on, kids. Tell the gentlemen thank you."

An obedient, if somewhat subdued, chorus of voices rose and fell, and then all four kids decided a bathroom run was in order before departure.

Eager to escape the moody cowboy, Rainy waited just inside the back doorway for the children. In minutes, they all returned carrying cans of soda and prancing around Nate's legs, clamoring for his attention as if nothing had gone wrong today.

Even though his color remained pale and he cradled his arm against his chest, Nate had made the effort to encourage the kids. He'd given them a cola and brought a smile to their gloomy faces. She had to appreciate that.

Nate Del Rio was the most disconcerting male she'd met in a long time. One minute he was gruff and the next he did something incredibly heroic or kind. She didn't know whether to hug him or kick him in the shins with her pointy-toed boots.

"Thanks for today," she said to the elder Del Rio, who insisted she call him Pop like everyone else. "I'm sorry for the trouble."

Not that Joshua's mishap would keep her from bringing the children here again, but she really was sorry the incident had taken the gloss off an otherwise shining day.

Pop waved her off. "Ah, stuff happens. Don't fret, Rainy. Kids gotta learn. That's why you brought 'em out here."

"Thank you," she said, smiling into hazel eyes much like his grandson's. "For understanding."

Which was more than she could say for the other Del Rio. The one with the killer dimples.

Feet tired from standing in heels all afternoon, she tottered a bit as she started toward the van, where four youngsters jockeyed for favorite seats. She was painfully aware that Mr. Dimples was standing in the yard, watching her.

"Rainy."

She stopped, drew a fortifying breath and pivoted.

Nate blinked at her, his expression uncertain. Rainy's heart fluttered.

She softened. "What?"

He waited two beats, eyes raking her face. Then he shook his head, his dimples flashed and his voice went soft. "Drive carefully."

Rainy figured it out on the drive home. Nate wasn't angry or cranky or rude. He just didn't want her to worry about his injury.

"Too late, Mr. Del Rio," she muttered.

"Huh?" Will, in the front bucket seat, turned in question. "Did you say something, Miss Rainy?"

"Talking to myself, Will." She glanced in the rearview mirror at the other kids, quiet for the moment. Katie's red head lolled to one side, her eyes droopy. In fact, they all looked worn out, a good thing when riding in a car. She'd broken up more than her share of energetic quarrels when the ride lasted too long.

"I feel bad for what happened," Will said, his fingers fidgeting on a now empty soda can.

"I do, too, honey." Even worse to know Nate had been injured in the process. "We'll have to think of something nice to do for Nate and his grandfather."

"I could offer to help out on the ranch. Feed horses and cows, muck out the barn and stuff like that." He pushed at the nosepiece of his glasses. "If you'd look after Joshua and Emma for me, I mean."

"That's not your job anymore, Will."

"I know." He glanced out the side window, his profile serious.

From what she'd learned of the children's pasts, Will had been their primary caregiver since he was very small. If the little ones caused a problem or lacked anything, he was blamed and often punished when and if the mother came home. His overblown sense of sibling responsibility weighed heavily.

"This needs to be a team effort. Let's see if we can come up with something we all can do."

"Like what?"

"Well," she said as she tapped her fingers on the steering wheel, chagrined to see dirt under her nails, "we could bake them a cake or some other goodie. I've heard bachelors don't get many home-cooked foods."

"Brownies." Even though he didn't smile, the child's face lit up with interest. "And a puppet show. Everyone likes your puppet shows."

Including a certain boy who could use a little more childhood in his life.

"Will, my man, you are a genius. Brownies and a puppet show it is."

"I asked them to come again next Saturday."

"You didn't." Nate shoved aside the cow-calf ledger he was working on to glare at his interfering grandfather. Four bull calves born this week without a problem. The Lord was blessing his hard work. Finally. Now if he could get Pop off his back about Rainy Jernagen so he could stop thinking about her, life would be good. "After what happened, today was enough."

He reached for the glass at his elbow. A pale brown mix of melted ice and watery root beer condensed into a ring atop well-worn wood. Nate pushed back from the table to get a refill.

Pop beat him to it, taking the glass from his hand and going to the freezer. Ice rattled.

"No use getting your tail in a twitch. Poor little kids was so upset. I figure they need to come back so's they'd know we wasn't mad at 'em."

Nate raised his eyes heavenward. His arm ached like nobody's business and he had a headache from thinking of all the things that could have happened if he hadn't been able to stop the Mule in time. That cute little boy with the big blue eyes and gentle ways could be laying in a hospital—or a morgue.

A shudder ran through him. Some memories weighed too heavily. He couldn't take a chance on repeating a nightmare.

He stalked to the sink and stared out at fat black, peacefully grazing cattle. Usually, the sight soothed him, edged out the mental flashes of Christine. Not so today.

"It's too dangerous, Pop."

"Living is a dangerous proposition, Nate boy. The roof might cave in any minute. Or a stampede of buffaloes could tear through the wall and trample us both to death."

Nate's lips twitched. Turning, he leaned his hip on the brown granite countertop. "There isn't a buffalo within fifty miles of here."

Pop shoved a glass of root beer at him. "That's what I'm trying to tell you. No use borrowing trouble."

Shaking his head, Nate laughed. "You make me feel better, even if you don't make any sense."

"Now don't tell me you aren't interested in seeing

that pretty little lady again. Cause if you do, I'll have to
remind you that lying is a sin." He opened the refrigerator and peered inside. "What do you want for supper?"

"Anything." Nate sipped the syrupy sweet pop, wel-
comed the fizz as liquid cooled his throat. "Getting
distracted by Rainy is what caused the problem in the
first place."

Pop straightened up, one hand holding to the top
of the refrigerator door. "So *that's* what's eating you.
You're blaming yourself for Joshua's curiosity."

Root beer soured in Nate's stomach. The responsibility was his, plain and simple. "He could have been
killed. On *my* ranch."

"Didn't happen." Pop jabbed a fat finger at him.
"Cast down imaginations, boy. That's what the Word
says."

Nate knew his granddad was right. He shouldn't
worry. He shouldn't always expect the worst to happen to people he cared about.

The notion caught him up short. He'd spent minimal
time with Rainy and her charges, but somehow they'd
gotten under his skin. He didn't like them there, didn't
want them intruding on his thoughts. He didn't need
anyone else to worry about.

Because no matter how much he prayed, his past
mistakes lingered behind his eyeballs as ghoulish reminders. He wasn't sure he could live through another
tragedy. Especially if he was the cause.

Pop plopped cellophane packages of bologna and
cheese onto the table. "Go on. Call her. Let her know
you aren't mad."

Nate pulled bread from the cabinet, adding the loaf to the pile. Cold cuts worked for him. He was in no mood to cook.

"I wasn't mad. Did she think I was mad?"

"Yep." Grandpop reached around him to where the phone hung on the end of the cabinet, its curly cord wadded into a mess. He handed the receiver to Nate. "Go on."

Nate stared at the dial pad for several seconds and then returned the phone to the hook.

Some things were better left alone. Thinking he was angry might not be such a bad thing if the notion kept Rainy Jernagen and her sweet smile at arm's length.

Sunday afternoon Nate opened his front door and came eyeball to eyeball with Rainy's sweet smile in the form of a giant yellow happy face puppet. He was certain the human behind the puppet was Rainy because she was accompanied by four much shorter puppets. And he smelled coconut.

His belly dropped into his boots. So much for avoidance.

Smiley's huge mouth opened. "A little birdie told us—" she started.

Up popped a crow puppet. "Cheep, cheep, cheep." Emma's blond hair peeked out from either side. "Cheep, cheep, cheep."

"Enough cheeping, Emma," Will's voice whispered from behind a cross-eyed pig. "Let Rainy talk."

"I want to be sure Nate hears me," came Emma's

stage-whispered reply. Mouth unmoving, the crow repeated, "Cheep, cheep, cheep."

Nate laughed in spite of himself.

Smiley cleared her throat. "A little bird told us that you did a very nice thing for someone. We came to say thank you."

"We brought brownies, too!" Joshua's face appeared from the side of a flop-eared dog.

Nate reached up and slowly pushed the yellow smiley downward until he was peering into Rainy's gray-blue eyes. "What is this, the Happy Patrol?"

The sweet smile he didn't want to think about appeared. "Something like that. Let us in and we'll entertain you with a skit."

No use fighting the inevitable. Rainy was a velvet bulldozer, and she'd mow him down and probably make him enjoy the experience. "Did I hear brownies mentioned?"

"My own special recipe. With chocolate chips."

"Double chocolate, huh? Having a rough day?"

The smile widened and she waved the happy-faced puppet. "You can decide after you taste them."

"Deal." He motioned them inside, quickly scanning the living room. He needn't have worried. With only two people to pick up after, the house stayed neat and tidy, the way he liked things. Everything in its place, unlike the chaos he'd seen at Rainy's. "Pop's not here. This is his day to visit the nursing home."

Rainy's gaze traveled lightly around the open ranch-style room, over the dark wood and leather furniture, the fifty-inch plasma television, the sturdy walnut tables, and came to rest on the native rock fireplace. Considering he'd collected the rocks himself, he was especially proud of that fireplace.

"Do you have someone special in the nursing home? A relative, perhaps?"

"Souls," he said. Then, seeing her quizzical expression, he explained. "Pop was older when he came to know Jesus. He feels older folks are often overlooked."

"I guess that's true," she said softly. "What does he do there?"

"Whatever they ask. Writes letters, reads the Bible, prays. Mostly he listens."

"Your grandpa is what I'd call a real Christian."

Nate had to agree. He wished he could be more like Pop.

Without a peep, Rainy's tribe of four lined up on his sofa like soldiers for inspection. She must have warned them to be on their best behavior.

"Yeah, Pop's a good guy," he said, motioning Rainy into a seat next to the hearth. He took the chair opposite her.

"So is his grandson. How's your arm?" Rainy leaned toward him, the yellow puppet speaking for her. "Don't try to tell me you weren't injured. I know better. Smiley knows everything."

Nate rotated the shoulder for effect. "A little sore. Tell Smiley it's nothing permanent."

"I'm glad. Smiley and I are both glad, aren't we, Smiley?" The puppet turned to face her and nodded, its wide mouth flopping open and closed several times before Rainy laid the toy in her lap and said, "Seriously,

Nate, what you did yesterday was amazing. Brownies and puppets are not enough to express how thankful I am."

What he'd done yesterday should never have happened, but he wasn't in the mood to go there. Rainy and her trouper of puppeteers cheered him. Why ruin a good mood? She was here and, short of throwing her out, she was likely to stay a while. He would avoid her next time.

"Brownies are a start," he said. "Are we going to eat 'em or admire 'em?" He lifted his eyebrows toward the container Joshua had placed on the coffee-table.

"We made those for you and Pop," Rainy said, "not for us."

"Ah, come on now. No fun eating brownies alone. I think that's a rule somewhere. Right, kids?"

Four sets of blue eyes shifted to Rainy and then back to the brownies. She laughed. "Little piggies. It's not as if you never get brownies."

Will raised his puppet.

"But, Miss Rainy," he said in an oinky pig voice, "you got to fatten us up. Skinny pigs don't win prizes at the fair."

Rainy's face glowed at Will's attempted humor. From what she'd told Nate, the boy didn't have much to laugh about most of the time.

"Will's right, Miss Smiley Face. I'm a rancher. I know these things."

"I can see I'm outnumbered." She eyed the fearsome foursome. "I have dinner in the Crock-Pot at home, so only one for each of you this time. Okay?"

"And milk," Nate said with a conspiratorial wink at the children. "Can't have brownies without ice-cold milk."

A row of blue eyes danced, but no one except Nate moved. He looked from the kids to Rainy and back again. She must have read them the riot act. "They can get up, Rainy."

"They're really sorry about yesterday, Nate. They don't want to do anything to upset you. They absolutely love coming out here and have talked nonstop about nothing else since."

The comment hit him right in the heartstrings. They were little kids. Good kids. Pop was right. Children were naturally curious. They made mistakes. Maybe he'd been too gruff.

"Yesterday's over, kids. Understand? I've made my share of dumb mistakes. Learn from them and move on. Okay?" He only wished he could take his own advice. He waited two seconds while his words settled in and then pumped his eyebrows. "Last one in the kitchen is a rotten egg."

Four small bodies erupted from the couch. Nate braced himself for a brawl—or, worse yet, one of Katie's Hollywood screams.

"Now you've done it," Rainy said, following him and the wild bunch into the big country kitchen.

The young ones skidded to a stop on the rock tile and with a cacophony of laughter and excited voices, pointed at Rainy. "You're last. You're a rotten egg."

She raised her smiley puppet with one hand and the

brownie container with the other. "But I have these. So what do you say? Am I still a rotten egg?"

Good-natured groans and mumbles and giggles rose from the children.

Nate trucked to the refrigerator for the milk, all the while observing the interplay between Rainy and her crew. A genuine affection flowed between them. His first impression of a harried woman with out-of-control kids had been way off. Rainy Jernagen not only had control in a firm, loving manner, she was...amazing.

Taking the milk carton from his hands, Rainy poured as she set a small glass in front of each child. He breathed a sigh of relief that Janine had left behind a complete set in one of her many comings and goings. Dishes weren't high on his shopping list. Certainly not kid-size dishes.

"Josh, grab us a paper towel over there, will you?" Nate nudged his chin toward the holder beside the sink. Will started to rise but sat down again, apparently realizing Joshua could handle the task. Solemnly, the younger boy placed a curling square of paper in front of each person. Katie was already peeling back the lid on the Tupperware container, her freckles popping with effort. Rainy lifted one finger in gentle reminder and passed the brownies from child to child.

Nate scraped a chair back from the table to join the party, the scent of baked chocolate tantalizing his senses.

"I didn't see you at church this morning," he said when she passed the Tupperware his way.

In truth, he'd done his best to avoid her, but that

had required an inordinate amount of crowd searching and attentiveness to his surroundings. Then he'd spent the rest of the service asking the Lord's forgiveness for thinking about her too much instead of concentrating on worship. No wonder he wasn't priority one with God.

"Children's Church," she said, cupping a hand under her chin to catch any brownie crumbs. "I presented a new puppet show today."

"How'd it go?"

"Good, I think. The class laughed and interacted with Brian the Brain, my genius puppet who thinks he knows everything."

"Does he?"

He took his first brownie bite. The power of rich, gooey double chocolate almost made him moan. He'd never had anything quite like Rainy's special recipe.

"No, that's the fun of it. Brian's arrogant about his intellect, so when the kids catch him making silly mistakes—and I make sure they do—they love it. He's a great tool for teaching life lessons."

"Am I meeting Brian the Brain today?"

She shook her head. "Uh-uh. Brian stayed home. You've already met today's entertainers. Normally, I'm a one-woman show, but the kids wanted to do this special skit just for you—as a thank you, an apology." She lifted her shoulders. "Because they like you. So they're helping today."

A few brownie crumbs dropped onto her paper towel. Poking at them with her index finger, she leaned close to whisper, "Don't expect anything fancy."

Her face was close enough that Nate noticed the spray of thick brown lashes fanning the crests of her cheekbones. And caught a whiff of that maddening coconut. The light, airy feeling lifted higher, filling his chest with warmth.

He didn't want to be attracted to Rainy, but he was. If only she wasn't so committed to kids....

Swallowing, he glanced toward the foursome gathered around his square table. They chattered among themselves while savoring their snack. The two girls each wore a milk mustache. Joshua swiped a sleeve across his mouth, coming away with a streak of chocolate on his cuff. Will frowned at him and handed over his clean paper towel, urgently whispering something. Josh looked down, saw the chocolate and scrubbed at the spot.

Nice kids. But Janine and Blake had been good kids, too, at one time. Now look at them. Excellent examples of why he should not get sentimental about Rainy's foster children.

"Are you ready for our show?" Rainy was asking as she wadded her paper towel and glanced around for a trash can.

"Whenever you are." He took the paper from her. "I'll clean this up later."

Rainy paid him no mind. In seconds, she and the children cleared away the glasses and towels. Then they adjourned to the living room for the performance.

Amid much nervous giggling from the youngsters, Rainy parked Nate in a chair. Then she and the children took positions behind the sofa across from him. As the only audience, he suffered a moment of discomfort. What exactly did they expect from him?

Four puppets popped into sight above the back of the couch. So commenced a skit about a super dog in a cowboy hat and a red cape who saves a foolish pink pig from running in front of a truck. Throughout the performance, the four children alternately giggled and shushed and forgot their lines. Thumps of movement shook the sofa.

Filled with cute one-liners, the show was a thinly disguised reenactment of yesterday's incident. Nevertheless, Nate found himself alternately amused and touched by the message of friendship, apology and forgiveness.

So when the skit ended and the five puppeteers rose for a bow, Nate rose with them, applauding. From the children's flushed and thrilled expressions, he figured they'd had limited accolades in their lives. The notion stung.

In that moment, the old feelings of responsibility pressed in. If he could make a difference in their lives, shouldn't he be willing? Wouldn't God expect it?

Some of the pleasure from the puppet show seeped away.

Sometimes God was a hard taskmaster.

Chapter Six

Rainy waited until the social worker pulled out of the drive before she closed the door. With a sigh, she leaned against the hard wood and smiled at a skinny, freckled, frightened eight-year-old boy named Mikie. The social worker had come for a scheduled visit to discuss Rainy's desire to adopt Katie. Katie, as usual, had screamed bloody murder the minute Mary Chadwick entered the house. Rainy had been tempted to join her when the social worker asked her to foster Mikie, at least temporarily.

The needs of the other four already kept her hopping, but how could she refuse? The little boy broke her heart with his quivering lips and proud, stubborn chin. No matter how crowded her house or how busy her schedule, Mikie needed someone to care. Caring for needy children was what God had called her to do.

She took Mikie into the boys' bedroom for introductions, making sure Will and Josh helped him feel welcome. Both boys went immediately to the closet for the air mattress and began to set up an area of the room for the newcomer. They'd been through this drill before.

The telephone rang. She grabbed it on the second ring. "Hello."

"Rainy? Guy Bartlett. How are you and the Brady Bunch?"

She twined the cord around her finger. "Wild and crazy as always. How are you?" And why are you calling?

The thought was short-circuited by Guy's next words. "Look, I was thinking. We had a good time that day after church. I was wondering if you might like to do it again? Just me and you without the kids."

Oh dear. Maybe he did want to be more than friends. A dozen thoughts filtered through her head. He was a good Christian active in her church. He liked kids. There was no real reason for her not to go out with him, and yet, she didn't want to. How did she say no without hurting a nice man?

"Um, things are hectic right now, Guy. I'll have to say no."

A short paused ensued. "Another time then? Maybe next week?"

His obvious disappointment made her feel horrid, so she said, "Let's talk about it later, okay?"

She needed some time to figure a way to let him down easy.

Another pause and then, "Sure. See you at church?"

Rainy forced a smile into her voice. "Absolutely."

She'd no more than replaced the receiver when the

phone rang again. Hoping it wasn't Guy with an alternative suggestion, she answered cautiously. "Hello."

"Hey, Slick," a dark, smooth baritone intoned. "My brownies are all gone."

At Nate's voice, Rainy couldn't ignore the leap of pleasure shooting through her veins. Funny how Nate had that effect and Guy didn't. "Are you a little piggie like my boys?"

"Oink, oink."

While she laughed and talked, Rainy absently used her sock-covered foot to dust the telephone table. Dust had a way of sneaking up on her. "Thanks for calling. I needed a laugh."

"Bad day?"

"Not bad as much as hectic." She told him about the social worker, Katie's persistent screams and the new boy. "To top it all off, we had a visit from our favorite police officer. Seems Katie's screams, even with the social worker on the premises, receive a lot of attention."

"Your neighbor again? What did you do to the woman, anyway?"

Carrying the cordless with her, Rainy checked to be sure Mikie was settling in. Will, bless him, solemnly rearranged a dresser drawer for the boy's meager belongings while Joshua plied Mikie with a handheld video game.

"Mrs. Underkircher is raising her only grandson alone and tends to spoil him a bit too much. He earned a low grade on his report card because he hadn't turned in a single assignment for over a month, even though I'd telephoned the home several times to discuss the problem. The low grade kept him off the honor roll. Which kept his name out of the local paper. Which caused him to be teased by another student."

"Woman, you should have your teaching license revoked."

Seeing that the children were okay, Rainy wandered into her bedroom for a few minutes of privacy and flopped onto a stack of seldom-used reading pillows. After teaching all day, attending a parent-teacher conference for Joshua and taking Katie to counseling, she was fried. Add the events of the last two hours and she was lucky to be breathing.

"Kathy Underkircher would agree."

"I was kidding."

Rainy stared at a cobweb above her bed. The fluffy little balls of dust were startling in the sunlight. Maybe she should shut the blinds. Instead, she looked around the room for something that would reach the ceiling, settling on a yardstick she used to measure the kids.

"I know you were joking. Unfortunately, Mrs. Underkircher isn't." She cradled the phone between her shoulder and chin and took a swing at the cobweb. "Somehow her vendetta turned personal. She claims I think too highly of myself, like I'm a saint or something because I take in foster kids."

"You are."

"Oh yes, Saint Rainy. This from the man who saw me totally freaked out over a flooded washing machine. And who has no idea that I'm trying to rid my ceiling of a giant cobweb at this very moment."

Crouching, she jumped and took another swing. "Missed again."

Nate's warm chuckle lifted her spirits. In fact, just hearing from him today after yesterday's impromptu, uninvited puppet show, thrilled her. Despite his occasional moodiness, she liked Nate Del Rio. She couldn't quite put her finger on the problem. He seemed to like the children, but he also seemed uptight with them at times.

She jumped again.

"Got it!" she shouted and then cringed. "Oops, sorry about the eardrum."

"No problem. I have another one."

Rainy giggled and fell back onto the fluffy lavender comforter. Right then and there she made a decision.

Nate probably hadn't been around kids much. That was why he didn't quite know how to react to them. That's why he was edgy at times and worried too much.

He just needed more exposure.

Nate didn't know for certain who started the phone calls, but he thought he might have been the guilty party. At the time, he must have been delirious on her double-dose brownies. That's the only excuse he could come up with for doing such a dumb thing. He thumped his head on the palomino's saddle, then mounted up. Somehow talking to Rainy on a daily basis had become a habit. One he looked forward to with growing enthusiasm.

Then yesterday morning he'd found himself standing on her front porch in the bright spring sunshine, red toolbox in hand as he dismantled her raucous-rock-band doorbell. Red tulips merrily mocked him from either side of the porch. Inside the house someone was playing a video game with sound effects. Next thing he knew, he was surrounded by kids jabbering away about school projects.

He'd been ambushed.

Now here they were again.

Holding the horse's reins at waist level with one hand, he leaned down to open the gate. Leather groaned and shifted as he rose in the stirrups, waiting for five more horses to plod past and out into open pasture on their first official trail ride.

With Nate riding alongside, Pop—with Katie stuck to his back like Velcro—led the single file parade. Rainy brought up the rear with Emma. The boys, including a newcomer named Mikie, rode in between.

Sweat broke out on Nate's neck. Pop and Rainy had talked him into this ride yesterday when she and the kids had driven out with a chocolate pie as thanks for fixing the doorbell. The pie was awesome, but he hadn't slept three hours last night thinking about all the things that could go wrong today.

They followed a well-trodden path made by the cows in numerous trips between the barn and the pond and beyond. Yo-Yo trotted alongside, his eyes bright and happy, his red tongue quivering in and out of his mouth.

Nate kept his attention roving from horse to horse and all around in search of hazards. As such, he caught the three boys watching him intently. With amused pride, Nate realized they were imitating him, each one sitting tall, reins in one hand, trying to perfect the cowboy posture. The difference was in relaxation. While Nate rode with one hand resting against his thigh, each boy gripped the saddle horn with a ferocity born of inexperience. As a result, they bounced like stiff little bobbleheads.

"Loosen the reins a little, like this," he said to Will, the closest to him.

Will nodded, serious as a heart attack, and adjusted his grip.

"This is supposed to be fun." A bug buzzed past his face. Nate swatted the air, coming up empty. "Relax and enjoy yourself."

"I am."

Yeah, right, Nate thought. Sweat beaded on Will's upper lip. The boy wrinkled his nose in an effort to adjust his sliding glasses and shot concerned looks toward his brother and sister. The kid didn't know how to relax. He always expected the worst.

Just like you.

The thought came out of nowhere and Nate shook it off. He didn't need his overactive sense of responsibility to horn in today.

He guided the group around the pond, where they spotted a pair of soft-eyed deer and a half dozen flapping, quacking ducks. The kids were excited to silence, a minor miracle to Nate's thinking.

He turned in the saddle. Rainy watched, too, both the animals and the children, with a gentle expression. She looked at him and mouthed, "Thank you."

Nate touched the brim of his hat, buoyed by that simple acknowledgment.

Maybe this wasn't so bad after all.

They rode farther into the pasture, over a ridge and into a shadowy line of woods along the creek. Nate wanted Rainy to see the area, certain she would appreciate its springtime beauty.

Dogwoods bloomed white and popcorn-like next to maroon redbud trees. Along the squishy, leaf-strewn riding path, bluebirds flashed in and out of blossoming limbs and sang in preparation for nesting. Tiny white and purple flowers jutted from the dark, damp earth. The smell was heady—green and moist and clean with nature's rebirth, yet ripe with the natural order of decay.

This was why he lived in the country and ranched. Days outdoors filled his spirit and soothed his troubles. He felt closer to God here than any other place on earth.

He glanced toward Rainy, wondering if she saw and felt what he did. Riding in and out of the leaf-dappled sunshine, her clear, pretty face was partly in shadow. She looked right and left, up and down, observing, listening to nature's wonder. When she took a deep breath and sighed, he had his answer. The notion that she, too, saw what he did filled a hollow longing beneath his ribcage. He didn't know why, couldn't begin to explain, but he relaxed in the saddle, content.

A low bawling sound broke the contemplative mood. Nate reined in the palomino. The horse tilted his head, listening, too. Yo-Yo paused in the trail, ears pricked up. The sound came again, high and plaintive, the cry of a calf. In two beats, the black and white cow dog hunkered low to the ground and, with a rustle of leaves, disappeared into the underbrush to fulfill his inborn job of protecting livestock.

"Better check that out, son," Pop said, riding up beside him. "Want me to go on ahead with our guests?"

They'd had their share of calves caught in barbed-wire fences, stuck in mud holes, or simply separated from mama. With coyotes always on the lookout for the young or weak, Nate took no chances with his registered stock.

By now, the other horses gathered around him.

"What is it, Nate?" Rainy asked. She looked like a rhinestone cowgirl in her fancy boots, jeans and a pink glittery vest. He'd plopped one of his hats on her head to make her laugh, and she'd amused—and pleased—him by wearing it.

"Probably a lost calf. Ride in easy so we don't spook him." He spoke as much to the children as to her. They all nodded their understanding.

"We gots to find her, Nate," Emma said, her blue eyes huge in her sun-kissed face. "Babies shouldn't never be without mamas. They get sad and cry."

The parallel between her situation and that of the calf was not lost on Nate. A lump formed in his throat. With a click of his tongue, he tapped Moccasin's flanks and rode on ahead.

By now, Yo-Yo had discovered the calf's whereabouts and yipped his find. Nate followed the sounds, his heart dropping to discover a mother and a newborn calf lying on the ground, the cow far too still.

Motioning to Rainy to wait with the children, he and Pop dismounted and approached the animals.

"Calf's brand new. Still wet."

"Mama's not looking so good."

Grimly, Nate flipped over her ear tag, discovering, as he feared, that she was one of his inseminated cows. The cow made no attempt to rise or protect her calf, both the norm, and he knew she wouldn't make it. Disappointment was a bitter taste in his mouth. He wasn't in this business to lose cows—especially now, when every penny counted.

The rustle and squeak of horses and leather brought his head up. His company dismounted, solemn and staring, to form a circle of mourning around the dying cow and her shivering black calf.

"Can we help?" Rainy asked softly.

He started to refuse and to send her and the children back to the house, but one look around the quiet circle changed his mind. "Why don't you fan out and gather dry leaves and grass for this little guy?"

As if the kids instinctively understood the need for stillness, they crept away, their colorful cowboy boots barely making a rustle on the soft grass.

By the time they returned, hands filled, the mother cow had heaved her last breath and Pop had headed back to the barn for the Mule. Nate felt as if someone had stepped on his chest. A registered Angus cow was worth a great deal of money. All he could do now was hope to save the calf.

The children gathered around him, uncertain. Their

eyes gleamed with sadness and the need to do something helpful.

Swallowing his own dismay, Nate motioned to them. "Come on. Baby here is waiting. Keep your voices down and be as calm as you can."

"What are we going to do?" Rainy asked, holding out her clump of dried grass. "Feed this to him?"

"City slicker," he said with a tiny smile, glad for the bit of humor. "He's too young to eat grass. We dry him. Warm him up, stimulate his circulation." He motioned toward the oldest boy. "Will, you and Emma bring yours and rub this side. We'll take turns."

Amazingly, the children did exactly as they were told with a minimum of noise and commotion. After a bit of rubbing, the wobbly calf struggled to stand, a good sign. Nate caught him around the chest and head, holding him still while the others rubbed the black fur to a dull softness.

"Can we name him?" Joshua asked. "He's a nice cow."

"He's not a cow," Nate corrected. "He's a bull, a boy."

"Oh." Joshua patted the calf's neck. "He's a nice bull. Can we name him?"

Nate made a habit of never naming livestock, other than for registration purposes. Sentimentality had no place in the cattle business. "Cattle usually get numbers, not names."

"Oh." Joshua's lips turned down. His small, dirty hand swiped uselessly at the bits of hay and grass clinging to his zippered fleece jacket.

Nate shifted on his boots, his glance moving from the small worried faces to Rainy and back to the hapless calf. The kids had gathered around the newborn, fingers trailing over him, reluctant to release their collective support. Dried but still trembling, the orphaned animal rolled big, brown eyes, and Nate was done in.

"Considering this little fella's been through a rough time, I guess you could name him if you wanted to."

Five heads snapped upward. "We can?"

Rainy's smile was warm and alive with approval. "Nate, that's so nice."

If she kept looking at him that way, her eyes all soft and glowy, he'd let the kids name every cow on the place.

"Will he get a new mama?" Emma asked, worry raising crinkles beneath her blond bangs.

Rainy placed a hand on the child's head, her smile fading to bittersweet. In one of their lengthy phone calls, she'd told him of Emma's fixation on mothers. She'd also told him of her hope to adopt the siblings and Katie, although all four were legal risk adoptions. Frankly, he thought Rainy was nuts for putting herself in a position to get her heart broken.

"Pop and I will have to be his mama."

This brought a round of giggles and snickers.

To cheer them, Nate turned an index finger toward himself in mock insult. "What? I don't look like a mama to you?"

While the other children laughed, Joshua rushed in to reassure. "Maybe not a mama, but you'd make a real good daddy."

Nate mentally flinched. Poor Joshua had no idea how wrong he was. Nate had been a dad all his life and he was lousy at it. Just last night, he'd been on the telephone for an hour trying to bail Blake out of another scrape. No matter how hard he tried, his siblings couldn't seem to get their lives together.

He was glad Rainy and her kids didn't know what a failure he was.

The calf bawled again and Pop rode up on the Mule, cutting off any need to respond. Thankful for the interruption, Nate loaded the now-squirming calf onto the vehicle for conveyance back to the barn.

Rainy touched his arm. "I have an idea."

He turned, dusting his hands down the sides of his jeans. "Trying to scare me?"

He wasn't joking.

Rainy bumped him with her side. "Don't say that. Hear me out. Will and Joshua joined the 4-H program at school. They've been trying to decide on a project for the fair next fall. Why not let them take care of the calf as their project? They could help you and, in the process, learn about ranching and animal care."

Nate could think of a thousand reasons why he shouldn't agree. Over the roar of the departing Mule, he started with one. "The calf has to be cared for every day. Fed at least twice a day."

"If you and Pop could handle the morning feeding, the boys could ride the bus to the ranch each day after school. I'd be happy to pick them up later." She hooked an elbow around the neck of each boy and pulled them close. "Being responsible for an animal is an excellent way to build self-esteem and integrity and all kinds of good qualities. An animal project would really be a good thing for them to do."

She looked so full of hope and good intentions. When Will and Joshua added their enthusiastic promises to be the best calf mamas ever, Nate felt his resistance slipping away. He knew he'd be sorry. He knew it was a bad idea. But, with a pull of dread in his gut, he gave in.

Ambushed again.

Chapter Seven

Rainy sat on an upturned bucket inside a barn stall watching Joshua and Will groom and feed the growing calf. All in all, Rainy thought the project was one of her best ideas yet.

Dubbed BlackJack because of his smooth black coat, the calf had grown from a spindly-legged orphan into a sturdy, friendly youngster in six weeks' time.

Joshua and Will had made up in enthusiasm what they lacked in knowledge, listening well when Nate or Pop taught them something new about livestock. Will, who had never enjoyed reading, had begun checking out library books on the topic and scoured the Internet for ways to turn BlackJack into a prize show calf.

Things were going well, indeed.

As part of their project, the boys were required to keep a daily record book, complete with photos. Every day after tending BlackJack, Will and Joshua took turns meticulously logging information. Everything from the amount and type of milk replacer to how much the calf weighed went into the book.

Today, Rainy had brought her camera for some photo updates. As she raised the digital, an overeager BlackJack butted hard at his bottle and sent Joshua onto his backside.

Foamy milk suds encircled the calf's mouth like shaving cream as he nudged at his human mama to get up and feed him some more. Rainy snapped a photo.

The cute shot got even better when Will flopped onto the hay-strewn floor, laughing.

"Mad calf, mad calf," he managed between bursts of laughter. "He's foaming at the mouth."

Rainy had few photos of Will in such a joyful moment so she snapped away, thrilled to see him behave like a normal, fun-loving fifth-grader. This project was good for him in more ways than she had ever imagined. During her months of caring for Will, he had not begun to relax until these weeks with BlackJack.

Outside in the corrals, Nate and Pop were "working cows," whatever that meant. A handful of high school boys from the agriculture program had been hired to assist. If the shouts and moos and thumps of bovine bodies in the metal chutes were any indication, the critters weren't too happy about being "worked."

Curious, she took a couple more shots of the boys with BlackJack and then left them to their job, going to the barn door. Directly across from where she stood, a cowboy herded an animal into a narrow passage. Then three other workers converged on the bawling creature with syringes, ear tags and tubes of medication. Dust and dirt swirled around the noisy activity.

Yo-Yo, the happy collie, snaked around the legs of calves, adding a nip here and there to make a rowdy one behave or move him forward in the chutes.

Camera dangling from her arm, Rainy raised a hand to shade her eyes, spotting Nate in the midst of the commotion. Broad-shouldered and handsome in a gray shirt, he shoved a final calf into the head gate. The trap door clanged into place. He made a notation on a clipboard.

Rainy stood still, enjoying the view.

The evening trip to Crossroads Ranch had become her favorite part of the day. And Nate Del Rio was the reason.

Funny that she found him, a country boy, so fascinating. But Nate was more than a ruggedly handsome face. Smart and responsible, funny and kind, Nate's heart was as soft as a warm marshmallow. He just didn't want anyone to know it.

He'd admitted how much he enjoyed volunteering for the Handyman Ministry, but he was a pushover with the kids, too. He'd also formed a habit of checking the oil in her car every week even though she could do the task herself. When she'd tried to compliment him for the kindness, he'd made some joking comment about women mechanics.

She raised her digital and snapped.

He looked up, lifted his hat in greeting.

Rainy's heart fluttered crazily. She waved, and Nate said something to Pop, who nodded. Then Nate leaped

over the steel corral and headed her way, shedding
a pair of leather gloves in transit. Yo-Yo spotted his
master's departure and slithered beneath an iron gate
to follow.

Okay, so she liked Nate. A lot. The more time she
spent with him, the more she liked him. They were
friends, but she wouldn't mind if they were more.
Sometimes she thought he felt the same. At other times,
she wasn't so sure. But something was going on between them.

The kids thought Nate was the coolest dude on the
planet.

Maybe Rainy thought so, too.

Maybe there was hope for an old maid schoolteacher
with four foster kids. They'd never exactly discussed
Nate's stand on the subject of foster care and adoption,
but he must be agreeable. He was letting the boys foster
BlackJack. That had to count for something.

While her thoughts tumbled around, Nate sauntered
toward her in the sunshine, his dusty boots striding in
that easy cowboy manner that had her wondering why
she'd never noticed cowboys before Nate. Her mouth
titled upward. She was noticing now.

"Hey, Slick, what's up?" he asked. He rubbed a ban-
dana over his sweaty face, stuck the red cloth in his
back pocket and grinned. His killer dimples made an
appearance, setting off the laugh lines around his eyes.

"Same old same old, Cowboy," she answered.

Their nicknames for one another had stuck, and
Rainy had to admit she liked hers. She even liked being

teased for some of the silly questions she asked about cows and horses and ranching.

She snapped another photo, earning a mock scowl. He reached out and slid the camera from her wrist. "My turn."

Rainy protested, ducking to one side when he raised the digital. "No way."

He laughed and snapped. "Smile pretty or suffer the consequences."

She made a face. He snapped again. This time she burst out laughing. He snapped that, too.

"I want a copy of every one of them."

"No way."

"You're repeating yourself." He took her hand and slid the camera strap onto her wrist. His fingers were calloused and rough against her tender skin, but his touch was light and easy. A zing of energy flooded her. Being in Nate's company had that effect.

They stood in the entry to the barn for several long seconds, saying nothing, grinning at each other. Nate leaned a shoulder against one of the doorposts.

Rainy took the other doorpost, bending a knee to prop her foot against the barn. From this spot, she could hear the boys and enjoy the sunshine with Nate.

"Riding the Mule yesterday was fun," she said.

A red wasp buzzed close. Using his hat, he slapped the insect to the ground, then smashed it with his boot toe. "We'll have to do it again sometime."

"I'd like that."

He'd taken turns giving rides to all of them, but hers had been the longest. She'd loved every minute of sitting next to Nate while they rumbled across the green grass. With four children around, time alone was not to be taken lightly.

"I got some news today." He replaced the Stetson, adjusting the brim low over his eyes.

"Good news?" she asked, not sure what this had to do with riding the ATV.

"I think so." He hitched his chin toward a fence line in the distance. "That land over there where we rode the Mule."

"Your leased property?" With a quiet intensity she hadn't completely understood, he'd detailed the eight hundred acres as they drove by ponds and a creek, stands of timber and loading chutes. His black Angus cattle roamed fat and content in the long, open areas of lush, green Bermuda grass.

"Right now I'm only leasing half. The lease runs out at the end of this year, but I have an option to buy the entire acreage. This morning I talked to the owner."

"He's ready to sell?"

Nate nodded. "He moved to South Dakota several years ago, so I've been expecting this. But Pierson was clear about one thing. He needs the money to invest in his business. So if I don't buy the property, he'll sell to someone else. He already has other offers."

She could see the prospect worried him. "Are you going to buy it, then?"

"I want to. I've wanted to for a long time. Buy the land. Add another hundred head of cattle." His face shone with quiet excitement. Rainy saw past the casual words to the dream inside. "I'm starting to believe I can make it happen."

"Sounds like a huge investment."

He nodded. "I knew sooner or later Pierson would sell, so I've been saving the down payment for a while. In the ranching business, a man either has to go big or keep grubbing with the small stuff. I want Crossroads Ranch to become the premiere organic beef ranch in this part of the state."

"Organic? That's awesome, Nate." Pushing off the door, she dropped her foot to the hard-packed earth. "I can see it now. Restaurants advertising organic steaks and burgers from Crossroads Ranch. Healthy and delicious."

Pleased amusement played around his lips. He joined her in the center of the entry and tugged her hair. "Thanks for the vote of confidence, Slick. I hope you're right."

Rainy hoped she was right, too. To her way of thinking, an honest Christian guy like Nate was good for the business world.

"I'd better check on the boys. They should be finished by now." They started walking that direction, taking their time, lazily enjoying one another's company.

"They're turning into good little ranch hands," Nate said, and there was pride and affection in his admission. "I can leave them alone with BlackJack now, knowing they can handle him."

They'd come a long way, indeed. "Think they'll win a prize at the fair?"

"Too early to tell. BlackJack's still a baby, but he's from good stock."

"Will the fact that he's bottle raised hurt him?"

"Some calves don't fare as well, but as I said, Will and Josh are trying to compensate. BlackJack should do fine."

"You've taught them a lot."

"Will comes in every day with some new idea he's read somewhere. If I'm not careful, he'll run me out of business one of these days." The quick flash of dimples showed he was teasing.

"You wouldn't believe his aversion to books before BlackJack. Before coming into the social system, he didn't attend school regularly, so reading is hard for him. He also didn't see any value in reading until now."

"You're good for them. They're thriving."

Happiness spread through Rainy like a smile on the inside. Nate had the uncanny ability to say the right things.

"I hope the courts agree."

"Are you worried about that? About them being taken away?"

She shrugged one shoulder, tilting her head. "I try not to."

"But you do."

"Yes, I do. I know I shouldn't. God has a plan for their lives. I don't want my wants to ever get in the way, but I've bonded with all four of these kids. Losing them would hurt."

"Would you ever give it up?" he asked, pausing just inside the shaded building. "Doing foster care, I mean."

There was something intense in the way he asked, some unspoken meaning that gave Rainy pause, made her wonder. She couldn't quite figure out what he meant.

She turned around then, looking back out at the pasture where calves kicked and bucked, in a hurry to rejoin their waiting mothers. Sometimes she wondered if her foster children felt that pull toward their birth mothers. Surely they did. They must. But they loved her, too. She was the person who'd provided the stable, loving, Christian home none of them had ever had before.

"Fostering is hard sometimes," she said, turning back to face him. "Dealing with the uncertainty, the heartaches. But I can't imagine a life without children."

A nameless emotion shifted over Nate's face. He glanced away, swallowed.

"That's what I thought," he said softly, as if to himself.

Rainy studied the side of his face, the strong jaw, the dimple creases she liked so much. For some strange reason, she felt as if he'd given her a test…and she'd failed.

Without another word, Nate headed deeper into the barn. Following behind, Rainy kicked a loose dirt clod at him. "Hey, Cowboy, did I do something?"

Nate looked over his shoulder. "Nah. Not you. Me. Come on. Time for the boys to muck out the stall. You gotta get a picture of that."

Though Rainy couldn't shake the feeling that she'd done something wrong, she let the subject drop. Side by side, she and Nate leaned their arms atop the stall's half door and peered at the scene inside. His elbow bumped hers. She tried to ignore the touch, concentrating instead on Will and Joshua.

The scent of fresh straw, bedding material for the calf, filled her nostrils. The little calf followed the boys around, nudging at them with friendly affection. Occasionally, Joshua or Will stopped working long enough to scratch BlackJack behind the ears. Yo-Yo belly crawled toward Josh, nudging with his black nose.

Nate tilted his head toward hers. "Where are blondie and the screamer today?"

Mikie had long since been returned to his mother and Rainy prayed every night that she'd embrace this second chance, stay away from her abusive boyfriend and make a good home for Mikie.

"Birthday party. A little girl from church." She checked her watch. "Don't let me forget to leave by six-thirty. The party is over at seven."

Pop appeared in the alleyway between the stalls and outside, his round, weathered face shaded by the broad-brimmed Stetson.

"We got company." He jerked a thumb toward the house. "Other than Rainy, I mean. She's homefolks now."

Rainy straightened, thanking him for the kind sentiment with a smile.

"Who is it?" Nate pushed away from the stall, dusting his hands down his jeans as he went to join his grandfather. Rainy followed the pair back out into the sunlight.

"Don't recognize the truck," Pop said. "But the driver looks like Janine."

Janine? Rainy frowned. Who was that?

She started to ask but noticed the tight line of Nate's mouth and changed her mind. Maybe later. A lot later.

A battered gray pickup truck came to a dust-stirring halt in the driveway beside the house. A young woman with a baby in her arms stepped out and came toward them. Richly tanned, with long, dark, curly hair and an ultra-slim figure beneath a black and white polka-dot sundress, the newcomer looked pretty enough to turn heads.

Rainy glanced at Nate to see if his was one of them.

It wasn't. Still bristling like a threatened cat, he made an unhappy sound in the back of his throat.

"Excuse me," he said tersely, his eyes locked on the woman and baby. "I'll be back."

He strode off to meet the newcomer.

Rainy knew she was nosy to listen in, but she couldn't seem to help herself. After Nate's odd reaction to the woman's arrival, she was curious. Maybe a little jealous, too. Nate had never mentioned any old girlfriends.

Nate's palomino edged a nose over the wire fence and whickered. Rainy sauntered close to stroke his velvety muzzle, an excuse, she admitted, to stay within hearing distance without appearing too obvious.

Voices from the driveway carried on the breeze. The woman's rose, strident and insisting. "I need the money, Nate."

Nate removed his hat and tapped it against his thigh.

The baby, a girl, reached toward him. He jiggled her tiny hand with his free one. The baby's toothless smile rewarded him, but Nate turned a concerned gaze on the woman.

By now, Will and Joshua had finished their chores and came to stand beside her at the fence. Feeling a little foolish, she was glad for their company.

"Who is that lady, Miss Rainy?"

"I don't know, Will." Not that Nate's company was any of her business, but she shamelessly tried to hear the conversation. Nate looked so troubled.

Unwanted thoughts raced through her head. Her heart sank. Who *was* this demanding woman with the adorable baby?

To her embarrassment, Pop must have noticed her curiosity. He joined her at the fence.

"That's Janine," he said without preamble. "Nate's sister. Wonder what she wants?"

With relief, Rainy now saw the family likeness. No wonder Janine was darkly pretty. "She's lovely. Is that her baby?"

"Yep. Little Bailey. Cute as a new kitten. Come on. I'll introduce you."

"Nate doesn't look like he wants company."

"Ah, he's all right. Come on. We might keep him out of trouble."

Shoving her fingertips into her back pockets, Rainy fell into step beside the rancher. "Keep him out of trouble? How?"

"I guess he hasn't told you much about his family."

"Just that his parents are dead and he has a brother and a sister. I can tell he worries about them a lot."

Pop snorted. "Too much, if you ask me, which you didn't, but I'm telling you anyway. He has some fool notion that he's the only one who can take care of them. Janine and Blake know how he feels and take advantage." He took a hitch at his jeans and sniffed. "Don't tell him I said that. He's touchy about it. Janine's a good girl, sweet as pie, but spoiled rotten and doesn't have a lick of common sense. Nate lets her get to him."

Rainy wasn't surprised. Nate was a born softy. "He cares about her."

"It's a whole lot more than caring. That's the bad thing about the whole mess." As they drew closer to Nate and Janine, Pop lifted a hand. "Quiet now. Don't want him knowing I said anything."

Rainy wondered about Pop's curious observation but she was so relieved that Janine was a sibling instead of a girlfriend that she didn't dwell on Pop's meaning.

Their boots crunched on the loose gravel. Nate must have heard because he turned, one hand on his hip, a scowl on his brow.

Pop made the introductions. "Let's all go inside and have a good visit," he said. "Janine and Rainy can get acquainted."

Nate's scowl deepened.

Janine shook her head. Loose, pretty curls danced around her shoulders. "Next time, Pop. Today I have to run. Nate and I have a little business to take care of first. You all go on inside without us."

Rainy recognized a brush-off when she saw one, but Pop said, "Nah, that's okay. We'll wait."

Nate narrowed a look at his grandfather. "Pop."

"Okay, okay." Pop kissed the babbling baby on the forehead and hugged Janine. "Talk to you later. Me and these cowpokes are hankering for a long, tall glass of sody water anyways. Isn't that right, boys?"

Oblivious to the undercurrent between adults, Will and Joshua grinned.

Rainy started to follow the boys inside, but Nate's voice turned her around. "Rainy."

He never called her that. "Yes?"

"You're not leaving yet, are you?"

She glanced at her watch. "Soon."

The baby in Janine's arms patted Nate's shoulder. He took her into his arms. At the sight of Nate holding a small baby, a funny feeling settled beneath Rainy's ribs.

"I rented a movie," he said, heedless of the baby tugging at his ear. "Thought you might like it."

She smiled. "Oh yeah? What's the movie?"

"A surprise. Come tomorrow prepared to stay. I'll even feed you."

"Feed me? As in pizza delivery, or home cooking?"

"Come and find out. You might be surprised."

Her smile widened. "I'll be here."

The next afternoon Nate hit the shower earlier than usual, and then dressed in clean jeans and shirt. Later, he'd whip up a Tex-Mex casserole to pop in the oven before Rainy and the children arrived. He couldn't wait to see her expression when she discovered he was a pretty fair cook. No pizza delivery for him.

"What are you getting all spiffed up for?" Pop limped in through the back door and tossed his hat on the couch.

"No use smelling like a cow lot just because I'm in the ranching business." He reached for Pop's white Stetson and hung the battered straw on a hook by the back door. "Why are you limping?"

"Cow stepped on my foot." Pop pulled two kitchen chairs face to face, collapsed in one with a gusty sigh and propped his boot on the other. "And don't change the subject. You never fancy up in mid afternoon."

"Nosy old man."

"I'd thump your head for disrespect if I didn't know you was joking." Pop eased his boot off, letting it fall to the floor with a thud. Dirt spattered the floor in a starburst. His big toe poked through a hole in a white tube sock. "You are joking, ain't you?"

"Sorry, Pop. You know I am."

"Good. Now tell me what's going on. Going somewhere?"

"Rainy's coming over."

"Comes over every day." Pop peeled the sock away with a grimace. The top of his foot was blue and puffy. With a knowing expression, he squinted toward Nate. "You like her, don't you?"

"We're friends. What's not to like?" Nate shrugged, turning his attention to Pop's injured foot. "That looks bad. Want me to run you in to the doctor's office?"

"Nah. Just a bruise. Hazard of the business." He motioned toward the sink. "Get me a bucket of hot water. A good soaking will fix me right up."

"Uh, Pop. Do you mind soaking somewhere else?" Nate rubbed the back of his neck, thinking of the dirt from Pop's boots. Now he'd have to clean the floor again. "Rainy's staying for dinner. And a movie. I'm cooking in here."

His grandfather leaned back in his chair and grinned what could only be termed a "possum-eatin'" grin.

"As in a date?"

Nate shrugged.

"Well now, if that isn't an answer to prayer, I don't know what is."

Nate narrowed his eyes in what he hoped was a warning look. "Meaning?"

Pop chuckled. "Sounds like more than friends to me. And I'm mighty glad to hear it. The Word says a man ought not to be alone. Needs a helpmate."

"You're alone."

"But I had your granny for a lot of good years. You keep floundering around, you'll miss out on all the good ones. I can tell you, Nate boy, Miss Rainy's a good one."

Nate couldn't argue that, but they did have one major problem. And he saw no way around it. "She wants to adopt kids."

"Nothing wrong with wanting young ones. That's one of the things that makes her special, shows what a fine woman she is."

"I wouldn't mind finding a wife, but I've had kids all my life. I'm done with that."

"You've had a set of pain-in-the-neck, overindulged siblings."

"Same thing."

"They're adults now, son. The sooner you let them grow up, the sooner you can think of yourself instead of taking care of them."

"I can't just turn them out like yearling calves. Not when they need my help."

"What do you need, Nate boy? You're not getting any younger or better looking. You got needs, too. Get to thinking on that for a change."

Pop's attempt at humor sailed right past him.

"What I need doesn't matter, Pop. You know what happened the one time I turned my back." His stomach started to churn in that old familiar way. "You *know* why I can't ever refuse them."

Pop studied him with a compassion Nate resented. He didn't deserve anyone feeling sorry for him. What happened had been his fault.

Pop laid his dirty sock across his knee and in a soft voice said, "Christine is gone, son. Martyring yourself won't bring her back."

The memory of his crucial decision, of his deepest, ugliest failure, jabbed into Nate like a hot knife. Pop knew better than to mention Christine. They never talked about her. Ever. Didn't he realize that Nate carried the guilt with him every moment of every day? Having her name shoved in his face, forced into conversation, was too much.

Swallowing back a groan of agony, he muttered, "I'll get that hot water."

He stalked to the sink and crouched to rattle around in the lower cabinet. The soft scuttle of chair and boot warned him of Pop's approach. The old man placed a hand on his shoulder.

"I didn't mean to upset you, Nate boy." He emitted a frustrated huff. "It's just…I want you to let go and be happy. That's all."

His shoulders were tight with tension, but Nate couldn't stay upset with his grandfather. For all his straight shooting, Pop cared deeply.

"Forget about it," he said, wishing he could. Wishing he could erase the wrong he'd done to his own sister. Wishing he could go back in time and change his response to that one phone call.

Digging an old blue dishpan from under the sink, he rose and stuck it beneath the faucet.

He couldn't change what he'd done to Christine. But he could take care of Janine and Blake. If that was his penance from God, he'd accept it. Even if it meant always being alone.

Chapter Eight

Rainy noticed a thin undercurrent of tension the moment she arrived at Crossroads Ranch. Nothing was said, and Pop was as jovial as always, but Nate seemed to have something on his mind. Rainy wondered if his mood had anything to do with Janine's visit the day before. She also wondered what Pop had meant when he'd said the siblings took advantage of Nate. Beneath all his cowboy macho, Nate had a soft heart, but she couldn't imagine anyone taking advantage of him without his permission.

"You two get the grub on the table," Pop said. "I'll go round up the boys." He pointed at Emma and Katie. "You cowgirls going with me?"

Emma batted long eyelashes. "Can we ride the four-wheeler?"

With a chuckle, Pop wagged his head. "Oh, I reckon so. Won't hurt nothing. As long as Katie here promises not to scream."

"She won't scream, will you, Katie?" Emma said, one small hand squeezing the other girl's upper arm.

Rust-colored freckles stood out against creamy, pale skin as Katie said, "Not if I can ride first."

Rainy's heart turned over every time she looked at her foster daughters. Emma was a sweetheart and, for all her difficulties, Kate was a precious little girl slowly learning to deal with life's frustrations with words instead of screams.

"Done!" Pop said with a chuckle and hustled the adorable pair out the back door.

Rainy went to the kitchen window and watched the trio cross the green grassy space between house and barn. She got more joy watching her little girls play than she had ever imagined possible. They were gifts from God, and she prayed they would be with her always.

"Is your granddad limping?"

Nate, busy assembling the ingredients for a green salad, glanced up. "Cow stepped on him."

"Ouch." Rainy turned away from the window to enjoy another sight—a cowboy in the kitchen. "What did the doctor say?"

"Pop hasn't been to a doctor in thirty years. He says bones heal whether a doctor says they're broken or not." With an affectionate twinkle in his eye, Nate stuck his chin out in a stubborn jut to imitate his grandfather. "God made 'em, He can fix 'em."

Rainy laughed and reached around him, snagging a piece of lettuce.

All day she'd looked forward to the evening with

Nate. More than once, she'd had to remind herself that this was probably not a date, but nevertheless, she'd rushed home after school. Like a giddy teenager, she'd changed clothes three times before settling on a magenta pullover tucked into jeans with a wide, fancy belt. Because Nate teased her mercilessly about her girly footwear, she'd worn a pair of hot-pink heels just for fun.

"What smells so amazing?" she asked. A blend of tomato and spices had been driving her crazy since the moment she'd entered the warm, fragrant kitchen.

"That, Slick," Nate said, gesturing with a paring knife, "is the house specialty, beef enchilada casserole with sides of Spanish rice and refried beans."

"Who's the cook? Don Pueblos?"

One side of his mouth tipped up. He turned the point of the knife toward his chest. "Señor Del Rio. Me."

She backed against the kitchen counter, crossing her arms as she leveled him with a disbelieving stare. "No, seriously. You ordered out."

"Hey! I do not order out. A man who doesn't like frozen dinners or driving into town to eat learns to cook or starves. Starving is not cool. So I wanted to impress you with my culinary expertise."

"Color me impressed. I expected something much less domestic from a—" She stopped, grinning sheepishly at the sexist remark about to come out of her mouth.

Busy tossing the salad around with a fork and spoon, Nate paused mid-stir, clearly amused. "I know what you were thinking. A man, especially a rancher, shouldn't cook anything except barbeque on the grill."

"Or hot dogs over a campfire," Rainy joked as she pushed away from the cabinet and began to gather up loose bits of lettuce. "Sorry for the stereotype. I guess I'm an old-fashioned girl in a lot of ways. At my house, Mom always did the cooking and cleaning. Dad did the yard and took care of the car."

"And never the twain should meet?"

Lettuce scraps in hand, she glanced around for the trash can. Nate pointed toward the side of the refrigerator. Sometime since the day of the puppet show, he'd rearranged. Nate was, quite possibly, a neat freak about his house. Rainy wondered if he'd ever dusted furniture with his sock feet. Probably not.

"That's why I have to call the Handyman Ministry so often." Rainy stepped on the pedal and the silver trash can *thwanged* open. "Daddy wouldn't teach me anything he considered man's work. A boyfriend in college taught me to change the oil in my car, and Daddy got so mad. He said the boy was too lazy to do the job for me."

"Boyfriend, huh? You've never mentioned boyfriends before." He placed the glass salad bowl in the center of the table, the red and green vegetables creating a colorful contrast.

"You've never mentioned girlfriends before." Rainy dusted tiny bits of lettuce from her hands into the trash and then *thwanged* the lid shut again.

"Nope. I haven't." With that maddening answer, he motioned to an upper cabinet. "Mind setting the table?"

"Not at all." She touched a pull knob. "Plates in here?"

"Next one over."

She opened the door and counted down seven plain white plates rimmed in black. "Are my chocolate pecan bars going to fit into your fancy Tex-Mex menu? Or should I take them back home?"

He made a harrumphing noise. "Don't even think about it. You'll never escape this house with anything but an empty plate."

Rainy smiled on the inside. Nate had a way of making her feel good about her simple talents.

Astoundingly efficient in the kitchen, he slid bottled salad dressing and croutons onto the table with one hand while straightening chairs around the table with the other. Rainy could not imagine her father doing any of these things.

She wondered then about Nate's family. With his mother and father gone, did the others come here for holidays? Did Nate cook for them? And what *had* Pop meant when he'd said they took advantage?

To her way of thinking families were supposed to help each other. Even though her folks lived an hour away, she knew they were there if she needed them. Would Pop consider that taking advantage?

Nate's voice broke into her thoughts. "How can you bake sweets all the time and still look the way you do?"

"Is that a compliment?" she asked, preening a bit as she took plates to the table.

"Don't let it go to your head." When he opened the

oven, a spicy, rich scent wafted forth. Rainy almost swooned.

"Too late. Already did. You paid me a compliment and here's one in return. You look nice, too. That emerald shirt turns your eyes green." Another reason to nearly swoon. Nate with green, green eyes above those dimples was breathtaking.

"Emerald?" He dipped his chin to his chest, pretending to stare at his shirt. "Is that what this is? I thought it was green."

"Ha. Very funny. Next you'll say my pullover is purple."

"It is."

"Magenta."

The oven door thudded shut. Nate moved closer, merriment in his expression, staring at her feet. "I suppose the shoes are magenta, too?"

"Nope," she said, enjoying the game. "Pink. Plain old pink."

With a grin and shrug, he said, "A man can't win."

"What fun would that be?"

They laughed into each other's eyes and the moment extended. Nate shifted slightly and Rainy had the lovely thought that he might kiss her. She'd thought it before, weeks ago, but the timing had been wrong. They hadn't really known each other then. Now she knew Nate as an honorable man who took relationships seriously. People mattered to him. Though he'd never said so, Rainy knew she mattered. The questions remained, how much and in what way?

She watched his eyes, mesmerized by the tenderness lurking in the green depths. Tenderness? For her?

A slight smile lingered on his lips, activating the dimples. He raised a hand, touched her cheek with the backs of his knuckles. Her heart fluttered, hopeful, expectant.

The oven timer *beep, beep, beeped*. They both jumped, and then laughed. With a wry expression, Nate turned away to answer the call.

A sliver of disappointment slid through Rainy.

She touched her fingertips to her cheek. Who would imagine a rough, tough cowboy could be so tender?

Just then, the back door banged open on its hinges. With an explosion of jovial noise, Pop and the four children clattered inside and the tender moment was lost forever as dinner was served.

But Rainy couldn't forget the caring look in Nate's eyes or the sudden burst of joy in her heart. When they bowed their heads to say grace, she struggled to keep her mind on the Lord and off the smooth rumble of Nate's baritone. A praying man was an enthralling attraction.

All through dinner she was acutely aware of him sitting across the table. Now and then, she'd look up from her plate to find him watching her, his expression interested and wondering. When he'd catch her staring—something she did far too often—he'd smile or wink and the expression disappeared.

After the meal and the dishes were cleared away, Rainy settled the children at the table to complete homework. As she did at home, she moved from chair to chair, helping each child. Will and Joshua, confirmed haters of homework, both grumbled and dawdled until Nate sat down between them.

"School's important, boys," he said quietly. "Don't give Rainy a hard time. She wants you to do well for *you,* not for her. She cares about your future. If you don't study hard and learn, life will be real tough when you grow up."

The two boys listened as if their lives depended on it. Then they bent their heads to the task and grumbled no more.

Gratitude filled Rainy. Will and Josh needed the counsel and example of a godly man. Rainy was more than glad that man was Nate Del Rio. Nate would make an awesome daddy.

There it was. A notion that had danced around the edges of Rainy's mind since that first day when Nate had rescued the children from the closet. Until this moment, she'd kept the thought hidden, forbidding it to bloom.

Even now, the revelation flustered her, made her all too aware of Nate's strong, masculine presence, of the dreams and longings she'd pushed aside, convinced they would never happen. She wanted to fall madly in love, not settle for anyone who would accept her and her kids. Her thoughts went to Guy Bartlett. After the last two turn-downs, he'd stopped calling, and she was relieved. Though she didn't begin to understand the reasons, she felt something with Nate that was missing with Guy and every other man. To escape her inner discomfort, Rainy leaned over Katie's shoulder and asked her to sound out the word *basket*.

Still, the idea wouldn't go away.

God must have a sense of humor, she thought, to let a city girl become enamored of a rancher, especially when that woman had given up on ever finding Mr. Right. She wasn't sure if Nate was the one, but the idea didn't scare her away.

Remembering his curious expression at dinner, she hoped the idea didn't scare *him* away, either.

When homework was nearly finished, Nate pushed back his chair and stood. "About ready for that movie I promised you?"

"I was starting to wonder if you'd made that up." She helped the smaller children stuff books and papers into their backpacks, then followed Nate into the living room.

"Check this out," he said, extending a DVD case. "Just for you."

"What is it?" She squinted toward the cover but couldn't make out the title. "A chick flick in my honor?"

He looked offended. "Not even close. I wouldn't be caught dead renting a chick flick."

Rainy laughed. "Oh, Cowboy, I'm going to make you eat those words. Give me that DVD."

She reached for it. Nate held the shiny plastic above his head, out of her reach. She jumped for it. He dipped to one side. Even in heels she didn't stand a chance against his superior height.

When he grinned like the ornery man he was, she slammed a fist onto her hipbone. "If you don't give me that right this minute, I'm going to do something terrible."

By now, Pop and the children had joined the fracas.

"Better give it to her, Nate," Will said. "She and Katie might start screaming."

"Me, too," said Emma, not to be left out.

As if terrified by the notion of three screaming females, Nate quickly deposited the DVD in Rainy's outstretched palm.

She looked down, read the title and started laughing. "*City Slickers?* Where in the world did you find this old movie?"

With a twitch of his eyebrows, Nate admitted, "I ordered it off the Internet. An edited version, especially for you."

Though secretly delighted to know Nate had been thinking about her enough to do such a cute thing, Rainy pretended insult. "You owe me, Cowboy."

"Ooh, I'm shaking." He extended both hands, giving an exaggerated tremble.

"Better be." She flexed a bicep, pointing at the pitiful bump. "Feel that muscle. Stainless steel."

Nate squeezed her upper arm, eyes widening in fun. "Dangerous. Mosquitoes beware."

With a head toss and a tiny sniff for good measure, Rainy settled onto the brown sofa next to Will while Nate set up the DVD player.

Will gave her a funny look, glancing from her to Nate. Then without a word, he moved to another chair. Nate, balanced on his toes in front of the TV, pivoted around, saw the only empty seat next to her and winked at Will. The boy grinned and hitched his chin toward Rainy in a not-so-subtle movement.

"What are you two up to?" she asked.

Nate scooted next to her on the sofa and pointed the remote toward the big screen. "No talking in the theater."

Will snickered.

"Good thing we're not in a theater." Rainy burrowed her shoulders deep into the couch cushions. The scent of Nate's clean cotton shirt followed her. "I love to talk."

"So I noticed."

"Hey!" She bopped him on the shoulder.

Nate captured her hand. Rainy stopped talking.

Why fight a good thing?

Though surrounded by kids, Nate was having a great time. He credited his good mood to Rainy, of course. Her reaction to the movie pleased him and he couldn't resist teasing her throughout.

The old comedy was about a group of city slicker friends who vacation on a working dude ranch and get into all sorts of funny situations. Some of the events paralleled a few of the blunders she and the children had made when first coming to Crossroads Ranch.

He thought her city girl mistakes were cute. Truth be told, he thought everything about Rainy was cute.

"Move over, Will. You're in my way." Emma shoved at her brother's shoulder.

Well, almost everything.

He liked the children. It wasn't that. Sometimes they

hit him right in the heart. There lay his concern. He didn't need any more heart problems.

A scene played out across the television. A mama cow died birthing her calf. Katie sniffed. "Like Black-Jack."

Rainy and Nate exchanged glances. They both knew Katie's response went far deeper than the orphaned calf.

A pinch of sadness dampened the laughter in Rainy's eyes. Nate stroked his thumb over the back of her hand, hoping to comfort her. He didn't know if it would, but Rainy's touch comforted him. The least he could do was return the favor.

Earlier in the kitchen, he'd thought about kissing her. Considering his ambivalent feelings toward her family, he shouldn't be thinking such a thing. But she made him smile and smelled so good, and her small, soft hand seemed tailor-made for him to hold.

Rainy was a strong, independent woman who didn't need anyone, but just the same, she made him feel necessary. Protective even. God-given male instinct, he supposed, but different from what he felt for Blake and Janine. He wasn't obligated to do things for Rainy; he wanted to do them.

She turned her attention back to the screen and giggled. The sound tickled Nate on the inside, like a bubble of happiness beneath his ribcage.

Miss Rainy was mighty distracting.

He should put an end to this budding infatuation before he fell in too deep. He should, but he didn't want to. Not yet, anyway.

The telephone jangled. Since Pop had disappeared into his bedroom to nurse the sore foot, Nate got up to answer, reluctantly loosing his hold on Rainy's hand.

As he reached for the wall phone, he glanced at the caller ID. Some of his pleasant mood leached away. Blake. His gut tightened.

"Is something wrong?" It was the first question he always asked. "Where are you? Are you all right?"

His grip tightening on the receiver, he turned his back and moved as far into the kitchen as possible. No use bothering Rainy with his problems. And his brother always seemed to have a problem.

"Sure, bro. Fine as frog hair. How are things at the ranch?"

Nate let out the breath he hadn't known he was holding. Maybe Blake's call wasn't another SOS. For all Nate's grousing, not every call was. Last week the two brothers had shared breakfast at the pancake house. Nate had paid, of course, but other than that, Blake had asked for nothing.

"Pop hurt his foot today, but he's tough." Nate recounted the situation, drawing a knowing laugh from Blake.

"I don't know how you put up with the old dude," his brother said. "Always preaching at you and waving the Bible under your nose."

Other than genetics, he and Blake had so little in common. "Don't start about Pop. If you'd listen to him, you'd be a lot better off."

In the adjoining living room, conversation began to flow again as the movie ended. He wanted to be in there with them, instead of standing here worrying about his adult brother.

When Rainy came into his life, she'd stirred up a lot of latent emotions. The jury was still out on whether that was a good thing or a bad one. Right now, he was enjoying his time with her more than anything he'd done in the last ten years. Maybe Pop was right. Maybe the time had come for him to focus on his own life for a change.

Shutting out the sound of Rainy's sweet laughter, he forced his attention to the call. If his brother wanted something, he wouldn't beat around the bush too long.

Sure enough, after about five minutes of useless chatter during which Nate's hopes rose, Blake got to the point. He wanted another loan. Nate closed his eyes in disappointment. His brother had a decent job. He should be doing well, but he lived far above his means and had a habit of buying into get-rich schemes that never panned out. From the occasional urgency of Blake's needs, Nate suspected he gambled, too, though Blake denied it, knowing his brother's aversion to the habit.

He hoped Blake stayed clear of illegal activities, but he couldn't be certain. That one worry was enough to wake Nate in the night and keep him handing over checks. Gambling debts of the wrong kind could get a man hurt.

A dozen times over, he'd tried to explain finance to his brother, but the advice only lasted until Blake's next payment was overdue. Sometimes Nate considered letting his brother lose his car or condo, but if he did, where would Blake go? How could he get to work? Blake had him by the conscience, and they both knew it.

Resentment bubbled up as hot as heartburn at the amount of money Blake requested this time. Nate would have to dip into his savings. Now, when he was so close to buying the Pierson land, the withdrawal would hurt.

He kept that information from his brother. Why bother? Blake cared nothing for this ranch.

Gritting his teeth, he agreed to meet Blake at the bank in the morning. He hung up the phone and leaned both hands on the kitchen counter to stare out into the darkness at the piece of property he wanted so badly. Would he always be saddled like a pack mule with his brother? Would Blake ever grow up?

Nate thought of a lesson in the Bible, though the story was foggy. Yet the words "my brother's keeper" rattled around in his head, weighing him down, obligating him.

"Is everything all right?" Rainy's voice came from behind him. He turned to find her standing close, her expression concerned.

"My brother," he said, rubbing both hands over his face as if he could wipe away the constant strain of being the oldest.

"You say that as if there's something wrong." She took his hands in hers, and that simple act eased some of his tension. "Can I help?"

She helped simply by being here. But he said, "Blake needs to help himself."

"Your brother and sister depend on you a lot, don't they?"

He twitched a shoulder. "No big deal."

She didn't seem to buy his answer. "Was that why you were so tense when I first arrived this evening?"

So she'd noticed.

He wasn't about to open the Pandora's box containing his biggest mistake and watch Rainy's looks of admiration turn to disgust. Instead, he told her about Blake's inclination to overspend and to run to Nate for help.

The television rumbled in the background, but Rainy focused on him, saying nothing while he dumped his tale of woe on her slender shoulders.

When he finished, she only asked, "How old is Blake?"

The question took him aback. He blinked. "Twenty-nine, why?"

What did age have to do with anything?

Head bent, she studied their joined hands, as if searching for the right words. Nate gazed down at the crown of her head, admired the way her hair shone beneath the kitchen light. Everything about Rainy Jernagen shone, from the inside out.

He was aware of many things at that moment, as though his senses had heightened with Rainy in the room. The lingering scents of spicy Tex-Mex and soapy lemon dishwater. The taste of Rainy's chocolate bars on his tongue. The incredible softness of her skin against his. Even the quiet rhythm of her breathing.

After a long moment, she met his gaze and said, "Nate, *I'm* twenty-nine."

The flood of senses fled, replaced by bewilderment. Nate frowned. "I don't see your point."

Gently, carefully, she said, "Isn't Blake—and for that matter, Janine—old enough to handle his own finances without depending on you?"

Nate tugged his hands away, fisted them at his sides, disappointed. He'd thought she would understand. "Our parents are dead. I'm the oldest."

Rainy's small, sad smile—a smile that never reached her eyes—confused him more. "You sound exactly like Will."

Was she judging him? Criticizing? He glanced over her shoulder to the living area, where Will and the other children watched TV. He didn't see the connection. She probably thought he came from a family of losers. Sometimes he thought the same thing, though she couldn't possibly comprehend what they'd all been through. What he had done to them.

"I'm all they have, Rainy."

"They have each other and Pop. Aren't they Christians?"

Her words were a gentle rebuke. At least, that's the way Nate perceived them. *He* had God to lean on. They didn't. He shoved a hand over his head, squeezed the back of his neck. On an exhale, he said, "Not yet. Pop and I are still praying."

She touched his shoulder in that soft way she had, gentle as a baby's, but her sweetness went all the way through him like a transfusion of honey. "I'll pray, too. I'll pray for you, as well, Nate. You're carrying a heavy load."

She had no idea. And Nate never intended for her to know the whole story. He liked her too much.

"You're carrying a pretty heavy load yourself." He looked toward the children sprawled around his living room. Next to the couch, Katie stood on her head while Emma steadied her legs.

"The kids?" She waved him off. "They aren't a load. They're a joy. I do what I do because I want to, not because I have to."

That was the difference between him and Rainy, he supposed. The responsibilities he resented, she embraced.

Rainy was a better person than him. No surprise there. He had a long way to go to be the man God expected him to be.

"Speaking of kids," she said. "These need to head home. School tomorrow."

He didn't want her to leave.

"Want to do it again sometime? Maybe Friday night?"

Yes, he knew he shouldn't. But he wanted to. No big deal. She was easy to talk to, and they were friends.

Yeah. Friends.

A little voice in his head mocked him. How many other friends had he ever wanted to kiss?

His *friend* tapped him on the chest. His heart somersaulted.

"Do I get to choose the movie next time? Something sappy and romantic. Or maybe sad and maudlin?"

He emitted a groan. "Spare me."

"Don't worry. I won't." She laughed at his grimace, then called toward the living room. "Gather up, gang. Time to roll."

To cover his sudden reluctance to part company, Nate stuck his hands in his back pockets and said, "I'd better walk you out. It's dark out there."

Rainy laughed as he knew she would and huddled close to him. "I'm sooo scared."

Nate grinned, sidelining his sibling woes. Having Rainy cuddled against his side, even as a joke, felt pretty nice—distracting, comfortable, right. To his knowledge, nothing scared this woman. She was a rock, solid in her faith and in the confidence that God had everything under control.

He figured it was true for someone like her. Someone good.

Yawning, the four children gathered their schoolbags and trudged to the van. The dome light glowed like a beacon as they climbed inside.

Nate and Rainy strolled along more slowly, hanging back for a moment alone. Nate had the most conflicted feelings, wanting Rainy near but needing to push her away.

He breathed in the cool April night, the scent of flowers sweet in his lungs. Sweet like Rainy. Out in the pasture, a mama cow mooed low and reassuringly.

Peaceful. Pleasant. He loved this ranch, loved country living.

For a moment, he wondered if a city girl could thrive here. Before the thought could bloom, he nipped it in the bud. Pop and his helpmate talk had put crazy ideas in his head.

In the shadow of the house, Rainy touched his arm. "I really had a good time. Thank you for inviting me. Us."

He stopped there in the darkness, sheltered by the night from prying eyes.

"So are you really going to force a chick flick on me Friday night?"

She grinned. "What do you think?"

He thought he was nuts for asking. Nothing good could come of deepening a relationship with Rainy Jernagen. Nothing at all. One or both of them would end up hurt, and he didn't want that any more than he wanted kids.

But when Rainy beamed that hundred-watt smile at him, he knew he would spend Friday evening with her.

He'd even watch her sappy movie.

Chapter Nine

So this is how it felt to fall in love.

That was the thought running through Rainy's mind as she turned the minivan into her housing addition, coming to a stop behind a yellow school bus. A dozen children emerged, their voices loud as they dispersed, calling to one another and the children remaining on the bus. Familiar sights and sounds to a schoolteacher.

Hands loosely draped over the steering wheel as she waited, Rainy glanced in the rearview mirror. Except for the silly grin on her face, she looked the same.

The difference was on the inside, in a heart so full she wanted to shout with joy. God had sent her four beautiful children to nurture, and now He'd sent Nate into her life to fill the void she hadn't known was there.

Twice today during a parent-teacher conference, her mind had wandered to the cowboy with killer dimples, and she'd lost track of the conversation. Embarrassed, she'd had to say, "Excuse me, will you repeat that?"

As soon as the parents had left, she'd written them

a glowing note about their child. Fortunately, the boy was an exceptional student, making the note easy to write. She'd never dreamed falling in love could make her lose her mind. She wasn't some teenybopper with a crush.

No, she was a grown woman with a crush. A serious crush.

The bus rumbled away, and Rainy proceeded to the low-slung house lined with flowers. Her foster children, including two sisters who'd since come and gone, had turned one flower bed into a small vegetable garden. Nate had helped, showing them the proper depth to plant, explaining the need for water and weeding.

He was amazing with the kids. She wondered if he even realized it.

Yesterday Nate had been gone when she'd driven to the ranch to pick up the boys. She had been embarrassingly disappointed.

According to Pop, "Janine hollered frog and Nate jumped."

When he'd phoned later, she'd tried to talk to him about his sister, but he'd changed the subject. Rainy now understood Pop's concerns.

She pulled into the driveway and shut off the engine. As she slid out of the van, dragging a canvas bag of papers to grade, she saw someone out of the corner of her eye.

Turning, she stifled a groan of dismay. For there, in the bright spring sunshine, came Kathy Underkircher. She stormed across Rainy's green patch of grass, her arms swinging at her sides.

Rainy sent a silent prayer heavenward. She needed all the help she could get when confronted by her neighbor.

Kathy, the young grandmother raising her only grandson, lived on a cul-de-sac at the end of the block. Rainy was always amazed that the woman knew everything that went on in the neighborhood, including how many foster children came and went at Rainy's house.

A reasonably attractive woman with dark hair and eyes, Kathy was stick-skinny and full of nervous energy. To Rainy's knowledge, she had no outside job. As a result, she stuck her nose into every area of the neighborhood. As president of the neighborhood housing authority, a voluntary position that Kathy seemed to relish so much she'd been seen measuring the length of someone's grass with a ruler, she often threatened to cite neighbors for the slightest infraction. Recently, she'd protested the vegetable garden, calling the tiny plot unauthorized.

Before Rainy could say hello, Kathy had her nose pressed against the van windows, peering inside with her usual scowl. "What have you done with those children?"

Though tempted to say they were locked in the cellar without food and water, where all children belonged, Rainy bit back the smart reply. No use antagonizing an antagonistic woman.

"The girls are at Brownies. The boys are working on their fair project." Determined to be a Christian no matter what, Rainy kept her face and tone pleasant. "How are you, Kathy? Today is a gorgeous day, isn't it?"

For indeed it was. Windless, a rarity in Oklahoma, with bright sunshine and a sky so blue she could almost taste it. Across the street, Sara Bishop pushed a red lawnmower, filling the air with the fresh spring scent of newly cut grass.

Kathy wasn't interested. Her nose quivered with indignation. "I've seen that man over here."

Rainy's stomach tightened. So much for niceties. "What man?"

"That cowboy in the big pickup truck. Making all the racket, noise pollution. Don't think you're fooling anyone, Miss Jernagen."

Rainy blinked, trying to follow. "I'm afraid you've lost me, Ms. Underkircher."

The woman's lips tightened smugly. "Play coy all you want. The DHS knows what I'm talking about."

Hair prickled at the back of Rainy's neck. She could deal with the woman's dislike, but an all-out character attack was a different matter. "Kathy, if you have something to say, say it. I know you're the person calling the police and social services."

"Someone has to look after the welfare of innocent children."

Emotion boiled up. Frustration, anxiety, outrage. Rainy tightened her grip on the schoolbag. The rough canvas bit into her fingertips.

"Let me assure you of this. I take care of my children. I love them. They're happy here."

Kathy tossed her head and sniffed. "I hear their

screams of terror. No telling what you're doing to them. Children belong with their real mother, not some high and mighty school teacher."

Rainy shut her eyes briefly, counted to three, and tried again. "I've explained Katie's problems to you. The social worker has explained them, as well. I'm sure you've noticed that Katie is making improvements." She adjusted the shoulder bag, which seemed to grow heavier with each unpleasant moment. "Please, can't you and I resolve the problem between us and leave the children out of it?"

"You'd like that, wouldn't you? You'd like for me to go away and let you go on mistreating children the way you mistreated my Conrad." Her face contorted in dislike. "Other people may think you're a saint because you take in foster children, but I know the truth."

Any conversation always came back to her grandson. "I'm very sorry if I caused you or Conrad any embarrassment, Ms. Underkircher. Truly."

She didn't know what else to do to resolve the issue. She wasn't going to apologize for doing her job properly, and she had no power over stories printed by the local newspaper.

Kathy ignored the effort at conciliation. She leaned forward, her green eyes as glittering and hard as cut glass. "Who is that man? I saw his truck here late Tuesday night and again the next morning. I told the DHS. We don't need that kind of thing in our neighborhood. What would the real mothers of these kids think if they knew what their children were being exposed to?"

Rainy squelched the urge to roll her eyes. The birth

mothers of these children were the reason she was a foster mom. These kids had experienced plenty of horrors before being placed with her.

She also remembered the reason Nate had come to her house Tuesday night and again the next morning. At her call, he had hurried over to fix a leak under the kitchen sink but didn't have the correct size pipe. After turning the water off for the night, he'd returned early the next morning to complete the repair.

But there was no use explaining the innocent situation to Kathy. She didn't want the truth. She wanted some sort of revenge. All the talking and explaining in the world would not satisfy her.

Giving up, Rainy said, "I really need to go, Ms. Underkircher. You'll have to excuse me."

Hiking up the canvas tote, she started up the walk to her porch. Kathy's voice followed her. "You won't be so smart when they take those children away for good and you lose all that money you're making off someone else's misfortune."

Rainy didn't look back, but Kathy had finally hit a nerve. Her back teeth clenched as anger boiled in her belly. She didn't take in foster children for the money. Every penny went to the children's needs. If she had her way and could adopt them, she'd receive nothing at all. And that was fine. *Fine.* Because she loved *them,* not the measly little checks they brought with them.

Inside the house, she dropped her keys and bag on the coffee table and slumped onto the couch. Her head in her hands, she took deep breaths and tried to calm down. Her jaws ached with tension as the familiar worry crept in. What would happen if social services believed Kathy's accusations? Would she lose the children?

Scriptures floated through her head—about not giving into anger, about loving her enemies, about trusting God with everything. Only last week she'd presented a puppet skit for Children's Church about getting along with difficult friends. With a self-deprecating huff, she thought maybe her puppets could teach her a thing or two.

Her doorbell sounded, a regular *ding-dong* since Nate had dismantled the hard rock music. She stiffened. If Kathy was back, Rainy wasn't sure what she might do.

Cautiously, she peered out, saw Sara Bishop from across the street and opened the door.

"Hi, Sara," she said, enormously relieved. "Come on in."

Sara, her face shiny with perspiration from yard work, shook her head. "No, thanks. I just wanted to make sure you're okay."

"You heard what Kathy said," Rainy said, chagrined.

"Everyone in the neighborhood hears her opinions on a regular basis." Sara pushed at damp bangs. Her brown hair stuck straight up in front. "Kathy's a loose cannon, Rainy, a pitiful woman with nothing to do but make others miserable. I know you take good care of the children who come here. I wanted you to know most people don't share her opinion."

Grateful, Rainy touched the other woman's arm. Sara's skin was hot and damp. "Thank you, Sara. That means a lot to me. I keep worrying that she'll complain so much the authorities will start to believe her. Where there's smoke there's fire and all that." She opened the door wider. "Are you sure you won't come in? I was about to make some tea."

"No, no. We have a baseball game tonight. I want to finish cutting the grass before Rodney gets home from work."

"And before Kathy cites you with failure to keep a tidy lawn."

They both chuckled. "Exactly. Better mow yours, too. It's over an inch and a half. Kathy will be over here with her ruler."

Though amusing, there was truth in the warning. "I'll have Will start on it tonight."

"Then she'll protest on the grounds of child labor laws." Sara laughed and stepped off the porch.

With a wave, she recrossed the street and cranked the lawnmower. At the burst of sound, flecks of grass whirlwinded around Sara's green-stained tennis shoes. Rainy stood in the door watching, thankful for a thoughtful neighbor.

But Kathy's visit had put a damper on her joy. It had also reminded her that Will, Joshua, Emma and Katie were not her children. Not yet. If anything went wrong, they might never be.

"Something bothering you?" Nate cut the wire on a bale of hay and kicked the alfalfa with the toe of his boot, scattering chunks around for the horses. Three equine heads dipped to munch. Rainy had arrived with

Emma and Katie a good thirty minutes ago and hadn't said a dozen words. "You're kind of quiet."

Normally, she talked his ears off, telling him about things that happened at school, a new puppet show idea, enthusing over his cows, his horses, his ranch. He looked forward to her chatter, if he was honest. The ranch seemed quiet, dull, even lifeless until she arrived.

He didn't understand why, but he simply felt better when she was here. Today something was wrong. He was certain.

"Come on, Slick, talk to Papa," he said, shooting her a grin intended to make her smile in return. "What's up?"

Absently, she ran her hand over the glossy bent neck of a bay horse. With an uncharacteristically heavy sigh, she told him about the confrontation with her neighbor, finishing with, "I've done everything I know to get on that woman's good side, and I've failed."

Nate gathered up several pieces of baling wire and rolled them into a loop. "Maybe she doesn't have a good side."

"I'm starting to think you're right. My mother keeps telling me to kill her with kindness, go the extra mile, etc., but I don't know what else to do. I've talked to her, sent her cards, baked her brownies—"

Nate held up a hand. "If the brownies didn't do it, she's hopeless."

That got a smile out of her. She climbed up on the metal fence and perched, a pair of yellow slip-on shoes hanging off the backs of her feet. "What if she jeopardizes my foster-mom status?"

Nate tossed the looped wire into a barrel. At the rattle, a fat crow perched on the eave of the shed squawked and flapped away. Nate glanced toward Emma and Katie, hanging upside down in the tire swing he and Pop had erected in a backyard oak.

"Can she do that?"

"Being single is already a strike against me. If she convinces social services that I'm doing something wrong…" Her voice trailed off. She bit her bottom lip.

Nate's protective hackles rose. Even though he wished she'd let someone else do the job, Nate didn't like the idea of anyone criticizing Rainy. She was amazing. Awesome. Real cute, too.

"You're a great foster mom. They're lucky to have you."

Though he could never do what she did, he also couldn't imagine Rainy without children around her. She was made to be a mother. In fact, he couldn't figure out why she wasn't married with a houseful of her own kids. Some guy was really missing out.

His protective urge turned green at the thought of Rainy with someone else. He had no right to feel possessive or protective, but he did.

He'd have to work on that, but right now Rainy needed his support. If he was a tad too happy about that piece of knowledge, he'd have to work on that, too. Later.

"What can I do to help?" Hadn't she asked him the same thing once?

Shaking her head, she banged the heel of her shoe against metal railing in a steady, clanging rhythm.

"Nothing, I'm afraid. She's seen your truck at my house. She thinks you and I have something illicit going on."

At the outrageous accusation, Nate bristled. "You can't be serious."

Rainy banged her shoe again and it fell off, tumbling to the dirt. "I wish I wasn't."

Nate retrieved the fallen shoe and caught her by the heel. "Here you go, Cinderella. You've lost your slipper."

He slid the shoe onto her foot but didn't release his hold. Sitting above him, Rainy leaned forward, placed her hands on his shoulders and smiled. For the first time since she'd arrived, the smile was happy.

Something warm and full pressed inside Nate's chest. He wanted Rainy to be happy—always.

"I guess that makes you my Prince Charming," she said.

Prince Charming? Him? Not even close.

"Come on, I'll help you down. I have a surprise."

"You rented another chick flick?" she asked, a twinkle in her eyes.

He made a rude noise, thrilled when she responded with a fullblown laugh. Now they were getting somewhere.

Bracketing her narrow waist with his hands, he lifted her down. "Remember when Emma and Katie said they wanted a calf to take care of, too?"

"You didn't get them a calf, did you?" She grabbed his arm. "Nate, they're too little for that."

He patted her hand where she grasped his upper

arm in a death grip. "Don't freak out until you see. I'll show you first and if you think it's okay, we'll show the girls. Deal?"

She looked dubious but followed him toward his surprise. He'd planned to wait a few days to give the gift, but Rainy needed the distraction today.

He opened the wooden door to a small storage shed he'd cleaned out this morning, keeping himself between Rainy and the animal inside. "I'm keeping him in here for now while he's so young."

She tiptoed up on her silly, impractical shoes, trying to see over him. Nate was too tall and wide for that. "Are you going to show me or not?"

"Tsk, tsk. So impatient."

Widening her eyes in joking defiance, she spun away as if to leave. He caught her arm, laughing softly, uncommonly happy, as he turned her back around and led the way into the dimly lit building.

A small bleat came from the corner. Rainy looked at him in question, but before he could say a word, a snow-white baby goat tottered into view. The little critter came toward him, bleating away, recognizing him as the meal giver. Nate touched the warm, woolly head with affection.

Suddenly, it was very important for Rainy to like his surprise. "Baby goats are supposed to make good pets. I thought Emma and Katie would like him. He's real gentle. A nice little fella. He won't get very big. What do you think?"

"Oh, Nate. He's perfect. *Perfect!*" Rainy threw her arms around him and hugged, knocking him backward several steps. "You are the most thoughtful, incredible, kindest man in the universe."

What else could he do? As he stumbled back to catch his balance, he took Rainy with him, wrapped her up like a present and held her close. Her coconut scent swirled around him in a cloud of pleasure, mixing with the scent of dust. What man could resist a woman who thought he was all that?

Other than the tiny goat nudging at his pants leg, he and Rainy were alone. One of those rare moments. Rainy gazed up at him. He gazed down at her, into eyes so full of light and love that he paid no attention to his previous reservations. He bowed his head and kissed her.

Rainy didn't take kissing lightly. In fact, she could count the number of guys she'd kissed on one hand. All those other times had been awkward and a little embarrassing.

Sharing a kiss with Nate was as natural as breathing. Only better. Everything in her wanted to burst out with the news that she loved him. But she didn't. Not yet.

"I've been wanting to do that for a while," he said, holding her lightly around the waist, his head bent so they were eye to eye, the tip of his hat shading them. His breath was warm and pleasant against her skin, the scent of him redolent of hay and leather.

"I've been wanting you to," Rainy admitted, not at all surprised when the words came out a little shaky. She rested her hands on his shirtfront, felt the smooth cotton and hard buttons against her fingertips.

She would always remember every detail of that kiss, she thought. Here in the small, dim shed, straw and dirt beneath her feet, the baby goat bleating, dust motes floating in the perforated sunbeams.

Nothing at all romantic about the setting, but Rainy considered it perfect.

Nate's supple mouth curved upward. "Want to do it again?"

"We have an audience."

"That old goat?" he teased, smiling wide, dimples deep, when she laughed at his clever reference to the new pet. "He won't mind."

Rainy tiptoed up and touched her mouth to his, a quick, light kiss before stepping away. "There you go."

He brought her fingers up and brushed them with his lips. Rainy nearly melted.

Forcing a lighter voice than she felt, she said, "Let's go tell the girls about their new friend. They're going to love him."

Two beats passed while Nate stared into her face. Then with a wink, he tugged her toward the door. "Whatever your heart desires."

That part was easy. Her heart desired him and the beautiful relationship growing between them.

They'd turned a corner today. For Rainy there was no going back.

Chapter Ten

Rainy's fingers shook with excitement as she held the day's mail in one hand and, with the other, jiggled the key in the front door. A gentle rain fell, washing the street in shades of dark and light, but even rain could not dampen Rainy's spirits. She'd been waiting a long time for the official-looking envelope from social services telling her she could begin the proceedings to adopt Katie. In another year, she hoped to do the same for the other three children.

"Katie, you and Emma change into play clothes while I read the mail." For once, she didn't have half a dozen things to do after school. Other than the regular evening trip to Crossroads Ranch, which was more of a treat than a task, she could relax for a few minutes.

"Can we have a snack?" Emma asked.

"Change first. Then you can each have some fruit and milk. Deal?"

"Then can we go play with Snowflake?"

"Sure," she said, smiling as Emma skipped happily down the hall with Katie right behind.

Emma and Katie had gone wild with excitement the day Nate had presented them with the goat, whom they'd quickly dubbed Snowflake. They'd danced around the pen stirring up dust and singing, "Nate, Nate, Nate is great" until Will had given both a quarter to stop.

Each day since, they looked forward to the trip to the ranch with exuberant delight, frequently taking along their own version of grooming tools—Rainy's old hair curlers. Barrettes, ribbons. Snowflake didn't seem to mind at all that he'd become their beauty parlor model.

Rainy looked forward to the daily outing, as well. But her enthusiasm had nothing to do with the animals and everything to do with the cowboy. Many evenings, unless school or church activities required their attendance, she and the kids stayed at Crossroads until dark. When other functions beckoned, Nate had taken to coming along.

Rainy thrilled with the belief that she meant as much to Nate as he meant to her.

Only last night, she'd sat next to him at a basketball game, yelling her throat raw for the Summervale Sonics. He'd taken into stride Emma hanging over his back and Joshua pestering him with questions about the game.

There had been an uncomfortable moment when Guy Bartlett had spotted her and climbed the bleachers to say hello. When he'd realized she was with Nate he'd behaved oddly. So had Nate. They'd reminded her of a couple of bristle-haired dogs, eyeing each other with polite suspicion.

Guy had become increasingly pushy lately, not wanting to take no for an answer, though he'd never bothered to ask if she was seeing anyone. As if no one else could possibly be interested. He was a decent man, one she disliked hurting, but hopefully he'd gotten the message.

After Guy departed, Nate had been different, protective, acting almost possessive.

Then, at one point when the Sonics fired a go-ahead three pointer, they'd erupted upward with the crowd to high-five each other. When they settled back onto the hard bench, Nate pulled her hand against his knee... and kept it there.

A family. They felt like a family.

And family was the reason for her excitement today.

Rainy ripped the thick envelope open, quickly scanned the letter before waving the papers at the ceiling and crying a delighted, "Thank you, Lord!"

Too excited to keep the news to herself, she grabbed the telephone and dialed, hoping, hoping Nate was in the house and not out in the pasture somewhere.

"Crossroads Ranch."

"Hey, Cowboy. Are you busy?"

"You sound...different. Is everything okay?"

"Everything is perfect. I'm so happy. I needed someone to share my good news."

A soft chuckle. "Share away. The bus hasn't gotten here with the boys yet, so I came in for a cold drink."

Rainy settled on her kid-friendly, fake leather sofa and curled her feet beneath her. "My adoption paperwork is in process. Pending court approval and if nothing goes haywire, I'll be officially Mom to Katie by the time school resumes in the fall."

A momentary silence hummed through the lines.

"Nate? Did we get cut off?"

"I'm here. That's great, Rainy." Was that hesitation in his voice?

An odd prickle of doubt teased the back of Rainy's mind. She tamped the worry down.

"I need to celebrate. Want to come over after the boys do their chores? I could order pizza. Bake some brownies."

Again that strange silence. "Sorry. Can't make it."

"Oh." Talk about deflating her joy balloon.

Then as if he knew he'd disappointed her, he said, "Something's come up. My sister called."

His sister. Again. Her disappointment turned to annoyance. "Nate, did you ever think of telling her no?"

"I can't."

"That's absurd. Of course you can. Unless she's truly having an emergency, dial her number and tell her you have something else to do."

His heavy sigh seemed magnified through the telephone. "I can't do that."

"Why not? Why do you let them run your life?"

"I'd much rather…" He blew out another breath, frustrated, trapped between his siblings and the woman he wanted to be with. Worse yet, Rainy had sprung the adoption thing on him, tying him into more knots.

"What is it, Nate? Talk to me."

He could do that much. He owed her that much. "When we were kids, Janine was injured in an accident. It was my fault. I owe her."

Nate didn't want to go into the ugly details. And he sure wasn't going to tell her about Christine, but she deserved to know why he was obligated to care for his siblings no matter the cost to his personal life.

"I was driving a tractor on my mother's family farm. Janine ran in front me. I hit her."

He shuddered at the memory of his four-year-old sister falling beneath the wheel of the tractor. "Broke her legs, crushed her pelvis. No one even knew if she'd survive."

"I'm sorry, Nate. That's awful." Her tone, annoyed before, had gone quietly horrified. "How old were you?"

"Nine."

"Nine! What was a nine-year-old doing driving a tractor?"

"My dad wasn't around much, so, as the oldest, his share of the work fell to me. It's a fact of farm life. Everyone works."

"I'm sorry for what happened. Truly I am, Nate, but you can't blame yourself for an accident that occurred when you were Joshua's age. Think about it. Would you let Joshua drive a tractor?"

"Of course not," he said. "He didn't grow up on a farm. I did." Joshua hadn't caused a sister's death, either. But Nate had.

"You need to let it go."

"I expected you to understand," he said, though his bitterness was not directed against Rainy.

He was trapped in this miserable situation with his brother and sister. He wanted things to be different, but they never would be. They were his siblings and therefore his responsibility.

"Nate?" Rainy spoke through the line, softly pleading. "I'm sorry. Your relationship with your brother and sister is none of my business. I should never have said anything."

Now he really felt like a jerk. She'd been excited when she first called, wanting him to share in her celebration. Instead of being there for her, he'd turned the conversation around to his own selfish concerns.

Proof positive that he'd been right all along. Nate Del Rio did not have what it took to make anyone happy. Not even himself.

The next afternoon, all four children in tow because of counseling appointments, Rainy arrived home to find a vase full of red roses on her porch.

"Bet they're from Nate," Will said, giving his glasses a shove for good measure.

"We don't bet," Rainy said automatically, though knowing Will's word choice was only a figure of speech.

"Well, if we did, I'd win." Will grinned an ornery grin and stuck his thumbs in his back pockets the way Nate often did.

Rainy thought his imitation of the cowboy was adorable. She'd begun to see other similarities between the man and the boy, as well. Will had never known a consistent father, and to her way of thinking, he had chosen a good man to imitate.

She slid the tiny envelope from its forked, plastic holder and took out the card, praying they weren't from Guy. She hadn't heard from him since the ballgame. Though sad to lose his friendship, enough was enough. Nate's signature was scrawled across the card with a message.

"Yes," she said to Will. "You'd win."

The children pressed in around her. "What does it say? Is it all lovey-dovey?"

"Joshua!" she said, turning surprised eyes on the nine-year-old.

"We're not babies, Rainy. We know he likes you."

Her heart skipped a beat. "I like him, too."

"Are you going to get married?" Will gnawed the corner of his lip and shifted his black backpack from his shoulders to the porch step. Did he like the idea? Or was he worried about it?

Before Rainy could think how best to answer, Katie lifted her face from sniffing the roses and said, "I never had a daddy. Can Nate be my daddy now?"

"Kids, hold on. Nate sent roses, not a wedding ring."

"First comes love, then comes marriage," Joshua said matter-of-factly.

"I haven't even read the card. He may say he's running off to Tahiti with a hula girl." She handed her keys to Will. "Unlock the door and let's go inside before the entire neighborhood knows our business."

Particularly Kathy Underkircher.

"Where's Tahiti?" Emma asked. "Is it close to Tulsa?"

Her heart light, Rainy laughed and followed the children inside, the spray of roses filling her head with their soft scent, the way a certain cowboy filled her heart with joy. She set the vase on the kitchen table and turned the card over to read.

"Congratulations on your good news. You're an amazing mother. Sorry I rained on your parade. Love, Nate."

Love. He'd written *love*. Did he mean it, or did he use the word casually, as so many people did today? Either way, Rainy was thrilled. He'd sent her roses and an apology.

Maybe she'd been too hard on him last night about his siblings. As the oldest brother, with no parents left to help, he felt obligated. One of the things she admired about Nate was his strong sense of responsibility and caring for other people. Wasn't that why he'd joined the Handyman Ministry? Wasn't that what helped make him a successful rancher and a committed Christian?

"Miss Rainy, there's something on the back of the card, too."

Emma stood at her elbow staring up at the card in Rainy's hand, her pretty blonde head tilted back.

Rainy flipped the card over and laughed. "Pizza is on the way. So am I. Please bake brownies."

Maybe he could do this. Maybe he could make this work.

With three pizza boxes stacked on one arm and

the hot Italian smell filling his nostrils, Nate stood on Rainy's porch. The roses he'd left earlier had disappeared and he smiled a little to himself, thinking of her reaction. He hoped she wasn't allergic or anything.

Inside the house, Katie's high-pitched scream rattled the windows. According to Rainy, the little redhead was down to about two screams a day, a big drop from every few minutes.

Rainy was a wonder woman with those kids.

A knot formed in his belly as the dilemma presented itself again and again. Falling for Rainy meant accepting these foster children. No, not accepting. Loving. Rainy was a love-me-love-my-kids kind of woman. Even if they weren't officially her kids.

Nate still didn't know if he could do that. He cared for Rainy. He liked being with her. Looked forward to that moment each day when her car came flying down the long drive to Crossroads Ranch, spewing dust and gravel in her rush to arrive.

Anyway, he liked to think she was rushing to be with him. Fool that he was.

They'd never actually discussed his feelings about kids, though nothing had changed his mind about not having any of his own. He liked her four munchkins. They'd grown on him. But he worried about them, too. He didn't like that part.

Now he was trapped into spending time with them. Sort of. Rainy with her pushy sweetness had shoved her way into his life and onto his ranch, bringing the kids along. Now they all had projects, reasons to be there every single day. When he wasn't scared out of his mind with worry, he enjoyed them.

He jabbed the doorbell again, concerned that no one had ripped the door open yet. Hadn't she read the card?

Truth was, he'd stopped minding about the kids' projects long ago. They gave him an excuse to see Rainy on a daily basis.

So the problem was exacerbated. He'd been praying a lot about what to do. Should he break things off before he got in too deep? Or was he already too late?

Before he could answer his own questions, Rainy opened the door, smiled her sweet smile and invited him into the celebration.

An hour later, the celebration turned to despair.

Rainy had just slid a pan of brownies into the oven. All four kids had chocolate batter somewhere on their happy faces. Her cowboy was leaning on the blue Formica, looking so handsome her heart was about to burst with happiness, when the doorbell rang.

"Grand Central," she said, grinning at Nate. Her doorbell rang often, usually neighborhood children coming over to play.

Surrounded by the kids, she opened the door. The social worker, briefcase hanging at her side, stood on the porch.

"Mrs. Chadwick, you're working late tonight."

"I'm sorry to bother you, Rainy," she said. "May I come in? We need to talk."

Something about the way the social worker said the

words warned Rainy that this was not a casual visit. Rainy let her in, motioning her to the couch.

All four children, wide-eyed as always when anyone of authority appeared, started to slither away. Nate appeared in the archway between the dining and living rooms. The children reoriented, moving to his side like iron filings to a magnet. In a flash of understanding, Rainy realized the kids felt safe with Nate by their sides.

Rainy made the introductions. Mrs. Chadwick, her smile a little weary, said to Nate, "Oh, so you're the cowboy in the big pickup truck."

Rainy and Nate looked at each other. "Mrs. Underkircher," they said at the same time.

Mrs. Chadwick raised and lowered her eyebrows. "Yes."

"Is that why you're here so late?" Rainy asked. "Is something wrong? More complaints?"

Mrs. Chadwick glanced at Nate who took the hint. "Should I leave?" he asked.

"That's up to Rainy." The woman placed her valise on the couch next to her and clicked it open. "The children, on the other hand, don't need to be present."

Rainy's stomach dropped. This didn't sound good at all.

Will pushed away from the pack, his skinny bird chest heaving. He stopped in front of the social worker, fists tight, chin up, eyes blazing behind the brown glasses. "You're not taking us away. We won't go."

Nate dropped a hand onto Will's thin shoulder. "Easy, buddy."

"No one's going anywhere today, Will," the woman assured him. "However, I need to talk to Miss Rainy in private, okay?"

No one was going anywhere *today.* At Mrs. Chadwick's carefully chosen words, cold fear trickled like ice water down Rainy's spine.

Please, Lord, she prayed silently. *Please don't let that be the reason for her visit.*

Nate, bless him, must have seen the panic rising in Rainy's face.

"The kids and I will go out back and shoot baskets or something," he told her, his gaze lingering for a long moment as if concerned about leaving her alone. Rainy desperately wanted him to stay, needing his support in a way she'd never expected to. His idea was better, though. The children needed him most of all.

"I'd appreciate that, Nate. Thanks."

"No problem. Holler if you need me." He gave the social worker a warning glance, then said to the kids with feigned joviality, "How about it, gang? Want to play a game of horse with a worn-out old cowboy?"

The children cast worried glances at the social worker and Rainy, but allowed Nate to shuffle them out the back door.

Though equally anxious about the unexpected visit from the social worker, Rainy's heart squeezed with gratitude that Nate would do this. The last time he'd played basketball with the children, he'd let Emma and Katie sit on his shoulders to shoot the ball. They'd loved every minute of it. So had she.

"He's very protective," Mrs. Chadwick said with a wry smile as soon as the back door clicked shut.

"He's a good friend. The kids adore him."

"Is he the one letting the boys raise a calf on his ranch?"

"Now the girls have a baby goat," Rainy said, eager to dispel any ugly rumors Kathy Underkircher may have started. "All four children are learning responsibility out there, taking care of animals, learning to ride a horse, observing good male role models. Nate and his grandfather have been good for the children."

The social worker held up a hand to stop Rainy's flow of words. "I'm not the one you have to convince, Rainy. You're one of the best foster parents we have."

"Sorry. I guess I'm worried that my neighbor will paint me with such a dark brush you'll start believing her. Or that something will go wrong with the children's adoptions."

The other woman looped a lock of short hair behind one ear and avoided Rainy's eyes. Tired rings circled her eyes. Rainy knew for a fact her caseload was enormous, working long hours.

"That's why I'm here. Something *has* gone wrong."

Rainy felt the earth shift. "But it can't have. I received an official letter about Katie yesterday."

The social worker's reply was gentle and compassionate. "So did Katie's birth mother."

A sick feeling began to churn in Rainy's stomach. "I thought she was in prison."

"She was. She's been released. When she received the letter, as was her right, she apparently became extremely upset and contacted a lawyer." Mrs. Chadwick handed Rainy a document from the valise. "She has filed to regain custody."

Rainy stared at the piece of paper as if it were a rattlesnake. As she quickly read through the official document, the bottom dropped out of her life. "She can't do this. They won't let her. Not after what she let happen to Katie—"

The social worker placed a hand on her arm. "I know, Rainy. I know. But legally, she has a right to protest the adoption."

"Can she take Katie away?" Rainy rubbed her throat, tight with emotion, determined to hold back the threatening tears.

"I won't lie to you. If the courts believe she has been rehabilitated and can give Katie a stable home, then she will likely regain custody."

"I've had Katie for so long. She's my little girl."

"Rainy, you've known from the beginning that this could happen. All of these children, not just Katie, are legal risk adoptions."

Rainy slowly shook her head from side to side, sick and shaking. A sour taste rose in the back of her throat. "I can't let her go, knowing what happened to her before. I can't."

"Then I suggest you contact a lawyer." Mrs. Chadwick closed her valise and stood to leave. "Remember, Rainy, I'm on your side. I will testify on your behalf. But if things don't work out, there are plenty of other children who need what you have to offer."

With that painfully true statement, the woman took

her leave, shutting the door behind her. Rainy sat on the couch, her insides trembling. Yes, there were plenty of needy children, but she loved Katie. And she feared for her little girl's safety.

For several minutes, Rainy sat frozen, unable to think, unable to react. She was vaguely aware of cars passing by outside, of the smell of baked brownies, of how cold her sock-clad feet had grown. Almost as cold as her insides. She shivered.

How in the world could she tell Katie? Or any of the children, for that matter. They'd be terrified that they were next. And what if they were?

Oh, Lord, oh, Lord, give me courage and strength and wisdom.

The back door banged open. Nate and the children came in without their usual exuberance. They must have seen Mrs. Chadwick's car pull away.

Nate took one look at Rainy and sank down beside her, taking her cold hand in his. "Hey, you okay?"

She shook her head and, in a whisper, answered, "No. Very bad news."

"Want to talk about it?"

She nodded, fighting back tears, not wanting to fall apart, but fearing she might. "Yes, but not in front of the kids."

"Miss Rainy." Will stood in the entry between the kitchen and the living room, his face anxious, twisting his hands. "I smell something burning."

"Oh my goodness, the brownies!" Rainy leaped up and rushed into the kitchen, yanked the scorched dessert from the oven with a potholder. This was too much. Too hard. She couldn't bear it. "I've burned them. They're ruined."

She burst into tears.

"Hey now. Hey." Nate took her by the shoulders, his voice stunned, maybe even scared. "Don't cry."

She knew the tears were not for the lost brownies, but the children wouldn't know that. She couldn't let them know. At least not yet. Not until she'd spoken with an attorney.

Oh, Lord, oh, Lord. The silent cry for help rolled over and over in her head.

She covered her face, her body quaking as she tried to regain composure. Without a word, Nate pulled her into his arms, one strong hand stroking her hair over and over again. His silence told her that he understood.

Rainy felt the presence of the children, felt their concern, their worry. They'd never seen her cry before.

"It's okay, Miss Rainy," Joshua said, patting her back with his small, warm hand. "I like burned brownies. We all like burned brownies. Okay? Don't cry. We'll eat every single one of them."

The child's desperate attempt to encourage and comfort touched Rainy to the soul. She cried all the harder. Bless his precious, tender heart. Regardless of his personal trauma, he never liked seeing anyone sad or upset. For his sake, if for no other reason, she had to pull herself together.

Rainy drew in a quivering *hu-hu-hu,* and looked over Nate's shoulder to the boy's worried face. On a shudder, she sniffed and said, "Oh, Joshy, I love you."

Blinking back new tears, she managed a watery

smile. The children, disturbed to see the usually up-beat Rainy cry over a pan of brownies, hovered around, patting and consoling. Will broke away and went to the counter to gaze at the steaming pan. Without a word, he took down a plate, got out a spatula, and set to work.

"They're still good," he said, adjusting his glasses. "Just a little toasted on the bottom. We can scrape that off. They'll be delicious."

"I love toasted brownies," Katie said, catching the spirit from Joshua and Will. She rubbed her tummy. "Yum."

Emma looked from Katie to her brothers and then to Rainy, expression puzzled. When Joshua nudged her, she blinked a few times. Then with false exuberance, she said, "Me, too. With milk. Lots of milk."

Her reaction was so cute Rainy chuckled. Seeing his chance, Nate jumped in, too.

"Sounds great to me. Toasted brownies and lots of milk."

Keeping one hand on Rainy's shoulder as though he expected her to topple onto the beige vinyl floor-ing at any moment, he slowly stepped away, reached for a paper towel and began to pat the tears from her cheeks. Rainy caught the towel and gently took over. She was feeling embarrassed enough without having Nate dry her tears.

Although the gesture was awfully sweet.

"I'm okay now," she said. "Thank you, all of you, for being so nice, but we don't need to eat burned brown-ies. I can make more."

"Oh, no, you don't." Nate's lips twitched with

humor. "Neither rain nor snow nor tears nor laughter will stop us from eating those brownies now."

"Nate," she said, with one final sniff and shiver. Her face felt swollen and distorted.

He pointed at her. "No argument."

So with a heavy heart bolstered by the love and compassion of four children and a cowboy, Rainy pulled up a chair and ate her share of slightly scorched, crispy-edged brownies.

The moment tasted absolutely delicious.

Chapter Eleven

Nate's guts were in a knot. This was exactly why he never wanted kids. Trouble. Heartache. Tears.

When the children eventually scattered to do homework and take baths, Rainy had told him the bad news. So, while putting on a happy face along with Rainy, he'd stayed until the children were tucked in bed and had fought down his own furious reaction while he read a bedtime story to a quartet of soap-scented, pajama-clad children. He'd never read a bedtime story before, and the emotion clogging his throat would have choked a horse. A Clydesdale.

"Surely the court will see what a great home you've given Katie and how much she's blossomed here," he told Rainy after the two of them had returned to the living room alone.

With the children in bed, the house had grown oddly silent. Silent, and still smelling of scorched chocolate. Which wasn't half bad, come to think of it. He would have eaten charcoal if he'd had to. Anything to see Rainy smile again.

"I can only hope," Rainy said. "Now I understand how a parent could take her child and run away during a custody battle."

"You wouldn't do that, would you?"

Rainy shook her head. "Running would only make things worse. Besides, I have the other children to consider. I'm scared, Nate. Scared of losing her. Scared of letting her go back to a life that hurt her."

Rainy had told him previously about the abuse Katie had suffered at the hands of her birth mother's boyfriend. He could understand her concern. The Neanderthal in him wanted to meet the guy in an alley somewhere and teach him a lesson. Little Katie was a screamer, but she was a doll face, too. She had taken a while to warm up to him, to trust that he wouldn't hurt her, but now the cute redhead dogged his footsteps, presented him with wildflowers and roly-poly bugs, and teased him by running away with his hat.

"Do you have an attorney?" he asked.

She shook her head. "No. I think there are a couple in the church, though."

"That's a good start. Want me to call Pastor Jim for a recommendation?"

"I'll do it." She sucked her bottom lip between her teeth and gnawed.

Nate was particularly fond of that lip and to see it gnawed in stress didn't set well. "Don't give up. We'll fight."

"Lawyers are expensive. The cost of a court battle

will be enormous." Wearily, she pushed both hands into the sides of her hair. "I'll get the money. I just don't know where."

"Do you have any savings?"

"Not much. Most of it was spent on Katie's private counseling."

"I thought the department of human services paid for that kind of thing."

"I wanted her to have the best in Christian counseling, and the system wouldn't pay for faith-based sessions. Dr. Baker has helped her more than anyone, so I don't regret one penny." She spread her hands wide, managing a sad smile. "But it's left me a little short of ready cash."

Nate's heart turned over. Acid indigestion, maybe from burned brownies, maybe from another source entirely, burned in his belly.

"I might be able to get a loan or take a second mortgage on my house. I don't know." Her lip quivered, just about doing Nate in for good. He'd never seen her cry until tonight. Never seen her anything but optimistic and peppy. If she cried again, he might have to do something drastic.

"Don't borrow trouble. Talk to a lawyer first. See where you stand. We'll get the money."

Her face brightened. "What's this *we* stuff?"

He was wondering the same thing. All he knew for sure was that he wouldn't let her fight this alone.

Three days later, Nate put the finishing touches on a boot shine as Pop ambled in from the garage, wiping his grease-covered hands on a red rag.

"Where you headed, Nate boy?"

"Town." He stashed the shoe polish beneath the sink. "Need anything?"

"Might pick up some oil for the hay truck, and maybe a box of those gummy fruit doo-dads."

"Gummy fruits? Since when did you start eating gummy fruits?"

"Ah, not for me," Pop said. "The kids is fond of them, especially that Emma."

Nate hid a grin. "Got you wrapped around her little finger, doesn't she?"

"No more than you are."

He jerked a shoulder. "You know how I feel about kids."

"Yep, probably better than you do. I also know how you feel about Miss Rainy." Pop opened the refrigerator and took out a pitcher of cold water.

Nate made a slow turn toward his grandfather. "Yeah? Well, I wish you'd share this great wisdom with me, because I sure don't."

Pitcher in hand, Pop stared long and hard until Nate glanced away. There was something going on inside his grandfather's head and to tell the truth, Nate didn't want to hear it. He didn't know what to do about Rainy. He didn't even know how he felt about her.

Fortunately for him, Pop let the topic go in favor of more pressing concerns. "Any progress on the custody hearing?"

Nate had told Pop the story, including Rainy's cash-flow problem. He hadn't, however, told his grandfather that he'd come up with a solution.

He sucked in a deep breath. The smell and flavor of fried bacon still hung in the air from the BLT they'd had for lunch. "She was turned down for a second mortgage."

"What a shame." Pop splashed milk into a glass. "Don't seem right that a woman trying to protect a child ought to be in this situation."

Nate felt the same way. In fact, he'd wrestled with the idea since the moment Rainy had called him, stressed over the startling sum of money required to retain a lawyer and to fight a custody battle. Last night, he'd prayed for hours and then had awakened long before daybreak to pray again. He knew what he had to do. What he *wanted* to do. No matter how much it hurt.

"I'm going to give her the money."

Pop lowered the drinking glass from his lips and slowly slid into a straight-backed chair. "Where do you plan to come up with that much cash?"

Nate went to the kitchen window and stared out. For months, years even, he'd gazed out this window, longing for the day he could buy the Pierson land. That day was on the horizon. Since the recent sale of this year's calf crop, the down payment was in the bank.

"You're going to give her your savings, aren't you?"

Nate hitched both shoulders. "I don't want to argue about it, Pop."

Saving that amount again would take years. Years of calf crops and careful living.

He heard the shuffle of chair against tile and then the movement as his grandfather came up behind him. A strong hand clapped him on the shoulder. "I figure

Miss Rainy will give you a fit or two, but you'll get no argument from me. I'm proud of you, son."

Yeah, well, Nate wasn't proud. He was shaken to the core. Sometimes he wondered if he was losing his mind.

"I'm not planning to tell her. She knows how much I want that land. She'd never agree. If the lawyer is paid by an anonymous member of the church, there won't be a thing she can do about it. Helping Rainy is the only thing that feels right. I know the idea sounds crazy, but I have to give her this. I need to."

"Prayed about it, I guess."

Nate made a noise in his throat. "All night. For days. The court date is next week. She has to retain a lawyer soon or give up her dream of adopting Katie."

"You're giving up a dream, too."

He knew that, and he knew it would hurt. But he would hurt a lot more if he didn't do this for Rainy. "There's lots of land. There's only one Katie."

"And only one Rainy."

"Yes, sir. Only one."

"I think that's called love, son." Pop squeezed his shoulder. "Bank closes at three."

The custody hearing wasn't what she'd expected.

There was no jury, only a judge and a couple of court workers, along with the attorneys, social services personnel and the parties involved. Unlike television trials, there were no histrionics, no great dramatic pauses, only a businesslike discussion of the facts surrounding Katie's life and that of her birth mother.

Rainy tried to listen to the proceedings, but she was so nervous her head roared and words turned to fog before she could absorb them.

Every few minutes, Nate squeezed her hand. She was thankful for his stalwart presence, just as she was thankful for the unexpected gift someone from the church had given by paying all of her attorney fees and court costs. An anonymous donor, her lawyer had said. She'd prayed a thousand blessings upon that generous, godly person.

The overzealous air conditioning unit made her shiver. Or maybe she shivered because of the nerves.

Legal voices droned on, asking questions, presenting documents and affidavits. Paper rustled and a woman coughed.

Rainy glanced across the narrow aisle at the cougher, Michelle Wagner, Katie's birth mother. Thin and very pale, the young woman resembled Katie, with blue eyes and a tilted nose, though her hair was a dull dishwater blond instead of a vibrant red. None of that mattered much. What mattered was Katie. The child had no understanding of what was transpiring here today. From the half dozen screaming sessions today, Katie suspected something was up, but she didn't know her future hung in the balance inside this room filled with strangers. Thank goodness, a social worker sat outside the courtroom with her, shielding her from the testimonies.

Witnesses on behalf of Katie's birth mother, including a psychologist, testified that she was emotionally healthy and stable, completely rehabilitated from her drug habit, and well able to care of Katie. She had an apartment, a job, and a therapeutic accountability group. If the witnesses were correct, Michelle was getting her life together. Part of Rainy was happy for the woman. Part of her was scared out of her mind.

Mary Chadwick, Rainy's social worker, took the stand and spoke in glowing terms about Rainy as a foster parent. Rainy smiled her thanks.

Then the Wagner attorney began to ask questions. Rainy's spirits tumbled as the lawyer extracted testimony about the complaints filed with DHS about Rainy, complaints from Kathy Underkircher. The social worker, looking distressed, glanced first to Rainy's lawyer, then to Rainy, and back to the judge. In clear tones, she tried to explain away the constant telephone complaints and the police visits to Rainy's home, but the damage was done.

Nausea rolled in Rainy's stomach. She was going to lose Katie. All because of Kathy's animosity. She must have made a sound because Nate shifted toward her with a questioning look. She shook her head and gazed down at her hands, which she was twisting in her lap.

Other testimonies came and went until Rainy's head throbbed and she wondered if the tension in her chest would explode.

At last the verdict was rendered.

While the court recognized and applauded the commitment and care given by foster mother, Rainy Jernagen, the birth mother, Michelle Wagner, had proven herself to the courts. It was the court's opinion that in the interest of the child, Katie Wagner was best served by living with her biological parent. Therefore, she was to be remanded to the custody of her mother, Michelle Wagner, effective immediately.

The single slam of the judge's gavel was like a fist in Nate's gut. Beside him Rainy slumped, too stunned at first to react. Then she began to shake.

Nate slid an arm around her shoulders. She didn't look up. She sat hunched over, head down, trembling enough to break his heart.

Across the aisle, a shriek of victory rose from Michelle Wagner. She flung herself into the open arms of a woman identified during the hearing as her sister.

What was the matter with that judge? Couldn't he see that Rainy was a better parent to Katie than this other woman could ever be?

But the decision was made. Rainy's lawyer was gathering papers, layering them into his briefcase. Feet shuffled, people exited the courtroom, voices rose and fell.

With a bracing inhale, a stricken Rainy ran her hands down her skirt and stood. Her eyes glowed with pain, but she didn't cry. The attorney and Mrs. Chadwick hurried toward her.

"I'm so sorry, Rainy," the social worker said, her face wreathed in dismay.

"Thank you for trying. You did the best you could. I don't blame you." She swallowed, her lips trembling. "You will keep a close eye on Katie, won't you?"

"Of course I will. Social Services is very diligent in such cases."

Rainy nodded numbly as the woman moved away to talk with the opposing group.

Rainy shook hands with her attorney, who also apologized. From her expression, she didn't want to hear it. She mumbled, "Thank you."

Nate wanted to say a lot more to the man, but he kept his peace. It wasn't the attorney's fault the courts had sided with the birth mother. Right or wrong, this was the norm.

Instead, Nate kept a light hand at Rainy's back, letting her know he was there if she needed him. She hadn't asked him to come today. She hadn't asked anyone to be with her, but Nate had come just the same. She needed him.

"I have to talk to her," she said to no one in particular.

Though visibly shaking, her face pale, she straightened her shoulders and moved toward Michelle Wagner. The other woman momentarily shrank back, wary. Mrs. Chadwick, who now stood conversing with the Wagners, put a hand on Rainy's arm as if to stop her from approaching Katie's mother. Rainy shook her off with a nod of reassurance.

"It's okay, Mrs. Chadwick. I mean no harm, but I need to speak with Ms. Wagner for a minute."

Nate watched in awe as a hurting but composed Rainy quietly introduced herself and said, "Katie is a very special little girl. She has been a gift in my life. I will never forget her."

There was no hostility, only tenderness and compassion, in Rainy's soft-spoken words.

Michelle Wagner slid a nervous gaze to her lawyer and back to Rainy. She swallowed but said nothing.

"I wish you every happiness," Rainy went on, and Nate was sure he'd never witnessed such decency and courage. "Truly. I'll be praying every day for you to be the mother Katie needs."

The other woman found her voice then. "I want to be."

"I know you do." Tears gathered, but didn't fall, as Rainy reached inside her handbag and withdrew a small hand puppet. "Whenever she gets upset and screams, this seems to comfort her. I put it on my hand and make funny pig noises while Piggy kisses her hair and cheeks and…" Her voice wobbled to silence.

"Thank you," Michelle whispered. "Thank you for all you've done to help Katie."

When Rainy's voice shook, Nate slipped her hand into his. "It was my complete and great pleasure. I love her."

With unshed tears glimmering, she gave a brief nod and, with heartbreaking dignity, exited the courtroom.

Chapter Twelve

She could still hear Katie screaming.

On the lonely drive home from the courthouse, Rainy played the scene over and over in her head. For Katie's sake, to ease the transition, the powers that be had allowed Rainy to talk to the child outside the courtroom. Everything had gone fine until Katie's mother took her by the hand and led her toward the exit, leaving Rainy behind. When Katie realized what was happening, she had screamed…and screamed… and screamed.

Rainy had nearly collapsed.

Without Nate's strong shoulder to lean on, she wasn't sure how she would have managed. Without platitudes or empty words, he'd offered to drive her home, to get her something to drink, to do anything she needed. Upon her refusal, he'd walked her to the minivan and watched as she pulled away.

She prayed all the way home, asking the Lord to

comfort and protect Katie. She'd also prayed for herself, to make some sense of all that had happened.

Now, she felt as if she'd swallowed a hot air balloon. Her chest was tight, her throat burned with unshed tears, and she wanted to disappear into the great somewhere and never return.

She couldn't, of course. For the sake of the other children she had to keep her composure. They'd be upset, frightened even. They'd need her reassurance. She felt helpless, knowing her reassurance could only go so far. No one could promise them the one thing they'd want to hear.

She pulled into her driveway and shut off the motor. As she stepped out of the van, her mother drove in behind her. With a sob of relief, Rainy gave in to the tears she'd been holding back since the verdict came down.

In another minute, her mother's arms were around her, and they were walking into the house.

"I'm sorry, sweetheart. I know your heart was set on adopting Katie."

Rainy wilted onto the couch, her forehead in her hands, staring down at the carpet. Her eyes clouded again at the sight of a pale pink Kool-Aid stain. Katie had spilled the drink there two nights ago. Afterward, she'd knelt right here on this spot with Rainy and scrubbed and scrubbed with a sponge, trying to clear away the stain. "I'm going to miss her so much."

"Daddy and I wanted her, too, you know. For a granddaughter. Now we have to trust that the Lord has something else in mind for her."

"I know. Since this began, I've prayed that the outcome would be whatever is best for Katie. I have to accept that this is the right thing. I don't like the decision, but I have to accept it."

"Why didn't you call me last night?" her mother said in mild admonishment. "I would have gone to court with you."

"I didn't want to worry you. I was hoping…" She let the rest go. They both knew what she'd been hoping for. "How did you find out? How did you know?"

"Nate called me. Told me what was going on. He thought you needed your mother. I'd say he was right." In her energetic manner, Mom bustled into the kitchen, returning with a glass of last night's leftover iced tea. "Here, drink this. Tea makes everything more palatable."

Bemused, Rainy took the glass but only stared into the cloudy mixture. "Nate called you? When?"

Mom checked her watch, a diamond bracelet affair Dad had given her on their twenty-fifth wedding anniversary. "More than an hour ago, I'd say. Such a nice young man. Very concerned about you."

Nate had excused himself at one point after the verdict came in. She hadn't realized he was sneaking off to call her mother. The thoughtfulness of his gesture eased some of her sadness.

No wonder she was in love with him.

The knowledge had come softly, slowly, but today in the courtroom with him beside her, stalwart and strong, the real meaning of love had settled over her like a warm flannel blanket, secure and comforting.

"I love him, Mom," she said, as if the beautiful words could erase some of the day's sorrow.

"Rainy Nicole!" Her mother's entire countenance brightened. "Oh honey, this is fabulous. Let's go shopping. You need shoes. And you can tell me all about this fabulous man who has finally won your heart."

Her mother's logic brought a much needed laugh. "Leave it to you to translate falling in love to a reason for shoe shopping."

"Honey, breathing is a reason to shoe shop. You need cheering up. This is a great excuse. Now, go splash some water on your face. I'm buying. A snazzy new pair of heels won't solve the problem, but shopping for them will take your mind off your troubles for a while."

"I can't. The children are at Nate's ranch. I need to go get them."

She didn't want to shop. She wanted to lie on her bed and stare at the ceiling. She wanted to walk around in the girls' bedroom and touch Katie's belongings. She also faced the painful task of telling the other children about the day's outcome.

"No excuses, darling. You're going. Nate would agree. In fact, he said, and this is a quote, 'Rainy's been strong for everyone else about as long as she should have to. She should take all the time she needs to rest and get herself together.' He'll take care of the kids until you come for them. No rush."

"Nate said all that?"

Lifting her perfectly arched eyebrows, Mom offered

a spunky smile. "I think maybe he's in love with you, too."

Rainy's heart fluttered.

"You think?"

Oh, she hoped so. Sometimes, like today, she thought he might be, but at other times he'd back away and she wasn't so sure. She threw her arms around her mother. "Mom, you are the best. Thanks for coming."

And thanks to Nate for intuitively knowing exactly what she needed.

Leaning against a post on his back porch, Nate watched Will, Joshua and Emma as the trio went about their chores and played with their animals. The black and white collie ran circles around them, thrilled as ever with their company. Once in a while, one of the kids would fall to the ground, arms around Yo-Yo's neck for a happy wrestling match and a doggy kiss. The sight squeezed him right in the solar plexus.

The trio looked lopsided without redheaded Katie. The whole world seemed lopsided after today's verdict. He still couldn't believe the judge had ruled against Rainy. Though the birth mother seemed to be getting her act together, anyone with eyes could see Rainy was the best mother for Katie.

Sometimes he wondered if his Christianity went deep enough, because he'd been tempted to tear into the judge and lawyers the way he would have done ten years ago B.C. That's how he always thought of the time before Christ came into his life. B.C.

He rubbed a hand over his aching chest and blew out a heavy, gusty sigh.

What was going to happen to Rainy when she lost the other three, too? Why did she put herself through this? Why did she take the chance of getting her heart broken over and over again?

He liked these kids. Okay, so he was pretty crazy about them. That was the problem. He couldn't protect them any more than he'd been able to protect Katie. He hated that helpless feeling. He hated the pain on Rainy's face and the empty place in his own heart. He hated that moment when Katie was taken away screaming and he hadn't been able to do a thing to save her.

Using the toe of his boot, he kicked at a flat rock. Helpless. Angry. Sad.

There was nothing he could do. Nothing. Even if he'd punched everyone in the courtroom, he couldn't have changed a thing.

No wonder he wrestled so much with the Lord's will for his life. Sometimes the old Nate tried to take over. Sometimes the new Nate thought God was too hard.

He was gonna miss that little redhead. Miss her funny face and her freckles. Miss her giggle.

Kicking out again, he missed the rock and connected only with air. Story of his life. Kicking at air, coming away empty.

With ranch work, the impending loss of the Pierson lease, and his brother and sister, he had enough to worry about without adding kids to the mix. He'd never, ever wanted to go there. Then Rainy had come charging into his life, all velvet and steel and sweetness, and he'd wanted to be her everything. Lately, he'd even begun to think he might enjoy being a dad.

There it was, plain and simple. He wanted to be something he could never be. As a result, he'd failed— again.

After today, when Katie had screamed her way out of the courthouse and Rainy had crumpled in his arms, Nate had faced the truth. He could never be enough for anyone. Hadn't he learned that lesson with Janine and Blake...and Christine? No matter what he did, it was never enough to make things right.

He'd foolishly thought he could make a difference in his siblings' lives. He'd thought the same thing with Rainy and her adorable passel of foster kids.

He'd thought wrong.

The door behind him opened and he heard the approach of footsteps. Nate recognized the slow, heavy boot shuffle as his work-weary granddad. Pop had spent the afternoon repairing a fence break in a water gap along the east side of ranch.

"You're looking mighty grim." Pop scraped a metal lawn chair away from the house with one hand and cradled a cup of coffee with the other. "I reckon things didn't go the way you'd hoped."

"The court ruled for the birth mother."

Pop hissed through his teeth. "Bad deal. Rainy's heartbroken."

It was a statement, not a question. "Devastated."

"You, too."

He didn't want to be, but his granddad knew him too well, sometimes better than he knew himself. "The whole thing stinks. The system stinks. Why take a budding rose from a greenhouse and put her in a dark cellar?"

"The Word says God has a plan for each of us, Nate boy. We have to trust that our prayers will cover Katie."

Trust. Nate was having a hard time with that today. He was a man of action. Taking care of people was his job. When he couldn't do that job, his imagination went crazy with worry about all the bad things that could happen.

Because, as he well knew, bad things *did* happen to good people.

"Why aren't you with Rainy?" Pop blew across the top of his coffee cup. Steam curled up from the potent black brew.

He'd tried to be. She'd turned him away. "She preferred to be alone. Said she needed time to process."

"You should've stayed with her anyway." Pop took a sip of his coffee and then propped his boot heel on the bottom rung of the porch rail and studied the scuffed, pointed toes. "Women are like that sometimes. They say one thing but mean another. Woman like Rainy wouldn't want to put you out."

Nate hadn't considered that angle. "I phoned her mother."

"A woman needs her man in times like this."

Nate slowly turned his head. "Don't do that, Pop."

His granddad held his gaze steady for several long, telling seconds. Nate's insides twisted and turned, flapping around like a kite in a hurricane. Sometimes he struggled between doing what was right and what he wanted. Sometimes he didn't know the difference. God had sent these kids into his life for a reason. He'd thought that reason was more penance for his mistakes. But he hadn't bargained on taking them and their foster mother into his heart and then letting them all down. Because, like it or not, that's what he'd end up doing.

"Do the young ones know yet?" Pop asked, hitching his chin toward the trio playing freeze tag with each other and Yo-Yo. The dog, of course, did not cooperate in the least and cocked his head in bewilderment at the sudden frozen status of his playmates. The baby goat had joined the fray, dashing this way and that, *bah-ing* with happy abandon. Today, Emma had tied a red bow around his neck and painted his toenails the same color. The ridiculous look would have cheered him any other time.

"They're bound to suspect something, but Rainy wants to tell them later, when she has her own emotions under control. She's making appointments with their counselors tomorrow."

"Smart gal, that Rainy."

Nate shifted his long body, feeling the hard, rough cedar porch timbers poke through the material of his shirtsleeve. "I have to let them go, Pop. To end it."

His grandfather knew him well enough to understand. He dropped his booted foot to the concrete porch and leaned forward, his coffee cup balanced on one knee. "Don't let something like this ruin what you and Rainy have going."

"It's for the best." Pop knew his sins. No reminders required.

"You regretting the money?"

Nate spun around, glaring. "No way. The lawyer was up front with me about our chances of winning. I knew the risk."

"Maybe that's what's eating you. You lost the case, lost Katie, lost the money, lost the land next door."

Nate hadn't looked at the situation that way. "I don't want to see Rainy hurt anymore."

"Then don't hurt her."

"This same scenario could happen again. Those three out there could be taken away from her. No matter how hard you hang on to someone, no matter how hard you try to take care of them, they can be taken away, and there is not a thing you can do to stop the heartache."

"Don't confuse what happened to Christine with these children, Nate boy."

Nate squeezed his eyes shut against the sharp twist of agony. Across the yard, Yo-Yo yipped a happy bark, and blond Emma giggled. Christine had been a little girl like that once, giggly and energetic and full of big-eyed charm. He'd been her big brother, her protector. Yet when she'd needed him most, he'd let her down.

Now he felt as though he'd let Rainy and Katie down, too, though there was nothing he could have done to change the verdict.

To his way of thinking, he wasn't good for Rainy and the children, and he never would be.

"I'm not what they need."

"What exactly is it that they need?"

"Someone who can take care of them. Love them. Be there for them." Someone like Guy Bartlett.

"From my point of view, you've been doing a pretty good job of it. Look out there, Nate boy." Pop waved a hand at the children. "Look at those young 'uns. Happy and free as robins in spring."

But one little redbird was missing. Though he knew he wasn't responsible for that turn of events, Nate felt guilty anyway.

He'd failed in taking care of Christine, and from the looks of things, he was failing miserably in taking care of his surviving siblings. No matter what he did to help them, they always needed more than he could give.

Rainy and her charges would be better off without him, without the baggage he carried, without the never-ending stress that Janine and Blake and his own mind pressed upon him and everyone he touched.

Heart heavy, he shoved his hands in his pockets and struggled to find a way to let go of Rainy Jernigan. It would be the hardest thing he'd ever done, but for his sanity and her well-being, he had to find a way.

Chapter Thirteen

A week passed and for Rainy, the house was brutally empty without Katie's freckled face and squeaky voice. The other children solemnly accepted the change, saying little. According to the counselor, they'd suffered so many losses, they'd come to expect the worst.

Their greatest concern was that they, too, would have to leave Rainy's care. Unfortunately, no one could promise them permanence, but Rainy had her lawyer on the job, doing everything possible to expedite the adoption. She'd been able to give them that much.

Yet, they clung more, wanted her closer. Joshua had bad dreams and Will became overvigilant, as if he knew Rainy couldn't safeguard his siblings anymore and the job had become his again.

She ached for him and prayed more than she'd ever prayed before, for the kids, for herself, for Nate, too.

Something had happened to him after the hearing. For a couple of days, he'd been so attentive in his efforts to cheer her. She knew he'd been devastated at

Katie's loss, though he'd never said as much. He'd been quieter, lost in thought, the way she often was.

Now, she was noticing a new difference in him that hadn't been there before. A distancing, as if he was trying to pull away from their relationship. They'd never spoken about the subtle change. Rainy was almost afraid to ask. She'd been so happy about falling in love, so committed to growing their relationship. She wondered if she'd done something wrong.

For the past two days, he'd been absent when she'd driven to the ranch to pick up the children. According to Pop, he was helping Janine move to a new apartment. Understandable. Janine constantly needed something or the other from her brother.

Yet when Rainy had telephoned him last night, he'd been unusually quiet and the conversation had dwindled away to nothing in a matter of minutes. Gone were the hour-long talks about anything and everything.

Perhaps he was worried about his sister. Or maybe he, too, still struggled to process the pain of losing Katie. Didn't men handle emotion differently than women?

A take-the-bull-by-the-horns kind of gal, Rainy decided to find out what was going on. Nate had been there when she'd needed him. So, maybe it was his turn to need her.

Rainy planted a new pair of aqua colored high heels in the soft soil outside the tack room. Inside the dimly lit space, Nate sat on an upturned bucket, bridles, halters and other tack strewn around him.

"Pop told me I'd find you here."

The older cowboy had been in the back lot showing the kids how to twirl a lariat. When he'd pointed toward the tack room, he'd had a gleam in his eye Rainy hadn't quite understood.

Nate glanced up, hands paused on a halter rope he was braiding. "Rainy. How you doing?"

Rainy. He'd called her Rainy. He never did that unless the mood was very serious. "The better question is how are you?"

One shoulder twitched. "As you can see, I'm all right."

Shadows troubled his dark eyes and there was something—*something*—he wasn't telling her.

"You don't seem all right." She waited two beats for a reply that never came. "Is it Katie? Are you still upset over what happened?"

He went back to weaving one strip of leather over another. "Aren't you?"

"Of course I am. It will take time to stop missing her." A lot of time, a lot of prayer to soothe the aching hole Katie's departure had created.

"But will you ever stop worrying about her?" Nate's voice deepened with emotion. "Wondering if she's safe? Wondering if her mother is staying on the straight and narrow?"

The questions were a jab at an already vulnerable wound. These were the things she prayed about daily. "I don't know. I keep clinging to the promise that God will never leave nor forsake her. That's all I know to do." She lifted her palms, let them fall. "Sometimes I feel so helpless...."

Nate shot her a look and then went back to the tack repair. So that was the problem. He felt helpless, too. For a strong, independent man such as Nate, feeling helpless was about as bad as it got.

Outside the tack room, one of the horses leaned against the sheet-metal building. The inside wall popped from the pressure. A wood bee buzzed in the sunlit doorway, searching for a place to drill.

Rainy went to her haunches, balancing on her toes in front of Nate. He didn't look up. His fingers continued to braid. Over, under. Over, under.

"Right now, we're all hurting," she said. "But please don't shut me out, Nate. Don't go all silent and brooding on me. We need to talk, to help each other get through this."

"Rainy, I—" He stopped braiding long enough to look at her, his expression pained. "I'm sorry."

Rainy blinked. "Sorry for what? You haven't done anything to be sorry for. What's going on in that head of yours?"

His chest rose and fell in a heavy huff. He put the neatly braided rope aside. "You're right. We do need to talk. Katie isn't the only thing that's bothering me."

Rainy's heart bumped. Something was more wrong than she'd anticipated. "You can talk to me about anything."

One hand rubbed at the front of his shirt. Work-roughened fingers whispered over coarse cotton. He took another deep breath. "I don't know how to say this."

"Straight out works for me."

"I care about you, Rainy—" he started.

She touched his knee. "I care about you too. A lot." Like in l-o-v-e. "You have to know that already."

"I do. That's what bothers me. You shouldn't. I can't."

"You can't what? Come on, Cowboy, you're scaring me. I thought we had something special going. If I'm wrong, say so."

He squeezed his eyes shut for one long moment. Rainy's heart thundered in her ears.

"You're not wrong."

Rainy almost wilted into the dirt with relief. "Then what is the problem?"

"Something we've never discussed and should have. Kids."

"We discuss the kids all the time."

"No. I mean, we've never discussed kids in the future. My fault. I take full responsibility. I should have told you sooner."

Rainy still didn't understand what he was trying to say. "Kids are my life. You know that."

He reached forward, took her upper arms in his strong, cowboy hands and held her gaze with his. "Kids are *your* life. They aren't mine."

Something shriveled inside. "I don't know what you mean."

"I care about you, Rainy."

"You said that already—"

"Let me finish. I don't want to hurt you or those kids out there. I'm nuts about them. That's the problem."

"You aren't making any sense."

"Then let me be clear." There was something hard in his voice. Rainy's pulse ratcheted upward. Foreboding crept over her like a black fog. Nate's jaw worked, his eyes begged her to understand. But how could she when she didn't know what was wrong?

In a dry whisper, she asked, "What is it, Nate? Please."

"I don't want kids," he said. "Ever."

Nate watched Rainy's confusion turn to shock. Slowly, she shook her head from side to side, as if denying the truth she hadn't wanted to hear. Nate thought he might die of self-reproach. He deserved to die. He never should have let things go this far. He should have been honest from the start. He'd foolishly believed he could be with her and never have to pay the consequences.

"You're not making sense." Her bottom lip quivered. "Everyone wants kids."

"I've had kids all my life, Rainy. I would have told you from the beginning, but I never expected to—"

Hurt radiated off her like sun off a metal roof. "To what?"

Love you. Love you so much that I can't take the risk of ruining your life.

But he couldn't say that now, so instead, he said, "Get...attached to all of you."

Nate wasn't sure what reaction he expected, but it

wasn't the one he got. She shoved his arms away and pushed up, stalked to the open door, looked out and then spun around.

"Nate Del Rio, that is the weakest excuse, as well as the most idiotic statement, I have ever heard. If you are tired of me and want me to go away, be man enough to tell me. But don't concoct some ridiculous tale."

Oh, man. Tired of her? He couldn't get enough of her. The day went on forever until the moment she sailed in, lighting up the place with her bright smile and brighter ideas.

Floundering, he said, "That's not it at all. Rainy, listen—"

But she was past listening. She stabbed a finger in the air. "Nothing you've said makes the least bit of sense. You say you love the kids, but you are *too* attached to them. What does that mean? Then in the next sentence you say you never want kids. How can you love kids and not want them? Tell me that."

"You don't understand."

"You got that right, Cowboy." When her eyes grew suspiciously bright and she tottered on the ridiculously high pair of blue heels, Nate nearly crumpled. He wanted to pull her close, to tell her that he didn't mean it. But he resisted the urge. Honesty in a relationship was essential.

Even if they didn't have a relationship. Which they didn't. They couldn't.

Yes, he was one confused dude.

"Will you listen to what I have to say?" he asked, almost desperately now that he'd made a mess of things.

He took her hand, tugged. Her soft skin, normally warm, felt ice cold.

"You know I will," she said and touched his cheek.

Of course she would. Rainy always listened. It was one of her gifts, one of the things he loved about her.

"I need to tell you something. Something that I hope will make you understand why I feel the way I do about being a father," he said. "Come in the barn, where we can sit and talk in private."

He didn't want an audience during this conversation, and the kids and Pop would come looking for them soon.

Still holding her hand, and surprised that she'd let him, he led the way through the outdoor lot and into the huge area inside the hay barn where large square bales of prairie grass piled to the ceiling.

Some kind of bird—a swallow, he thought—was nesting in the rafters. The creature flapped wildly, swooped a dive-bombed warning over their heads, then disappeared into the blue sky.

Rainy perched on a hay bale, shoulders tense. Hope and confusion radiated from her in equal amounts. Nate felt like the jerk he was. The best he could hope for was her understanding. If she hated him, he deserved it. He swallowed, his throat as dry as trail dust.

He'd kept Christine's death bottled up for so long, he couldn't find the words.

"You look as if you're going before the firing squad," Rainy said softly. "It can't be that bad, can it?"

He sucked in a lungful of grass-scented air, exhaling

in a gust. "Yes, it can. It is. I've never talked to anyone about this before. Except Pop."

And they didn't really talk about that awful time. They tiptoed around it.

Her fingers pressed into his forearm. "You don't have to tell me."

Her kindness was killing him.

"Yes, I do. I want you to understand why I can't have kids. That it's not you. It's not the kids. It's me. It's what I did and what I have to do." He picked at a piece of hay, pulled it loose from the bale. "You've met my sister Janine, and you know about Blake, my brother."

Her chin dipped in agreement. "You have a nice family."

He made a noise in the back of his throat. "They're pains in the neck."

Amusement eased her worried features. "But you love them."

"Yeah, I do. I loved Christine, too." The name slid off his tongue easily, but the taste was bittersweet.

Rainy cocked her head, amusement fleeing as she intuitively went on alert. "Who's Christine?"

"Christine—" his throat worked "—was my baby sister."

Rainy's eyes registered the verb tense. Her fingers tightened on his arm, a subtle touch of encouragement. "Was?"

He nodded. Was. Past tense. Gone forever.

"What happened?"

His gut clenched. "She was murdered."

The ugly words hung in the warm barn, as grievous now as then.

"Oh, no. *Nate*." The horror in Rainy's voice matched the guilt in his heart, but Rainy-like, she scooted close, looped her hands around his elbow and leaned her forehead against his shoulder in a brief hug.

Just that little bit of tenderness melted him. How did a man get the courage to break away from such a woman?

"What happened? Who would do such a terrible thing?"

Holding back a tidal wave of emotion, he told her the basics, the words shooting out in staccato rhythm.

"She was hitchhiking. A monster offered her a ride. Three days later a hunter found her body. In a shallow grave. In the woods." His fingers bit into the rough fabric of his jeans. "She was nineteen. And beautiful." He shook his head, remembering. "Nineteen."

"Dear Jesus," Rainy murmured, and he knew the words were a prayer. For him. She gazed at a spot somewhere behind him, deep in thought. "I can't imagine what your family has suffered."

Suffered. Yes, they'd suffered.

"Because of me. She died, and they all suffered—because of me."

Rainy's gaze snapped back to his. "That is not true."

"I wish it wasn't, but it is. She had car trouble." He scrubbed his hands over his face. "She was always having some kind of crisis."

"The way Janine and Blake do now?"

He nodded. "She called me from the side of the

highway, wanted me to come pick her up and fix her car. I'd warned her before she left that her car needed repair and shouldn't be driven. She hadn't listened. She never listened to me. Until that phone call."

"What do you mean?"

"I mean," he said, his voice raspy with contained emotion, "I told her that I was tired of running to her aid. The stalled car was her problem. Not mine. I didn't care if she had to hitchhike to the nearest garage." He tilted his head and looked up into the rafters. "I told her that, Rainy. I said the words that sent her straight into the hands of a murderer."

"You had no way of knowing what would happen. You can't blame yourself."

"No? Well, I do. It's my fault she's dead. If I had done my job… If I had answered her cry for help…" He squeezed his eyes shut at the brutal onslaught of crime photos flickering through his head. "She died because her brother was too busy watching a football game."

More than anything, Rainy wanted to comfort this broken man. Once again, she slid her arms around his shoulders, resting her cheek against his shirtfront. Nate's heart thundered beneath her ear. His chest rose and fell like a man in torment.

She couldn't begin to imagine what the Del Rios had experienced. Nothing that heinous had ever happened in her own family. Thank God. But now, some of Nate's behaviors became crystal clear. No wonder he worried about the children getting hurt on the ranch.

No wonder he pampered his sister and brother as if they were helpless ten-year-olds.

"The man who took her life is solely to blame. No one else." Soothingly, she stroked her fingers over his whisker-rough cheek. "You are not responsible."

He turned his head so that they faced one another, whisper close, his tormented soul visible in his eyes.

"I wish I believed that, but I don't. If I had answered her call, she would be alive today."

"And you're still punishing yourself, letting the guilt eat you up."

"I let her die, Rainy. My baby sister. A person's life is a lot to make up for."

"Is that what you're doing? Trying to make up for her death? Is that why you jump every time Blake or Janine call?"

"Can you blame me? What if I don't respond and history repeats itself?"

"They're adults now, not teenagers. They can take care of themselves."

"You don't think families should help one another?"

"Of course I do. That's not what I meant, and you know it. They take advantage of you, Nate. Even Pop thinks so."

He pulled away from her and bolted upright. The muscle beneath his eye jerked as he stared blindly at the dust motes dancing around his scuffed boots. From her spot on the hay bale, Rainy battled with the need to comfort him and the conflicting need to shake him out of the past.

After a long, troubled moment, she said, "I'm confused. I don't understand what all this has to do with kids. With why you don't ever want to have children."

His shoulders raised and lowered, but he didn't turn back to her. "I can't be what you need, Rainy. Don't you get it? I couldn't take care of Christine. I'm doing a lousy job with Janine and Blake." He was doing a lousy job with Crossroads Ranch, as well, but he didn't want her to know about that. "I'd be a lousy father, too."

He heard the rustle of movement behind as she came to stand beside him, twining her arm through his. She felt good there, as though she belonged by his side.

"You know what?" she said, tugging gently on his elbow, her voice soft and sympathetic. "Losing Katie was hard. But I'm going to survive. I'm going to go on loving and giving and doing what I can to make a difference. I can't just curl up and quit."

"I don't see your point."

"The point is, what happened to your sister is too terrible for words. But, Nate, it happened, and you can't change it. You have to do what I have to do with Katie. Give the pain to God and let it go. Move on with your life, be the best you can be in her memory, but let her go. You didn't die with your sister."

Nate jerked away, stunned that a woman as kind and understanding as Rainy would say such a cruel thing.

"You have no idea what you're talking about," he said, his jaw tight enough to break a molar. "I'm to blame for my sister's death. That's a far cry from a custody dispute."

"You're being ridiculous." Her voice rose, her eyes snapping. "You did not kill her any more than you make bad choices for Janine and Blake. They make them for themselves. You aren't accountable for them."

"You're wrong."

"And you're sounding like Will. Stop being a martyr, Nate. Stop thinking the world depends on you to take care of it. That's God's job. You have so much to offer, so much to give, but not like this. Get over the past and move on."

Now she'd gone too far. No caring human being ever got over the murder of a loved one. Ever. Drawing on hurt and anger, he said the words that would set her free.

"The kids still have projects. I won't deny them that. I won't be here, Rainy. I'm done. We're done."

And before he could fall on his knees and beg her forgiveness, he stalked away.

Chapter Fourteen

Devastated, her heart bleeding all over the place, Rainy somehow managed to gather the children together to leave. Nate had disappeared into the house, and she wasn't about to follow him inside for a repeat performance. His parting message had been as clear and cold as glacial water. They were done. The beautiful emotion growing between them would never blossom into full flower. He wanted nothing to do with her anymore.

Maybe the relationship had been in her imagination all along. Maybe he'd never cared one whit for her or the children.

But he did. She knew he did. He'd even admitted as much.

Right before he'd tossed her out.

Blindly shoving the car key into the slot, her hands shook.

Rainy didn't want to cry in front of the children, but

they all knew something was wrong from the moment they'd climbed into the van to drive home.

"Are you mad at us, Miss Rainy?" Joshua inquired, his blue eyes too big for his face.

With one hand gripping the steering wheel, she patted him reassuringly with the other. "No, darling. You're the best kids in the universe."

She was positive Nate thought the kids were fabulous, too.

Perhaps she should have kept her mouth shut. Maybe she'd gone too far. Who was she to tell him how to fix his life?

The woman who loved him, that was who. As such, she felt a responsibility to tell him the truth. Hanging on to his guilt had done nothing but hurt him and make parasites out of Janine and Blake.

A part of her wanted to turn the van around, go back to the Crossroads, and tell him she'd been wrong. But she wasn't. She was sorry for upsetting him, even more sorry for what his family had endured, but she wasn't wrong. He needed to let his past go and embrace the future. The decision, though, was his. All she could do now was pray for him.

And for her own aching heart.

Nate couldn't sleep. Long after midnight, he dressed and let himself quietly out the back door. Yo-Yo, curled into a comma on the porch, awoke and raised his head in question.

"Go back to sleep, buddy," Nate said softly.

But of course, the dog rose, shook himself, stretched

and sidled up to nudge his head beneath Nate's hand. By habit, Nate rubbed the warm, soft neck, taking mild comfort from a pal who demanded nothing but love.

Rainy wanted too much.

And he simply did not have it in him.

The night was cool and soft, scented with dogwood blooms, and lit by an impossible number of glimmering stars against a black chalkboard sky.

God was up there, he thought, as he stood with his head tilted back. Tonight, he needed to be close to God, to know the Lord was his Father, not just his Master and King.

Without much consideration, he ambled to the barn and saddled Moccasin, the sure-footed old Palomino who could find his way blindfolded around the Crossroads. With Yo-Yo trotting happily alongside, he rode out into the pasture, passed the gates, passed the black, lumpy shadows that were cattle and onto the Pierson lease.

In a matter of months he'd have to find a new lease or sell some of his stock. He wanted to resent the loss, but he couldn't. When he'd told Pop he believed Rainy and Katie were worth the money, he'd meant it. They were worth everything. Couldn't Rainy understand? She was valuable, special. He could never be the man she deserved. If money could bring Katie back into her life, he would gladly sell everything he owned to make it happen.

Their conversation from this afternoon swirled around inside him, painful and cutting. He'd thought she would understand. Janine and Blake needed his influence as well as his help. He couldn't turn his back on them.

He rode on, slowly dawdling along the creek bank where recent spring rains caused the water to flow musically, trickling over rocks and roots. A hoot owl called. To the Native Americans in the area, the owl's cry was bad luck. Nate didn't believe that, but the lonely sound added to his melancholia.

After a while, he prayed, spilling out his confusion and anguish. Rainy had no right to say the things she'd said. She had no way of knowing what his life was like or how he felt to know his indifference had caused Christine's death.

After a while, he sagged in the saddle, physically weary but still mentally tangled. The Lord didn't have any answers for him tonight.

He rode back to the barn to put the horse away, giving him a handful of sweet feed for his efforts. Hands in his pockets, Nate strode toward the house. Yo-Yo dogged his heels, a silent, unobtrusive, accepting companion.

The back porch light flared on. He blinked, blinded for a second.

"Something wrong, Nate boy?" Pop stood in the open back door.

No use avoiding the inevitable. His granddad knew him too well. Anytime Nate took a night ride, something was troubling him.

"Didn't mean to wake you," he said, stepping up into the light. A frog hopped across his boot and out into the darkness. Yo-yo gave the critter a glance but didn't bother. Instead, the collie flopped, with a sigh, into his corner of the porch and curled up with his head on his paws, facing the men.

Pop arched his shoulders in an awakening stretch and scratched at the back of his head. "You want some coffee?"

"Are you serious? I can't sleep, Pop. Coffee will only make matters worse."

"If you can't sleep anyway, you might as well have a hot jolt of java." He motioned toward the inside. "I got a fresh pot perking."

"Motor oil," Nate mumbled as he slid into one of the metal lawn chairs.

"I heard that."

They both chuckled softly.

"So, are you going to tell me what happened between you and Rainy?"

Nate cocked an eyebrow. "Think you're smart, don't you?"

"I seen her tear out of here this evening without the usual lollygagging the two of you do."

"We don't lollygag."

Pop made a rude noise. "Lying's a sin."

"Leave me alone, Pop."

"Not until you tell me what's going on. I kind of had my heart set on that girl."

So had he. "It's not going to work out."

The admission was harder to make than he'd expected. A lot harder. In the next few minutes, accompanied by the sound of Yo-Yo's snore and the occasional low of contented cattle, Nate told his granddad about the conversation.

Pop listened without interruption. When he finished, the older man pushed off the porch post and shuffled inside the house, returning with two oversized mugs of black, black coffee.

"Drink this," he said, handing a mug to Nate. "It'll put hair on your chest."

Nate's mouth twitched. Pop had told him that same thing years ago when he was a teenager, longing to grow up.

Hands wrapped around the warm cup, he took a sip, then grimaced. "Pond sludge."

Pop grinned, delighted. "Good stuff. Rivals those fancy espresso places."

"Right. Pond sludge latte. Gotta be a top seller."

They sipped in companionable silence, Nate glad to have his granddad's company. Brooding alone hadn't helped.

After a bit, Pop loudly slurped at his coffee, a signal that he was about to speak.

"Rainy's right, Nate boy."

Nate bristled but didn't reply.

"When Christine died—"

"She was murdered, Pop." Nate's hand flexed on the mug handle. "She didn't just die."

Pop waved off the comment. Once the old man started, he was going to have his say. Might as well let him.

"No one needs to tell me, son. I know what happened. That's not the point. The point is this. When she died, you got some wild-haired notion that you could have saved her."

"I could have."

"Nope. You couldn't. Get that settled in your hard Del Rio head. I don't know why we had to lose Christine, but we did. You didn't cause her murder, but you've spent years paying for it as if you had. I see what you do. I know why you do it. All of it."

Nate had no idea what Pop was talking about, but he was getting more uncomfortable by the second. He took another sip of fortifying pond sludge.

"Here's what I think, Nate boy." Pop drained his cup with an *ahhh* and plunked the stoneware onto the concrete porch. "You got a works mentality."

Nate tilted his head, figuring Pop would explain himself. He did.

"That means you think you got to work your way into God's good graces, especially when it comes to Janine and Blake. But the same goes for Rainy's kids and the Handyman Ministry, and a host of other things you do."

"The Bible teaches us to serve others."

"Not as a way of winning God's favor. Scripture says we're saved by grace, not by works. The Lord loves you because you're His, not because you sacrifice your own happiness for your brother and sister."

"I like helping people." Most of the time.

"Nothing wrong with that. It's the motive that counts. In here." Pop tapped a thick finger to his breast bone. "We both know you resent the way Janine and

Blake expect you to drop everything and come running."

That much was true. He loved them and worried about them, but he resented their dependence, too. Still, they were his brother and sister. He was the oldest. If he didn't look after them, who would?

"God doesn't blame you for Christine's death, son. Neither does anyone else. Don't you think it's time to stop blaming yourself, let go of the past and take hold of the good things God's trying to give you?"

Nate's gut knotted. He wanted to believe Pop was right. With all his heart, he wanted to believe. But he didn't.

Rainy cranked the volume on the CD player as she made the turn onto the graveled road leading to Crossroads Ranch. Her favorite Christian group, Third Day, belted out, "Don't you know I've always loved you," an encouraging reminder that God's love and grace were sufficient. No matter how sad she was about the loss of both Nate and Katie, God was still right here, surrounding her with his eternal, overwhelming love.

Determined to be happy, to embrace the good, she smiled through tears at the heavens. Though some might think her silly, she waved at the sky and said, "Thank you, Father."

Peace in the storm was not just a phrase preachers tossed around, but a reality to Rainy. She'd never understood before, but now she did. Oddly enough, the trying days of late had taken her faith to new heights. God was faithful when no one or nothing else was.

As she approached Nate's property line, a sign caught her attention, but she was going too fast to read it. She braked to a stop, dust swirling up around the windshield. Wryly, she thought of the five dollars she'd spent on a car wash yesterday.

She reversed the van, easing backward until she was parallel with the big red and white sign. Country Realty. For Sale.

Third Day kicked into one of her favorites, "Cry Out to Jesus," but she reached over and turned the volume down.

As she stared at the puzzling sign, her eyebrows drew together in a frown. She checked her location again, though she knew very well she was parked in front of the Pierson lease, the property Nate intended to purchase. Why was a For Sale sign needed? Nate had already proclaimed his intention to buy the land. He had the first option. No one else could buy this acreage.

After a few seconds in which she came to no conclusion, she drove on to the ranch to collect the children.

As usual, the black and white collie rushed out to greet her, barking a few times for good measure. To her amusement, Snowflake, who now had the run of the property as if he, too, was a dog, scampered around the side of the long, low house. A small bell jingled from a red collar around his neck.

She parked the van next to the big cedar and got out, knowing that if the animals appeared, the children would not be far behind. Sure enough, all three barreled toward her. Will carried a baseball and bat. Emma wore someone's oversized ball glove on her head. Joshua toted the white ball, skidding to a stop in front of the van to toss it high into the air. Head back, he feinted from side to side, both hands extended until the ball thudded to the ground in front of him.

Will laughed. Rainy hid a grin. "Did the sun get in your eyes?"

"Nope," Joshua said, bending to scoop up the ball. "I just missed it."

Rainy stooped for a hug. "This is your first year to play. You'll get the hang of it."

"He's getting better, Miss Rainy," Emma said. "The ball doesn't hit him on the head anymore."

"Well, there's something to be said for progress." She ruffled Josh's hair and then grabbed each of the other two for their afternoon hug. When she'd first gotten the trio, none of them quite knew what to do with her displays of affection. Now, they expected them and had learned to reciprocate.

"Where's Pop?" she asked.

Just then the older cowboy limped around the house. "I'm coming."

"Why are you limping? Did you hurt your foot again?"

"Ah, it isn't nothing." He waved off the idea of injury. "Twisted my ankle."

"Working with the cattle?" she asked.

"Nope. Chasing a fly ball." He rubbed his chin and chuckled. "That Will's got a power swing on him. Can hit a ball plumb to the pond."

So Pop had been playing ball with the kids. Without thinking better of it, Rainy hugged the older man.

"What was that for?" he asked, looking pleased.

"For being such a nice man."

"Does that mean you'll bring me some of your fancy brownies next time you come?"

The request brought an ache to her heart, but she didn't let it show. The brownies were Nate's favorites. Since the breakup, she'd baked far too many of them. Half the neighborhood, her students and her Sunday School class had benefited from her fits of stress baking. She'd taken them everywhere but here.

"I'd love to make some brownies for you, Pop. You'll have them tomorrow." She motioned toward the van. "Load up, kids. Time to go." Before Nate arrived. Seeing him hurt too much.

"Whoa, now," Pop said. "You can't leave yet. We're in the third inning. Will and Joshua are winning. Me and Emma deserve a chance to catch up."

"What's the score?"

"Twelve to five," Emma said with disgust. "Me and Pop need help."

Rainy pressed her fingertips over her smile. "Oh, my."

"I have an idea, Miss Rainy," Joshua said. "You can play on their team and maybe they'll have a chance. They're good. But Will is like a pro or something."

She noticed the way Will's narrow shoulders straightened at the compliment. This was good for him, building his confidence.

"And I'm a tad bit gimpy," Pop added, his eyes twinkling merrily.

Rainy knew when she was being manipulated, but

she didn't mind at all. "How can I refuse? We can't stop a game in the third inning. Lead on, mighty Yankees."

With a whoop of joy, the three kids, followed by a jingling goat and an overzealous collie, started toward the back yard. Rainy and Pop followed at a slower pace.

"Maybe you should go inside and put ice on your ankle," Rainy suggested.

"Nah, it's all right." He waited two beats until the children were out of earshot to say, "So, how you doing, Rainy? I mean, really doing, since all this nonsense with Nate?"

"I'm okay. Sad. Disappointed. But God is closer than ever." She stopped long enough to pull a bright yellow dandelion. "Is Nate okay?"

"Nah, he won't ever be okay until he gets his mind straight. I tried talking to him. He's got a hard head sometimes."

She sighed, rubbed the soft wildflower against her cheek. "Do you think he'll ever realize he wasn't to blame for his sister's death?"

"I'm talking. And praying. Janine and Blake don't help. They keep him burdened down, feeling obligated. He has the fool notion that he's not good enough for you or some such nonsense, that he can't be enough for them and for you and for all these young ones of yours at the same time."

"I know." And she was helpless to change his mind. "He's unhappy. I don't want that for him. I love him, Pop."

He patted her shoulder. "I know you do. I believe he

feels the same. That's what's got him in such a turmoil. My grandson's at a Crossroads in more ways that one."

Rainy hoped Pop was right, but she was beginning to have doubts.

They rounded the corner of the house where Will and Joshua were carefully realigning the three bases and home plate. The bases appeared to be pieces of an old horse blanket.

Rainy, still ruminating on Pop's "Crossroads" comment, remembered the troubling For Sale sign.

"I saw something odd on my way out here today," she said.

"Yeah?" Pop removed his hat to swipe a hand over a perspiring and balding head.

"A For Sale sign on the Pierson lease."

Pop plopped the hat in place, his expression changing from interest to wary.

"That place is Nate's dream," Rainy went on. "No one else can buy it out from under him, can they? Why is there a sign up if he has exclusive first option?"

Pop rubbed at his ear, face averted to watch the children. Rainy got a funny, suspicious feeling in her stomach, though she couldn't for the life of her understand why.

"Pop? What's going on with Nate's land?"

The old cowboy shifted his weight onto his good leg. "Well, it's like this, Miss Rainy. Nate let the place go. He's not going to buy it."

"Not buying it? How can that be? He's saved for years to buy that property, to expand, to grow the best organic beef in the state." She thought of the excitement in Nate when he'd told her about the expansion, of the times he'd dreamed out loud, sharing his plans for the future. "This doesn't make sense. Why would he change his mind?"

Again, the silence. When Pop spoke, he seemed to be saying something she couldn't quite comprehend.

"If you really want the answer—and I think you should—you'll have to ask Nate."

Nate wiped a forearm across his sweaty brow. The sun was high and hot this afternoon. He'd spent the day separating cattle and was bone tired. Tired was good. It kept his mind off other troubles. Namely Rainy. He missed her. Missed their talks, their Friday-night movies. Truth was, he missed everything about her.

Will, Joshua and Emma tumbled off the bus each evening full of school news and childhood energy. No matter how hard he tried to let Pop handle them and their projects, the three siblings tracked him down wherever he was.

To make matters worse, Rainy kept right on coming to the Crossroads every night. She and the kids and Pop had a grand time without him. On those chance occasions when their paths crossed, her smile fell away and she gazed at him with hurt in her gray-blue eyes.

He was such a jerk. Surely, she understood that now. Understood that he was not good for her.

But seeing her was a sweet torment that kept him awake at night.

As such, he'd taken to staying away from the ranch or far out in the pasture until dark.

This particular evening, he'd had no choice but to come in from the field. His horse had pulled up lame.

On foot, he led Moccasin through the gates and across the wide, empty lot. From somewhere near the house, he could hear the kids playing, their voices carrying high and joyous on the still air. Yo-Yo yipped happily. The dog was crazy about those kids and had even taken to lying beneath the cross timbers of the ranch each afternoon, waiting for the bus to rumble into view.

A woman laughed, warm and joyful.

Rainy.

The ever-present knot in his belly tightened. He left Moccasin in the stall and walked to the corner of the barn, looking toward the house, where the voices seemed to originate.

He did a double take. There they were, all of them including Pop, playing the craziest game of baseball he'd ever imagined.

The goat, who followed Emma with the same devotion that Yo-Yo gave the boys, dashed down the baseline after the little girl, bleating like crazy. His jingle bell bobbed and tinkled. When it appeared Joshua would catch the ball and put Emma out, Snowflake gave him a hearty butt, knocking him on his backside. Yo-Yo rushed to his defense, alternately barking at Snowflake and licking Joshua's dirty face.

All the players fell down laughing.

Nate laughed, too. He started forward to join the

fun, then caught himself and turned back toward the barn and the limping horse.

Some things were better left alone.

Chapter Fifteen

The thunderstorm arose suddenly, as was common in Oklahoma. Though the afternoon had been hot and humid, a harbinger of stormy weather, the dark clouds boiled together in a matter of minutes.

One clap of thunder and a crack of distant lightning sent three wide-eyed children scurrying toward the house from the calf barn. Nate, who'd been stacking sacks of horse feed in the bins watched them run, full-out, legs pumping toward the house. A few seconds later, Pop limped out behind them. The old man refused to see a doctor for his ankle, claiming that it, like his foot, would heal in God's time. Before Pop reached the back porch, the dark skies opened with a downpour, soaking him.

The horses stirred in their stalls, restless at the sudden crackle of electrical energy sizzling in the air. A bolt of lightning zigzagged overhead, the accompanying crash of thunder startling and magnificent. Nothing like a good Oklahoma thunderstorm to clear the air.

Since boyhood, Nate had enjoyed the wild unpredictability of Oklahoma weather, finding thunderstorms invigorating, exciting.

He finished his task and stood inside the horse barn, watching water run off the metal roof, breathing in the fresh rain scent, stirred by the awesomeness of nature.

Pop would check the TV for severe weather alerts, but by all signs, this was one of those fast and furious, gone-in-a-few-minutes cloudbursts. The sun would probably be shining before Rainy got here. Even if it wasn't, Rainy brought sunshine with her, from the inside out.

As always, something inside him reacted when he thought about the woman he couldn't have. She'd been wrong to take him to task the way she had, though he was struggling to remain angry. She didn't understand. That was the problem. No one did.

After a few minutes, the rain had not abated and Nate began to worry. Probably better get to the house and make sure there were no tornado warnings. Hand clapped to the top of his hat, he loped the hundred yards to the house. The cold sucked his breath as rain soaked his shirt.

Thunder rumbled. He braced himself for the lightning strike. By the time his boots thumped onto the porch, pea-sized hail pinged against the house and bounced across the yard, dotting the green grass.

The back door opened and Will's face peered out, anxious. "You're gonna get wet."

Nate grinned and shook like a dog. "Already am."

A sprinkled Will jumped back. "Ew."

Amused by the boy's reaction, Nate stepped inside and shucked his boots on the kitchen tile. "Anyone look at the weather on TV?"

"Pop did. He says it's just a thunderstorm. Nothing to worry about."

"Would you grab a towel for me, then?" Nate motioned toward the back of the house, but Will was already gone. He knew where things were. In seconds, the boy returned, tossing the fluffy terry cloth to him.

Patting the excess water from his face and chest, Nate followed Will into the living room. The rest of the crew was scattered about on chairs, on the floor, etc. Emma had curled up with her reading book. Rainy would be glad to see that. Josh stood at the big front windows staring out. Was he worried about the storm? Or watching for Rainy?

"What do you see out there, partner?" Nate asked.

"Hail. Big hail." Joshua tapped a finger on the windowpane. "Look at it bouncing around."

"Like golf balls," Will said, going to stand beside his brother.

Nate placed a hand on each child's shoulder. "You boys scared?"

Both shook their heads in denial.

"I think it's kind of cool," Joshua said. "I might want to be a meteor—meterol—a weatherman when I grow up."

"Yeah?" Nate said. "Good plan. I like weather, too."

He'd even considered studying the subject as a profession after high school. That had been before Christine's death, before Janine and Blake had proved themselves inept without him. Not that he regretted his decision to raise cattle instead of going to college. He was happy here. Most of the time.

"Come on, Josh," Will said, tugging on his brother's arm. "Let's go play a game until Rainy comes."

For all his protests to the contrary, Nate figured Will didn't really appreciate the thunder and lightning as much as Joshua did.

"Later," Josh said, fascinated by the show outside his window. "I want to watch the storm."

Will shrugged, looking at Nate as if he thought his little brother was loony, but said, "I'll get a game out. You want Chinese checkers?"

"I don't care." Joshua jerked a shoulder, but didn't take his eyes from the window as he said in awe, "Look at those hailstones. I wonder how big they are."

Will made another face and headed toward the back of the house, where Nate kept a stack of board games. For some reason, he'd started collecting the things during the past couple of months. He and Rainy had enjoyed a crazy, laugh-filled time playing Scattergories one night.

Annoyed to be thinking of her again, he grumbled. "I gotta change these wet clothes. Pop, will you thaw out something for dinner and put on some fresh coffee?"

Pop shoved off the couch and headed toward the kitchen with a chuckle. "You claim I make terrible coffee."

"You do," Nate called with an answering chuckle

just before closing the bedroom door. A rumble of thunder followed him.

As he dressed, the rain abated and a glimmering of light slithered through the mini blinds. The storm was passing. Good. He didn't like the idea of Rainy driving through heavy rain and hail, even if the storm was mild.

The overhead lights flickered once—no big deal after a rainstorm.

He buttoned his shirt and reached for dry boots. A deafening crash rattled the windows. The boots clattered to the floor. He yanked the door open and rushed into the living room. Pop, Emma and Will, all wearing identical stunned expressions, met him there.

"What was that?" he asked, taking in the saucer-sized eyes of the two children.

"Don't know," Pop said. "Lightning maybe?"

"Maybe, though the storm is letting up," Nate said. "Struck close by, I'd say."

"Yeah. Real close." Pop relayed a silent message.

Nate nodded. "I'd better check outside. Make sure the animals and barns are okay." Lightning on a hay barn could cause a mean fire in a hurry. He glanced at the children. "Where's Joshua?"

"He was right there a minute ago," Will pointed toward the window. "Watching the hail."

"Joshua?" Nate called. No answer.

His expression worried, Will ran toward the bathroom but returned in a second's time. "He's not in there."

A tingle of fear prickled the hair on Nate's neck.

Joshua was not afraid of storms. He was not hiding in the back of the closet.

"If he's not in the house, where is he?" Pop asked.

"The hail," Will said softly, eyes growing even wider. "He wanted to get some hail when the rain stopped. To measure it."

At that moment, a high-pitched wail lifted above the conversation, and Nate knew.

"Oh no." He was in a dead run before he reached the front door.

The big cedar tree next to the driveway angled across the front yard, split at the trunk. Beneath it was Joshua.

His heart hammering in his ears, Nate rushed to the fallen child. Water soaked his socks. As he stumbled to his knees in the wet grass, Pop, Will and Emma came up behind.

Emma set up a wail. "Joshie's hurt."

"Hush, child," Pop said, patting the top of her blond head, though his concern focused on the cedar-trapped boy. "Josh boy, where are you hurt?"

"I—I—I don't know." Joshua's voice was thin and shaky. "The tree is smashing me. I can't get out."

Nate pushed at the prickly cedar branches, sliding his hand over the wet, rough grass, until he touched Joshua's foot. "Hang on, buddy. We'll have you out in a minute. I'll move the tree, and Pop will pull you out. Okay?"

While listening for Joshua's wobbly agreement, he signaled a silent message to his granddad. *The boy could have broken bones. Take it easy.* Pop responded with a nod.

As Nate put a shoulder to the enormous old cedar, Will appeared, adding his slight weight to the effort. Nate was proud of him for that. Later, he'd let him know.

With muscles quivering, they lifted the splintered cedar a few inches, enough for Pop to gently ease Joshua into the clear. The boy began to cry.

Thunder rumbled overhead and the sky had darkened again.

"Let's get him inside." With great care, Nate scooped the shivering child into his arms. Joshua's back was as soaked as Nate's socks.

Once in the house, he gently placed Joshua on the sofa and began to assess the damage. Scratches on his face and arms. A bruise on his shoulder, which appeared to have taken the brunt of the falling limb. Nothing looked permanent or serious. Thank God. He couldn't bear for anything terrible to happen to one of Rainy's kids.

Keeping his own rampaging emotions under control, he said softly, "What happened out there, Joshua?"

Joshua's lips trembled as tears slid along the side of his nose and into the corners of his mouth. "I don't know. I went to grab some hail. I thought the storm was over. Then I heard a big boom and the tree hit me."

The child rotated his shoulder, touching it gingerly with his opposite hand.

"Lightning must have struck it," Pop said.

A tremor of horror was replaced by more gratitude

as Nate realized how close the boy had come to a life-and-death situation. Thanks to a merciful, loving God, the lightning had not struck Joshua.

"Is he all right?" Will hovered next to the couch, his face white and pinched. Emma stood at one end, stroking Joshua's hair over and over again.

"Looks like he will be. He's one tough cowboy, aren't you, Joshua? He can take on a bolt of lightning and a giant cedar tree and come out the winner." Nate winked at the shaking child. "I don't find any broken bones, but Miss Rainy may want to have you checked out by the doctor."

Will crumpled to the floor and thrust his face against his upraised knees. His glasses pushed to one side at an odd angle. "I'm sorry, Joshua. I'm sorry. I shouldn't have let you go."

By now, Pop had brought a damp cloth and was carefully cleaning Joshua's scratches as he checked for more injuries.

Nate turned his attention to Will.

"Whoa, now. What's this all about? Little brother will be fine."

"I knew he wanted to go out there. I shouldn't have let him. It's my fault he got hurt."

Nate sat down on the floor beside the older child and draped an arm over the shaking shoulders. "Will, that's not true. This is not your fault. Joshua did what he did. You can't take the blame for his actions."

"I'm supposed to take care of him."

"No, you aren't. That is not your job, Will."

The boy raised his head and looked at Nate with

red, guilt-ridden eyes. He shoved angrily at his dirty glasses. "I'm the big brother. It *is* my job."

The big brother. Guilt-ridden and overresponsible.

Nate felt as if he'd been hit in the gut with a ball bat. Hadn't he said these same words a thousand times? Hadn't he walked in Will's shoes?

"No, son. No."

He squeezed his eyes shut and pulled Will against his side. None of this was Will's fault but the boy carried the burden for all of his siblings. Just as Nate did.

Dear Lord, have I been wrong all this time?

While he sat on the hardwood floor consoling the child, the telephone rang. He patted Will's shoulder. "Hang tight, my man. I'll be back."

Pop waved him off. "You look after the kids. I'll get the phone."

Nate urged Will to his feet. Keeping his hands on Will's shoulders, Nate scooted both of them onto the couch next to Joshua. "See, buddy, he's all right. Aren't you, Joshua?"

Rubbing at a long scratch on his cheek, the younger brother nodded. Just then, Pop hollered from the kitchen. "Blake's on the horn. Wants to talk to you."

Instead of the usual leap of worry that something terrible had happened to his brother, something new and unfamiliar passed over Nate. Truth. Freedom. "Ask him if it's an emergency."

A grin twitched Pop's mouth. "Only to him. He forgot to pay his cell phone bill. Six hundred dollars."

"Six hundred—" Nate caught himself. He was the

big brother. He should take care of it. For the first time in his life, he recognized the lie behind those words.

As clearly as if the clouds had disappeared and the sun illuminated a path, Nate recognized the parallel between his mind-set and Will's. They were both wrong. He was no more responsible for his brother and sister than Will was to blame for Joshua's accident.

"Tell him he's on his own." Nate stilled himself against an onslaught of guilt. It never came. "From now on."

Pop blinked at him in wonder before a slow, satisfied smile spread across his weathered face. He spoke into the receiver for several more minutes, then disconnected and returned to the living room where he clapped a broad hand on Nate's shoulder.

"I don't know what brought that on, Nate boy, but all I can say is it's about time."

All these years, he'd blamed himself, carried the burden of familial responsibility that was not his to carry. As a result, the things he'd done for his siblings were out of guilt and fear, not love, and as Rainy had tried to tell him, he'd hurt them more than helped them. He'd made them weak and dependent.

He'd failed. Not because he hadn't tried hard enough or done enough, but because he'd left God out of the equation, thinking he had to handle everything on his own.

He gathered Rainy's three children into his arms, recognizing the love he'd been holding back.

"God help me," he muttered. "I have been a foolish man."

Part of faith was being able to give the things and the people he loved to God and trust that the God who made the universe could care for them far better than one guilt-ridden cowboy.

Rainy couldn't figure out what was going on in Nate's head. He'd followed her to the A.M.-P.M. Clinic to have Joshua's shoulder X-rayed, adding support, looking after Emma and Will in the waiting room, and generally behaving as if he'd never shut her out of his life.

By the time she arrived at her house, it was nearly ten o'clock. The kids were exhausted and emotionally overwrought, but thankfully, Joshua's shoulder was only sprained and bruised. As a foster parent, she'd had other close calls, but this one was the most serious. She was so glad Nate and Pop had been present when the accident occurred. The kids loved and trusted them. So did she.

She sneaked a glance at the tall, perplexing cowboy. As if it were the most natural thing in the world, he was sitting on the edge of Will's twin bed, talking in low tones. She couldn't hear what was being said, but Will's serious mind was taking everything in.

Across the room, she helped Joshua into his Scooby pajama top, being careful of the bruised arm. Then she tucked him into bed.

"You have a lot to be thankful for tonight, Joshua," she said as she kissed his soap-scented forehead.

"Yeah. A lot." His big blue eyes looked from her to Nate and Will and then tiredly closed.

After a heartfelt prayer of thanks for his safety, which Rainy silently affirmed, he said, "Thank You, too, for Nate. I'm glad he was there to take care of me. I think I love him, Jesus. I wouldn't mind having him for a dad."

Rainy's eyes flew open. She glanced across at Nate, but the cowboy apparently hadn't heard. Thank goodness. He'd made himself clear on that subject.

"And Jesus—" Joshua went on, heedless of the turmoil he'd initiated "—please bless my brother. Tell him it wasn't his fault. I was the dummy who went outside. Okay, I'm done now. Thank you. Amen."

Rainy stood, gazing down at the beautiful boy. "I love you, Joshua."

A tiny smile appeared as his lids drooped.

"I love you…" Before he could finish the thought, Joshua was asleep.

Rainy pushed the damp hair away from his forehead and kissed him again before leaving the room.

Emma had fallen asleep on the ride home and was already in bed. Rainy rubbed weary hands over her face and through her hair. What an evening.

She had two cups of hot chocolate in the microwave when Nate came out of the boys' bedroom. Back turned to the cabinets, she heard his boots *tap-tapping* on the tile. Maybe now she could find out what was going on with him tonight.

As she removed a bag of marshmallows from a shelf, her own smiley-face puppet appeared over her shoulder.

"Hey, Slick," the puppet said in Nate's voice. "How you doing?"

Touched, amused, she leaned her cheek against the puppet for a brief moment, fully aware that Nate's hand was the recipient of her affection. "Tired, but thankful. How about you, Mr. Smiley?"

There was a pause before Mr. Smiley slid away. Rainy felt the loss clear to her tired feet.

"I'm sorry Joshua was injured on my watch," Nate said.

Rainy slowly turned around. Nate was standing inches away, his eyes darkened with emotion, the smiley puppet dangling at his side.

"You can't watch them every second. They're boys. Boys are adventurers. Don't blame yourself."

"I'm not."

"That's a first."

"Yeah, it is."

He looked as weary as she felt, his hair disheveled and his shirt smudged with dirt and smelling of cedar sap. Yet an aura of peace emanated from him such as she'd never seen before.

Something was going on with Nate Del Rio. Something good. A ray of foolish hope energized her.

"Is Will all right?" she asked, stirring the cocoa. "Joshua mentioned that he thought he was somehow to blame for the accident."

The reaction was typical of Will. He carried the burden of his brother and sister as seriously as Nate did.

The parallel had occurred to her before.

Rubbing a hand over the top of his hair, mussing the

brown stuff even more, Nate nodded. "I straightened him out about that."

He had? Mister I'm-Responsible-for-the-World had straightened out Will's similar thinking?

She handed over a mug filled with hot cocoa and floating marshmallows. "How did you do that?"

Eager to rest her weary body, Rainy led the way into the living room, where she curled her feet beneath her on one end of the couch. Nate perched on the edge at the other end, his elbows on knees, the cup in both hands. The puppet lay inert between them, its wide eyes and permanent smile looking up at them with happy interest.

"I told him about me," he said, studying the rising steam from his cocoa. "About how I'd been wrong for a long time and didn't know it. About how he and the Lord had opened my eyes today."

Rainy blew across the top of her mug. "I'm afraid you've lost me."

He looked up then, caught her gaze with his and held on. "I hope not. With everything in me, I hope I haven't lost you."

Rainy's heart skipped a beat. What was he saying? That he was sorry for the breakup? That he cared? She tilted her head as the ember of hope became a flame. "Nate? What's going on?"

"I was wrong, Rainy. About us. About Janine and Blake. About everything." He set the cup aside. "I love those kids in there."

"I know you do." She'd always known. No matter how he denied the emotion, everything he did screamed love.

His jaw worked for a few seconds. His nostrils flared.

"I love you, too."

The beautiful words floated across the space like colorful balloons in a blue, blue sky. Rainy's throat filled with emotion. She wasn't sure what had transpired, but she was too happy to care.

She smiled. "Feeling's mutual, Cowboy."

He squeezed his eyes closed for one brief moment, shaking his head. "I don't deserve you, but if you can forgive me, if you can give me another chance, I promise to do things a lot differently this time."

Nate rose and took the cocoa cup from her hands, setting it next to his on the coffee table. Kneeling before her on one knee, his fingers, warm from the hot drink, entwined with hers.

"So what do you think? Will you give this dumb cowboy another try?"

Rainy studied his beloved face, soaking him in. As much as she loved him, he had to understand one important thing. She wouldn't back away from the calling God had placed on her life to minister to children. Not even for him.

Nate jiggled her hand. "Help me out here, Slick. You're too quiet."

"I come with baggage, Nate. You know that. God willing, I'm going to adopt those three in there. And I'll go right on taking in foster children as long as God wants me to."

"Wouldn't it be easier if you had a partner to help out?"

She was almost afraid to believe this was for real. "I can't settle for any old partner, Nate. Only someone who loves these kids and is as committed to them as I am."

Nate picked up Mr. Smiley, working his giant, grinning mouth.

"I know a guy like that," Mr. Smiley said. "Good-looking dude. Owns a ranch. Crazy about you. Crazy about your kids. Come on, Miss Rainy, what do you say? Throw the guy a bone."

Rainy grabbed the puppet, stopping the onslaught of words. "What happened to the cowboy who never wanted kids? The one who said kids are too much trouble?"

"Lightning struck. God spoke. I listened." He took her hand in his and squeezed gently. "I've been battling the idea for a long time. Ever since we met, I guess, and you pushed your way into my heart."

"I do not push." She bunched one shoulder. "Well, maybe a little."

"Like a velvet bulldozer." His killer dimples flashed. "After Katie was taken, I got cold feet, thinking I couldn't take the hurt. But today, when Joshua was under that tree, I realized I was going to love him no matter where he was. He might as well be with me as my son."

Tears pushed up behind Rainy's eyes. "Nate Del Rio, I love you so much. You big jerk."

He kissed her on the nose. "Did you just agree to marry me?"

"Did you just ask me to?"

A grin spread across his handsome features.

"Yep," he said in wonder. "I sure did."

Rainy traced the whisker-roughened jaw line, touched the firm crease of dimple next to his mouth. "Will you answer a question for me?"

"Anything. Anything you want. As long as you'll be in my life, I'll do anything."

"Why did you let the Pierson lease go?"

She could tell she'd shocked him. He rocked back on his heels. She tugged him back. "I saw the For Sale sign. I asked Pop and he said to ask you. So I'm asking."

"You don't need to know."

His answer told her everything. "You were my secret donor from the church, weren't you?"

"Your happiness is worth more to me than any piece of land ever could be."

So he'd sacrificed his dreams and every penny he'd saved for her and Katie and their lost cause.

"Oh, Nate. You wonderful, generous, incredible man. No wonder I fell madly in love with you."

She leaned forward and wrapped her arms around his neck. "You gave up your dream for me and Katie and got nothing in return."

With a tenderness that brought tears to her eyes, Nate cupped her face. "No, my darlin', you're wrong. I got everything a man could want."

Epilogue

Nate thought the courtroom looked the same. Cold. Austere. Formal. Only the atmosphere was different. Anticipatory. Happy.

He glanced at the woman snuggled close to his side on the hard wooden bench. His chest swelled with love for his bride of three months. She was nervous, but in a different way than on that terrible day of Katie's custody hearing. Glowing with excitement, Rainy fussed over first one child and then another until all three squirmed.

The kids looked perfect, like Easter portraits. Emma was princess gorgeous in a frilly yellow dress with white patent-leather shoes and ribbons in her hair. Will and Joshua looked as handsome and studious and neat as bankers in blue dress shirts and black slacks.

Nate couldn't hold back a grin at Will's pained expression, as the boy tugged at the necktie pressing his Adam's apple. Nate tugged at his own just for good measure. Will noticed and his eyes crinkled behind the plastic frames.

"When is the judge coming?" he whispered to Nate.

"Soon." Nate reassured his soon-to-be-son with a pat on the knee.

Son. Will would be his child forever. As would Joshua and Emma.

The wonder of it moved through him, as warm and cleansing as summer rain.

He could hardly believe the way his life had changed in the past year. On Valentine's Day, he and Rainy had married in a simple church ceremony filled with love and spirituality and family blessings. Then, with Pop happy to play granddad to the kids, the newlyweds had honeymooned in beautiful Cancun, a wedding gift from Rainy's parents.

Now, his once tidy, quiet ranch was lively with children and toys and schoolbooks, along with Miss Rainy's puppets and chocolate baking.

Kathy Underkircher and her bitter complaints had come to nothing. Thank God. Now Rainy and the children were safely away from her prying eyes and ears, a fact that gave him immense satisfaction.

Blake and Janine had been stunned when their older brother insisted on having a life of his own. To their credit, though they still struggled they were gaining ground, slowly becoming independent adults—and happier for the change. Last Sunday afternoon Janine and the baby had come for a visit and had left much later without requesting anything but Rainy's recipe for brownies.

With Rainy by his side and the Lord as his guide, Nate knew he would never go back to his self-imposed martyrdom.

"All please rise. This court is in session. Judge Bohannon presiding."

Rainy's fingers jerked in his and he winked at her.

The serious-looking judge scanned the gathered assembly, his gaze landing on Nate, Rainy and the children. Emma lifted a small hand and waved at the man. His responding chuckle relaxed them all.

In minutes, the proceedings were over. The judge offered his congratulations and proclaimed Will, Joshua and Emma to be the lawful children of Nate and Rainy Del Rio.

Before the black-robed jurist had swept from the courtroom, the three children erupted in celebration, hugging and high-fiving everyone in sight. Even the social worker had tears of happiness in her eyes.

Rainy threw herself into Nate's arms in exuberant joy. With a laugh, he lifted her high into the air. As he settled her to the earth again, three children attacked his legs. He and Rainy formed a circle, embracing their sons and daughter.

"Grab a hand," he said, his voice gruff with emotion.

Over the months of bonding, the children had come to understand. In a circle of family, they bowed their heads while Nate quietly gave thanks, heart full enough to burst, mere words inadequate.

Why had he ever thought he didn't want this? How could he have ever been so blind?

When the prayer ended, Joshua looked up at Rainy.

"Can we tell him now, Miss Rainy?" He shook his head. "I mean, Mom."

"Yeah, Mom," Will said, trying the name on for size. "Let's tell Dad the news."

A quiver of something new and wonderful moved through Nate. Dad. He was a dad.

"Yeah, Mom," Emma said, not to be outdone. "Tell Dad."

Man, he liked that word. Nate looked from one member of his new family to the other. "Tell Dad what? Are you already keeping secrets from the old man?"

Rainy's face was radiant. "A good secret. You're going to like this. I promise."

She reached inside her purse and removed an envelope which she handed to him. The kids gazed on, expectant, smiling.

Nate turned the envelope over in his hands. "What is this?"

"Open it and see." By now, Rainy was jiggling up and down, as eager as a kid on Christmas.

He removed the legal-looking paper and quickly scanned it. He gazed up, bewildered. "This is a contract to buy the Pierson property."

"Mom bought it for you, Nate. I mean, Dad," Will said. "She bought it for our family."

"You couldn't have. How could you have?"

Rainy's sweet smile would stay with him forever. "When I put my house up for sale, I contacted Mr. Pierson, explained the situation, and convinced him to wait a little longer before selling to anyone else."

"Convinced him?" Yes, he could see that. His velvet bulldozer could persuade the feathers from a peacock.

"Then when my house sold," she went on, very pleased with herself, "he and I made the deal. My profit from the house easily covered the down payment on the land, with some left over for those cows you wanted to buy."

"I can't believe this." But he held the legal evidence in his hands. "You did this for me?"

"For you. For me. For all of us, cowboy. Your dreams are my dreams now."

He couldn't hold back. There on the front lawn of the courthouse surrounded by three giggling, whooping children, he pulled his beautiful bride into his arms and kissed her.

As her warm, loving lips met his, Nate Del Rio lifted his heart to God in praise for the day a city slicker and her passel of children bulldozed their way into his life—

And made him like it.

* * * * *

Dear Reader,

I'm often asked if I write myself into my stories. This is one book where I did, at least to a small degree. Like the heroine, Rainy, I love to bake, especially chocolate. Also like Rainy, I tend to bake when under stress. Below is the recipe for Rainy's (and my) favorite brownies. I hope you like them, too.

Rainy's Chocoholic Brownie Recipe

Melt 1/2 cup semisweet chocolate chips with 1 stick of butter or margarine. I do this in the microwave but you may also do it on the stovetop over low heat.

Stir in, mixing well after each addition:

1/4 cup flour
1/4 cup cocoa
1/2 cup brown sugar
1/2 cup sugar
2 eggs
1 tsp. vanilla
1/2 cup pecans or walnuts (optional)

Spread in a sprayed or greased 8x8 baking pan. Bake at 350 degrees for 40 minutes. To test for doneness, an inserted toothpick will come out crumbly-moist. Do not overbake.

Enjoy!

Linda Goodnight

Questions for Discussion

1. According to his grandfather, Nate struggled with a "works mentality." What does this mean? Have you ever known anyone who thought they had to work their way into God's favor?

2. Discuss some of the ways Nate "worked" for God's favor. Did his efforts do him any good?

3. At one point, Pop reminds Nate that motive is everything. What did he mean by that? Is it possible to be a Christian and have a resentful heart?

4. Many Christians serve their churches or fellow man in some way. Is this the same as "works mentality"? Discuss the difference.

5. Nate says he never wants kids. Why does he feel that way? Are his feelings justified?

6. Rainy believes God has called her to be an adoptive parent even though she is single. What is your position on single-parent adoptions? Why? Are there any instances of adoption in the Bible?

7. Kathy Underkircher, Rainy's neighbor, causes problems for Rainy over a perceived slight. Was there anything else Rainy could have done as

a Christian to win Kathy's approval? Should a Christian always turn the other cheek?

8. The foster child, Katie, is returned to her birth mother. How did you feel about that? Was this the best choice for Katie? Is a birth parent always a better alternative than an adoptive one?

9. How is the word "Crossroads" in the title significant to the story? Discuss both types of crossroads in Nate's life.

10. Did any other characters experience a "crossroads" during the course of the book? Explain.

11. Nate suffered terrible guilt over the death of his sister. Do you think he was to blame in any way? Could he have prevented her death? Was he wrong in not responding to her call?

12. Do you think each person has an appointed time to die and nothing can prevent it? Or can the action of human beings determine matters of life and death? Whichever you choose, is there scripture to back up your beliefs?

13. Nate believes he isn't one of God's favorite people. Do you think God favors some Christians over others? Why or why not? Can you find scripture references concerning God's favor?

The Baby Bond

When you pass through the waters,
I will be with you; and when you pass through
the rivers, they will not sweep over you. When you
walk through the fire, you will not be burned;
the flames will not set you ablaze. For I am the
Lord your God, the Holy One of Israel, your Savior.
—*Isaiah* 43:2–3

During the writing of this book,
I was blessed to have the help of
an awesome group of real-life heroes—
the men of B Crew, Fire Station One in
Norman, Oklahoma. Captain Lenny Mulder,
Driver Keith Scott, and firefighters Matt Hart
and Cody Goodnight answered any and
all questions, discussed scenarios and even
let me ride along on a call in the new fire engine
Thanks, guys. You're the best!

Chapter One

Nic Carano leaped from the fire engine as soon as the truck came to a rolling stop, heedless of the sixty pounds of turnout gear weighing him down. Along with the captain, the driver and two other firefighters from Station One, he'd been the first to arrive on a very bad scene. Flames shot out of the front windows of an old two-story Victorian. Fully involved. Being devoured by the beast. Smoke plumed upward like gray, evil genies. With a sinking heart, Nic realized fire crews had only arrived and they were already behind.

Almost simultaneously, Engine Company Two wailed onto the scene and "pulled a spaghetti" as a pair of firefighters, moving in opposite directions, circled the structure with the two smaller lines.

Someone said, "We've got people inside."

Nic's adrenaline jacked to Mach speed. He glanced at his captain, and noticed the fire reflecting gold and red in the other man's pupils. Without a word, Nic tapped a finger to his chest. Ten minutes ago he'd been asleep in his bunk. Now he was wide awake and revved for takeoff.

"You and Ridge do the primary." Captain Jack Summers's graying mustache barely moved as he spoke. "No heroics."

His captain knew him well. Nic wanted in. He wanted to face the beast and win. Maybe he broke a rule now and then, but Captain knew he'd never endanger the crew. He and Sam Ridge, a quietly intense Kiowa Indian had gone to the academy together and practically read each other's minds.

If there were people inside, they would find them.

He and Ridge charged the house, pulling hose. Engine Company Two axed through the front door. The beast roared in anger. Nic and Sam hit their knees, crawling low into the dark gray blindness. As nozzle man, Nic went first, spraying hot spots while Sam rotated the thermal imaging camera left to right around the rooms.

The whoosh-hush of his own breathing filled his ears. *Darth Vader,* he thought with humor. Otherwise he heard nothing, saw nothing.

"Front room clear," he said, feeling his way through a doorway to the left and into the next room.

"We got casualties." His partner's terse words jacked another stream of adrenaline into Nic's already thundering bloodstream. He aimed the hose in the direction Sam indicated and crawled through the smoke to a bed. Two people lay far too still.

In moments, he and Ridge had shouldered the victims and were back outside. A man and a woman.

Young. Maybe his age. He discerned no movement, no rise and fall of rib cage. Smoke, he figured, because they looked asleep. The woman was blond. In Scooby Doo pajamas.

Paramedics took over, working frantically. But Nic's gut hurt with the knowledge: they'd arrived too late.

Nic clenched his jaw against the emotion. Fury at the fire. Fury at himself for being too late.

Though he'd been on the force for five years and he'd been taught to stay detached, firefighters were human. This could be one of his sisters.

"I'm going back in," Nic said grimly. "There may be kids upstairs."

More victims was always a possibility. He could only hope the smoke hadn't gotten that far yet.

The captain gripped his shoulder. "Parrish and Chambers can go."

Nic shook his head, already changing to fresh air tanks. "Me and Ridge. We started it. Let us finish it."

The captain's radio crackled. Lifting the black rectangle to his lips, Summers motioned toward the inferno. "Go. Don't do anything stupid."

This wasn't the first time Nic had heard the warning. And it wouldn't be the last.

He and Sam made the stairs in double time. Fire danced below them, taunting and teasing. The firefighters outside were doing their job, knocking down the worst. Smoke rolled as wild and dark as Oklahoma thunderheads.

The thin wail of a smoke detector pierced the crackle and roar of the blaze. Downstairs had been ominously silent. No detector. Or one that had been disconnected. Nic's teeth tightened in sad frustration.

Again, moving clockwise, they searched two rooms before Nic heard another sound. He stopped so fast, his buddy slammed into him.

"Did you hear that?" Nic asked.

"Can't hear anything over that detector but you, puffing like a freight train."

Nic pointed with his chin. "Scan over there."

Sam raised the camera. "Bingo."

The noise came again, a mewling cry. "A kid?"

"Baby." Sam shifted the viewfinder into Nic's line of sight. "And he's kicking like mad."

Nic wasted no breath on the exultant shout that formed inside him. Handing off the nozzle to his partner, Nic approached the crib and had the crying child in his arms in seconds. His blood pumped harder than the engine outside, consuming way too much air. "Let's get out of here."

Sam scanned the rest of the room as they exited, hosing hot spots along the way. A crumpling roar shook the floor beneath them. They both froze. Nic tucked the baby closer, waiting to see if the flooring would give way and send them plummeting down into the inferno.

Sometimes Nic wondered if his afterlife would be like that: A trapdoor sprung open and a long fall down into the flames.

Pray, Mama, he thought, knowing Rosalie Carano prayed for him all the time. He was her stray son, the one who danced on the borderline between faith and failure. Often she told of waking in the night to pray when he was on duty. He hoped she'd awakened tonight.

With the fire below them, eating its way up, it was only a matter of time until the second floor would be fully involved or structurally unsound. If it wasn't already.

"Move it, Sam. This little dude is struggling." Everything in him wanted to break protocol and give the baby his air mask. He'd do it, too, if he had to and worry about the consequences later. Nic reached toward his regulator.

A gloved hand stopped him.

"Don't even think about it, hotshot," Ridge growled, reading his intention. "You're no good to him dead."

Ridge was right. As always. Neither of them knew what might transpire before they could escape. Firefighters had been trapped in far less volatile situations.

Nic gave a short nod and started down the stairs, the infant tight against his chest. Almost as quickly, he jerked to a stop and slung his opposite arm outward to block Sam. "Trouble."

Big trouble.

Heart jackhammering, Nic spoke into his radio. "Firefighter Carano to Captain of Engine One. Stairs have collapsed. We have an infant, approximately three months old, conscious and breathing, but we have no means of egress. I repeat, Captain, we have no means of egress."

A moment of silence seemed to stretch on forever. The baby had stopped struggling. Gone quiet.

Pray, Mama. Pray for this kid.

Nic was reaching for his air mask again when the radio crackled. "Firefighter Carano, you have a window on D side, second story. We'll send up an aerial."

He dropped his hand.

"10-4." Now to find the window. Fast. Though the upstairs smoke remained moderate, the darkness was complete. Without the imaging camera, he was as good as blind.

Keeping the baby as low to the ghostly haze as possible, Nic felt his way around the walls through the upper rooms, working toward what he hoped was D side. His partner found the exit first and opened it with a forcible exit tool. Glass shattered, the sound loud and welcome. The baby jerked. Cool night air rushed in.

Nic yearned to reassure the frightened infant. Through the plastic of his visor, he looked down into the wide, tearing eyes. Poor little dude would probably grow up with a terror of *Star Wars.*

The ladder clattered against the outside. Nic handed the child to Sam and climbed out, grateful for the flood of light as he reached back for the baby. He always appreciated life and light and fresh air a lot more after an entry such as this.

In seconds, he was down the ladder and on the ground. Paramedics whisked the baby out of his arms and started toward the ambulance. Nic followed, ripping away his helmet and mask as he walked.

His legs felt like deadweights inside his turnout boots.

"He gonna be all right?"

The red-haired paramedic, Shannon Phipps, nodded, her busy hands assessing, applying oxygen and otherwise doing her job with rapid-fire efficiency.

"You done good, Carano," she said.

Nic knew he was expected to shoot back a wisecrack so he did. In truth, all he could think of was the tiny boy in blue sleepers who would never know his mother and father.

"We'll get him to the hospital," Shannon said. "But I think he'll make it. Listen to that cry."

Nic nodded, watched the paramedics load and slam doors. Heard the *whack-whack* of a hand on the back indicating the ambulance could pull away.

He jogged to his captain, equipment thudding, and then, as the ambulance started to leave, he stepped in front of the headlights. The driver slammed on his breaks and rolled down his window.

With a frown, the paramedic said, "Carano, I should have known it was you. You maniac, what are you doing?"

"Make room," he said. "I'm going with you."

This can't be real. This can't be real. Please, God in heaven, this can't be real.

Cassidy Willis's mind chanted disjointed prayers and denials as she stumbled down the corridor of Northwood Regional.

Janna and Brad would be waiting for her. They would laugh and yell a very cruel "April Fool." This was not real. Her sister and brother-in-law could not be dead.

A nurse stopped her. "Miss, are you all right?"

Cassidy nodded numbly.

"Fine." The word came out as a croak. "I need room twelve-fifteen. Alexander Brown. My nephew."

Comprehension and a heavy dose of compassion registered behind the nurse's glasses. She knew baby Alex was an orphan now.

An orphan. Oh no. Could she live through this torment again? She'd already lost her parents. Janna had been her family, her best friend, her sister. They'd had each other when life had been too hard to bear.

Cassidy closed her eyes and swayed. The nurse looped an arm gently through hers. "I'll walk you down. You must be devastated."

Devastated. Devastated. Like a recording stuck on repeat, the word reverberated and replayed in her head.

All she could do was nod and stumble on, going through the motions. Doing what had to be done.

Whatever that was.

Alex. Baby Alex needed her. He was alone. All alone in a violent world that had stolen his mommy and daddy. A mommy and daddy who had loved him fiercely.

She felt lost. Alone. Just like Alex.

At the door of the room, she paused and sucked in a deep breath, hoping for strength, settling for vague sensory input. Hospital food. The clatter of trays coming off the elevator. Breakfast.

It seemed like hours since the sheriff had appeared at her door. But morning had just arrived, the dawn of a new and terrible day. A day she could not bear to face.

Maybe she was still asleep. Still dreaming. That was it. Bad dreams about death and destruction were all too common to her.

Wake up, Cass. Wake up.

The urging didn't work. She was still standing outside a thick, brown door inside Northwood Regional Hospital staring into the gentle eyes of a nurse. Wishing she could slide to the floor and die, too, Cassidy faced the fact that this nightmare was the real thing.

"Is Alex…?" How did she ask if he was horribly burned or hooked up to tubes and wires? If he was suffering?

The nurse nodded, understanding Cassidy's concern. "He was far enough away from the fire to escape the worst. He suffered some smoke inhalation, but nothing that breathing treatments won't resolve in a few days. He should recover well."

With a push to the center of her glasses, the kind woman left the rest unsaid. Alex had slept in the remodeled nursery upstairs. His parents slept downstairs in the unfinished portion of the old house. The fire must have started on the bottom floor, sucking their lives away while they slept, exhausted from the chore of remodeling the beautiful old Victorian into a bed-and-breakfast. A dream that would die with them.

The nurse hovered, leaning close to whisper, "He came in with the baby. I hope you don't mind."

Cassidy paused, perplexed, the flat of one hand against the cool wooden door.

"Who?" She had no relatives close enough to have arrived already. Not anymore. No one but Alex.

"The firefighter. He won't leave."

Cassidy tensed. The last thing she wanted was a firefighter hanging around to remind her of what she and Alex had lost this horrible night. She wanted the man to get out, to leave her in peace. But she hadn't the strength to say so.

"I'll handle things from here. Thank you." Her voice sounded strangely detached, as though her vocal cords belonged to someone else far away in a big, empty auditorium.

"If I can do anything…"

Cassidy managed a nod. At least she thought she did as she pushed the door open and stepped inside.

The eerie quiet that invades a hospital deepened inside the room. Pale morning light from the curtained windows fell across a bulky form. Still dressed in the dark-yellow pants and black boots of a firefighter, stinking of soot and smoke, a man had pulled a chair against the side of Alex's crib. Turnout coat hung on the back of the chair, his dark head was bowed, forehead balanced on the raised railing. One of his hands stretched between the bars, holding Alex's tiny fingers.

Too exhausted and numb and grief-stricken to think, Cassidy paused in the doorway to contemplate the unlikely pair—a baby and a fireman. What was the man doing? Sleeping? Praying? Why was he here?

Unexpected gratitude filtered in to mix and mingle with her other rampaging emotions. After the night's tragedy, she could hardly bear to think about anything related to fire—even the men who fought it—but she was very glad her four-month-old nephew had not been alone all this time.

The fireman roused himself, lifting his head to observe the sleeping baby and then to turn and look at her. Cassidy's first impression was of darkness. The same black soot covering his clothes smeared his face, so that Cassidy had a hard time discerning his age or looks. His eyes, though reddened behind the spiky eyelashes, were as dark as his nearly black hair. Only the fingerprint cleft in his chin stood out, stark white against the soot.

With another look at the baby, the man carefully slid his fingers from Alex's grip and stood. He wasn't overly tall, but his upper body was athletic and fit beneath the navy Northwood Fire Department shirt. Weariness emanated from him.

"Are you the aunt?" he asked. "They said he had an aunt." He glanced back at Alex, swallowed. "My sister has a baby."

Then he stopped as if the word *sister* was too strong a reminder of the night's loss.

"Yes, I'm his aunt. Cassidy Willis."

She moved to the raised crib and gazed down at the child with her sister's dark-blond hair and Brad's high cheekbones. What was she going to do now? What would Janna want her to do? Who would be mother and father to her sister's little boy?

"Is anyone else coming to be with you?"

Gripping the rail with both hands, she struggled

to think. Her brain was a fog. Her emotions jumbled, but mostly numb.

"Brad's parents."

"Brad?" he asked gently, standing close as though he thought she'd faint. The scent of smoke seeped from him in insidious waves. Her stomach churned, fighting down a memory. She'd hated the smell of smoke before. Now she hated it even more.

"Alex's father. My sister's husband, Bradley Brown."

"Ah." He didn't have to say the words. She could hear his thoughts. Brad Brown was dead along with her sister.

"His parents live in Missouri, just over the state line. They'll come."

"Have they been notified?"

She looked at him then, lost. Notified? Of what? "The fire?"

"Yes, ma'am."

"I gave their information to the sheriff." At least she thought she had. Those moments in her small living room with the solemn sheriff were a painful blur, a slow-motion torture of trying to comprehend the loss, of answering questions, of understanding that Alex needed her and she had no time to grieve.

She knew little about Brad's parents except that they lived in Joplin and had raised a son who loved her sister. The pair of them had been building the one thing Janna and Cassidy had always dreamed of—a real family.

"The sheriff will make sure they are notified."

Good. She wasn't certain she could speak the words that resigned her sister to eternity. *Dead* was such a powerful term, as if saying it aloud made it so.

"They're probably on their way now. My grandmother. I called her." For whatever good it would do.

Grandmother Bassett had been detached from her life and Janna's, an austere provider who sometimes seemed surprised to find them living in her house. She'd taken them in as orphans, but she'd been too busy with her business and her own social circle to be a parent. Though a good person in her way, Eleanor Bassett did not know how to comfort and nurture. If she came at all, she'd do so only to issue orders.

With a shudder of hopelessness, Cassidy realized she had no one now to understand and share her pain. No one to help her make decisions for Alex. No one but God. And at the moment, God seemed far, far away.

Oh, Janna. My beloved sister.

"Isn't there someone close? You shouldn't be alone."

She'd always had Janna. They'd run to each other when trouble came. "No one, but I'm fine."

For most of her life, she'd depended on no one but Janna or herself. Leaning on others, asking for help, did not come easily. She could handle this, the same way she'd handled the loss of her parents and growing up in a home that was less than warm. Without God, she wasn't sure she would have survived to adulthood. This time, the burden was almost too much to bear.

Her body sagged. She crossed her arms in an attempt to remain upright.

The firefighter touched the back of her shoulder. "I could call someone for you. You need your family."

He had no idea. She opened her mouth to reply that she had no family now, but she would be all right. He should go away and leave her alone. Leave her to think things through, to figure out where to go from here.

Baby Alex chose that instant to stir. Both adults turned their attention to the crib. Dressed in a hospital gown decorated with yellow ducks, he looked small and helpless. Murky blue-brown eyes blinked up at Cassidy. She touched his reaching hand and felt his strong grip against her fingers. Her heart turned over with love and regret.

"He doesn't seem to have suffered any permanent effects," she murmured, more to herself than to the fireman.

"He's a tough one. A fighter." The man reached inside the crib again as though he couldn't keep his hands off the tiny survivor. Alex kicked his feet, happy with the attention. "His eyes are still red. They were streaming from the smoke when I brought him down."

"You?" Of course, now his presence made sense. She turned slightly, caught the hint of emotion in the man's face. This close, she could see he was about her age and was probably nice-looking beneath the grime. "You rescued Alex."

Which meant he must have seen Janna and Brad, too. She wouldn't ask about that.

"Handsome little dude." His full bottom lip curved.

As if insulted, Alex's small face puckered and he began to cry. Cassidy reached inside the crib and lifted him into her arms, thankful that he was not attached to the wires and tubes she'd feared.

He cried louder. She bounced him up and down, feeling as helpless as he did. She was his aunt, not his mother. What did she know about soothing a baby? She'd spent time with him, but Janna had always been nearby, ready to take over when the crying commenced. It had been a standard joke between her and her sister. Cassidy played with Alex. Janna did all the hard stuff.

"It's probably breakfast time, don't you think?" the fireman asked.

Oh dear. Breakfast. Cassidy's stomach fell to her toes. "I don't know what to do."

He shot her an odd look, as if everyone knew what to do with a hungry baby. "Give him a bottle, I guess."

Cassidy bit her bottom lip, both embarrassed and dismayed. "Janna was nursing him. He's never had a bottle."

In fact, Janna had never left her son with anyone, not even Cassidy, for more than a few minutes. Alex was her child of joy and promise, the beginning of the big family she and Brad had wanted. If Cassidy was honest, Janna was living the life both sisters had longed for.

"Oh. That does present a problem." He held up one finger. "Sounds like a job for the nurse."

He pushed the button and issued the order for formula as though he did this every day. Maybe he had kids of his own.

"Thank you. I hope Alex can deal with the change,"

Cassidy said, juggling the fussy child up and down, up and down, praying the nurse would hurry with that bottle.

"It may take some time, but he will."

He must be a dad, she thought. Nice guy, firefighter, baby expert. Not hard to look at, either. Interesting fellow. "I never did get your name."

"Carano," he said. "Nic Carano. Fire Station One."

Cassidy blinked. He couldn't be. No way. This firefighter who had rescued her nephew was Nic Carano?

Notorious Nic?

Chapter Two

"I remember you," she said, trying to reconcile the helpful firefighter with the Notorious Nic she remembered.

He'd dated half the girls in her sorority house. All at once. Nic Carano, the fun-loving life of the party who went through girlfriends faster than frat boys through a keg of beer. She'd been very careful to be sure she wasn't one of them.

Nic was not her kind of man. If she had a kind. Unfortunately, building her career in graphic design left her little time to date. If she did, it would not be a man like Notorious Nic, no matter how nice-looking and charming he seemed.

The door swished open and a nurse attired in blue scrubs appeared with a bottle, patted Alex's head and disappeared again. As if she had a clue what she was doing, Cassidy tilted the baby into a cradle hold and slid the nipple into his squalling mouth. Alex shoved back, twisting his head, fighting the strange silicone.

"You look familiar to me, too." Apparently unperturbed by Alex's crying, Nic went on talking as he pushed a chair behind Cassidy's knees. Gratefully, Cassidy slid onto the seat. She hadn't realized she was still standing. "College maybe?"

Cassidy nodded. "Kappa Kappa."

"Oh yeah." He grinned. "My favorite sorority. You lived there?"

He asked as if he were puzzled, as if he hadn't dated her so how could she have lived in the Kappa Kappa House.

For one thing, she'd been too focused. For another, she'd been too smart to get involved with a man who was all charm and no substance. Though loath to admit it, her social life had been limited to a few shallow, quickly fading relationships, a couple of them regrettable. The Lord had forgiven her, but she was taking no chances on making the same mistakes again. Handsome, charming, shallow men were off-limits.

Alex grew frustrated and thrashed in howling protest. Cassidy jiggled the bottle, trying to calm him. She'd had no idea feeding a hungry baby could be this difficult.

"Come on, sugar. I know it's different, but you'll get the hang of it."

She tried again, sliding the nipple onto his tongue. He jerked away, pushing at her hand.

"Want me to try?" Nic held out his arms. "I've got a little experience."

"You do?" Now that was a shocker.

He winked. "Trust me. I'm amazing."

Right. Trust him. How many girls had heard that line? Trusting Nic was the last thing on her agenda. In fact, the sooner Fireman Fun and Games disappeared, the better. She had enough to deal with.

"I appreciate all you've done, Nic. Really." She jiggled Alex harder. "But you must be exhausted. I can handle things from here. You look like you could sleep for a week."

Alex screamed, a cry that would bring police, and fire and rescue in any other setting.

Fire and rescue was already here, holding out his arms, with a funny little quirk at the corner of his mouth.

If Nic comprehended her efforts to get rid of him, he didn't show it.

"Come on. Let me try. Me and the little dude are buddies. I can sleep when I'm dead."

The word *dead* lingered between them, harsh and dark. The night's tragedy slipped back into the room. As though water flowed through her veins instead of blood, Cassidy's arms went weak.

What was she going to do without Janna? What was Alex going to do without a mother who knew how to soothe him when he cried?

"Hey," Nic said, his voice soft and concerned. She raised her eyes to his and he must have seen her helplessness. Without asking again, he took Alex from her.

Cassidy sat, limp and devastated, trying to think of anything except that ugly word—*dead*. Her head was like an echo chamber bouncing the word back a thousand times. *Dead, dead, dead.*

Swallowing a cry of anguish, she focused on Nic Carano, cradling her nephew against his chest as if holding a baby was the most natural thing in the world.

Did that mean Nic Carano was now married with children? That the wild and crazy jokester without a care in the world was not only a firefighter, he was a dad?

The image didn't fit. The party boy she remembered did not have either "responsibility" or "settle down" anywhere in his vocabulary.

Right now, however, he was using his charm to convince Alex to accept the unfamiliar bottle. He pressed a dab of formula onto the infant's lips and then stroked the corner of his mouth with the nipple. As if by some form of communication known only to the male species, Alex turned his face and latched on.

"Attaboy," Nic murmured. His gaze flicked up to Cassidy's. "Look at him go."

Cassidy should have felt better. Instead, her depression deepened. If she couldn't even feed Alex, how could she care for him? And if she didn't, who would? She was no more parent material than Nic Carano. Nor did she possess his natural ease with people.

"How did you do that?"

Nic shrugged. A small smile gleamed white against his dirty face. "Told you," he said easily. "Uncle Nicky's got the touch."

"Are you this good with your own kids?" she asked, not because she cared about his life one way or the other, but to keep from thinking about Janna and Brad.

Nic drew back in feigned alarm. "The Caranos have

enough rug rats running around the place without me adding to the numbers. I'm *Uncle* Nicky. Not Daddy Nic."

That sounded more like the Nic she remembered. Naturally he would love to play with the little ones, but he wouldn't want to take on such a responsibility. The guy probably still lived at home so his mom could do his laundry.

"No matter where you learned, I appreciate your expertise. I'm kind of lost."

Lost and more afraid than she'd been since that night in the Philippines. And almost as helpless.

Shoulders sagging, she closed her eyes. Janna's pretty face laughed behind her eyelids.

Somehow Nic managed to hold Alex and his bottle as he leaned toward her, stirring the sickening stench of smoke. "Are you sure you're gonna be okay?"

Cassidy nodded, numb and empty. She would never be okay again, but what could Nic Carano do about it? What could anyone do?

"I'm sorry." He tilted his chin toward the baby. Alex gazed up at him with wide, earnest eyes, still sucking for all he was worth. "Sorry for both of you. I wish there was something more I could do."

What good was sorry? She was sorry, too, but Janna was still gone. There were no words to describe how shattered she felt, how special Janna was or how much both she and Alex had lost last night.

Insides chilled, Cassidy drew her crossed arms tightly against her body as if to ward off reality. She longed to go to sleep, wake up tomorrow and discover this had all been a bad dream.

"Where do you go from here?" Nic asked gently. "I mean, who's going to care for the little dude?"

The "little dude" had finished off his bottle. As if handling a baby was second nature, Nic set the bottle on the floor, lifted Alex to his shoulder and patted his back. Alex made gurgling, satisfied noises, oblivious to the drastic change in his life.

"I don't know what we'll do." She didn't want to think about the future. She could barely deal with the here and now. "Brad had no siblings and there was only Janna and me in our family." She thought about Brad's parents. They might be willing to raise Alex.

"My sister's a social worker. She might be able to help."

The idea of a social worker frightened Cassidy.

"No," she said a little too sharply. "No social services."

She trembled to think of her nephew growing up lonely and unloved the way she and Janna had. Alex deserved a loving home and family, not a parade of foster homes. She would choose. She would make the decision. Somehow.

"Forget I brought it up. Today is way too soon to think about that."

"I never dreamed this would happen to Janna," she murmured.

"No one ever expects a tragedy of this magnitude. Not even us firefighters. These things happen to other people. Not to us. Or so we think."

Almost to herself, Cassidy said, "I don't understand why God would let this happen."

Again, she thought. Twice in her life she'd lost those closest to her. It wasn't fair. She'd always considered God to be a good and loving God, the Father she'd lost as a child. Now she was left floundering to understand. Had she failed in some way? Was she being punished?

"You got me there," Nic said. He tapped Alex on the nose and waited for the toothless smile before settling him on his lap to face Cassidy. Alex made a goo-goo sound, waving his arms in poignant happiness as he recognized her. "My mom would say all things work to the good for those who love God, but I have to admit I don't get the whole God thing."

Cassidy, too, was having a hard time believing that anything good could come from the death of two young, caring, godly people and the orphaning of their son.

"So you aren't a believer?"

His smile was crooked. "Oh, yeah, I believe."

Cassidy heard the unspoken "but" at the end of his proclamation, though she didn't understand it.

From her missionary parents, she'd learned to love, revere and serve God all the days of her life. Regardless of her questions, God was the only answer. He was her anchor, her only hope. Though she couldn't begin to understand, she had to believe God was with her. The alternative was hopelessness. How could anyone face an uncertain future without His strength and courage to sustain them?

She was about to ask Nic that very question, when

he crinkled his nose. "Uh-oh. Change time." Averting his head, he pushed the baby in her direction. "Uncle Nic does not do diapers."

His lighthearted comment was a welcome diversion. She smiled in spite of herself.

"Firemen are supposed to be brave."

He made a face. "Brave is relative. Give me a nasty, dirty fire any day, but not a nasty, dirty diaper."

A nasty, dirty fire. Nic's words brought back the pain, as sharp and plunging as an ice pick. She wished he would go away. He was a walking, talking reminder of death.

She'd had enough of death to last a lifetime.

Holding Alex, she abruptly stood, turning her back on the gear-clad firefighter. "Thanks for all you've done, Nic. I'll take it from here."

Her words were a stiff dismissal he couldn't possibly miss this time.

A moment of silence stretched behind her. She didn't turn around. If she did, she would apologize, and he would stay longer. He had to go and take his ghoulish job with him.

"If you need anything—"

Why did he have to be nice? "I won't. Bye, Nic."

She was giving him the brush-off?

Nic shifted on his feet, his boots heavy, his body weary. He wanted to be ticked, but he tamped down the reaction. Cassidy Willis was living a nightmare he couldn't begin to comprehend. She looked so shattered that for a minute or two there, he'd been tempted to take her in his arms and comfort her. With most women, he would have done exactly that, but the classy-looking blonde exuded a cool aloofness that kept him at bay. For some reason, she wanted him to leave, but he couldn't do that, either. Not yet anyway.

Normally, he didn't get involved with fire victims, but last night the baby boy had gotten to him in a big way. As he'd waited in the emergency room, the child had clung to him, calm only as long as Nic was present and touching him. The little dude seemed to intuitively understand that his parents were gone and that Nic had saved his life.

Then when the aunt had stumbled into the room, the soft heart that sometimes got Nic into trouble had done a weird flip-flop, like a banked bass. Compassion, he supposed, but he was intrigued, too, though he had to admit, all women intrigued him. Ladies were a gift from God. Might as well enjoy them. But Cassidy Willis was different from his usual lady friends. Perhaps not in looks—she did have those—but in demeanor.

He'd known she was the aunt right away. She resembled the woman in the Scooby Doo pajamas he'd carried out of the burning house. Only where Alex's mother had been dark-blond, Cassidy's hair was sleek platinum, the kind that required considerable maintenance. Pampered sorority girl hair that went perfectly with her fancy acrylic nails.

She also had the kind of blue eyes men dream about, as vivid as his mama's pansies. At the moment they were filled with anguish.

She must have been heading out for a jog when the

news arrived because she wore a running outfit. From the looks of her slim form and pro athletic shoes, Cassidy Willis was a serious runner.

Too bad she couldn't run away from the situation. Her world had turned upside down and she was coping pretty well, he thought. Well enough to want him to leave.

He was kind of offended at that. Most women wanted him to hang around. This one wanted him to leave.

In any other situation, he'd consider that a challenge.

Maybe he did anyway.

Her back still turned as if he wasn't in the room, Cassidy reached beneath the crib, found a box of baby wipes and a clean diaper. He should go. He needed to go. Hanging out in hospitals with orphaned babies and bereaved women wasn't his idea of a party.

Still, he felt this *obligation* to do something for her and the little dude.

Cassidy's polished beauty was right up his alley, but her looks were the farthest thing from his mind. He wasn't after a date. He had a couple of those already. He was after—Nic didn't know for sure what he was after.

For reasons he could not explain, he couldn't walk away and forget this pair. He should. He wanted to. But something irrevocable had happened last night and he couldn't live with himself if he didn't do s*omething* for them. Besides, his big, pushy family would have his head if he didn't look after a damsel in distress.

Maybe that was the problem. Family expectations, as usual, were his undoing.

"Hang on," he said, though she clearly wasn't leaving and had effectively shut him out. "I'll be right back."

He jogged out of the room, only to reappear in seconds bearing a pen and notepad. The nice nurse at the desk had been all smiles and obliging. He grinned and patted his chest with the flat of one hand. Must be the uniform.

He scribbled on the sheet, ripped off the page and handed it to Cassidy.

"Here you go," he said. "That's my cell and my house. Call if I can do anything."

The way Cassidy stared at his broad scrawl made Nic wish he'd taken more interest in penmanship.

"Thanks." She pocketed the piece of paper without enthusiasm.

"I'm serious," Nic said, backing toward the door. "Call. I have a whole army of family who'd be glad to help."

She nodded but returned her attention to the baby.

It wasn't the reaction Nic was hoping for, but he'd done his duty. His conscience could rest. He needn't give Cassidy Willis another thought.

Maybe.

Chapter Three

Nic met the angular, suit-clad woman in the hallway coming in as he was leaving. When she stopped at the nurse's desk and asked for Alexander Brown's room, Nic knew she must be the grandmother Cassidy had spoken of. A sense of release settled over him. Cassidy and the baby needed this woman's company.

Coming from a very large family, he couldn't imagine having so few relatives. In fact, he'd tried to imagine it a few times but with the Carano bunch, he never had a moment's peace. They were in his business more than he was. At times he resented them for that, but situations such as this one made him appreciate the circle of love.

Which did not mean he wasn't going to move out on his own as soon as he found an apartment. No matter how his parents argued that it was not necessary. No matter how economical the arrangement might be, no matter how expensive apartment rentals were, Nic needed his own space. Space to study for another go at medical school exams. Space to be away from the prying eyes and pressure of second-generation Americans who expected him to be something more than what he was. Much as he loved them, a big family could be trying.

With a quirk of his lips, Nic admitted to himself that he would, however, miss his mama's cooking.

He was pushing the elevator button when he heard the older woman ask in a high and nasal voice, "Has anyone telephoned child welfare? That baby will need to be adopted out."

He pivoted for a better look at Cassidy's grandmother. The woman looked as though she had swallowed a glass of vinegar and was sorely annoyed to be in this place. Not grieved, annoyed.

Maybe he'd been wrong about Cassidy needing her family.

He squeezed the bridge of his nose with his thumb and forefinger, thinking, fighting the temptation and losing so fast his head spun. He needed to head home, clean up, catch some Zs. He and Lacey and Sherry Lynn were on for a Redhawks game tonight. This was none of his business. Cassidy didn't even want him here. She'd practically tossed him out on his ear.

But baby Alex had wanted him, and the little dude was the one in jeopardy.

Besides, as Nic and his firefighter buddies always said, he could sleep when he was dead.

With a tired sigh, he headed back down the hall to the baby's room, knowing he was about to stick his nose where it did not belong. Mama would say he was going to get it cut off one of these days.

The thought put a spring in his step.

The never knowing when was part of life's adventure.

With the flat of his hand, Nic pushed open the door to room twelve-fifteen and followed the vinegar woman inside.

Cassidy turned from the crib in surprise. Her gaze slid past her grandmother to him. "Nic. I thought you'd left."

"I did."

She patted Alex's back and covered him with a blanket. "Did you forget something?"

"Yeah."

She glanced around the small room. "What is it?"

He ignored the question. "Is this your grandmother?" *And did you know she wants to put Alex up for adoption?*

Vinegar lady slid a critical glance over his dirty face and uniform. Her nostrils twitched in distaste. "A fireman, I presume?"

His mama would throttle him if he was rude to his elders. Vinegar lady didn't know how lucky she was. "Yes, ma'am. Nic Carano. I'm a friend of Cassidy's."

Cassidy's eyes widened at the word *friend*, but she didn't deny him. "Nic, this is my grandmother, Eleanor Bassett. Grandmother, Nic rescued Alex from the…house."

Again, Mrs. Bassett settled narrowed blue eyes on

him. The blue eyes were about the only thing she had in common with her granddaughter.

"Thank you, Mr. Carano." The gratitude seemed to pain her.

"Nic," he said. Poor Cassidy, if this was her comforting family, she was in a world of hurt. The woman hadn't so much as hugged her.

"I suppose the Browns have been notified." Mrs. Bassett perched her narrow backside on the edge of a chair and folded her hands atop an expensive-looking handbag. Dressed in a business suit the color of zucchini, she appeared ready to conduct a board meeting. *Or*, Nic thought with a hidden grin, *be chopped into a salad. Add a dab of oil to the vinegar and voilà, lunch.*

"Yes, Grandmother." Cassidy's face, so pale before, was now blotchy red. "They've been notified."

If he was a guessing man, he'd say vinegar lady made her granddaughter both anxious and unhappy.

She was starting to do the same to him. Nic Carano did not like to feel either of those emotions. The woman needed an injection of fun. Or cyanide. The bit of internal sarcasm tickled him. He would laugh later.

Mrs. Bassett checked her watch. "They should be arriving soon. If I can drive from Dallas, they should be able to get here from Joplin in equal time."

"They've lost their only son, Grandmother."

"Yes. A shame, too. Bradley was a good boy. That wind is awful today. My hair's a mess. I'll have to call Philippe for a recomb." She patted the brown fluff around her face. "There are so many details to take care of. I hope they arrive soon. I have a dinner party tonight. We need to get the problems ironed out today."

"Well, I certainly wouldn't want you to miss a dinner party on the day of your granddaughter's death." Cassidy's words were quietly spoken, but the resentment was clear. So were the red splotches covering her cheeks and neck.

What had he walked into? And why didn't he hit the road before the war broke out?

One look at Cassidy, standing sentry beside Alex's crib, hands white-knuckled against the railing, gave him his answer. She was fighting to hold herself together, as much for her sister's baby as for herself. Aunt Cassidy needed his support, whether she wanted it or not. Baby Alex needed him even more.

"Don't be sarcastic, Cassidy. It isn't ladylike." Vinegar lady opened her purse and removed a card. "This is my attorney. He can help work out the details."

Nic crossed his arms and leaned against a wall, glad to have some plaster to hold up his fatigued body. Cassidy glanced his way as if just remembering he was there. Something flickered behind those baby blues. He gave her a wink of encouragement. She glared back, clearly not wanting him to stay. Call it macho, call it stubborn, but the notion made him even more determined to stick around.

"I don't know what you mean, Grandmother." Cassidy took the card, studied the face, turned it over and then back again. "Why do we need a lawyer?"

"Issues of estate. The problem of Alexander."

Cassidy's hackles rose. She stood up straighter. "Alex is not a problem."

"You know what I mean, dear. He'll need new parents, although the Browns may have some notion of taking him on."

Taking him on. That's the way Grandmother had thought of her and Janna, as unpleasant responsibilities she had incurred. The notion would have hurt if Cassidy hadn't always known.

"No," Cassidy said with surprising firmness. "Not strangers."

"Be reasonable, Cassidy. The child is still young enough to be acceptable to adopters."

"I don't want someone to take him because he's acceptable. I want him to be loved."

Grandmother huffed; her mouth puckered tighter. "I was afraid you'd be like this. You and Janna could be so stubborn at times, binding together in your fits of determination."

Trembling with fatigue and emotion, Cassidy pressed a hand to her forehead. A dozen issues she'd never considered or discussed with Janna filtered through her head. The only thing she knew for certain was that she, not Grandmother, needed to make this decision. She prayed she was strong enough to stand against the powerhouse woman whose iron hand ran a company with several hundred employees.

Nic, whom she'd almost forgotten, surprised her by pushing off the wall and coming to stand beside her. He brought the nauseating scent of smoke with him. Why had he come back when she'd been more than clear that she neither needed nor wanted his interference?

He took one of her hands. She knew she should yank it away, but she was too weak and empty to fight both Nic and her grandmother. When the firefighter gave her fingers a squeeze, she realized how cold she'd become since Grandmother's arrival. How sad that a virtual stranger—even one she didn't particularly like—could provide more comfort than her own flesh and blood.

Considering that painful fact, maybe Grandmother was right. Perhaps adoption was the answer.

She pulled her hand away, knotting it with the other in front of her. Nic's eyes bore into the side of her face, but she kept her gaze trained on Alex.

Dear Lord, help. My mind is so scattered right now.

As though someone had asked for his input, Nic said, "You need some time to think. Nothing should be decided today when you're still in shock."

Grasping that tiny bit of good sense, Cassidy nodded. He was right. She was running on fumes and emotion. How could she make an intelligent decision about Alex's future in this condition?

Grandmother did not agree. "The sooner you settle things, the better. You have a busy career and Alexander has nowhere to go. I am simply not up to taking on another child."

"Grandmother, please," she interrupted before Eleanor could begin her diatribe on the supreme sacrifice she'd made when Cassidy's parents died. Cassidy was determined that Alex would never feel the sting of believing he was an intruder living in someone else's home. She wanted better for her nephew and with God's help, she would figure out something.

Eleanor had opened her mouth to say more when Beverly and Thomas Brown entered the room. Both of them looked completely shattered. Cassidy rushed to greet them.

"I am so sorry," she said to Brad's mother. "I don't know what else to say."

The matronly woman fell against her with a sob. "I can't believe this. I kept hoping we would get here and discover some kind of ghastly mistake had been made."

Hadn't she prayed for the same thing?

Thomas, a portly man, stood by looking helpless, his jowls droopy with sorrow. "How could this have happened?"

"I don't know," Cassidy said honestly. "I suppose the fire marshal will investigate."

She glanced at Nic, amazed that he hadn't left. He nodded and extended a hand to Thomas. "Nic Carano. I was at the scene last night."

"Did you see them?" Beverly, eyes puffy and red, pulled away from Cassidy to face the fireman. Her short brown hair, shot with gray, was in disarray as if she'd run her hands through it over and over again in her distress. "My son and his wife?"

"Yes, ma'am. I brought them out."

"Are they certain of the identities?"

The heartbroken mother was grasping at straws,

hoping for a miracle that would not come. Cassidy's stomach rolled, sick with grief.

"I don't know about that, ma'am, but I can assure you they died peacefully and easily in their sleep. Smoke inhalation. No pain. No suffering. No fear."

Thomas clapped a huge paw onto Nic's shoulder, mouth downcast, as he drew in a shuddering breath and then nodded once. "Thank you for that. It helps."

The atmosphere ached with sorrow.

"Yes, sir."

"Nic rescued Alex, too," Cassidy said, glad for the first time that Nic had returned to the room. His professional ease and knowledge of the situation seemed to be exactly what the devastated Browns needed.

"Thank you, Nic," Beverly said and hugged him. The firefighter embraced her as if he'd known her forever. No surprise there. Nic Carano was comfortable with people, especially women.

Cassidy's grandmother had kept her peace for about as long as she could. "We need to plan services, I suppose."

The other four turned to look at her. Perched on the chair like a queen on her throne, Eleanor would run the show or die trying.

Somehow Cassidy stumbled through the visit to the funeral home, the preparations for the services and the double funeral four days later. In the midst of making all sorts of arrangements and decisions she hadn't realized were necessary, she'd warded off Grandmother's attempts to "deal with the issue" of Alex until after the funeral.

She and the Browns had taken turns sitting with the baby at the hospital where they'd discussed the painfully few options for her nephew, but none of them were emotionally ready to make a permanent decision.

To Cassidy's discomfort, Nic Carano had returned every day as well, sending the baby into an excited display of arm and leg pumps and slobbery smiles. Cassidy, on the other hand, suffered a pain the size of Dallas. Every time she saw him, she had an unbidden vision of the yellow-clad fireman carrying Janna from the house, limp and dead. He was too much of a reminder of that night, of her sister's last hours and moments.

Out of uniform, he looked different, more like the wild and crazy Nic in funny T-shirts she remembered. She couldn't understand why he kept coming around. Surely not to see her. Having had her fill of womanizing playboys, she'd let him know from the start that she was not interested.

Alex was the only explanation. Through the shared tragedy, Nic had bonded with the child. That's all it could be.

Until today, the doctors had kept her nephew in the hospital for observation and respiratory therapy. Two hours ago, he'd been discharged into Cassidy's care—temporarily.

Now on this pleasant April afternoon, she sat on the off-white sofa in her tidy living room with Alex asleep in her lap, feeling as if she were a house of cards, ready to tumble at the slightest breeze. The grandparents were on their way to make the decision.

"Oh, baby boy," she whispered to his peaceful, innocent face. "What is going to become of you?"

Earlier, her pastor had stopped by with a word of counsel and a prayer for comfort and guidance as she made important decisions in the days ahead. He'd prayed for Alex, too, that God's will and perfect plan would unfold. To her way of thinking, God's perfect plan should have been Janna and Brad raising their son together. Yet, she'd found relief in Pastor John's prayers. Since the accident, praying had been difficult.

Heart as heavy as it had ever been in her life, Cassidy dreaded the family meeting that would decide Alex's fate.

A bitter laugh escaped her throat.

"Family," she muttered with a shake of her head. "Some family you have, baby."

Beverly and Thomas Brown were fine people, but Beverly's heart wasn't strong. She'd had two bypass surgeries already. They couldn't raise an infant and had admitted as much, though they loved Alex with all the grandparent love in the world. Eleanor, thank goodness, had never even considered "taking him on." Had she wanted Alex, a moving freight train could not have stopped her.

Grandmother wasn't a bad person, just a focused, determined businesswoman who'd never forgiven her only daughter for marrying a penniless missionary and then dying in a "heathen" land. Janna and Cassidy had borne the brunt of her unforgiveness.

With a shudder, Cassidy made up her mind that her nephew would never live that way. She wanted him to have love and family and warmth and support. A dear cousin in Baton Rouge was interested in adopting Alex, but Louisiana seemed so far away. Cassidy wanted him nearby, close enough that she could be part of his life.

If only she were married or had a less demanding job. If only she possessed the natural mothering instincts of her sister. If only her future weren't laid out before her like a tidy road to the top of her game.

But it was. Regardless of the crazy thoughts going through her mind every time she looked into Alex's face, she had no business raising a child.

"Lord," she whispered, smoothing her fingers over Alex's velvety forehead. "Show me what to do. Make Your plan clear. I'm dreadfully confused."

Grandmother had declared today the final day she would "worry" about this situation, because she had business to attend to. Though Cassidy had urged Eleanor to return to Dallas and let her and the Browns decide, Grandmother wouldn't hear of leaving until the issue was settled.

"I take familial duty very seriously," she'd insisted with an insulted sniff. Behind her back, Cassidy had rolled her eyes.

Someone pounded on the door. Cassidy jumped. Baby Alex jerked and threw his arms out to the side but didn't wake.

"They're here, lamb," she told him, stomach churning to know that after today, she would be separated from this baby she'd loved since before his birth.

Having no crib, and worried he would roll off the sofa, Cassidy placed Alex on a blanket on the floor, and then went to the door expecting to find the Browns or her grandmother waiting.

Instead, the handsome face of Nic Carano grinned down at her. In a snug black T-shirt imprinted with "Slackers give 100%, just not all at once," he looked firefighter fit and beach tanned.

Cassidy's stomach fluttered in a troubling and inappropriate response.

"Hey," he said, slouching against her door.

Charm absolutely oozed from the man.

"Nic?" Her voice was cool to the point of frost. Maybe he'd get the idea. "What are you doing?" *And why won't you go away?*

"Went by the hospital to see the little dude and they said he'd escaped with a beautiful blonde."

She refused to fall for the compliment. It rolled from his silver tongue far too easily. "I brought him home this morning."

"I called the sibs." With a jerk of his thumb, he indicated an oncoming barrage of humanity. "Told them a friend needed some baby stuff and here they are."

A parade of people she didn't know had piled out of cars and were trailing up the sidewalk like smiling, supply-laden ants. Each carried something that related to an infant.

Cassidy was dumbfounded. "They're bringing those things for Alex?"

Oh dear. What did she do now?

The dimple in Nic's chin widened. "Unless you wear Huggies and onesies and play with bathtub toys." He shook his head, one hand up to wave off the remark. "Scratch the last comment. Everyone needs a rubber ducky."

Against her own better judgment, Cassidy laughed. "Nic, you're a nut."

With a cocky grin, he turned and hollered down the stairwell. "Come on up, folks. She's laughing. I don't think she'll shoot."

While Cassidy wrestled with the wisdom of letting Notorious Nic into her house, a ribbon of chattering, jostling Caranos, all toting various baby items, trudged up the steps and into her space. Nic stood in the doorway like an affable traffic cop, rattling off introductions as three men and three women passed through. Even with six, Nic declared that some of the family had to work today.

"These are only the goof-offs," he said with affection.

Cassidy, confused, touched and annoyed in equal amounts, could only watch in stunned amazement. How many Caranos could there be? Where did they get all this stuff? Why would they give it to her?

A man Nic introduced as his father, Leo, paused in the living room to ask, "Where do you want us to put everything?"

With his blue-collar physique and thin ring of hair around a shiny bald head, Leo Carano would have been perfect in a sitcom set in a pizza parlor.

"Anywhere," she said, and then, discombobulated, changed her mind. "No, wait. The guest bedroom."

What was she doing? Alex wasn't here to stay. The furniture would only have to be moved again.

Before she could tell them as much, a beautiful, full-figured woman reminiscent of Sophia Loren stopped with a box of baby clothes in her arms.

"I'm Rosalie," she said, hitching her chin toward Nic. "This rascal is my baby boy."

No wonder Nic was so handsome.

"Now, Mom," Nic said with considerable humor. "Don't start telling stories."

Rosalie cocked an eyebrow at him. "Then stop lazing in the door and go help your brothers. Cassidy won't remember who was who anyway. Later, we'll get acquainted. Anna's bringing pizza."

Pizza? Somehow she had to stop the madness and tell these people that she could not accept their generosity. Alex was not here to stay.

A painful knot formed in her throat.

"Nic," she started.

"Gotta go," he said, cutting her off.

With a parting wink, he saluted his mother before bounding down the steps. On the way, he shouted general insults at his brothers. They shouted back, all in good fun.

Cassidy watched in fascination at the family dynamics. Teasing, working together, the bond of love between them was practically visible. Her heart ached with the knowledge that this was the kind of life Janna and Brad had been building for Alex. Now what would he have? Where would he go?

Rosalie returned from the bedroom, empty-handed. "I think my Nicky likes you."

Liked her? No way. "He likes the baby, I think. He rescued him from the fire and they seem to have formed a bond."

It was the only explanation she could think of, the only acceptable one.

"Precious angel from God." Rosalie looked over at Alex who didn't seem to mind that an army of Caranos were tromping all around him. "You'll be a fine mother for him, I'm sure."

"Oh, I can't keep him. That's what I've been trying to say."

The woman was taken aback. "I'm sorry. I thought Nic said you were the aunt, the only sister of the baby's mother."

"I am. It's just that…"

Rosalie tilted her kind face to listen. Cassidy stumbled through her litany of reasons.

"I've already missed four work days. I can't keep a baby. I'm single. I don't know anything about babies. My job is demanding. I'm working my way up to creative director. That's even more demanding. Alex deserves…" Realizing she was babbling, Cassidy clamped her lips together.

Rosalie patted her arm. "It's all right, Cassidy. Alex deserves love. Everything else is negotiable."

Cassidy opened her mouth to say more but nothing came out.

"You'll do the right thing. God will guide you."

She hoped she could count on that.

"But what about all these lovely things? I can't keep them."

The woman waved her off. "As long as you need them. We know where they are." Then Rosalie stuck her head out the door and called down the stairs. "Come on, boys. This baby does not need to sleep on a floor with all of you tromping around like Bigfoot. Bring that up here."

Two men who looked remarkably like Nic pulled a baby crib from the back of a pickup.

Cassidy felt a moment of panic. This was getting out of control. Did she need a crib?

One of Nic's dark-haired sisters, Mia, if she remembered correctly, asked, "The baby is awake. Do you mind if I pick him up?"

"No. Please. I—" Cassidy blinked, as confused as a minnow in a whirlpool.

Her heart continued to race as load after load of baby paraphernalia, much of which she could not identify, found its way into her apartment. By the time the pickup and two cars were unloaded, the guest room was crammed with baby items.

With relentless cheer, the Caranos went to work organizing and setting up. The men clanged away at the crib, arguing over the direction of the springs and screws. The ladies folded sweet-smelling clothes and placed them inside a small chest.

The Caranos were like a tidal wave, overwhelming in their power. Cassidy gave up the battle. She'd deal with this later.

"What is this thing?" Nic asked, holding up a device with a dangling electric cord.

"Baby wipe warmer." Mia's full lips curved in amusement at her clueless brother. "Now that my little one is out of diapers I don't need it or most of this other stuff. Thank goodness."

"Sweet," Nic answered and found a place for the warmer on the baby changer. "Right here okay, Cass?"

No one called her Cass.

"Perfect," she muttered, helpless to say otherwise.

Nic efficiently filled the machine from a package of wipes, plugged it in and then wove his way through the maze of working Caranos and baby stuff to her side.

Smelling like baby wipes, a fact that made Cassidy want to giggle, the macho fireman plopped down on the floor and tilted a roll of Life Savers toward her.

She was on her knees next to Rosalie sorting onesies by size.

"Overwhelmed yet?"

She dug a cherry candy from the wrapper. "A little."

"Want us to disappear?"

What could she say? To tell the truth would be both unkind and lacking in gratitude. Suspecting she would live to regret the decision, she said, "Stay."

"Sure?" He popped a lemon Life Saver into his mouth.

Trying not to remember who he was or his role in her sister's death, Cassidy controlled the urge to send him away. She slid the candy onto her tongue and sucked at the sweetness.

During the hour since the Caranos had swept into her life with their friendly laughter and kindhearted intentions, she'd pushed aside the terrible circumstances that brought them here. For this little while she'd witnessed the inner workings of a real family, the kind she and Janna had dreamed of. For the first time since Janna's death, she'd felt almost human. That's why she'd let them stay. She'd needed to feel normal again.

Now the sorrow came back in a rush.

Nic was silent beside her as though he guessed her thoughts. Guilty, troubled, hurting, she folded and refolded the onesie, never taking her eyes off the tiny garment.

I'm a mess. She, a woman who had long known what she wanted and where she was going, now floundered like a baby bird fallen from the nest.

The intrusion of a single, high-pitched, nasal voice jolted Cassidy from her brooding.

"What is all this?" Eleanor Bassett stomped into their midst, the heels of her alligator pumps thudding ominously on the beige carpet. Beverly and Thomas Brown peeked in behind her. Ignoring them, Grandmother swept one arm imperiously around the bedroom filled with boxes, diapers, bottles, a changing station, a crib and a lot of people.

Nic leaned into Cassidy's ear and whispered, "Cruella de Vil. Hide the puppies."

Squelching a gust of sudden and surprising laughter, Cassidy pushed at his shoulder and stood. He came up with her, eyes dancing above an expression as innocent as a rose. He'd probably gotten away with a lot of things because of that face.

"Grandmother, come in. I'd like you to meet the Carano family." She'd almost added "friends of mine" and yet she hardly knew them. This amazing group that had baffled her with their display of generosity to a bereaved aunt and an orphaned baby were basically strangers.

Introductions were made and Grandmother perched on the rocker, ready to take over. The Caranos, while polite, didn't seem all that impressed.

"Cassidy, we've come to discuss the situation. Although I see no reason whatsoever for you to have purchased all this frippery, shall we adjourn to the living room and leave these people to their work?"

The Caranos exchanged amused glances, aware they had been relegated to the position of hired help.

"Grandmother, the Caranos are friends." There. She'd said it. "They donated these items for Alex."

"Oh. Well." Eleanor tilted her nose down a notch. "Unnecessary given the situation, but thank you. How generous. Now, Cassidy, as I was saying, let's adjourn to the living room. I need to get back to Dallas tonight. The Forkner merger is set for tomorrow and I have tons of paperwork to prepare."

Cassidy looked from the woman who'd birthed her mother to Nic's sister who held Alex. The blue-clad baby reached chubby arms toward his aunt. Cassidy's heart swelled with an undeniable emotion—love. Her knees started to shake. Could she do this? Could she let

Grandmother ship him off to virtual strangers? Could her heart let him go?

The answer came loud and clear. No. She could not.

Lord, help me. She was about to jump off a building without a safety net.

"Grandmother. Mr. and Mrs. Brown." She sucked in a steadying lungful of Nic-scented air and let it out slowly. This was the right thing. The only thing. "I want to keep Alex."

Nic squeezed her elbow.

Buoyed by that simple gesture and the growing confidence that no one else could love Alex the way she would, Cassidy took her nephew from a gently smiling Mia and kissed the top of his head. His warm baby smell filled her senses and settled in her heart.

"That's ridiculous, Cassidy. You have no business with a child. You have a busy, growing career."

That was one of the dozen problems she hadn't figured out—yet.

"Something will work out."

"Well now, if that isn't a well-considered plan." Grandmother's nostrils flared in sarcasm. "You're single, Cassidy. You cannot raise a child and that is all there is to it."

The Caranos had grown quiet, eyes averted as they busied themselves with work, trying not to listen. All but Nic who stood at her side like some kind of warrior, which was ridiculous given that this was Notorious Nic. Despite his job, Nic wasn't a fighter. He was a player.

Still, his solid presence was oddly strengthening.

She, who had rarely won a battle with Eleanor Bassett, quelled the trembling in her bones.

"I promised Janna and Brad."

"Promised them what?" Grandmother's mouth puckered. Vertical lines, like spokes in a wheel, circled her lips. "To give up your own life?"

Cassidy's chin rose a notch. She could feel the red blotches creeping up her neck. She hoped Grandmother didn't take them as a sign of weakness. She was anxious, not weak.

"I promised to take care of Alex if anything should ever happen to them." With the stress and confusion of the past few days, she'd forgotten the conversation and the piece of computer-printed paper until this moment.

"Oh, for goodness' sake." Eleanor waved at the air in dismissal. "No one would hold you to some silly, sentimental promise."

"I would. I believe God would, too. Janna and I knew from experience that the worst could happen. She loved Alex so much, she wanted to be certain he would never—" She stopped before she could say too much. Her grandmother had tried. Hurting her now had no value. "We even put her wishes in writing with the nurses as witnesses. I have the paper in my safe-deposit box, if anyone wants to see it."

The day after Alexander Bradley Brown was born, Brad and Janna had handed her a document asking her to act as legal guardian if anything should ever happen to them. She'd wanted to laugh it off, but she and Janna knew that life didn't always play fair.

"We think it's a wonderful solution, Cassidy," Beverly Brown said, coming close enough to stroke Alex's hair. Tears filled the woman's eyes. "This is what we've prayed for, though we didn't want to pressure you. You're young and healthy, and you love this baby."

"You'll always be his grandparents," she said, aching for Beverly's loss. "He'll need you in his life."

"Thank you, honey," Beverly whispered. "We want that very much."

Without a word, she slid Alex into his grandmother's arms and watched her cradle the infant tenderly. Tears shimmied loose and slid silently down the woman's ruddy cheeks.

Grandmother Bassett, however, was determined to have her way. "You're running on emotion, Cassidy Luanne. This can't last. Then later, you will be sorry you made such a drastic mistake."

With a sharp pang, Cassidy realized Grandmother spoke from experience. She considered taking Janna and Cassidy into her home a "drastic mistake." That final, cruel comment gave Cassidy the last bit of courage she needed.

"Loving Alex could never, *ever* be a mistake."

Regardless of her single status, regardless of the demanding career, regardless of her goal to be a premiere graphic designer, and though she knew nothing at all about raising a baby, Cassidy Willis would find a way to give her sister's son the loving home he deserved.

Chapter Four

Nic tossed down the remote, skirted the semicircle of recliners pointed at a television set and headed into the kitchen area of Station One to dish up the lasagna. Four tough, manly firefighters followed like puppies. Tonight was his night to cook at the fire station, and thanks to his mother's recipes, Nic's cooking was favored by the other men.

"Not as good as your mama's," Captain Summers teased, his mustached mouth so full his words were mush. "Passable."

Above high cheekbones, Sam Ridge's brown eyes glittered with amusement, but he said nothing. Such was Sam's way. If he strung twenty words together during a twenty-four-hour shift, everyone sat up and listened. Nic always figured he and Ridge got on so well because Nic liked to talk and Sam liked to listen. Pretty sweet deal.

The Kiowa took an extra slice of buttered garlic bread, lifted it toward Nic in appreciation and returned to his chair to eat and watch reruns of *MASH*. If they were lucky, no calls would come in before they'd finished their meal.

During Nic's rookie year, Mama had appeared at the fire station to supervise the kitchen on his night to cook. Now that Nic had the recipes down, Mama still came around on occasion with pastries or breads from the family bakery. The other men lived for the times Rosalie Carano swept into the station to see "her boys," as she called all of them.

Lately Nic wished Mama wouldn't come around so often. Though he laughed at the good-natured teasing, the mama's boy comments were growing thin.

Nic dished up a healthy dose of steaming, cheesy casserole, his belly whimpering in anticipation. Other than a few medical calls, a couple of motor vehicle accidents and a grass fire, today's shift had been slow, both a blessing and a pain. Nic liked to be busy. Taking care of the station, the engines and the equipment was part of the job as was ongoing training, but he liked the adrenaline rush of a callout.

From the corner of his eye, Nic caught movement at the outside door. A luscious brunette, long hair blowing in the fierce Oklahoma wind, swept into the station. Behind her came a short, perky redhead.

Ah, well, he thought with a grin, *there are other types of adrenaline rushes.*

"Mandy! Rachel!" Nic said. "What's going on?"

One of the cool perks of being a firefighter was that citizens could drop by any time. Even gorgeous girl citizens who only came in to flirt.

He could deal with that.

Rachel, the leggy brunette, swept her hair back with one hand. "Came by to see you, what else?"

From the circle of recliners came the usual hum of interest. Sam and the other firefighter, "Slim Jim" Wagner, momentarily lost interest in Nic's lasagna.

Mandy, the perky redhead, opened a tiny purse and extracted a brochure. "We're getting up a group to go to the beach. Are you game?"

Trips to anywhere entertaining were right up his alley. After a long, windy and cold winter, some fun in the sun sounded pretty sweet. "When?"

"This weekend." She waved a photo of blue water lapping at sunny, white-sand beaches. "Three days at a friend's condo right on the beach in Galveston."

This weekend. He'd planned to drop by and check on Cassidy and Alex this weekend. Not that Cassidy was all that hot to see him. Fact of the business, he'd called her a couple of times since she'd made the decision to become Alex's permanent guardian, but she never answered the phone.

Weird.

He hoped she didn't have caller ID. The implications of that would be ego-crushing.

She'd sent cards to him, his parents and siblings expressing gratitude for their help. Nic would have preferred a phone call. One of those gushy-breathed, "Oh, Nicky, thank you so much for being there for me and baby Alex." But what did he get? A formal card with all the warmth of January.

He must be losing his edge.

He thought she liked him okay, but he also felt a kind of pushing away, as though she was too polite to say so, but she didn't want him around.

A terrific, fun-loving guy like him, he thought with humor. What wasn't to like?

Rachel's voice intruded on his aberrant thoughts. "So are you going with us, Nic?"

What had they been talking about? Oh yeah. A trip somewhere. "If I'm not on duty."

Rachel rolled her eyes. "Nic, it's this weekend. Remember? I have your schedule. I know when your four-days are. None of us want to go without you."

Ah, sweet. His ego was feeling better by the minute. Why was he letting a cool blonde and a toothless baby mess with his head?

Nic clapped his hands together. "Sounds good. You make the plans. I'll make the party."

Both girls laughed. Rachel tossed her hair over one shoulder. Nice hair. Nice girls. Fun times.

"You ladies up for a plate of my lasagna?"

Rachel touched her flat belly. "Can't. We're dieting. Swimsuit time."

"Don't know what you're missing." Slim Jim lifted his nearly empty plate above his recliner.

"Yes, we do," Mandy simpered. "Nic is a fabo cook."

"He'll make someone a great wife one of these days," Captain Summers added, his tone droll. "Did he tell you ladies about his new baby?"

Both women froze. Nic wished he'd had his camera phone ready to catch their shocked expressions.

"Get lost, Captain," he said mildly, and then to the girls, "He's kidding."

Yet, the mention of baby Alex started that strange yearning inside of him all over again.

Cassidy was a zombie.

"How's that design coming, Willis?" The art director of McMann's Marketing, Shane Tomlinson, was a go-getter, a type A personality who wanted everything done yesterday. On a normal day, Cassidy was right there with him.

But there was nothing normal about this week or the one that had preceded it.

"Fine," she muttered and reached for her coffee cup, hoping to appear cool and in control.

"Good. We need it ASAP." He tapped the top of her desk and wandered off to hassle another designer. Thank goodness.

For the past ten minutes, Cassidy had sat at her station staring mindlessly at the same rotating graphic. How was she supposed to create a new website for the Sports Emporium when all she could think about was sleep and Alex?

After four days and four of the longest nights of her life, she and her nephew had yet to establish a workable routine.

Workable? What a laugh. They had no routine at all. Alex cried and refused to sleep from dark to dawn. Cassidy rocked and sang and prayed and wondered if she'd lost her mind to think she could raise a child and keep her high-pressure career in fourth gear.

To make matters worse, after taking a week off, she was far behind. And today was the first day Alex had attended day care.

She glanced at the clock on her computer, then reached for her cell phone. She had the number on speed dial.

"Bo-peep Daycare," a chipper voice answered.

"This is Cassidy Willis. I'm calling to check on Alex Brown."

There was a slight pause. "Miss Willis, didn't you call about fifteen minutes ago?"

A lot could happen in fifteen minutes. "Is he all right?"

"He's asleep."

"That's what you said the last time."

"Babies generally nap for a couple of hours at a time."

Not at her place, he didn't. "Are you sure he's okay?"

"Positive."

"Will you check? I mean, right now. Go stand over his crib and look at him. Make sure he's breathing."

The day-care worker emitted a taxed sigh. "Stop worrying, ma'am. We take excellent care of our children."

That's what they all said. Yet, she'd seen the news reports, the horrors of day-care abuse. Bad things happened in some of them. How was she to know if Bo-peep was a good one or a bad one? Yes, she'd checked references, toured the facility, talked to other moms, but still…

"Please. Put the phone up to Alex's ear so he can hear my voice."

She didn't want him to feel abandoned.

"He's asleep. You don't want me to wake him, do you?"

"No, of course not." Yet she wondered at the woman's reticence. Was she hiding something? "Are you sure he's all right?"

Again that pause, only this time when the woman spoke, she was defensive. "Miss Willis, Alex is doing fine, but if you are that concerned, I suggest you come to the facility and have a look for yourself."

With a stammered thank-you, Cassidy snapped her flip phone shut and stared into space, deep in thought. After a couple of minutes, she dragged her purse out of the bottom drawer and jumped up. On her way out she passed Shane Tomlinson's office. She called, "Something important came up. I'll be back in twenty minutes."

Before her surprised boss could ask about the new web design or remind her that she was days behind in work, she rushed out the door and down the elevator.

At ten o'clock that night Cassidy sprawled on her couch eating a convenience-store burrito while Alex gurgled happily on his play mat. Classical music, Beethoven's *Für Elise,* tinkled from the music box as colored lights responded to Alex's movements.

She felt like a hammered banana while Alex was rested and ready to rock and roll.

He looked up at her and smiled.

That quick her spirits lifted. Stuffing the last bite of burrito into her mouth she slid onto the floor beside him. No matter how exhausted, frustrated or lacking in confidence she might be, one smile from that face and she was mush. Sometimes she stared into his precious, innocent eyes and saw her sister. With every look, every splashing bath, every time he caught her finger in his little fist, Cassidy fell more in love. Terrified, inadequate, but in sappy, sloppy love.

No wonder her sister had been so happy. But how had she juggled taking care of Alex with working on the B and B? How did she manage to appear fresh and rested when, at times, she must have been as frantic and exhausted as Cassidy?

The answers would forever remain a mystery. Perhaps birth mothers received some influx of hormone that kept them going.

A hormone Cassidy lacked.

Lying on her belly, she talked to Alex, played with him and then tried once more to get him down for the night.

Her head ached from lack of sleep. The tension in her shoulders was tight enough to snap. Her eyes burned.

She gathered a wide-awake Alex close to her chest and rocked him in the bentwood rocker.

"Come on, lamb, help Aunt Cassidy out. I'm so tired. I have to work tomorrow, you know. If I don't work, I won't be able to buy those cans of formula you're so wild about."

She rubbed his rounded belly with the flat of her hand. He seemed to like when she did that.

Her fingernails, she noticed, were looking rough, but when would she have the time or energy to go to the nail spa? Her roots needed to be touched up, too. Hopefully, in another week Alex would be on schedule.

"Ready for sleepy-pie?" It sounded like a dumb thing to say, but lately Cassidy found herself saying all kinds of gibberish. What exactly *was* sleepy-pie?

With a shake of her head, Cassidy laughed at her giddy thoughts. At the same time Alex swung his hand, catching hold of her hair. Cassidy's head was yanked sideways. Tears smarted at the corners of her eyes. With painful care, she managed to peel back each tiny finger until she was free again. Alex laughed up at her.

"Come on, buddy. Please. Go to sleep. I'm going to lay you down in your crib like a big boy and turn on your favorite lullaby." She did so, simultaneously activating the video monitor over his bed.

He gooed happily, arms and legs waving. Slowly, breath held, she backed to the doorway. So far, so good. She snapped off the light. Only the tinkling lilt of Brahm's lullaby shimmered in the quiet.

With a relieved exhale, she tiptoed down the hallway and fell facedown, still fully dressed, on a down comforter that had cost three days' pay. Normally fussy about anything on top of that cover, right now she was too tired to care.

From the monitor at her bedside came the continuing sounds of lullabies and baby noises. All was well in the nursery. Maybe tonight was the night Alex would sleep.

Cassidy thought about getting up to read her devotional, something she hadn't done since Alex moved in. Instead, she muttered a half-baked prayer, eyes closed, body beginning to float away. Thank goodness. Rest.

The banshee cry shot a stinging bolus of adrenaline into her brain. She sat straight up.

"No. Please," she whimpered like a kicked pup. "Don't cry."

But the sounds from the monitor grew louder and more furious.

"What could he want?" He was fed, changed, warm. What could be wrong with him?

Cassidy brushed limp hair from her face and stumbled into the baby's room. "What is it, sweetheart? Tell Aunt Cassidy."

If only he *could* tell her. If only she understood his signals. Janna always said she could tell the difference between every cry.

"Not me." Every cry sounded the same—painful to the ears and nerves.

Maybe she didn't have the mother gene. "Lord, I'm trying. Show me what to do."

Such a pathetic prayer, she almost felt guilty for praying it.

"I want to make him happy. I want to be a good mom." She lifted Alex's stiff, screaming body against her shoulder. "I love you, Alexander Brown. I love you."

She began to swing her body back and forth, back

and forth in what she hoped was a soothing rhythm. Alex kept crying.

Out on her feet, ready to collapse, she considered taking him into her bed. But if she lay down on the bed with him, she might fall asleep. Wasn't that a bad thing to do? Wouldn't she be in danger of rolling on him or something horrid like that?

Alex stiffened his whole body, pushing back from her shoulder to scream into her ear. His red, contorted face indicated something was wrong. But what?

She slid into the rocker again. What if she rocked herself to sleep and dropped him? The high-pitched crying rose a notch. Not much chance of falling asleep right now.

Arms heavy, head aching, she rocked and prayed. Alex found no comfort.

Her heart ached, too, knowing that Janna would have known what to do. Brad and Janna should be here, loving their baby, tending to his needs, not her. Not a workaholic aunt whose only venture into care-giving was a dozen exotic house plants.

She needed help. But who? Last night, she'd phoned every coworker she could think of. Some had laughed at her. Some had offered advice that hadn't worked. The trouble was, most of her friends were single.

"I know you miss your mommy, Alex." Tears pressed at the backs of her eyelids. "I miss her, too."

Alex jerked his knees to his chest and screamed.

Cassidy paced to the front window, murmuring words of comfort and slips of prayers. Light from an apartment below and to the right of hers beamed like a beacon of hope.

James and Marla were still awake. Maybe they would have an idea.

Desperate, Cassidy muttered, "Any port in a storm."

The late April night was glorious. Usually, she would have sat out on the stairs and breathed in the scent of blooming lilacs and watched a handful of cars slide past. Not tonight.

In minutes she was pounding on the door of the apartment below. Loud barks greeted her as the door opened.

"Cassidy, hello." Marla was in her robe. The tiny woman of Thai heritage looked back over her shoulder toward the living area. "It's Cassidy, honey."

An indistinguishable male rumble answered.

Dismay drifted through Cassidy. She shouldn't have come. "Were you already in bed? Marla, I'm so sorry."

"No problem. We were watching *The Late Show*." She waved Cassidy inside. "What's going on?"

As if she couldn't tell, Alex lifted his face from Cassidy's shoulder, went momentarily silent while he took a long, searching look at Marla and then belted out another cry.

Two fat English bulldogs plopped onto their bottoms, heads cocked to one side in fascinated silence.

Marla's exotically beautiful eyes looked at Alex as if he were a Martian. "Why is he crying so hard?"

Cassidy's face crumpled in disappointment. "I was hoping you might know."

"Me? My babies are bulldogs, Cassidy, not humans."

"I know, but…" At a loss, Cassidy puffed out a sigh. "I guess I was desperate."

A tinkle of laughter erupted from Marla's lips. "To come to me, you surely were. I never even babysat."

"Me neither."

"Want me to hold him for a minute? You look like you're about to collapse."

"I am." Tears burned Cassidy's eyes as she handed him off. "I love the little guy. I'm just not a very good mother."

"Hey." Marla patted Cassidy's arm. "Give it some time. This is new for both of you."

"Maybe I should take him to the hospital," Cassidy said.

"Is he sick?" Marla's voice rose above Alex's crying.

"I don't think so. Anyway, he was all right when I picked him up at day care and they said he'd had a good day."

She didn't add that this was after she'd "dropped by" the place four times on unannounced visits. Every time he'd been asleep. She'd started to wonder if they drugged him. He certainly didn't sleep like that for her.

"Hmm. Well, I don't know. It seems pointless to take him to the emergency room for crying. What about a nice cup of chai?"

Cassidy's humor returned. "For me or Alex?"

Marla giggled. "Both of you. That's my solution anytime I'm upset. Chai, massage, pray." She held up a finger. "Good idea."

The tiny woman turned and yelled, a surprisingly loud noise coming from such a small body. "James, come in here. We need to pray with Cassidy."

Cassidy realized then that this was really why she'd come downstairs to the Taylors' place. James and Marla were the only other believers she knew in the apartment complex. The three of them, along with Janna and Brad, had shared a monthly cookout, Bible study and time of fellowship. She needed her neighbors even more now that Janna and Brad were gone.

James, a blond giant as opposite as could be in looks from his tiny, dark wife, padded barefoot into the living room wearing baggy shorts and a T-shirt. Both bulldogs jumped up, tags jingling, to greet him. He placed an enormous hand on one's head.

All this time, Alex continued to fuss, sometimes quietly, sometimes with earsplitting cries.

Marla, her face an amusing mix of horror and compassion, handed Alex off to her giant husband. Again, Alex stopped crying long enough to examine the new stranger. The two bulldogs sniffed at the baby's dangling feet.

"Let's pray while he's quiet," James said. Before Cassidy could get her eyes closed, he began. "Father God, Cassidy is new at this parent stuff. She needs some help. Guide her, give her wisdom."

"And some sleep," Marla said. "Every night."

"Yes, Lord." James picked up the tag-team prayer. "And help Alex adjust to his new situation and sleep like a baby, too. In Jesus' name."

All three said, "Amen."

"He isn't crying." Marla stroked a tiny, pink-nailed hand over the back of Alex's smooth, round head.

"Is he asleep?" Cassidy asked. Please say *yes*.

James leaned away from the baby and looked down. "No. Wide awake. One out of two isn't bad. At least he's quiet."

"For now," Cassidy said, taking him from the man's arms.

Though she hadn't accomplished anything as far as understanding Alex's problem, Cassidy felt better. James and Marla were unorthodox in some ways, but they had hearts for God.

"Thanks, guys." She turned to leave. "Go finish your show. I hope you haven't missed too much."

"We're good. TiVo," James said with a grin. Cassidy noticed the remote protruding from his T-shirt pocket. "This thing with Alex will work out. Don't worry."

Easy for him to say.

With a bulldog at either side, he opened the door and all three faces—one large human and two fat canines—kept guard while Cassidy walked down the sidewalk and up the stairs to her apartment.

A siren split the night. Cassidy shivered and slammed the door, locking it. Someone somewhere was in danger.

Alex's fussing started up again.

So much for bothering the neighbors. But they had prayed, and with her fuzzy brain of late, her own prayers seemed to bounce off the ceiling. She only hoped God was listening and would show her what to do.

The sirens grew louder, reminding her of that tragic night and of Nic Carano.

She didn't want to think about it or about him. The fire had brought back terrible memories of the time she'd been alone and terrified, trapped under a mountain of rubble while the smell of death and distant smoke moved ever closer.

She shivered. For years, she'd tucked away the fear, but Janna's death had brought the memories back with a vengeance. Everyone she loved died tragically. Though in different ways, fire had been involved both times.

Fireman Nic was a reminder she didn't need.

But his family had brought her a baby book filled with advice. She'd been too busy and tired to read it.

The Caranos. Her exhausted mind drifted to Rosalie, the warm earth-mother woman whose babies probably had never cried. Like some sitcom mother of the fifties, Rosalie would have cradled one child, fed another, played with two others and baked a delicious Italian dinner for the family, all while running a bakery single-handedly and keeping a pristine house.

Nic's mother would know what to do with a baby who cried and refused to sleep at night.

A teensy bit of guilt nagged at her. Nic had phoned a few times. She hadn't answered or returned his calls. He probably thought she was a snob. How could she explain that who he was and what he did for a living struck terror in her heart?

She couldn't, of course. Her fear was irrational.

Hopefully, Nic considered that she was busy adjusting to a baby in the house.

The notion almost brought a sob. Adjusting? No one was adjusting around here. Her work suffered. Her appearance suffered. Even her miniature lemon tree was droopy.

How had Rosalie Carano become a superwoman?

With Alex against her shoulder, she paced, trying to remember what she'd done with Nic's phone number.

When she found the slip of paper in the bottom of her purse, her shoulders sagged.

She had no right to call him. She didn't want to call him.

But who else?

She battled her conscience. It was too late at night to call anyone. She'd already bothered the neighbors. And phoned her handful of good friends.

Alex shuddered against her, then wailed louder.

Was it incredibly rude of her to call a man she was trying to avoid?

More like incredibly desperate.

A guy like Nic would either be on duty at the fire station or out having fun. He would be awake. She could find out from him if it would be all right to call his mother.

Though aware that her brain was not working on all cylinders, Cassidy dialed anyway.

The line *brrred* in her ear. Twice. Three times. Cassidy bit her lip. What if she got his voice mail? What would she say? "Nic, I need your mother. Alex won't go to sleep, and I'm about to die over here?"

Pathetic. A stupid idea.

She must have been delirious to even consider calling Nic Carano.

Ready to hang up, she was lowering the receiver when a *snick* sounded.

A slightly slurred voice, deep and grumbly, muttered, "Party Central."

Chapter Five

Nic pushed back the blanket and sat up, pressing the receiver to his ear. What was that racket? After the trip to Galveston, he had been dead asleep and had considered not answering the phone at all. Now he was glad he had. Someone was in trouble.

"Who is this? What's going on over there? Do I need to call 9-1-1?"

He swung his feet over the side of the twin bed—the same twin bed he'd slept in since he was twelve. His high-school baseball trophies still lined a shelf in the corner.

Sheesh, he thought. *Nic, when are you going to grow up, man, and break out of here?*

"Nic, I need your help."

The voice sounded familiar. Fumbling with the lamp at his bedside, he clicked on a light and squinted at the caller ID.

"Cassidy?"

"I'm sorry to call this late. You're probably busy."

Busy? His blurry eyes found the clock. Yeah, he was busy. Catching *Z*s. "Not busy at all. Just got back from the beach. What's going on over there?"

And why are you calling me? Not that he was complaining about hearing from her, but the timing was weird. Real weird.

"Alex won't stop crying."

Nic's ego whimpered. No woman had ever called to tell him about a crying baby. "Give him a bottle, maybe?"

"I did. I changed him. I rocked him, I walked him. I'm dying, Nic." The desperation in her voice was apparent. "I haven't slept in a week because Alex cries all night. I don't know what to do anymore."

Nic had visions of the breathy, gushing phone call he'd dreamed of getting from the sleek blonde. This was not it.

He got up and stumbled around his bedroom, kicking a lump of clothes out of the way, rubbing his chest as he shook off the cobwebs of sleep.

Certain he was missing something in this conversation, he asked, "Want me to come over?"

"No!"

"You said that too fast. Broke my heart right in half."

"Nic. This isn't funny. Is your mother up? I thought she might be able to give me some advice, but I didn't want to wake her."

She hadn't minded waking him though. Hmm. Interesting.

Suddenly wide-awake and feeling zippy, Nic said, "I'll be there in ten minutes."

"No, Nic. Your mom—" but before she could finish, he laughed softly and disconnected.

The woman intrigued him. And he was a sucker for Alex. Why not be a good little fireman and rush to the rescue?

Timing himself, Nic arrived at Cassidy's apartment in eight minutes. He could hear the little dude through the door. *Man, oh man*, he thought. No wonder Cassidy was on the verge of hysteria. The noise increased when she let him inside.

Without giving the motion any consideration, he took the baby from Cassidy's arms. "You look beat."

"I am."

She must be really tired. Most women of his acquaintance would be offended at such a comment.

The half-moons below Cassidy's eyes were dark and hollow, more so since the last time he'd seen her. Her eyes were bloodshot, her hair limp and disheveled.

He had the uncomfortable thought that she was pretty anyway. He must be as tired as she was.

"What's the matter with the little dude?" he asked, patting the baby's stiff back, the blue onesie pajamas soft beneath his fingers.

"I have no idea. That's why I wanted your mother."

"Mom would know." He led the way into the nursery and laid the red-faced, bawling baby on the changing table. "Maybe Uncle Nicky knows, too."

He wasn't a paramedic-turned-med-school wannabe for nothing.

"What?" She sounded on the edge—on the edge and leaning over the railing ready to jump.

Alex kicked and thrashed, inconsolable as Nic ran a gentle hand over his rigid tummy. "Feel how firm his belly is. Maybe he has a tummy ache."

Cassidy came up beside him, her side warm against his. She smelled like orange blossoms. Sweet. Very sweet.

Normally when Nic noticed a girl's cologne, he paid her a compliment. Not tonight. Though his nose couldn't help enjoying her scent, his focus was baby Alex.

"What do we do for him?"

"Not sure. Comfort him as much as we can until he gets over the worst of it, maybe?"

"Should I take him to the hospital?" she asked over Alex's intermittent outbursts.

Nic gazed down at the infant. "For a tummy ache? Nah, I don't think so. Seems like I remember my sisters talking about colic. Could he have colic?"

"You're asking me?" Her voice rose an octave. She looked frantic enough to cry. Nic couldn't stand for a woman to cry.

Digging hard into the recesses of his mind, he dragged up conversations between his sisters and mother. Baby and kid stuff came up a lot at his house, though he hadn't paid all that much attention. Still, with that many kids some of the info was bound to have stuck.

"If he has colic, I don't think there's much you can do."

"What's caused it? Did I do something wrong?"

"I remember my sisters discussing diet changes."

Nic stroked the squirming infant with one hand as Cassidy gazed up at him. Blue. Her eyes were the prettiest shade of blue.

"Alex certainly has had those," she said. "And a lot of other changes. Poor lamb. I feel so bad for him. He's stuck with an aunt who doesn't have a clue."

Nic blinked and dragged his gaze from Cassidy's blue, blue eyes to Alex. "Tell you what."

"What?"

"You get some sleep. I'll look after Alex."

Cassidy was already shaking her head. "I have to learn to cope. He's my responsibility."

She nudged him aside to check Alex's diaper, changed him, then lifted him against her shoulder. Nic didn't appreciate the brush-off. She'd called him over here. He wanted to do something.

So much for the trusty-firefighter-to-the-rescue scenario he'd imagined. This woman was messing up his knight-in-shining-turnout-gear fantasy.

"Does he cry like this every night?" He followed her into the living room, wondering what he was doing in Cassidy's apartment at two in the morning and why he didn't just hit the road? She didn't want him here.

No, wait, she *did* want him here. She'd called him.

Yep, she was definitely messing with his head. And he was just stubborn enough to stick around and see what happened.

Besides, he felt sorry for the little dude.

"He cries off and on every night from bedtime until morning. Then he sleeps like a rock at day care." Cassidy gnawed a pretty lip with white, even teeth. Some orthodontist had made a mint off Grandma Cruella. "Anyway, the day-care workers say he sleeps all day. I don't trust them."

"Why not?"

"How can he sleep all day when he's awake or crying all night?"

"There's your answer. He's tired. He has his days and nights confused."

"Oh." Drooping with fatigue, she sagged into a chair and propped Alex on her lap facing Nic. "Makes sense. But I still don't like putting him in day care. Janna never wanted that. She would be appalled."

Bad deal, but what choice did she have? "Necessary evil, I guess, for a single parent."

"I guess."

Cassidy's whole body was a study in exhaustion. Nic couldn't take it. Sure, he was a tad weary from three days of fun in the sun, but erratic hours had never bothered him. They were part of a firefighter's routine. On for twenty-four hours, off for a day, on again, and off for more days. A crazy life that fit him to a tee.

He reached for Alex and plopped down with him on the small couch, propping his feet on the ottoman. If she was too stubborn to get some sleep, at least he could give her some respite from Alex. The baby couldn't help having a bellyache and being confused with all the changes in his life.

With Alex over his shoulder, he patted and talked, the way he had done with his gaggle of nieces and nephews. Uncle Nic had been the favored babysitter. Well, maybe not by his siblings, but definitely by the kids. Even when they were infants like Alex, he'd enjoyed them, knowing when the going got rough, he could hand them back to their mothers.

He made up silly songs in the baby's ear, singing low and soft as he patted. Cassidy looked at him from beneath drooping eyelids and smiled. "That one didn't rhyme."

"What are you talking about? I won a third grade poetry contest. I am a master at the rhyming couplet. Convertible and Corvette in the same poem would make the Bard green with envy."

She laughed softly. A pretty sound. Had he heard her laugh before? If he had, he must not have been paying close attention.

He was paying attention now.

The last thing Cassidy remembered was thinking how cute Nic was and how delirious she must be to allow a firefighter—especially this one—in her apartment.

Slowly returning to consciousness, she adjusted the angle of her neck. A crick was in the making. She'd fallen asleep sitting up in a chair, listening to Nic Carano sing to Alex.

Nic Carano. Oh my goodness.

Her eyes popped open.

The darkly handsome firefighter no longer occupied the couch across from her. She glanced around the dimly lit room. Someone had turned off all the lights except for a small reading lamp.

"Nic?" she whispered. "Nic?"

Fear stood her on her feet. Nic was gone. So was Alex.

Hurrying now, she rushed into the nursery and nearly collapsed with relief. The baby lay in a hump, knees drawn up and tiny backside in the air, a blanket covering him. His back rose and fell in restful slumber.

Tiptoeing, afraid of waking him, she went through the apartment to check the door locks and then to make sure the smoke detectors were functioning. Finding all secure, she looked out into the parking lot. Nic's truck was gone. A car slid past on the street below, its lights washing the concrete in pale yellow before disappearing.

According to the artsy clock above her sofa Cassidy had slept several hours. Her alarm would go off soon.

Amazing. How had she slept so soundly while sitting up in a chair? She hadn't even heard Nic leave.

Heading toward the shower, Cassidy rubbed both hands over her groggy face.

She'd fallen asleep with a man in her apartment—a playboy firefighter, of all people—and Alex in pain. What kind of mother was she?

Guilt-ridden, Cassidy spent too much of the following workday telephoning the day care and researching four-month-old babies on the Internet. Then she made a long list of parenting dos and don'ts and scheduled an appointment with a pediatrician. Even though Alex had been thoroughly examined before dismissal from the hospital, Cassidy figured another exam was in order. This time she knew what questions to ask.

On her lunch break, which she had never taken before the baby came into her life, she drove to Bo-peep day care and played with Alex.

Her boss frowned when she walked in after an hour's absence. "I need those mock-ups today, Cassidy. We have a production meeting with Carters at two and the design team meets after that."

"Right." She was a perfectionist in her job. Shane knew that. "I'll get it done." Somehow.

While Nic was comforting Alex last night, she should have whipped out the laptop and gotten busy on this project. But what had she done? She'd fallen asleep.

Since the fire, her creativity had gone flat. She was going through the motions, plugging in clichéd ideas that would get her nowhere. The company expected original, top-notch work from her. They'd always gotten it.

By the time the workday ended, she'd managed to throw together a couple of ideas, which she emailed to Shane's in-box. Her eyes burned and her neck ached. Four hours of sleep had been better than none, but she was still fatigued to the point of dropping. She wished for the time and energy to go for a run.

After picking up the baby and stopping by the supermarket for diapers, formula and a few groceries, she realized her running days might be over. She couldn't run and leave Alex alone in the apartment—even if she had the energy.

As she trudged up the stairs, baby in one arm, plastic grocery sacks dangling from her elbow and diaper bag and purse over the opposite shoulder, reality struck. Being a good mother was the hardest, most unselfish job on the planet.

And she had a lot of adjustments to make.

"You're worth it, though, my lamb," she said to the boy balanced between the crook of her elbow and her hip. She was determined to read and study and do everything in her power to become the best possible mother to this child who held her heart. No matter how much he cried, no matter how much sleep she lost, there were those special moments when he smiled or laughed and cooed up at her with recognition and pleasure. Then her heart filled with profound joy and the belief that together they would be a family. Somehow. If she could get it right and keep her job in the process. She owed that much to him and to Janna.

"Aunt Cassidy will do better, sweetie, I promise." She shifted him higher, balancing while she fumbled with the key.

An amused voice jolted her. "Talking to yourself?"

Cassidy jumped and dropped the keys.

Arms and ankles crossed, Nic Carano leaned against the railing outside her door. He wore a crisp, maize-colored shirt unbuttoned over a navy blue T-shirt that said, "Certified Hokey Pokey Instructor."

Cassidy ignored the sudden butterflies in her stomach. Nic looked as neat and fresh as a catalog model. She felt like the bottom of a clothes hamper.

"You scared me."

With a charming grin and easy grace, he retrieved the keys and unlocked the door.

As she stumbled awkwardly past, lugging too much stuff, Nic snatched the baby, swinging him high overhead. "Hey, Alex. How's my man?"

Alex gurgled happily, toothless mouth wide open. The sight was precious, endearing, and Cassidy's heart turned over with profound love for her sister's child.

"Be careful," she said. "He'll spit up in your face."

Nic's shoulders bunched. He grimaced and slowly returned Alex to a level position. "Was that the voice of experience?"

"Unfortunately." Cassidy dipped her head in wry concession and dropped the load of bags in the doorway. Her place was a mess. Baby toys scattered here and there. Unfolded laundry piled on the table. This morning's coffee cup and Alex's dirty bottles cluttered the sink. Until last week, she'd been a perfectionist here as well as at work. Anyone with off-white furniture had better be neat. Today she was too tired to care. "Sorry the place is a disaster."

"It is?" Nic's honest bewilderment made her laugh.

"Does that mean your apartment is less than tidy?"

"Room. I don't have an apartment. My mom says I'm a pig, a throwback to Great-Uncle Dominic." Still holding Alex, he plopped down on the sofa in the same spot he'd occupied last night. Alex grabbed Nic's bottom lip and pulled.

"You still live with your parents?" Hadn't she figured him for the type?

"For now." Nic extracted his lip from Alex's grasp and handed the baby a rattle. "I'm looking around. Time to get out on my own."

No kidding. She shuddered at the very thought of still living in Grandmother's house.

But then, the Carano family wasn't anything like her grandmother.

"The apartment directly below this one is open." As soon as she spoke the words, Cassidy wished them back. What was she thinking? She didn't want Nic Carano for a neighbor. She didn't even want him here now.

"That a fact?"

"Well, ummm," she stammered. "It's probably rented by now."

He studied her for a few seconds. Then he grinned. The cleft in his chin drew her attention. "You trying to discourage me?"

"I don't know what you mean."

Nic kept staring, eyes dancing with amusement.

She tugged at the collar of her blouse, aware of the heat that crept up her neck. Certain the dratted blotches would pop up on her skin any minute, Cassidy turned away, busying herself with straightening the living room.

"Why *did* you come over today?" she asked. And why did Notorious Nic have to be the firefighter who rescued her nephew? "I mean, there's really no need.

I appreciate all you've done, coming to my aid last night, but—"

"Are you telling me to hit the road?"

Hands filled with baby toys, she paused, "No!" *Yes.*

"Good. You were about to hurt my delicate feelings." He grinned at the statement. A man with his self-confidence would never believe he wasn't wanted. "Probably of more importance to you than my tender ego is this. I bring good tidings and words of advice from my mom, the baby expert."

All thoughts of getting rid of Nic fled. Cassidy stacked the colorful toys into an empty clothes basket and shoved it against the wall.

"What did she say?"

Nic dangled a set of plastic keys in front of the baby. "According to Mom, Alex has a big adjustment to make. Because of the new formula, he probably *is* having some colic like we thought last night, but the bigger issue is he's missing the familiar. He may only be a few months old, but he knew his mother and father. Now, when he's tired and nighttime comes, he looks for them. He wants them."

An ache of sorrow, never far away, surged inside Cassidy. She missed them, too. She wanted them, too. How much more, then, would a tiny baby long for his mother and father?

She slid onto the sofa to stroke Alex's hair. "She's right. He does. I hadn't realized it but he checks out every new face as if hoping to find Janna or Brad."

Both adults gazed at Alex. Nic spoke. "Sad deal."

Her heart heavy, Cassidy murmured softly, "I can never replace them."

"Don't beat yourself up. You're doing the best you can in a tragic situation. Mom says for you to just keep keeping on. In time he'll bond firmly to you and everything will be great."

In time. She didn't have time. Her job was floundering. Her body was a wreck. Beyond her work and Alex's care, she had the issues of Janna's estate to deal with. Talking to Grandmother made things worse, not better. She had no time.

More than anything she wanted Alex to be a happy, healthy, well-adjusted child. She prayed that she had what it took to give him that. God would not have put her in this position if she couldn't handle it. Would He?

Nic's cell phone played the "Looney Toons" theme. Nic whipped the phone from his pocket and held the music out for Alex's reaction before speaking into the mouthpiece. "Party Central."

Immediately Cassidy was aware that a female was on the other end. She tensed.

For some inexplicable reason listening to Nic chat up a girlfriend in her apartment made Cassidy uncomfortable.

She got up from the sofa, went into the kitchen and began slamming cabinets and rattling dishes. There was so much to do. Besides, she had no desire to hear Nic flirt with one of his girls. Really. He was exactly as she remembered—an irresponsible charmer. Not that she cared. Not that she was interested.

She was simply grateful for his help. Last night,

she'd been out of her mind to call him. Now, she'd have to be rude to get rid of him. But she couldn't do that. He and his family had been godsends—literally sent by God to help her and Alex in their time of need.

So now what was she supposed to do?

Wrinkling her nose at the sour smell, she dumped clabbered formula from a bottle she'd found in the bottom of the diaper bag and added the nurser to the others in the dishwasher.

An arm snaked around from behind her and added yet another bottle to the dishwasher. Cassidy jumped. She hadn't heard his approach. "Will you stop sneaking up on me?" *And will you stop forcing me to think about you?*

Standing a tad too close, he grinned, unrepentant. "You smell good."

She made a face, but her pulse tripped. "If you're fond of baby puke."

Nic laughed. He had a great laugh. "Look, I gotta go."

No surprise there. His entourage had called.

"But first, I have an idea."

"This came from your conversation with—what was her name?—Brittany?"

Drying her hands on a paper towel, she glanced around him, past the table and chairs into the open living area. Alex rested in his swing, grabbing happily at the overhead circus animals, the swing tick-tocking to the tune of "The Greatest Show on Earth."

"Brittany's a pal. We hang out."

344   *The Baby Bond*

A pal? Uh-huh. Bet Brittany didn't think that way. "So what's your idea?"

"I'm on duty tomorrow."

Cassidy stiffened at the reminder. Fire. Death.

"Can't come over."

Cassidy fluttered a hand against her chest. "You're breaking my heart."

Nic's lips twitched. "Smart mouth. We're talking about the little dude here. He's wild about me. What will he think if Uncle Nic doesn't stop by?"

"Modest," she said, rolling her eyes. But Nic was right. Alex lit up and hushed up when Nic played with him. "Don't worry about it. Now that I know what's wrong, I can handle everything."

Nic's voice gentled. "We all need a little help now and then, Cassidy." He touched her arm. Cassidy stepped back, breaking contact. If Nic noticed, he didn't react. "So what I'm thinking is this. The folks are having a cookout Sunday after church. You're invited. I'll pick you up about one o'clock. Baby advice from renowned Carano experts will flow. Many hands will hold and play with him, giving you a break. What do you say?"

What she wanted to say was "No way, get out. I don't understand why I'm letting you in my house." What she actually said was much nicer. "Life is crazy right now, Nic. I don't think so."

"All the more reason to come." He started toward the door, stopping to hand Alex a rattle before moving on.

"Thanks, Nic, but I can't."

He opened the door, then turned and pointed. "Think about it. I'll call you."

His footsteps echoed down the stairwell. Cassidy closed the door and looked at the baby happily babbling to a plastic lion. "Did Notorious Nic just ask me out?"

Chapter Six

A curl of smoke snaked beneath the rubble of wood and brick where the ten-year-old lay trapped beneath a demolished school building. Cassidy could see the terrified, dirt-covered girl. Poor baby, she thought, and then with horror realized the child was her.

Her pulse jackhammered.

Somehow it had happened again. The earthquake had come back for her.

She struggled, fighting the rubble. Not again. Not again.

"Mama! Daddy!"

The acrid smell of smoke crept closer. Fire was coming. She couldn't see it but it was coming. And she couldn't escape.

Something above her shifted. She tried to look up, but all was dark. The building trembled. Cassidy tensed, praying that nothing else struck her. She was thirsty. Her head pounded like the distant hammering.

Her legs and back ached, too, from the weight holding her captive beneath the school building—or what was left of it. Where were her friends? Where was her teacher? Where were Mama and Daddy? Why didn't they come?

"Somebody, please," she whimpered. Dust and ash flowed into her mouth.

Then the fire was upon her with its monster roar, licking at her face and hands. She was hot, burning.

She screamed…and bolted upright in bed.

For a second she didn't know where she was. She blinked into the darkness. All was quiet. No fire. No hammering. No painful press of rubble. Only the silky slide of sheets against her legs.

Realization flowed in and with it relief, sweet enough to taste. She was safe. She was an adult, not a helpless child, alone and trapped beneath a crumbling school.

Shaking all over and drenched in sweat, Cassidy rubbed both hands down her face. Her heart thudded loudly in the silence.

"A nightmare," she whispered into the darkness. The earthquake hadn't returned. She'd been dreaming again as she hadn't done in years.

Somewhere nearby, a siren wailed, a haunting cry of despair.

Cassidy kicked back the sheet that had wadded and tangled around her legs and went to the window of her second-floor apartment. The sirens must have awakened her. Either that or they'd invaded her subconscious and set off the dream.

She blew out a long, shuddering breath.

Nic Carano was on duty tonight. He was out there somewhere, facing the beast, facing death. She didn't want to worry about him, but she did. He'd saved Alex. He'd tried to save Janna.

Grief washed through her at the thought of her beloved sister, gone forever. She sagged against the window.

Though the night was warm, the smooth wood beneath her feet was as cold as her insides. With a shiver, she wrapped her arms around her waist and stared out into the dark night. Streetlights cast eerie shadows onto the parking lot below. No one stirred in this residential neighborhood.

Another siren added to the mournful cry.

Someone in this pleasant, upscale city had awakened to a living nightmare. Nic was out there with them.

"Father in Heaven," she whispered against the cool windowpane. "Don't let anyone die tonight. Surround them with your protection. Just as you protected the children of Israel from the fiery furnace, protect Nic and his crew and the people they're trying to help."

Yet the prayer didn't stop the quaking in her middle.

A week ago she wouldn't have given Nic Carano a thought. Regardless of her resistance, he'd charmed his way into her life. He'd been kind to Alex. Now he could die. In the short time they'd been reacquainted, she'd already heard stories about his antics. Nic Carano was not a cautious man.

She put a hand to her throat. This was why she

couldn't let Nic come any nearer. This was why she'd refused his invitation. The danger was too great.

Trying to shake off the morbid thoughts, Cassidy padded into the nursery. The glow of the angel night-light illuminated Alex's round, cherubic face. Fist against his bow-shaped mouth, he stirred and made sucking noises but didn't awaken with his usual howl. For once, the baby slept soundly. It was the aunt who couldn't rest.

Reassured that Alex was safe, Cassidy moved from room to room checking each smoke detector. Satisfied that all were activated, she returned to bed.

In the dark silence, Cassidy willed her heartbeat to slow, willed her mind to stop circling around the nightmare and prayed for Alex's rescuer.

Sleep didn't come for the longest time.

Cassidy had thought about the nightmare—and Nic—all the next day and finally satisfied her concerns that evening by phoning Rosalie Carano. Nic was fine, as she'd known he would be, and then she'd felt a little silly for calling. True to her nature, Nic's mother had been warm and wonderful, a fact that made Cassidy acutely aware that she'd rarely had a mother to turn to in times of need. It also made her aware that there was more to Nic than he let on.

She and Rosalie had ended up talking about the Lord and babies and finally about Nic. Cassidy hadn't wanted to hear charming stories about the firefighter, but courtesy bade her listen.

As if that wasn't bad enough, by the time Sunday

rolled around, the troublesome firefighter had telephoned twice and appeared on her doorstep another two times. He was becoming a pest. An attractive pest, yes, but an uncomfortable one, as well.

What did the man want anyway? Certainly not her. He had a host of women at his beck and call. Besides, if she was in the market for a man—which she wasn't— Nic could not be the one. He had two strikes against him. He was Notorious Nic with a girl for every day of the week, and more importantly, his job gave her nightmares. She would never, ever date a man who risked death every time he went to work.

Alex the traitor, however, went into ecstatic gyrations at the sound of Nic's voice. The baby was too young to associate the man with the event that had changed his life forever. Unfortunately for Cassidy, she remembered all too clearly.

Yet, Nic still came over. He still called. And the bond between him and Alex grew exponentially.

"We're not going to the cookout, Alex, and that's all there is to it," she said to the baby cradled in her arms. Muddy blue-brown eyes gazed earnestly back at her as his greedy mouth pulled on a bottle of formula.

"No use making a fuss," she went on. "Like half the female population of Northwood, you are enamored of Nic's charm. You simply don't understand the problems the way I do."

And understand she did. Nic brought back too many memories, too much pain. Being around him had uncovered the shallow grave of buried trauma. Twice more this week she'd had nightmares. Though these were a combination of the earthquake that had stolen her parents and the fire that killed Janna, they were both vivid and terrifying. The residual effects lingered for hours afterward, stealing any hope of sleep.

Cassidy squeezed her eyes tight against the visions. She was so tired, like a minnow swimming upstream against a flood.

That morning in church she'd experienced a few minutes of peace and comfort. People were kind, thoughtful, interested in the tragedy that had made her Alex's guardian, but once outside the church doors, Cassidy felt alone again. She was certain the feeling was magnified by the unrelenting fatigue.

If only she had time to lie down and take a long, long nap. Three weeks' worth.

Alex waved his chubby arms as if to remind her that he was with her. A bubble of love replaced her melancholy thoughts.

Without Alex she might have sunk into despair and never come out again.

"I love you." Cassidy leaned forward to kiss the slobbery face, an action she'd have considered a little disgusting a few short weeks ago. Now, everything about Alex struck her as precious and beautiful. In unexpected moments like this, a kind of love she couldn't explain flooded over her in sweet waves.

The telephone jangled. Holding Alex in one arm with the bottle stuck under her chin, she answered the phone with the opposite hand. "Hello."

"Cassidy. This is Grandmother."

Cassidy's shoulders tensed. "How are you, Grandmother?"

"The question, dear, is how are you?"

"Coping."

The nasal voice pounded at her. "Exhausted? Frustrated? Realizing that raising a child is not an easy task?"

All that and more, but she was not about to admit as much to Grandmother.

"We're getting along great," she said with false cheer. "Alex is a wonderful baby."

A moment of silence hummed between them. Cassidy remained quiet, determined not to let her grandmother know how difficult things had been.

"I know of a good family here in Dallas that would be willing to take him." Eleanor's tone was crisp and businesslike, as though she was selling real estate.

Cassidy's jaw tightened against the wash of pain. Had Grandmother ever loved anyone? "We've discussed this. Alex stays with me permanently. The subject is closed."

"Don't let sentimentality ruin your career."

Sentimentality?

Cassidy felt the soft roundness of Alex's body cradled against her, felt the movement of his little feet against her side, heard the sweet murmurings he made whenever she fed him. She glanced down into his beautiful face, aching with a love she couldn't explain to anyone, much less Eleanor Bassett. Grandmother had no clue what she was missing.

Cassidy knew if she didn't get off the line now, she'd say something regrettable.

Holding the phone tight enough to whiten her knuckles, she said, "If you'll excuse me, Grandmother, Alex and I have an outing planned. Thank you for your concern."

Without giving Eleanor a chance to reply, she replaced the receiver. It was only then that she realized Alex's great-grandmother had not even asked about him.

Heart heavy, though she should have expected this from Eleanor Bassett, Cassidy finished feeding Alex and then changed him.

Grandmother's words were a reminder that her career was indeed going down the tubes. Friday, she'd missed another half day's work to take Alex to the pediatrician. Her boss had rejected the designs she'd submitted, asking for new ones by tomorrow. In addition, the advertising firm needed several other logos and brochures for which she was primarily responsible, and she'd missed a meeting with a key client. To move up the ladder, she had to perform, and this week, for the first time in her career, she'd been reprimanded by her superior for poor performance.

Her head hurt from trying to be a good mother while also trying to be more creative in her work. Women who did it all were superheroes.

Someone pounded on the door and a male voice called, "Open up. Your ice cream is melting."

And if she didn't already have enough problems to solve, there was Nic Carano.

Braced to remind him that she had, indeed, refused to attend his family's cookout, Cassidy opened the door.

Nic, in a black T-shirt inscribed with "First things first, but not necessarily in that order," held a pink ice-cream cone in each hand. His maize-striped overshirt was unbuttoned as usual. Black hair shining in the sun, he looked good. Real good.

Ah, the beauty of Italian heritage. It should be outlawed.

Alex surged forward, nearly wrenching himself out of Cassidy's arms. She grappled to hang on.

Nic grinned, teeth white against his olive skin. "Trade you."

Ignoring the unwanted flare of attraction, Cassidy took one of the cones and slid Alex into the firefighter's hold. "How did you know to buy strawberry?"

"A guess. You don't look like the chocolate type."

She turned and started inside, feeling him there behind her.

"I could be vanilla," she shot over one shoulder.

"Oh, no." He shook his head as he followed her into the living room. "No one could mistake you for plain vanilla."

She spun around, cone pointed at him. "Is that a compliment?"

His eyes twinkled below one quirked eyebrow. "Maybe."

Okay, enough already, Cassidy, she thought. *No flirting allowed, no matter how charming and cute and hunky he might be.*

As a distraction, she tasted the soft ice cream. The cool burst of strawberry tantalized her tongue.

Cassidy rounded the back of the off-white couch, stopping there to lean. Having furniture between her and Nic might be a good idea, especially considering how her skin tingled and her pulse jumped around like frogs on a sidewalk.

"I thought you were going to a cookout," she said.

"I am." Balancing Alex easily in one arm, Nic took a giant lick of his double dip. "Good stuff, huh?"

"Great stuff. Thank you. But won't ice cream ruin your appetite?"

"Never put off the good things in life. Dessert first. Burgers later."

Making himself at home at one end of the couch, Nic crossed an ankle over one knee. Then he propped the baby in the resulting valley. Alex bicycled his arms, as if trying to reach the ice-cream cone.

"Think it's okay if Alex has a bite of this?"

He was asking her? "I don't know. Should babies have ice cream?"

Nic's shoulders lifted. "It's milk."

"True."

Though she had reservations, about both the ice cream and the man, Cassidy gave up the battle and settled on the opposite end of the couch to watch as Nic dabbed a bit of strawberry ice cream on Alex's tongue. The baby's face contorted, his tongue worked in and out. Pink melted ice cream slid down his chin.

Nic laughed, a rich sound that warmed a cold place

inside Cassidy. The reaction startled her. She didn't want to *see* Nic, much less be attracted to him.

She whipped a wet wipe from a box on the end table and caught the drip before Alex's clean shirt could be soiled. The action put her shoulder to shoulder with Nic, the top of her head resting just below his chin. She could hear him breathe and smell the scent of warm cologne mingled with cold strawberry ice cream.

Oh dear.

Abruptly, she moved away.

Nic noticed. Contemplative eyes the color of French roast coffee watched her.

Cassidy's pulse stuttered. Her breath stuck in her windpipe. She dropped her gaze, wanting to reclaim Alex and run away, though there was no escaping her jumbled emotions.

After another uncomfortable second in which Cassidy searched for something clever to say, Nic crunched the edge of his waffle cone and raised an eyebrow. "Ready to head over to my place?"

Not on your life, buddy.

Drawing upon the cool demeanor that had won her the title of "ice queen" in college, Cassidy shook her head. "Can't. I'm sorry. When you knocked I was getting ready to put Alex down for what I hope is a long nap so I can work."

Nic paused on his way to another bite of waffle cone. "Work? On what?"

"Designs for a major client. I've fallen behind." She didn't add the rest. If she didn't catch up, her chances for promotion to creative director this year would be down the tubes.

"You're turning down an afternoon of fun with a terrific guy like me in favor of work?" His expression was comical. "This is painful."

"Call Brittany. Or Rachel." Both women had phoned more than once in her presence.

The comment had the opposite effect she'd intended. Nic seemed delighted.

"Are you jealous?" he asked, grinning like a maniac. "I'd feel a lot better if you'd say you are."

Not even close. The one thing she would not ever be was one of Nic's entourage. If he was the least bit interested in her, which he couldn't be, she would run in the other direction. Nevertheless, the notion that he might be made her more anxious than her own unacceptable attraction.

Keeping it light, she quipped, "Jealousy keeps me up at night."

"Oh, good. I thought Alex was doing that."

She made a face. "Funny."

"Yeah, I'm a funny guy. A barrel of laughs." For a minute, his relentless cheer faded.

Cassidy blinked at the change, wondering if there was a serious side to Notorious Nic. The idea made her more uncomfortable.

"Anything I can say to convince you to go to the cookout?" he asked after a minute. "You could use some R and R after the weeks of stress. And there's always that expert baby advice I promised." He placed a palm over the left side of his chest. "Along with mending my broken heart, of course."

He was kidding. He had to be kidding, but the man was charming to the max. Convincing, too. An afternoon of mindless relaxation sounded like a dream, but not with Nic Carano.

"I can't. Really, Nic. Thanks anyway."

"Another time maybe?"

Why was he so insistent?

She raked splayed fingers through the top of her hair. "Probably not."

"Okay. But you don't know what you're missing." He sighed, resting his chin on Alex's soft blond hair. "Mind if I take the little dude then? The folks were pretty taken with him."

So was Nic, which should eradicate any concerns she had about his interest in *her*. This was about Alex, the baby he'd bonded with during a tragedy.

Nic Carano was not interested in her as a woman. He had plenty of those.

Any twinge of disappointment on her part was purely wounded pride.

"I don't think that's a good idea." She didn't want her baby out of her sight, much less hanging out with a playboy fireman.

"Ah, come on. You'll have a chance to rest and work without interruption."

"A run," she said without thinking.

"Huh?"

"Since Alex came along, I've not had time to run."

"Great then. I'll take him. You run, rest, work, whatever."

"No!" How had she gotten into this? "Nic, I don't want to seem ungrateful, but I'm not ready to be away from Alex any more than I have to be. Understand?"

He tilted his head to one side, clearly *not* understanding. "No, but I respect your decision."

Without further argument, he handed the baby to her and headed for the door.

Feeling inexplicably guilty, she followed him. Was he angry? Upset? Hurt? "Thanks for the ice cream."

With a final wink and a quick salute, he pounded down the metal steps, open shirt flying in the breeze.

If she'd hurt his feelings, she was sorry. He'd been nothing but kind. At the same time she was relieved to have him gone.

Maybe he wouldn't come around anymore. Maybe she'd seen the last of Nic Carano.

She hadn't.

Tuesday morning as she dragged herself down the stairwell toward the parking lot, toting more than her body weight, she spotted a swarm of familiar dark heads on the sidewalk. She squinted through the over-bright sunlight, shaking the cobwebs out of her sleep-deprived brain.

The Carano brothers? Surely not. Why would they be at her apartment complex at seven in the morning? Must be someone else.

In her foggy-headed condition, the newcomers could be the royal princes and she wouldn't recognize them. She needed coffee, but since Alex, those little extras had gone by the wayside. She'd barely gotten the two of them dressed, him fed, the diaper bag packed and her hair and makeup in place. She didn't dare arrive late to work another morning.

Suddenly, the man she did not want to think about came jogging up the steps looking poster-boy neat, his affable smile in place.

"You look grumpy," he said.

She glared at him. How dare he look happy and handsome at seven in the morning?

"I am. Go home."

With an annoying grin, he relieved her of all baggage except her purse and Alex. "I am home. Or I will be by noon."

Cassidy stopped dead, one foot on a step and one on the ground. A frisson of worry tingled up her spine. "What are you talking about?"

"The apartment you mentioned. I've finally made the break."

His words registered. Her heart tumbled to the concrete and lay there, shuddering. This couldn't be happening. The man she didn't want to be attracted to was now going to live too close to ignore.

"You rented the apartment below mine?" The words came out as flat as her mood.

Nic didn't notice. With his usual blithe spirit, he said, "Great, huh? Now I can pop up and see Alex any time. If you're really good, I might even babysit for you while you run."

That part sounded good. The rest, not so good.

Plodding on to her Camry, with Nic tagging along talking a mile a minute, the possibilities whirled inside Cassidy's head.

A firefighter living below her. The firefighter who was a walking, talking memory of one of the worst nights of her life. The firefighter who couldn't seem to take no for an answer.

Lord, she thought, the Bible says, *You'll not put more on me than I can stand. This is getting real close.*

Nic jogged ahead of her, too cheerful for anyone this early in the morning, and opened the back car door. Without saying a word, though she was reluctantly grateful for the extra hand, Cassidy strapped Alex into his car seat. When she turned to take the diaper bag and laptop from Nic, he had bounced around the car and was putting them on the other side.

"Thanks," she said grudgingly and got into the driver's seat.

Nic, all smiles and oozing charm, stood between her and the opened door, one elbow leaning on the upper edge. He bent toward her. He smelled good—like a recent shower and some subtle men's cologne. "What time do you get home?"

"Six," she answered, her mind occupied with noticing him more than she wanted to. "Why?"

"Lasagna. I'm great with lasagna."

He wanted to cook for her? "I might be running late. Work is backed up."

"No problem. Lasagna will wait."

"Oh, well…" What did she say to that?

"Hey, Nic," a male voice called. "Are you going to move this couch or romance the neighbor?"

Great. Everyone in the apartment complex probably heard that remark.

"Bye, Nic." Cassidy reached for the door handle. Her elbow bumped his side.

He stepped back and shot her a jaunty salute. Right before he shut the door, he said, "It's going to be great being neighbors."

Great was not the word Cassidy had in mind.

Chapter Seven

"Come on, Nic. A trip to the lake won't be any fun without you."

Rachel drew her long brunette hair over one shoulder and looked at him with big, sad eyes. She and Mandy had dropped by with a pan of fresh chocolate brownies and a housewarming gift—a color-changing mood bowl.

"For chips and dip and conversation," the girls had said.

Whatever. He'd probably eat Cheerios out of it in the morning to find out what kind of mood he was in. Or maybe run the bowl upstairs and have Cassidy eat from it and check out her mood, which changed with the wind. She had been none too excited this morning to discover he was moving in below. What was with her anyway? One day she was begging him to come over and the next she wanted him out of her sight.

Challenging woman. No wonder he liked her.

"Nic, are you listening to me?" Mandy cocked her

head, pouting a little. Her pout usually got to him. Not today.

"Sure I am." He grinned and reached for one of the brownies. "What did you say?"

She bopped him on the arm. Chocolate crumbs scattered on the floor. "You were a million miles away. What's going on with you?"

"Moving, I guess. Pretty busy around here." He stuffed the brownie into his mouth all at once and wiped his fingers down the legs of his jeans. Had he remembered to eat lunch?

"We came to help." Rachel motioned toward a stack of cardboard cartons lining the wall in the living room. "Show us where you want the things in these boxes and we'll put them up."

He waved them away. "Nah. I'm good. Thanks anyway." *And when are you leaving?* The last thought came out of nowhere. Normally, he liked having his friends hang out.

"If *we* put things up," Mandy said, poking through a box of linens his mother had donated. "He'll never find them."

"True." Rachel twisted the ends of her hair. "Guys have their own system."

"Yeah," Nic said, fingering the mood bowl. "Toss it in a drawer or under the bed."

"Nic!" Both girls laughed.

"Come on, Mandy." Rachel hiked a tiny silver purse over one shoulder. "Nic doesn't have time to play today. Let's go."

Nic was relieved. As much as he liked his friends,

today he wanted some downtime. He had a million things on his mind and none of them was a trip to the lake or a party. Man, he must be having some kind of crisis.

He checked the mood bowl. It was still white, whatever that meant.

Setting the dish aside, he edged the girls toward the door as subtly as possible.

"Are you sure you won't go with us tomorrow?" Mandy asked when they were out on the sidewalk.

He didn't like to disappoint anyone, but he had things to do. Lately, he wasn't in the mood for their constant fun and games. He needed to study if he was going to pass his med school entrance exam next go-round, one of the main reasons for renting this apartment. Not that he would share that information with Rachel and Mandy. He had a reputation to uphold.

Most people, including his family, doubted he had what it took to get into medical school in the first place. If he failed again, they'd never know. If he passed, they'd finally see him as something besides a goof-off.

Maybe he needed to prove something to himself, as well.

"You'll have a great time," he told the girls. "Don't even think about me."

Resigned, the pair hopped into a yellow sports car and backed out, bracelet-bedecked arms waving out the windows.

With a relieved sigh, Nic started to close the door

when he saw Cassidy's blue Camry pull up. All of a sudden, he was in the mood for company.

He jogged down the sidewalk to the parking lot, waited for her to kill the motor and then he opened the back door. The little dude was asleep, his head lolling to one side so that Nic felt sorry for him.

Cassidy pivoted around in the seat to stare. "Are you trying to kidnap my baby?"

"Rescuing. His neck is breaking." He unlatched the harness and gently lifted Alex into his arms, his attention on the series of straps holding the car seat in place. "I'll come back later and check your car seat. Did you have it professionally installed?"

Cassidy stepped out of the car and slammed the door. "No. This is the car seat your sister gave me."

"My bad. I should have installed it properly for you that day." He tapped his chest. "Certified baby seat installer."

She laughed.

He shot her a mock scowl, feeling zippier by the minute. She looked pretty standing in the sunshine, her sleek blond hair catching the light. When she moved, a pair of big silver earrings danced around her face.

Even after a day's work and with bags under her eyes, Cassidy looked good to him. He was a little worried about that. He liked girls and thought every one of them was pretty, but Cassidy had started to stand out from the crowd. Before, all the girls were friends, pals, good times, but there was something different with this lady.

Nic looked forward to finding out exactly what that

delectable difference *was*. Nothing serious, nothing heavy, but he was intrigued.

Alex woke up and turned sleepy eyes on him. He was fond of the little dude, too.

"Don't laugh," he said. "Firefighters take a course in this stuff. Safety first. I know my way around a baby seat."

"I learn something new every day." Cassidy pulled the diaper bag and laptop from the opposite side of the backseat. She was tired, as usual. He could see the fatigue hanging off her like weights. Strong lady, this one. A do-it-or-die-trying kind of woman. He liked that about her.

"Well, add this to your list." He followed Cassidy up the stairs where he took the key and opened the door.

She trudged inside and dumped the load on a red stuffed chair, the rare splash of color in the off-white room. "What?"

He handed Alex to her. "I'm going down to finish up dinner. The place is still a mess but the food will be awesome. I promise. You and my main man here spend some quality time, take a little rest, and then come on down."

"I should stay home and work."

He'd known she would argue and he was ready.

"You have to eat anyway." She was thin enough without skipping meals. "Come on, a relaxing, painless dinner, and then you can come back up here and work yourself into a coma. I'll even show you my mood bowl."

He'd meant the last crack to be funny. She didn't bite. "Why are you doing this?"

"I told you. I'm a great guy. Irresistible." He hoped she was buying this load of garbage. He wasn't sure why he needed to do things for her but he did. Maybe he felt responsible because he'd been there the night of the fire. Maybe the reason was a smiley-faced orphaned boy whose eyes sparkled as though Nic was the greatest thing since milk. Or maybe it was Cassidy herself. Whatever the reason, he wanted to find out.

"Did you get everything moved in this morning?"

"My brothers helped. We dragged everything inside. I'll need a few days to set up."

She kicked her shoes off and settled Alex on a play mat next to the red chair. A push of the button and classical music poured out with a tinny sound. Mozart, maybe, but what did he know of classical music, other than his dad's favorite operas?

"Didn't your friends help you unpack?" She gave Alex's back one last pat and straightened.

"Friends?"

Cool blue eyes scrutinized him. "The two girls who were leaving as I drove up?"

The question tickled him. "I love it when you get jealous."

One finely shaped eyebrow twitched. Man, she had pretty eyebrows.

"You wish."

Did he? Maybe. "Want me to take Alex down to my place while you grab a nap?"

She was shaking her head before he could finish. "Thanks but no."

He knew she'd say that. She didn't want Alex out of her sight. "All right then. Come on down when you're ready. I have a present for you."

Surprised interest lit her expression. "A present? What is it?"

Nic grinned. A present was always good for persuading the reluctant. "You'll find out. See you in a few."

Cassidy plopped down on the couch for fifteen minutes with her feet up while she stewed about the problem of Nic Carano. Having him pop in or call had been bad enough, but now the guy was right downstairs and showed no signs of leaving her alone.

To make matters worse, she liked him. Somewhere beneath all that fun-and-games charm was a solid man, maybe a little off-center but dependable in the most surprising manner. She didn't much like thinking of him that way, but what else could she think? He'd been there when she needed him. Even with his reputation as a loose cannon, he'd saved Alex's life. How much more responsible could you get than that?

The thought depressed her. There was the main reason she couldn't let herself get too involved with Nic. Besides the females flitting around him like pretty painted butterflies, his career put him in danger every time he went on duty. She couldn't bear the thought of caring about someone else who might die tragically.

Yet, Nic was here, there, everywhere. What was she supposed to do about that?

Rubbing the ache in her temples, she came to a decision. There was nothing she could do about having Nic Carano as a neighbor. She couldn't very well have him evicted. So, she would simply block out any knowledge of his profession and be a good neighbor, a friend, but nothing more. As long as she kept an emotional distance, she was safe.

She hoped.

By the time she and Alex arrived at Nic's apartment nearly an hour later, Cassidy felt better, at least enough to look forward to eating a real meal for a change. There was something about having a man cook for her that inspired a surge of energy.

When he spotted Nic, Alex went into his usual ecstatic bounces and squeals. Cassidy, in spite of her good intentions, couldn't really blame him, though she kept her reaction under better control.

"The lasagna smells incredible," she said, nose tilted as she sniffed the air.

"Mama's special recipe." He waved them inside with a loaf of Italian bread. "She learned it from her mama who immigrated from Sicily after the war."

"Not many guys can make lasagna." Going down on one knee, Cassidy settled Alex on the carpet next to the couch. From there she could see him no matter where she was in the combination living/dining room.

"All five of us kids cut our teeth in the family bakery. A Carano who can't cook would have to change his last name."

"Where's my present?"

"Impatient woman." Shaking his head, he *tsk-tsked.* "Later, gator. If I give it to you now, you might run off."

With a smile acknowledging the humor, Cassidy quickly and, she hoped, surreptitiously surveyed the room in search of a smoke detector. The apartment layout was similar to hers, so escape routes would be the same. Reassured, Cassidy pushed up from Alex's side.

"I brought one for you." She offered Nic a small potted plant from her collection.

He looked at it as if it were the mystery meat in the school cafeteria. "What's this?"

"A plant, you goob."

"I figured out that part. I mean, why?"

"A housewarming gift. It will oxygenate your apartment."

"Oxygen is good." His head bobbed a couple of times. "Will you come over and water it for me?"

She ignored the question. "This is a Venus fly trap. His name is Michelangelo. He eats flies."

"No kidding? Real flies?" When she nodded, he considered the greenery with new respect. "Awesome. No sprays or swatters. And *zap,* dead fly. How sweet is that?"

"I thought a guy would appreciate the dead fly part." She took the plant away from him and glanced around for a place to set it. Boxes and clothes and a variety of odds and ends lay scattered about the place. Cassidy maneuvered around the biggest piles to plop

Michelangelo in the middle of a very cluttered table. "Can I do something to help with dinner?"

"Everything is under control. Grab a glass of soda or whatever you want from the fridge and relax. Check out my mood bowl." He indicated an ordinary-looking white bowl on the counter. "Maybe you can tell me what to do with it."

"Mood bowl?" She studied the bowl, pretending to be serious. "Is it designed to determine mood or set the mood?"

"You got me. But I think it works. I've been in a good mood ever since you arrived."

Cassidy pulled a silly face, "Ha-ha. Cute."

Looking amazingly proficient in the kitchen, Nic responded with his usual cocky grin. Before she'd arrived, he'd tied a dish towel around his waist which did nothing to detract from his masculine good looks. Now, he slid a white quilted oven mitt onto one hand—a replica of the Arby's restaurant mascot, complete with a printed-on face. Cassidy smiled. Now that was the Nic she remembered.

Taking a can of diet soda from the fridge, she held up another. "Want one?"

"Sure. Not the diet stuff, though. I bought that for you."

She blinked. "How did you know?"

"I'm observant. You had a can in the cup holder of your car."

"Impressive."

He pulled a beautiful dish of lasagna from the oven.

The smell of oregano and spices was strong enough to make Cassidy's stomach leap with excitement.

"I haven't had a home-cooked meal in—" she paused, not wanting to go there. Her last home-cooked meal had been made by Janna. "—a long time."

"You should have come to the cookout at my folks'. Lots of great homemade stuff."

Without being asked, she found the box containing dishes, took out a couple of place settings and scooted an array of odds and ends to one end of the table. Finding no napkins, she opted for paper towels, a roll of which lay on top of a box. Not exactly up to Grandmother's formal style, but pleasant and functional.

"Sit." Nic surprised her by politely pulling out a chair and waiting until she'd obeyed.

"Alex—" she started.

"Alex is fine where he is. I've got my eye on him. Stop worrying."

Sure enough, the baby lay on the blanket where she'd placed him, pushing up with his chubby arms to watch the adults with interest. From somewhere two colorful toys had appeared. Had Nic put those there?

"I could help get the food on the table." But her back ached from lugging Alex around, and it felt wonderful to sit and do nothing for a few minutes.

"Nope. You're my guest. I can't impress you if I don't do it all myself."

So she watched with interest as the ever-surprising Nic efficiently prepared dinner, casting frequent glances at Alex, and kept up a running conversation about her job, their mutual friends in college and his family.

"Tell me," Nic said as he sat down at her elbow— the only other clear spot on the table—and pushed the food in her direction. "Is Alex sleeping better at night? Or maybe I should ask if you're sleeping better?"

She took a hearty helping of the steaming lasagna. "A little. We're starting to adjust."

"I hear a 'but' in that sentence."

"It's hard, Nic," she admitted, aware of how easily she could talk to this man. "I never realized how much work being a mother is."

"You're also holding down a full-time job."

"True. But if I don't pick up the pace at work I won't have a job at all, much less advance in my career."

"Is the problem serious?"

"Frighteningly so. I missed an important deadline with a client."

"Not the end of the world."

"It wouldn't be if other things weren't going wrong and falling behind."

"Anything I can do to help?"

What an interesting question. She shook her head. "I appreciate the offer, but I'm on my own."

Nic snagged a chunk of the fresh bread he'd brought from his family's bakery and slathered it with real butter. "Yeah, about that. Would I be prying to ask what happened to your parents?"

Over the years, she'd encountered the question dozens of times. She never let herself think deeper than the surface.

With little emotion, she swallowed a bite of cheesy lasagna and said, "They died when I was ten and Janna was seven."

"Wow, bad deal. So that's how you came to live with Cruella de Vil?"

"Nic," she tried to scold, but her lips quivered with humor. "Grandmother did her best. She just isn't that good with children."

"Or puppies." His eyes danced. "Sorry."

"No, you aren't."

"Well, no. I'm not. So, what happened? To your parents, I mean. Car accident?"

Cassidy fiddled with the salad on her plate. Most people let the topic drop when she did. Not Nic. He had to pry. "They were missionaries teaching in a Christian school in the Philippines. There was an earthquake. The building collapsed."

The buttery bread paused halfway to his lips. "Oh man. Cass."

The sympathy in his dark eyes got to her in a hurry. A trembling started way down in her bones and the flood tide of emotion rumbled like a threatening volcano.

Cassidy licked her suddenly dry lips. "I haven't talked about this in a long time."

No one knew of the terror she'd sublimated in childhood, scolded by her grandmother, called a baby for being afraid in the dark. Thank God Janna had been spared and had never really known what Cassidy had gone through. She'd been in the States, quarantined with chicken pox.

Nic chewed and swallowed. "You don't have to tell me if you don't want to."

Did she? She wasn't sure. She stabbed a piece of lettuce, swirled it around in the Italian dressing. In the far recesses of her mind, the dying cries for help stirred to life. A shiver of dread threaded down her spine.

Nic remained silent but she felt his gaze on her, steady, patient and compassionate.

"I survived," she murmured, plain and simple, almost hard. "They didn't."

Nic carefully laid aside his fork. "You were with them then?"

"In the same building. They were on the bottom floor. I wasn't." The lasagna began to lose its flavor. She didn't know why she'd started talking about this. She pressed a hand to her stomach.

Chair legs scraped loudly against the tile as Nic moved his chair closer to hers. "Hey."

With a touch gentle enough for Alex, he smoothed a hand over her head, letting it rest on the ends of her hair. His empathy throbbed between them, both surprising and welcome.

"You were alone in a collapsed building? How long? What happened?"

Throat tight, she swallowed. "About two days. In the dark. Under bricks and rubble."

The implication pulsed in the room, broken only by the sound of Alex's movements.

Now that she'd begun, she needed Nic to know. Maybe then he'd understand her fear and leave her alone. Maybe she could scare him away.

More than that, she needed to talk about the unspeakable. No one, not one person had ever listened all the way through.

"I couldn't see or move," she said, in a voice that sounded oddly detached. "But I could hear things falling and shifting, and I could hear the cries and moans."

"Others in the building?"

She nodded. The light pressure of Nic's fingers against her hair encouraged her. He listened with such intensity, she could almost believe he cared.

"After a while, the sounds faded away." She'd known somehow in her ten-year-old mind that the people around her were dead. Terrified, she'd called for her parents. They never answered.

"You had to be scared." He stroked her hair again. "So scared."

"I was. The smoke was the worst. I could smell it growing thicker and thicker but I could never see any flames. I kept thinking I would be burned alive with no means of escape. Later I discovered the fires had been far away in another section of the city. Wind had carried the smell everywhere."

But the scent of smoke stayed with her, a haunting kind of torture made worse by the loss of her sister.

"How did you get out?"

"Rescue workers heard me crying. I was transported back to the States. My parents were found later, but Grandmother never shared the details." For years she'd harbored the fantasy that her parents had survived and would be coming for her.

"First your parents and now your sister," Nic murmured softly. "No wonder you're overprotective of Alex."

"Everyone I love dies, Nic." She turned her face, saw her pain reflected in Nic's dark eyes. "I don't understand why I'm still here and they're all gone."

She hadn't meant to say the words, but they were true. Why had God spared her but taken everyone else?

"Not everyone, Cass." Nic gestured toward Alex who had rolled onto his back and was happily exploring his upraised feet. "Maybe you're here to raise that little boy the way your parents and your sister would have wanted."

"That's the only thing I can think of. But his own parents would have done a better job than I'm doing."

"Don't sell yourself short." He leaned closer. Cassidy's pulse ratcheted up a notch. Nic had the softest eyes. She swallowed, suddenly nervous about the expression she saw in those espresso depths. Before she could think of a reason to move away, Nic reached out and brushed back a loose strand of her hair. His fingers grazed her cheek, a rough-gentle touch that raised goose bumps.

"I think," he said, "that you are one strong, amazing woman and Alex is a lucky little boy to have you in his corner."

At the gentle words, tears formed, threatening to spill over. She didn't need this. Couldn't bear to let go in front of Nic.

She used the mention of Alex as an excuse to escape the throbbing emotion.

"The baby," she said lamely.

Before Nic could assure her that Alex was fine, she pushed away from the table, breaking contact with Nic's eyes and fingertips. As she reached for her sister's baby, Cassidy suffered from an uncomfortable truth. Maintaining an emotional distance from her new neighbor might not be as easy as she'd hoped.

Chapter Eight

Study. He had to study.

Nic kicked back in the brown leather recliner commandeered from his brother Adam's overcrowded apartment and propped an enormous medical tome on his chest. A double jolt of java waited at his elbow for those times when he went cross-eyed.

Moving out on his own was going well so far. The apartment looked pretty good with its hodgepodge of furnishings donated by family and friends, all of whom dropped by on a regular basis. Too regular for a guy who wanted to secretly cram for his medical school entrance exam.

Today, everyone assumed he was out of town. He hadn't exactly lied to anyone, but he'd hinted at a rock-climbing expedition with a couple of his firefighter buddies. Anything to get some peace and quiet so he could study. Grateful, he bowed his head to the book.

He read two pages about synapses and ganglions

before his mind wandered to Cassidy. She occupied his thoughts way too much lately.

She'd gotten to him the other night when she'd told him about her parents. He had thought his heart would rip right through his T-shirt when she'd talked about being buried alive. As a firefighter, one of the worst fears and the most planned for scenarios was the danger of collapsing buildings. But he'd never lived through it. She had. Worse yet, she'd been a child, alone and scared and trapped.

He hadn't been blowing smoke when he'd told her she was amazing. Her faith amazed him, too. He'd heard people with far less heartache rage against God for their troubles. Cassidy had never done that. She'd questioned, but she'd stood strong.

Watching Cassidy over the past few weeks had got him to thinking about his own relationship with God. It wasn't that he didn't believe. He did. But his brothers claimed he was riding on his parents' prayers instead of his own. He didn't know about all that but it was food for thought.

He sighed and dragged a hand down his face.

How was he supposed to study when the orange blossom smell of Cassidy's hair, the silky texture of it beneath his fingers, kept intruding?

The woman didn't even like him.

He'd wanted to comfort her, had been sorely tempted to kiss her, but she'd bolted like a startled deer.

After all she'd told him, one thing stuck in his peanut brain like a thorn, and he'd turned it over and over inside his head. While she was trapped, she'd smelled smoke and feared burning alive. Then a house fire had taken her sister. He'd also noticed a smoke detector in every room in her apartment.

Could Cassidy be fire-phobic? Was this why she jumped every time he got close?

Nah. The notion didn't make sense. He didn't cause fires. He prevented them, put them out. She should feel safe with him, not threatened.

Firefighters were the good guys. That's why he loved his job.

The medical book grew heavy in his hands. He stared down at it. Yeah, well, he loved being a firefighter, but he'd love being a doctor, too. Time to get serious.

He started reading again, revisiting scientific principles, absorbing as fast and as much as he could. When brain overload threatened, he paused to ponder all he'd studied and to sip the cold, stout coffee.

Contrary to popular belief, his IQ was greater than his shoe size. Some folks would be shocked to know that.

He chuckled and rotated his neck left and right, listening to the crackles. Without giving it much thought he cataloged the anatomy of a neck ache. The upper portion of the trapezius as well as the levator scapula had stiffened to create tension, thereby contracting against cervical vertebra one through four.

Movement past his front window caught his attention. He turned his head, grimacing at the stiffness, and then sat up straight. The recliner emitted a metallic pop. His feet hit the wood floor with a thud.

Was that Cassidy?

He jogged to the door and yanked it open. Sure enough, his gorgeous neighbor was journeying down the sidewalk pushing a familiar navy-blue stroller complete with an alert, bright-eyed baby. Nic's mood elevated and he hadn't even looked at the white mood bowl.

"Hey, lady."

She turned toward him, the movement catching the light in her sun-drenched hair. She was dressed in running clothes, complete with classy sunglasses and a bright-blue headband.

He didn't know a single woman who compared with her. Or at least with the way he felt around her. The rest were friends, contrary to another popular myth. Friends with Cassidy was a start, but there was something else going on there, too.

Nic got a funny feeling beneath his rib cage. He must have fried his brain on the books.

Cassidy pushed the shades up on top of her head, a classy, movie-star action. "Nic, I thought you were gone for the weekend."

She was paying better attention than he'd suspected. Nice.

He struck a casual pose, leaning on the edge of his open front door. "Changed my mind. I had some study—" Nic caught himself in time. "—stuff to do."

He wasn't ready to admit his med-school failings to a woman he wanted to impress.

The thought startled him, but once it had taken form

he realized it was true. Weird. He'd have to figure that one out later.

"Oh," she said. "You're busy. I guess I shouldn't keep you then."

Was that disappointment lurking behind that beautiful smile?

He pushed off the door and sauntered outside. The bright May morning drew him almost as much as the woman and child. "Where are you headed?"

"For a run. This stroller has worked out great." She patted the shiny metal handle. "Did I say thank you for thinking of this?"

The jogging stroller had been a brilliant idea, even if he *had* thought of it himself. His sister-in-law owned one and he'd known it was the answer for Cassidy's need to run and still be with Alex. He'd given the gift the other night when she'd told him about her parents, a stroke of genius that had broken the bizarre tension between them.

"About a dozen times, but guys like gratitude. Go ahead and thank me again."

She bent to adjust the awning over Alex's face, but not before Nic saw the gleam of humor. He crouched next to the baby to say hello. Alex flopped both arms and grinned.

"Things must be going better with Alex," he said.

He wanted to ask about the other night, to make certain he hadn't crossed some invisible line, but he didn't. Not yet. Sooner or later, he'd bring up the topic again. If she'd developed a phobia of fire, he wanted to know.

"We're getting there. Slowly." She grimaced but there was humor behind it. "Very slowly."

He squinted up at her. "The fact that you have enough energy to run again must mean something."

"True. Your mom reminded me that exercise energizes. And that I have to take care of myself in order to take care of Alex." When he frowned, confused by her mention of his mother, Cassidy went on. "Didn't she tell you I've called her a few times?"

"No." And he felt a tad annoyed that she hadn't. But then, he hadn't been hanging around the home place as often lately, either.

"Your mother has truly been an answer to my prayers. I've never met anyone quite like her. She even prayed with me on the phone one day when I was in a panic over a rash on Alex's bottom." She bit her bottom lip and looked away. "You're blessed to have a mother like her."

Nic thought of the times around the kitchen table when both his parents had counseled and prayed with him about some problem or another. Now he understood how fortunate he'd been. Cassidy hadn't had that.

"Family can be a pain, but yeah, they're a blessing, too."

"She invited me to have dinner with your family tomorrow after church."

Nic perked up. Sunday dinner with the fam was sounding good. "Are you coming?"

Her mouth tilted at the corners. "I said yes."

"I think I'm offended," he said lightly, though truth

lurked behind the words. "You wouldn't go when *I* invited you."

"Your mother has helped me a lot. She's a wise woman."

He turned both index fingers to point at himself. "And I, her son, am a wise guy."

As he'd intended, Cassidy laughed. She bumped his foot with the toe of her shoe. "Are you ever serious?"

He thought of the MCAT book waiting inside.

"You would be surprised." He chucked Alex under the chin and rose to a stand. "Mind having some company on your jog?"

"I thought you had stuff to do."

"Stuff that can wait." He'd been up until two that morning cramming. A break was overdue. "We don't get many perfect days like this."

She glanced out at the street where cars sailed by, their metallic paint reflecting the bright sun. "Well…"

There she went again, throwing up barriers.

"Never mind. I don't want to intrude." He backed off and turned away, disappointed but annoyed, too. If she didn't want him around, fine. He wasn't exactly lonely.

"Nic." Her voice hesitated, uncertain.

He glanced over one shoulder, head tilted in question. It was her call.

She blinked twice and then smiled. "Got any running shoes?"

A grin started down in his belly, rose in his chest and landed on his face. He held up two fingers. "Two minutes."

Without analyzing the pure rush of pleasure, Nic hurried inside, donned running shoes and a Yankees cap and was back on the sidewalk in less than the allotted pair of minutes.

"Let's roll," he said and then laughed, looking at the stroller. Cassidy laughed, too. "No pun intended. Are we headed to Pride Park?"

"Yes." A block from the apartment was a park with a circular running track around the play area. They started in that direction. He crowded her out of the way and took over the stroller. The wheels clattered against the concrete walk. The baby's head bobbed and jostled, his eyes drooping with the rhythm.

"How are things at work? Catching up yet?"

"I wish." She didn't elaborate, a bad sign, he figured. Instead, she asked, "Why aren't you out with your friends this weekend?"

He looked at Alex and then at her, the grin in his belly still in full bloom. "I am."

Weird, but true. He was right where he wanted to be.

Cassidy got butterflies in her stomach when Nic said things like that. She knew he was teasing. He was always teasing. Notorious Nic's idea of fun could not be a stressed-out neighbor and her sometimes cranky nephew. From the gaggle of girls, and if she was fair, an equal group of guys, who had roamed in and out of Nic's apartment since he'd moved in, Cassidy was certain he could find better entertainment.

"My grandmother called again this morning," she said as they waited at the corner for the light to change.

"Sorry to hear that." A red sports car roared past, going far too fast. Nic braced an arm in front of her and scowled at the disappearing Camaro. "Dude. Slow down." To her he said, "Grandma still pressuring you?"

Cassidy wrinkled her nose at him. "Sometimes I wonder if she's right, if I'm cheating Alex out of a real family."

Easily pushing Alex's stroller with one hand, Nic took her elbow in the other and guided them across the busy street. "Don't do that. Don't sell yourself short."

"I want what's best for him."

"That would be you. *You* are a real family. Small but mighty."

She was starting to believe him.

After they stepped up on the curb, Nic dropped his hold. She realized then how protected and safe she'd felt for those few seconds. Notorious Nic was working his amazing charm on her and she couldn't seem to stop reacting to him.

She didn't understand the reaction, either. She had friends and a busy life. She didn't need Nic's attention.

After the other night when she'd told him things she'd never told anyone, he had been in her thoughts constantly. On the days he didn't bounce up to her apartment with some silly quip or tale of wild adventure or jokingly asking to borrow a cup of sugar, she missed him.

Dumb. Real dumb.

At times like this, she could forget he was a firefighter. Almost.

An hour later they returned to the apartment complex, drenched in sweat and laughing. Cassidy had never enjoyed a run in quite this manner. She'd raced Nic, beating him in a short sprint, though he'd cried foul, claiming the wheels on Alex's stroller gave her an unfair advantage. She'd laughed so hard, she'd had to sit down on the track, arms over upraised knees to get her breath. No doubt, he could have smoked her if he'd wanted to. The man was in amazing physical condition.

Nic had jogged forward, backward, sideways and around her in ever narrowing circles until he'd collapsed on the blacktop surface next to her, panting, the grin on his handsome face causing her exercise-pumped pulse to skitter. No wonder he could have any girl he wanted. Besides being darkly handsome, Nic was a ton of fun. She was working harder than ever to also remember that he had about as much substance as a dandelion puff. Somewhere along the line he'd put a dent in that strongly held opinion.

Dangerous. Very dangerous to be thinking of Nic as a solid man with deep feelings and beliefs. He was a Christian. She'd gotten that much out of him during one of their late-night talks when Alex wouldn't sleep, she couldn't and Nic had chosen not to. Like most things, though, he didn't take his faith as seriously as she did.

"Come on in," he said when they reached his apartment door. "I have bottled water in the fridge."

"My kingdom for your water," she joked.

Nic lifted the stroller over the threshold and led the way. Once inside, he extracted Alex and sat him on the floor. "Is he okay here?"

Cassidy reached inside a pouch on the back of the stroller, took out several toys and placed them in front of the baby. "He is now."

"Make yourself comfortable. I'll grab that water."

She moved around the room, taking in the changes, hearing the suction of the refrigerator door and the clatter as Nic moved around.

"Everything looks different. I'm impressed."

A beige couch, a deep-maroon leather chair and a couple of occasional tables were set up around an interesting area rug in shades of beige, maroon and navy. All the boxes and stacks of household goods and clothes were gone.

"Did your girlfriends put everything away?"

"Friends who are girls. Let's get that part cleared up." He came around the recliner to hand her a bottle of cold water. "But no. I did everything myself."

"Even the wall hangings?" A clever assortment of photographs from Nic's various adventures had been grouped along one wall. The opposite wall held some sort of graphic design in colors that blended with the hodgepodge of furnishings. Her artistic eye found the choices intriguing.

She uncapped the bottle and took a long drink, letting the cold chill the back of her throat. Condensation frosted the plastic and dampened her hand.

Taking his own bottle of water, Nic dropped onto the sofa. "Painted the design, too. Saw it on HGTV, but don't tell anyone." He patted the couch. "Sit. Cool down."

"What's the deal? Real men don't watch design shows."

"Right."

Amused, Cassidy sat, curling one foot beneath her. "Your secret is safe with me."

As she leaned her head back against the microfiber sofa and relaxed, a large, thick book that looked for all the world like serious study caught her attention. Curious, she leaned to pick up the text. It weighed a ton.

She read the title. "MCAT? Nic, what is this?"

Nic gulped half his bottle of water and then dragged the back of his hand across his mouth. His fingers froze in place as he realized what she was looking at.

"Pay no attention to that man behind the curtain," he said in a silly Oz-like voice.

"Nic, be serious." She hoisted the heavy textbook. "Is this yours?"

With a shrug, he tried to laugh it off. "Found it laying around. Thought I'd see if I could learn some big words to impress the girls."

"You're studying to take medical school entrance exams," she said in stunned wonder.

The completely incongruous concept ping-ponged around inside her head. Nic Carano studying to be a doctor? Notorious Nic? This was crazy.

"Nic? You are, aren't you?"

Nic responded by rubbing his temples and then dragging both hands over his face, which was now somber. "Promise me you'll keep this to yourself."

"Why? Nic, this is awesome, amazing."

"And surprising?"

"Well, yes, that, too. You don't exactly present yourself as the serious student type."

"Which is why I'd like to keep this between us, if you don't mind."

"No one else knows?"

He shook his head. "No one."

"Not even your family?" They were so close. Surely he'd told them.

"*Especially* my family."

She placed her half-empty bottle onto the coffee table and wiped a moist hand over her shorts. "I don't get it. Your family would be thrilled."

"That's the point. They'd be thrilled to know their baby boy, the son with mostly air in his head, was finally trying to make something of himself like the other kids have."

"Okaaay, forgive me, but I'm still not getting it." She leaned toward him. "Why wouldn't you want to share that with them?"

"I do. I want that more than I can tell you. When the time is right." He sucked in a lungful of air and blew it out slowly through pursed lips. "This won't be the first time I've taken the test." His eyebrows rose and fell in a wry facial shrug. "Or the second."

Understanding dawned. "Now I get it. You're afraid of failing again. Of letting them down."

"Bingo."

Nic looked so shaken by his admission that Cassidy couldn't help herself. She scooted closer and placed a hand atop his.

"How close were you to passing?"

Nic gazed down at where their hands touched, turned his palm up and laced his fingers with hers. The motion felt right.

Now Cassidy was the shaken one.

"Real close. I'm taking an online review class this time, plus the book study. Unless I'm a complete idiot I should do okay. But I can't just pass. I need good scores to get into the state programs."

This was a new side of Nic. Anyway, it was a side of him she'd tried not to see before. Now she realized the serious Nic had been there all along. This was the man, after all, who'd pulled Alex from a burning building, the man who'd sat by a strange baby's bed until a relative had arrived. A man who'd cheerfully rounded up baby furniture and clothes for a complete stranger.

"Your T-shirt lies," she said gently, still stunned by the wrenching paradigm shift. Her carefully held opinions of Notorious Nic, fueled by his self-deprecations were tumbling like stacked dominoes.

Puzzled, Nic's eyebrows came together before he dipped his chin and read the slogan on his shirt. "I took an IQ test. The results were negative."

With his usual humor, his lips twitched. "That remains to be seen."

Cassidy squeezed his fingers, felt him squeeze back. Funny how something as simple as holding hands could suddenly take on new meaning. She'd taken his hand to comfort him, as he'd comforted her that awful morning at the hospital and again the other night. Now that he'd let her past his facade of fun and games for a look into the complete Nic Carano, Cassidy had to face an unwanted truth.

She swallowed hard, her heart thudding in her throat at the stunning revelations going on inside her. Nic Carano was not only a lot of fun to be with, he was a much deeper guy than anyone suspected.

Trouble was, she didn't want him to be deep and complex. Even though he might aspire to medical school, there was no guarantee he would make it. No guarantee he would trade a life-threatening job for a life-saving one. Worse yet, his entourage of girls called or texted him constantly.

She didn't need any of this in her already tumultuous life.

He squeezed her fingers again and smiled. Cassidy suffered a sinking sensation strong enough to leave a hole the size of the Grand Canyon.

She liked Nic Carano…far more than was prudent.

Chapter Nine

The man was full of surprises.

On Sunday morning when Nic had shown up at her door dressed in a pale-yellow shirt and crisp navy slacks offering to drive her to church, Cassidy had nearly choked on her breakfast bar. All through the service, she was aware of him sitting too close, aware of the fresh scent of shower, shampoo and masculine warmth, aware of the timbre of his voice lifted in song.

Lord, forgive her. As hard as she fought it, he was definitely a distraction.

Now, here they were in the ample backyard of his family's home where she had received the most shocking surprise yet.

On arrival, Nic had introduced her to his family, some of whom she'd met. Altogether Nic had two sisters, Anna Marie and Mia, plus two brothers, Gabe and Adam. All except Adam were married with families, so an abundance of children ran around the backyard. She hadn't yet matched the children with their parents because every adult seemed equally interested in every child. A toddler boy with curly dark hair clung to Nic's leg. A little girl with the face of an angel sat atop Adam's broad shoulders, thrashing his back with a long weed and yelling, "Giddyap, horsie."

Several small ones ran in, out and between lawn chairs in a squealing game of freeze tag, while a couple of teenagers worked on a dilapidated go-cart turned upside down in the far corner of the yard. Occasionally, one of them called for help and one of the brothers or their father, Leo, jogged over for a consultation.

Mia's husband, Collin, along with Leo and a slim young man named Mitch, manned the grill where the scent of hamburgers sizzled in the air. The Carano brothers drifted past a few times to add friendly advice and insults before drifting off to other pursuits.

The ease with which Rosalie and Leo related to their children and grandchildren fascinated Cassidy. She'd never been this easy with her grandmother. No one seemed overly concerned about soiled clothes or too much noise. In fact, noise seemed to be the common denominator among the Caranos. Everyone talked at once, gesturing with expressive hands. Laughter punctuated the conversations like exclamation points. Somewhere a radio belted out contemporary music.

Nic played yard darts with a half dozen other people but occasionally wandered over to where Cassidy stood talking with Rosalie and Mia as they prepared a table full of food "for the masses," as Rosalie put it.

Once, Nic draped an arm over his mother's shoulder and kissed her cheek. In return, she patted his, the mother–son love a visible, lovely thing. Emotion surged inside Cassidy. Though she'd been young when her mother died, at times like these Cassidy remembered the feeling of being loved unconditionally. The longing for a warm, loving family of her own almost choked her.

"You taking good care of my neighbor?" Nic asked, eyeing both his mom and sister. This afternoon his bright red T-shirt proclaimed, "I'd give my right arm to be ambidextrous."

Mia, whose full, wide mouth seemed to either be smiling or talking all the time, said, "We're telling her about your naughty childhood."

Nic drew back in pretend horror. "She'll have me evicted."

The full mouth laughed. "Remember what the Bible says. 'Be sure your sins will find you out.'"

"I," he declared dramatically, slapping one hand against his chest, "am a dead man."

With a teasing wink at Cassidy, he snitched a strawberry from the fruit plate Mia was arranging. She slapped his fingers. He drew back with a laugh. "Mom, Mia hit me."

Rosalie handed him another strawberry and shooed him back to his game.

"See what I have to put up with," she said, fondly gazing after her baby boy. "He likes you a lot, I'm thinking, Cassidy."

Her stomach dipped. "Nic likes all the girls."

"Mmm. Or maybe *they* like *him*. You may be surprised to know he's never been serious with anyone."

Actually, she was surprised, but she said, "Nic is rarely serious."

As soon as she said the words, she realized they were neither fair nor entirely true. They were the stereotypical Nic, not the real one. Sure, Nic knew how to have a good time and he could be wild and crazy, but she'd met the real man beneath the flash and dash.

The notion that Notorious Nic had never had a serious relationship was...interesting, to say the least.

"He went to church with you today," Mia said. "Do you know how long it's been since he's done that?"

Cassidy shook her head, remembering how distracted she'd been by the handsome man seated next to her. "He doesn't go with you?"

"Not in a while. He claims his job interferes, and I'm sure it does. But Nic has drifted." Rosalie's dark doe eyes saddened. "It breaks my heart to see one of my children ambivalent about the Lord."

It bothered Cassidy, too, but she got the idea Nic was searching to find his own way instead of leaning on his parents' faith. She couldn't fault him for that.

"Did you know," Rosalie went on, "that you are the first girl he's ever brought to a family gathering?"

Cassidy nearly dropped the tomato she was slicing. "You can't mean that."

"On my family's honor." Rosalie touched her heart.

Mia grinned at Cassidy. "The look on your face is priceless."

"I—" Cassidy blinked rapidly, trying to make some sense of the revelation. "I'm not sure what that means."

Rosalie patted her shoulder. "It means, dear child,

that my wayward boy has feelings for you. I've been praying for a beautiful Christian woman to come along and give him a reason to settle down."

Cassidy managed a shaky laugh. Rosalie had no idea how impossible a relationship between her and Nic was. "Nic is attached to Alex. Not me."

Rosalie slid a spoon into a bowl of sliced melon, dark eyebrows drawing together in question. "You don't like my Nic?"

"Well, yes, of course I do. He's great." *He's funny and warm and generous. He's even changing diapers now.*

Oh dear.

The man in question jogged toward her. Cassidy's pulse danced a jitterbug, an effect she blamed on Rosalie's insinuations.

He reached out and snagged her hand. "Come on, Cass. I'm getting cremated in this game. I need a partner."

As his strong, firefighter's fingers wrapped around hers, the word *partner* took on an entirely new meaning.

"What do you think of this one?"

A few days later, Cassidy still had Nic Carano on the brain, but tonight she was trying to concentrate on the teen group gathered at her place.

Cassidy spun sideways in her rolling desk chair to look at the freckled teenager. Angie leaned over the computer to peruse the design Cassidy had created for her MySpace page.

"I love it. You're good at this, Cassidy."

With a laugh Cassidy said, "Considering this is my bread and butter, I'd better be."

She didn't add the bitter truth that her career had taken a turn for the worse lately. No use worrying her Bible study girls. Regardless of her boss's expectations, Cassidy had come to the conclusion that she wanted a life outside her career. If that meant cutting back, she'd have to do it. Alex was her life now. Her career was not. Unfortunately, Shane Tomlinson was not at all happy to hear of her newfound dedication.

Angie, purple highlights in her hair shining under the light, twisted toward the six other girls lounging around the kitchen table. "Come look at the cool page Cassidy created for me."

Cassidy listened to the oohs and ahhs of the teens. Tonight was the first time in the more than a month since her sister's death that she'd resumed the weekly Bible study with the girls from her church. In truth, the meeting was more of a Christian mentoring group than anything, though she always presented a short, relevant lesson from scripture. By spending quality time listening to the girls, she'd been delighted to watch them grow as Christians.

In the process, she'd grown herself. Though she still questioned the losses, she'd felt the love and compassion and peace of God surrounding her with such sweetness. And He'd sent people into her life—people like the Caranos—when she'd needed them the most.

The Caranos. Once more, her mind drifted to last Sunday and the pleasant afternoon she'd spent with

Nic and his big Italian-American family. They were the kind of family she and Janna had longed for all their lives. The kind of family she wanted to give to Alex but couldn't.

Her gaze went to the baby happily being passed from one girl to the next. Alex babbled something in her direction. Love bubbled up inside Cassidy. She'd been busy and active before he came along, but Alex had added a new, unexpected element of joy. As difficult as the adjustment was, she couldn't imagine her life without him now.

"It's so cool of you to do this for us," one of the other girls said, breaking her train of thought. "Will you change mine next week?"

"Sure, if we have time."

Cassidy had never told them, but she designed their online pages not only for their enjoyment, but as a means to monitor what was going on in their lives. Over the past year, she'd been able to head off some trouble areas for a couple of the girls and to talk to them about inappropriate visitors to their pages.

"Someone's coming up the stairs." Angie started toward the door. "Maybe it's Melissa."

Cassidy, too, was concerned about the absent Melissa. According to evidence on her MySpace page, Melissa was hanging around with a questionable crowd.

"How can you hear footsteps with all this chatter going on?" she asked.

Almost before Cassidy finished the question, Angie opened the door and Nic breezed inside.

"Whoa," he said, skidding to a stop. "Is this a party?" He smiled, accenting the dimple in his chin. "And why wasn't I invited?"

Seven teenagers giggled, turning wide-eyed, speculative gazes on Cassidy. The heat of a blush climbed up the back of her neck.

That day at the cookout, Rosalie and Mia had put the craziest thoughts in her head. Thoughts that hammered away at her, threatening to undermine her resolve to remain emotionally distant from a guy with two strikes against him.

Nic didn't help matters in the least. The fact that he was a firefighter was offset by his application to med school. If he got accepted, he would no longer be a fireman and, therefore, no longer be in imminent danger. She could actually date him without fear.

As soon as the thought arrived, she cast it down, aghast. Fireman or not, he would still be Notorious Nic.

Or would he?

To make matters more unsettling, their relationship had changed dramatically since she'd discovered his fear of failure and the secret longing to please his family. Who would have thought Nic Carano, the man who faced raging fires, zip-lined in Mexico and had once ridden a Brahma bull, would be afraid of anything? The notion tugged at her heart.

So much so that she'd even spent several hours this week sitting at his kitchen table, drilling him on terms she could barely pronounce. Behind the smoke and mirrors, Nic was a very bright man.

Add to that the innuendos from his family and Cassidy was one confused *chica*.

"Nic," she said, a little too breathlessly, a little too happy to see him considering they'd jogged together yesterday. "I thought you were on duty tonight."

"Excuses, excuses. I traded shifts with a buddy who needs off tomorrow. His wife is scheduled to have a baby." Without missing a beat, he dazzled the girls with a wink and another smile as he whisked Alex into his arms. Holding the baby at arm's length, he wiggled the chubby body back and forth saying, "Hey partner, what's shakin'?"

Mouth wide with pleasure, Alex drooled. Cassidy rose, grabbed a tissue and swiped.

"You're getting good at this." Nic beamed at her.

Foolishly, she beamed back. "You know what they say about practice."

"Too late. You were already perfect."

The hum of speculation around them grew louder.

In self-defense, Cassidy introduced Nic to each of the girls. They simpered and cast sideways glances at each other.

Fighting not to roll her eyes, Cassidy said to her neighborly intruder, "Did you need something, Nic? Or are you only passing by?"

They both laughed at the inside joke. Nic had started it when he wanted an excuse to come up for a visit, though the only reason to climb those particular stairs was to arrive at her apartment.

"Passing by, hoping to take you and Alex out for ice

cream." Alex grabbed hold of his ear. Nic paid him no mind. "I need to talk to you about something."

Cassidy studied Nic's face, trying to gauge what he was not saying. This was his serious side. She was beginning to recognize the difference. "Can I take a rain check on the ice cream and come down later to talk?"

"Works for me. I'm not going anywhere."

"No company?"

He grinned. "Only you."

A skitter of awareness danced through her, both happy and anxious. She grinned back, glad that Rachel and Mandy and Nic's usual gaggle of female company had been nowhere around for the last week.

She cocked a hip. "Got popcorn?"

"Theater butter, guaranteed to clog your arteries."

"EMT to the rescue?" What in the world was she doing? Flirting?

"CPR could be called for at any time." He pumped his eyebrows. His gaze dropped to her mouth. "I'm good with that."

She imagined he was. The thought of kissing Nic tingled every nerve ending in her body.

The ripple of giggles from the teenagers brought Cassidy back to reality. Goodness. Nic was causing her to lose her sense of decorum.

"Go away, Nic."

He chuckled knowingly, but handed Alex to the nearest teenager and backed toward the door. "See ya."

After the door closed behind him, Cassidy almost wilted into the carpet.

The teens attacked like a friendly school of sharks. A volley of mingled comments shot at her.

"Are you dating him? He's a hottie. Like a movie star or something. That dimple in his chin made my knees weak. Why didn't you tell us about him? Are you in love?"

"Girls, stop!" She held her hands against her hot cheeks, laughing but embarrassed, too. "Nic is my neighbor. My friend."

"Oh, right. That's why you went all dreamy-eyed when he walked in."

"Yeah, and did you see the way he looked at her?" Angie wiggled her fingers as though she'd touched something hot. "Ooh-la-la!"

"We know flirting when we see it."

Cassidy gave up and let them speculate.

How could she be expected to explain her feelings for Nic when she didn't understand them herself?

When the last of the teenagers left, Cassidy glanced at the sunburst clock above the couch. The hour was later than she'd expected and it was almost time to put Alex down for the night. A consistent routine, she'd discovered, made a world of difference. But she'd promised Nic.

"Want to go see Notorious Nic?" she said to Alex. The little dude, as Nic called him, bicycled his arms and legs with enthusiasm as if he understood.

With Alex against her shoulder she trotted down the steps to apartment seventeen. The door opened before she knocked.

"I saw the girls leave," he said by way of explanation.

"Thank goodness," she joked. "I was starting to think you could see through walls."

"Does this mean I've reached superhero status?" He leaned forward to nuzzle Alex under the chin. Having Nic this close brought back her wayward thoughts.

She ignored his question as a buzz of energy danced between them. Nic must have noticed, too. He lifted his face from Alex but didn't move away. Dark, dark eyes studied her. Serious eyes.

The jitters in her belly got worse.

"Where's my popcorn?" she managed, dismayed by the breathless sound of her voice.

Nic backed off, a funny quirk to his lips. "Coming right up. Grab a seat while I stick the bag in the nuker. You want a Coke?"

Cassidy kissed Alex on the forehead, laid him on the play mat that had recently appeared in Nic's apartment without explanation and followed Nic into the kitchen area. "Too late for caffeine. How about water?"

"Works for me, too." He motioned toward the fridge. "I'm on shift tomorrow. Gotta get up early."

"Tap water is fine. We'll save the bottles for running."

"We. I like the sound of that."

"Don't get cocky. I only let you come along to entertain Alex." She cast a quick glance at the baby. He was doing mini-push-ups and drooling on a terry-cloth fire truck.

The popcorn began to pop, the scent filling up the

apartment. Nic sniffed the air. "Man, I love that smell." When the microwave *pinged,* he removed the bag, holding it by the top with the tips of his fingers. "Hot, hot. Good thing there's a firefighter on the premises."

The comment cooled Cassidy's enthusiasm. She wished he wouldn't remind her of the primary reason why she shouldn't be here. He was on duty tomorrow. Anything could happen.

She found a glass bowl in the upper cabinet and held it out while he dumped the popcorn. "What did you need to talk to me about?"

Nic's hands paused on the now empty bag. "In a minute. Wait until we sit down."

A worse feeling crept over Cassidy.

Nic blew into the popcorn bag, twisted the top and slammed his hand against the bottom. *Pop!* Even though she'd seen it coming, Cassidy jumped.

She jabbed an index finger toward him. "If Alex starts crying, you've lost your superhero status."

Nic peered over at the child who seemed unfazed by the unexpected noise. "Superhero status, huh? So now you admit it."

"I admit nothing." Pretending haughtiness, she pitched a piece of popcorn into her mouth before going to the couch.

Nic settled close. Real close. Cassidy knew she should probably scoot away but she didn't want to. Not yet anyway.

"Alex is trying to sit up alone now," she said, more for something to fill the silence than to start a conversation about baby development.

"I noticed. It's kind of cute when he topples over."

She chuckled. "I know. It's like watching slow motion. One minute he's up, and then slowly, slowly he leans sideways."

"The leaning tower of Alex." Nic tossed a piece of popcorn into the air and caught it in his mouth.

Cassidy applauded, making fun. "A man of many talents."

He aimed at her. When she didn't open her mouth, he tossed anyway. The popcorn bounced off her chin.

They both laughed.

"Nic, this is fun, but I can't stay long. I need to get up early in the morning and try to get some work finished before I go to the office."

"Still behind?"

"Yes. And my boss is not a happy camper. He says I'm ruining my career."

"Are you?"

"I don't know. I love my work but it doesn't consume me like before. My mind is in a dozen places instead of totally focused on the job."

"Life isn't all about work."

The comment was something she would have expected from Nic before, but now she knew his goal and the efforts he'd taken to reach it. "Let's don't talk about this. Tell me why you wanted me to come down."

"All right." He pressed both palms against his thighs, shoulders arching before reaching for a piece of paper on the end table next to his medical guide. "Got this today."

"What is it?" She leaned forward and saw the words

fire marshal across the top. Dread pulled at her insides. She must have gasped because Nic snagged her gaze with his.

"You asked to see the report when it came in."

She nodded, unable to speak just yet. With each passing day the grief had settled more and more into a deep, abiding ache instead of screaming agony. Yet, not a day went by that she didn't remember the fire that had stolen her sister and Alex's parents.

"Are you okay?" Nic touched her cheek, brought her gaze back to his. "Can you handle this?"

She nodded again, not sure at all.

"Cass," he said softly, studying her face. "Is it the memory of your sister or the idea of fire in general that upsets you most?"

Her lips went dry. "Both."

"Talking about fire scares you, doesn't it?"

She shuddered, suddenly cold though the room temperature was pleasant. "Terrifies me."

Nic's fingers trailed down her arm to grasp her hand. "For a while I thought it was me, but now everything makes sense. The smoke alarms in every room of your apartment, even the way you've tried to push me away."

"I didn't try—" But she couldn't lie. Nic was an intelligent man. He'd known she wanted to avoid him. "The problem isn't you."

"It's my job, isn't it?" Nic loosened his grip on her hand and leaned forward, elbows on his thighs, to stare at Alex. A subtle shift in mood had occurred that Cassidy didn't understand.

"Firefighting is dangerous, Nic. I'm glad you'd rather be a doctor."

Normally any hint that she might be concerned about him would instigate a wisecrack about his ego or some other sassy Nic remark. This time he let the opportunity slide and instead made a funny little huffing sound.

In a distant voice, he said, "Yeah. Good thing."

Several seconds ticked past while Cassidy contemplated Nic's odd behavior. Alex flopped over on his back and gurgled, a reminder of the time. The baby needed to be in bed. So did she.

Though she had no great desire to hear the ugly details of her sister's death, she might as well get it over with. "Will you tell me about the report now?"

Nic's gaze flicked to her and then to the page in his hand. After a couple more seconds, he shook off the strange mood.

"The cause of the fire was pretty much what we thought. No arson or foul play. An electrical short. It started in the downstairs front bedroom."

Pain pierced Cassidy's heart. "Where Janna and Brad slept."

"Yes."

Cassidy closed her eyes, imagining the menacing flames that sucked the life from her only sibling. Her throat threatened to close. "No wonder they didn't have a chance."

"They didn't. That part's a mercy, Cassidy. As hard as it is to believe there could be good in this, that part is good. Toxic gas took them quickly."

The horror of such an insidious killer made her nauseous. Deadly fumes that sneaked up on her beautiful sister while she slept, dreaming happy dreams of her home and husband and baby.

"But why didn't the smoke detectors work?" she asked, tormented by that one thought. "I bought them myself. I helped Brad install them the day they moved in."

She'd tried so hard to keep her tiny family safe. Dear, accommodating Brad had thought she was overcautious and paranoid on the subject of fire, but he'd done the work on the spot to appease her.

"The one in Alex's room worked properly," Nic said. "I heard it myself. Someone had removed the battery from the one downstairs."

With a groan, Cassidy pressed a palm against her forehead. "Dear Lord, why? Why?"

But she knew why. Janna complained about the instrument's sensitivity. When she cooked certain foods, the alarm reacted.

"We'll never know for sure who disengaged the battery. Unfortunately, it's a common occurrence. We see it all the time. Let me tell you, finding a nonfunctioning smoke alarm makes a firefighter crazy."

"Me, too." That's why she had one in every room of her apartment and hanging over her desk at work. Brad and Janna had refused to be that "paranoid," they'd called it.

"Janna loved scented candles," she said, trying to piece together the truth that killed her sister. She shuddered. "I hate them. I begged her not to buy any at all, but she thought they were perfectly safe. She wouldn't burn one while I was there because she knew they upset me, but I know she used them. Vanilla," she said sadly. "The house always smelled of vanilla. Maybe one of them caused the alarm to sound so she took the battery out and forgot about it."

"Yeah, it's possible." Absently, Nic popped a knuckle. The sound was loud in the quiet room. "Whatever the reason, I'm sorry, Cass. For you, for Alex, for her. She was beautiful. Like you."

The sadness in Nic's remark shook her. She'd never considered that a tragic scene would also have affected him. She'd only considered how he reminded her of her sister's death. Not of how much he'd done, and how he'd tried to save her family.

"You carried her out," she murmured. "Oh, Nic. How awful for you."

His jaw tightened. He swallowed.

With mingled sorrow and gratitude, she touched his cheek. Their gazes collided.

"Hey," he said softly. "You're crying."

Cassidy hadn't realized she was, but now she felt the wetness rolling down her face. Unable to speak, she shook her head and tried to turn away. Nic would have none of it. He pulled her to him, pressed her cheek against the soft cotton of his silly T-shirt. His hand stroked the back of her hair, comforting.

"Cry if you need to, baby. You don't always have to be strong."

As if she'd needed permission, Cassidy let the tears come. Part of her wanted to feel foolish for the long overdue reaction to her sister's untimely death. Another part of her knew she needed this cleansing.

While Nic stroked her back and hair and murmured reassurances, she cried for her sister and Brad, for baby Alex's loss of his parents, for her own parents long dead.

When the siege ended, she remained in Nic's arms, reluctant to pull away. Funny how safe and comforted she felt in a fireman's strong, fit arms. No, not just any fireman's, but Nic's alone.

The thought was both scary and enticing.

Beneath her cheek, Nic's strong heart beat steady and sure. He smelled of cotton and popcorn and that special something that was Nic's alone. Something comforting and good.

"I'm okay now," she managed through a throat still clogged with emotion, the sound muffled against Nic's chest. She sniffed, a little embarrassed.

As she leaned back a tiny bit, Nic's hands slid around to cradle her face.

"Are you sure?" he asked, peering intently into her eyes.

She nodded shakily.

"Thank you," she whispered. "I needed that."

Nic's thumbs traced the tracks of her tears and stroked the corners of her mouth. Her lips tingled in response.

"You know what *I* need?" His voice was husky and warm.

Before she could venture a guess, he lowered his

face, his breath a feather-touch against her lips. She knew in that instance he was going to kiss her.

Cassidy tried to think of all the reasons why he shouldn't.

She tried…and failed.

Chapter Ten

Fire Engine One swung around the tight corner on the return to the station. The inside reeked with the smell of burned rubber. The fire at the tire manufacturing company had taken hours to subdue, and even now one engine company remained on the scene to kill hot spots.

Nic glanced across the seat to his buddy, Sam Ridge. What he saw brought a laugh. "Man, you should see your face."

Black soot smeared his high cheekbones and rimmed his mouth and eyes.

Ridge's mouth twisted. "Can't be as bad as yours."

The captain, seated in the front, swiveled. "None of you boys are winning any beauty contests. Not even your women will recognize you."

His friend harrumphed but said nothing. Nic knew what the captain didn't. Ridge didn't have a woman, although plenty of ladies noticed his native good looks and long, athletic form. Nic knew his friend had reasons for steering clear of the female population. His wounds ran deep.

As for Nic, his thoughts immediately went to Cassidy. She'd freak out if she smelled this smoke and fire all over him. He'd be sure to grab a shower and plenty of cologne before he jogged up the steps to bug her.

Cassidy. He smiled, aware that his teeth gleamed snow white against his sooty skin.

Last night, he'd kissed her. He'd thought of little else today to the point that his captain had commented on his quietness during the fire call. He, who usually jabbered and bounced around as hyper as a rat terrier, was struck dumb.

Nic wasn't sure what the big deal was. He'd kissed plenty of girls over the years, though if he admitted it, none in a while. Not since Cassidy and Alex began to occupy all his time as well as his thoughts. Kissing Cassidy was different, though. Not that he could put his finger on what that difference was.

Weird. He wasn't sure what was going on in his head or maybe in his heart, but one thing was for sure, he'd never felt this way about anyone else.

That fact made him a little nervous.

His cell phone ripped into his latest download, the creepy movie theme from *Jaws*. The sound always brought a smile to his lips and usually a shiver from the ladies. He kind of liked that.

Ridge shook his head and grinned before turning to look out the window.

Nic flipped open the instrument. "Party Central. Elvis speaking."

"Nic. Adam." His brother's tone was short and serious, not at all like Adam. Nic's radar went up.

"What's up, bro?"

"Got some bad news."

All the flippancy went out of Nic. He sat up straight, tensed by the sudden foreboding in the back of his mind. His brother wasn't one to exaggerate. "What's going on? Is everyone all right?"

By everyone, he meant family. Had there been an accident? One of the kids. Oh, please, God, not that.

"Mom's in the hospital."

"What?" His hands started to shake. "What happened? Did she have an accident?"

"Look, I'm sorry to tell you on the phone, but we're trying to get the word out. We need to start the prayer chain. Nonstop."

The words scared Nic even more. His throat tightened. Mom was the rock, the family hub, the one to whom everyone went with troubles. She couldn't get sick or hurt.

"Adam. Brother. What's the matter with our mama?"

A long pause pulsed through the phone. Nic was aware of passing cars, of people on the sidewalks, of Ridge and the captain staring at him, of the awful stench of burned rubber.

Finally Adam's strained voice said, "When your shift ends, come to the hospital. Nicky," he paused again and sucked in a quivering breath, "Mom's got cancer."

* * *

Cassidy carried an assortment of plastic shopping bags from the car to the apartment complex. Today was Saturday and she'd found great bargains in the baby section at Penny's. Alex was outgrowing clothes so fast she could barely keep up. Thanks to Mia and Anna Marie she had a few things but, in truth, she enjoyed shopping for Alex more than for herself.

"'Cause you're so cute," she said, kissing his chin. He responded by grabbing a hunk of her hair.

As she passed the walkway to Nic's apartment her attention was drawn to the dark window. He wasn't home. A frisson of disappointment shimmied through her. He'd been on duty last night. She'd expected him to sleep most of the day. Instead, he was gone. Probably out with friends.

The disappointment deepened, frustrating her. She hadn't seen Nic since he'd kissed her. She should have known their relationship was moving into the personal zone, but somehow she'd managed to ignore her feelings. She'd been bowled over by the avalanche of emotion one tender, achingly sweet kiss could generate.

She'd known from the beginning that a charmer like Nic had been her weakness in college. But she was sure she'd learned her lesson well. Now she worried about falling for another guy who could sweet-talk her into things she shouldn't do.

The idea frightened her. At the same time she wondered if she was being fair. He'd kissed her, not asked her to move in with him. Maybe she was overreacting.

But to Cassidy kissing was a big deal. As hard as

it was to admit, she wouldn't mind kissing him again. And again.

At the top of the stairs she set her shopping bags on the landing to unlock the door and hoist Alex higher onto one hip. As she maneuvered the key into the lock with one hand, a car door slammed in the parking lot below. She glanced down to see Nic exit his truck. Her heart lurched.

Resolved not to behave like one of her Bible study teens, she pushed the door open and took Alex inside.

On the return trip for the bags her traitorous eyes searched for her neighbor, finding him. Something in the way he moved drew her attention. Plastic bags dangling from both arms, she leaned over the railing to observe.

Nic didn't walk with his usual jaunty step. He wasn't whistling or singing some silly song. Instead, he moved slowly as though his feet weighed a ton. He looked forlorn, depressed even.

The notion stunned her. Nic was a lot of things, but she'd never seen him depressed. Something was wrong.

All self-consciousness fled. She took the bags inside, changed Alex's diaper, washed his face and hands and then hurried downstairs.

Nic had been there for her, not once, but many times since the fire. If something was wrong, friendship demanded she return the favor.

The apartment was dark, but she knew he was in there. She banged on his door. "Nic. It's Cassidy."

A minute passed before he opened the door.

"You look awful," she blurted.

Some of his old humor gleamed for a few seconds. "Sweet talker."

She pushed past him, going into his living room where she turned to face him. His apartment smelled like reheated pizza.

"What's wrong? Can I help?"

Nic slowly closed the door, leaned there for a moment as if gathering strength before coming toward her. "Sit. I could use a friend right now."

Never taking her eyes off him, Cassidy lowered her body onto the couch. The firm cushion squeaked a tiny bit. She settled Alex onto her lap facing Nic, hoping the baby would cheer him.

As much as she hated knowing, she had to ask about his job. He had been on duty last night. Cassidy shuddered to think about it. "Did something happen at work? A bad fire?"

"No, no fire. It's my mom."

"Rosalie?" His answer shocked her. "Nic, what's wrong? Is she sick?"

"Yeah. Bad sick." He raked a hand down his face, rasping out a ragged breath. "Cass, she has breast cancer."

Blood drained out of Cassidy's head. She felt weak with the implications. Weak and frightened. What did one say in the face of such a terrifying diagnosis?

"Nic, I'm so sorry. What can I do? What do you need?" She grabbed one of his hands. "Anything. You name it."

His expression distraught, he shook his head. "I don't know. The family has a prayer chain."

"I'll pray. Every day, I promise. We will expect God to do something amazing. He will. I just know it." She knew prayer worked. It had sustained her more times than she could count, the most recent still ongoing. "Can we go see her?"

Absently, he jiggled Alex's outstretched hand, but Cassidy could see his mind was elsewhere.

"I just came from the hospital. The doctors came in and talked options. Scary stuff."

"How advanced is the cancer?"

"They're still testing to be sure, but the news is not good. Mom, I discovered, has known something was wrong for a while but didn't say anything to anyone but Dad. She's been to the doctor a lot this month." He stared down at his hands and then back up at her. "I didn't even know."

"She didn't want you to worry."

"But I should have noticed. I should have paid more attention. This is my mother!"

At the sharpness in Nic's tone, Alex started babbling like crazy and reached for him. This time Nic noticed. Almost desperately, Nic pulled the baby against his chest and clung to him in a way that pierced Cassidy's heart.

"I don't know what to do," he said to her over Alex's shoulder. "Mom's our anchor."

Hurting for him, Cassidy stroked his arm over and over again, trying to convey some sense of comfort. "Maybe it's your turn to be strong for her."

"Yeah. Yeah, I guess that's true." He rested his cheek against Alex's fuzzy blond head. "You know about being strong. You're a good example."

"Sometimes you don't have a choice."

"We always have a choice. You could have caved to the pressure from your grandmother."

"Yes, but look what I would have missed." She rubbed a hand down Alex's back, the striped T-shirt rumpled beneath her fingers, the tiny jean shorts and soft denim shoes adorable. "The reward far outweighs the sacrifice."

"I'm afraid that won't be true this time." He moved the baby from his shoulder to his lap. Alex leaned forward to press his open mouth against Nic's knees, bobbing up and down. Nic's strong grasp held him safely even though the baby's bottom rose in the air. "I'm scared, Cass. What if she dies?"

"Medical science is doing amazing things today with breast cancer. I know several survivors." She took the straining baby from him and propped him between them on the couch. "And you know what else I know?"

He shook his head, looking at her through blood-shot eyes.

"I know a big, big God and so does your mother." She touched his cheek. "So do you, Nic. You should talk to Him about this."

"Yeah, I've been thinking about that, too."

"I can tell you from experience that He's there and He cares about your pain. For a while after the fire, I struggled to make sense of the senseless. I wondered why God had done such a thing, but finally my pastor helped me understand that God didn't kill my family. The Bible says Jesus came to give life, not to take it. He loves me. I'm His child. He wouldn't hurt me on purpose. Bad stuff just happens. There's no doubt about that, but Jesus is right here, longing to comfort and strengthen and carry you through this."

Nic bit his bottom lip and looked away, but not before she saw the yearning in his eyes.

She squeezed his hand, tears forming on her lids. "Will you let me pray with you?"

She'd prayed with her teen girls as a group but she'd never done this before. As self-conscious as she felt, Cassidy knew this was the right thing to do.

"It's been a while," he said softly. "Do you think He'll listen to a prodigal son?"

She laced her fingers with his. "I have no doubt at all."

Later that evening, Nic returned to the hospital. This time Cassidy went along. He was still scared out of his mind and disappointed that Cassidy's prayer hadn't automatically fixed the problem. But he'd watched Cassidy come from shattered despair to strong resolve and finally to peace. Tragic circumstances hadn't broken her. They had made her stronger.

God, she claimed, had been there for her in those awful hours when neither she nor Alex could sleep, when she feared that she didn't have the ability to mother a child, when the weight of dealing with funerals and autopsy reports and grief had threatened to drown her.

All his life, he'd been surrounded by believers and a Christian family with rock-solid faith, but Nic hadn't given God much thought in a long time. For as long as he could remember he'd been taught that God was the answer to every need. Somewhere along the line, he'd drifted away, too busy with enjoying life to think about God. It seemed like a sorry deal to run to Him now, asking for help and maybe even a miracle. Cassidy assured him the Lord didn't care about the circumstances. He simply wanted to help His children as a loving parent would.

And boy, did Nic need help now.

He pushed open the door to his mother's hospital room and waited until Cassidy, carrying Alex on her hip, passed through, her orange blossom scent tickling his nose. Much more pleasant than hospital smells.

The whole Carano gang was here again, jammed into the small space like Italian sausages.

Mama was propped up in a hospital bed, looking far too healthy to be stuck between white sheets with an IV dripping into one arm. The sight knotted his gut. He wanted to throw up.

"Don't come in here with that long face, Nicholas Alexander," his mother said.

Cassidy shot him a funny look. He'd never told her his middle name was the same as Alex's first one.

"How ya doing, Mom?" he asked.

"Better than you. Come here." Rosalie raised her free arm.

Nic bent to receive her embrace, his heart hammering into his throat. He wrapped his arms around her shoulders and held her for several seconds, absorbing the moment, the fleshy softness and ever-present bakery smell of his mother. He thought of all the hugs he'd taken for granted over the years, forgotten even. Never again. Every moment with her was precious now that he had to face the fact that even she was not immortal.

"I love you, Mom," he whispered.

She patted his cheek. "I know you do. I love you, too. Have you had supper? You look tired. Dad brought sandwiches and pastry from the bakery."

Nic laughed. Leave it to his mother to make sure everyone was fed even from her hospital bed. "We'll eat later."

Rosalie motioned to Cassidy who hung back at the foot of the bed, a gentle smile curving her lips. If she felt out of place with his family, she didn't show it. And he'd never been so glad to have her company as he was tonight.

"Cassidy, make him eat. He's too thin." Mom shifted in the bed, her body whispering against the linens. "Mia, hand that platter around. Gabe, we need drinks."

"This isn't a picnic, Mom," Nic reminded her.

"Why not? We're all here. Food's here." She gestured around the room, a smile dancing in her dark eyes. "In Carano language that means, let's party."

He knew what she was doing and he loved her for the effort. Mom never wanted anyone to worry about her. Family was her everything.

With a jolt, he realized he'd been trying to run away

from the very thing that mattered most in life—his family's love and care and interest.

"She's right, gang." He clapped his hands once, rubbing them together for good measure. Though his heart wasn't in it, if Mama wanted a family party, he'd give her one. "Gabe, you buy the drinks."

"I figured as much," Gabe grumbled in jest. "I pay. You eat. Right?"

"That's the way the system works, bro," he said, determined to liven things up for his mother's sake. "Adam will go with you to the machines in case you run out of money."

Adam shot his father a grin. "Dad comes, too. He's the one with the fat wallet."

Leo, whose stricken expression had begun to abate with the banter between his boys, patted his back pocket. "I knew I should have left this at home. My sons become rich lawyers and they still pick my pockets."

Nic squelched a flare of envy. Dad never missed a chance to brag about his successful lawyer sons. Someday maybe he'd have reason to be proud of Nic, as well.

"Go, go, you silly men." Rosalie shooed them with both hands. "A person could starve to death while you argue."

The grim reminder of death, even in jest, dampened Nic's spirits. He forced a grin as his brothers and father disappeared into the hallway.

"Come on, ladies." He grabbed a wad of latex gloves from the box next to his mother's bed and handed one to Cassidy and his sisters. "Blow these up. We need balloons."

Rosalie wiggled her fingers toward the baby in Cassidy's arms. "Let me have that little one for a while."

Cassidy handed over the baby, who stared around in interest at the unfamiliar surroundings while Rosalie clucked and cooed at him.

Holding the floppy glove to her lips, Cassidy blew until the fingers filled and stuck straight up. All the while, her heart ached for Nic. Playing to the opinion that he was the clown, the never serious son, Nic broke into full party mode, joking, teasing, filling the room with an energy she knew he didn't feel.

She was the only one present that knew he was taking the MCAT again tomorrow morning, bright and early. He'd intended to study tonight. Now she wondered how he would concentrate on the exam when his mind and heart were here in this room with his mother.

"Woody Woodpecker." Nic grabbed her glove balloon and scrubbed a red marking pen over the protruding fingers. He added two huge eyes and a wide, smiling mouth. "See?"

His mother laughed and his sisters groaned.

He was shattered, devastated by his mother's illness, but if they wanted a party Notorious Nic came on the scene and gave them one.

The beauty of that kind of love made Cassidy want to cry.

It also made her feel something deep in her heart

that she had never intended to feel. Something strong and sweet, lovely and fearsome.

And she had no idea what to do about it.

Chapter Eleven

Rain pounded the window next to Cassidy's bed. Lightning flickered, followed by a rolling boom of thunder.

Over the baby monitor she heard Alex begin to cry. With a sigh, Cassidy rolled over for a look at her alarm clock. The number four glowed red. She groaned aloud. Alex had been doing much better, usually sleeping until six, but the storm must have wakened him.

The crying grew louder. She cocked her head to listen. Though he was probably hungry, this cry sounded different. He must be scared. Poor lamb.

Cassidy shoved back the sheet and padded through the dark apartment into the nursery. The angel nightlight glowed, guiding her inside.

"Shh, darling boy, I'm here. Shh." She switched on the small, dim lamp next to the changing table, blinking for a few seconds. In the shadowy room, the baby-scented air hung cool and damp. Thunder rattled the windows. Lightning flickered like flames of fire across the floor.

Cassidy's nerves jittered. Nic was on duty tonight.

As she lifted the baby from the crib he quieted, but a new worry eclipsed all others.

"You're hot." She frowned and pressed a cool hand against his forehead. Too hot.

After carrying him to the changing table, Cassidy took his temperature and replaced his wet diaper. He fussed, whimpering, almost a moan. The sound frightened her.

Holding the thermometer toward the lamp, she squinted at the digital readout. "One hundred and one point four."

Her mind worked, trying to remember the books she'd read. Was that high for a baby? Was it in the danger zone? She knew normal but how high was high?

For a moment, she considered phoning Rosalie. Then, with a heavy heart, she remembered. Even she had come to count on the wisdom and strength of the Carano matriarch. Little wonder the hospitalization and diagnosis were so difficult for Nic and his siblings. She had to believe Rosalie with her valiant spirit and powerful faith would beat the disease.

Alex started to cry harder. Though he was hot, his skin prickled in the cool night air. Cassidy quickly slid his feet and arms into a pair of cotton pajamas and then hurried to the telephone. With the receiver in hand, she paused. Who could she call? It was far too late to contact anyone except Nic and he was on duty. Even if he knew what to do, he couldn't rush to her rescue this time.

Finally, she phoned the hospital emergency room and spoke to a nurse who advised her to give the baby some acetaminophen and take him into the pediatrician's office in the morning if he didn't improve. Not especially comforted, but somewhat relieved, Cassidy did as the woman suggested, fixed Alex a fresh bottle and sat down to rock him. At times like this, she realized why God intended for children to have two parents. Moral support took on an entirely new meaning at four o'clock in the morning.

The minutes crawled on while outside the storm raged. Thunder rumbled like a distant airplane. Lightning flickered through the blinds, illuminating the baby's fretful expression. Cassidy rocked and prayed. At seven, Alex's temperature had not improved but he'd fallen into a fitful slumber.

After placing him in the crib, she reached for the telephone once more, this time dialing her boss. He wasn't going to be happy but she had no choice.

"Shane, this is Cassidy Willis."

"Yes?" The art director's voice was cool.

"I won't be in to work this morning. Maybe not this afternoon, either. Alex is sick."

A long silence hummed through the receiver. Cassidy's fingers tightened. Her boss had been less than cordial of late. "Shane, are you still there?"

"I heard you, Cassidy." A loud sigh expressed his annoyance. "Look, we've got a problem here."

She had a problem. A sick baby. "I wouldn't take

off if it wasn't necessary. You've worked with me long enough to know that."

"Six months ago, I would have agreed, but you've changed. Your production has decreased, you're missing work when we need you most and, frankly, I need someone I can depend on."

The words were clipped and sharp as though he'd been storing them up, prepared to unleash the volley at the right time. Apparently, this morning was the last straw.

"A child can't help getting sick." She kept her tone even but her insides shook. "Other mothers have to deal with this."

"That's the point. They deal with it. Someone else looks after their sick kids while they work."

She didn't have anyone else. Even the day care wouldn't take Alex with a fever.

"I'm still making the adjustment to motherhood, Shane. Cut me some slack. In time conditions should improve."

"We don't have time. We're on a deadline."

He was being especially difficult this morning. She was tempted to ask if he'd had his coffee yet. "I'll work late tomorrow."

"I need you here today." The frosty tone was unrelenting.

"I understand that. I wish things were different but I can't come in." She disliked missing work, but what else could she do? Alex had to come first. "I'm sorry."

"So am I, Cassidy. This is a business. We have deadlines and clients who expect top-of-the-line, on-time work. If you can't do your job, perhaps I should look for someone who can."

Cassidy stiffened, incredulous. "Are you threatening to fire me?"

His huff of frustration grated on her nerves. "I'm stating facts. You have choices to make. Come to work or don't. Keep your job or don't. Your choice."

The threat scraped through her like nails on a chalkboard. Decide between a sick, orphaned baby and her job? What kind of choice was that?

Three months ago, the decision would have been swift and easy. She would have done anything to feather her career cap. This morning with her arms still achy and damp from holding Alex's hot, fussy body, she had to do what was right and best for him, regardless of the consequences.

Suddenly, the job wasn't so important, the drive to the top less enchanting.

"You know what, Shane? You're right. I have a choice to make." Drawing in a deep, quivering breath and praying like mad, she jumped into the abyss. "I choose Alex."

"Don't be stupid, Cassidy. I'm not asking you to give up the child."

"No, but you're asking me to choose work over a sick baby. I won't do that. Now, if you'll excuse me, I have a pediatrician to visit. And you have a position to fill."

With a trembling hand, she hung up the phone and blew out a long, shaky breath. Now she'd done it. She was jobless. She not only would never climb to the top of her game, she had jumped off the middle rung and removed the ladder.

Her grandmother would have a fit.

Tears pushed at the backs of her eyelids. She blinked them away. The decision was made and she'd worry about the results later. Right now, her nephew was burning with fever, his eyes glassy and bright, and she was the only one around to help him.

That was far more important than designing a logo for a chain of restaurants.

By the time she'd changed and fed Alex, who ate little, the worst of the thunderstorm had passed and a steady shower of rain washed the morning. Cassidy debated on carrying an umbrella but between Alex, his diaper bag and her purse, she had no hands left. Making sure Alex was covered, Cassidy backed out of her apartment for the mad dash to the parking lot.

The smell of rain on warm concrete mixed with the exhaust fumes of passing cars. Cold rain pelted her from above, prickling the skin on her arms. Her hurried steps splattered droplets onto her pants legs.

As she bent forward to place Alex in his car seat, water dripped from the car roof down the back of her shirt. Gasping at the sudden cold, she shivered.

Footsteps sounded to her left. Then something popped at her back. Though she could only see his navy pant legs and gleaming black shoes speckled with water, Cassidy knew her visitor was Nic, still dressed in his work uniform.

And he was holding an umbrella.

"Taking your shower outside this morning?" The baritone voice was amused.

"Don't be funny. I'm having a lousy day." She snapped Alex into his carrier, covered him with a light blanket and touched his forehead once more. The fever still burned.

As she straightened, her side bumped Nic's solid torso. The morning air was chilled, but he exuded a welcome warmth. Cassidy relented. Regardless of her reaction, she was relieved to see him.

"Sorry. Thanks for coming out with the umbrella. I thought you'd be asleep already."

His shift ended at seven and it was now eight-thirty.

"I was about to come up to your place. I saw your car in the lot and figured something must be wrong if you didn't go to work."

The words brought back the too-recent confrontation with her boss. Or rather, her former boss.

Oh dear, she really had quit her job. She closed her eyes for a second. When she opened them again, Nic had moved closer, eyebrows drawn together as he studied her face.

They were standing next to her car crowded beneath a black umbrella, so close she could see the night's scruffy growth of beard along his upper lip and feel the rise and fall of his breathing. Rain patted the concrete outside their intimate circle. The memory of their shared kiss trembled in the morning. Cars on the street swished past. Water pooled along the street's edges sprayed in an arc behind their tires.

She was tired of handling everything alone and Nic

was so wonderfully available. Cassidy resisted the urge to lean into him.

Almost tenderly, Nic rubbed his free hand down her chilled arm and then held on to her wrist. Just that small gesture, that single touch of his warm skin, comforted her.

"I see that look," he said, his brown eyes deepening to velvet espresso. "What's wrong?"

"Everything," Cassidy admitted, biting her lip to hold back the tears. "Most importantly, Alex is sick."

Nic's pose changed. He tensed and leaned around her to gaze through the car window at the dozing baby. "With what?"

"Fever. I can't get his temperature down, and he's fussy and won't take his bottle."

"Are you headed for the hospital?"

"Pediatrician's office."

He reached around her and opened the passenger door. "Get in. I'll drive."

"Nic, you don't have to do that." But she really could use the moral support. "You worked all night. You need to sleep."

With a cocky grin he said, "You know what I say about sleep."

Yes, she knew. He could sleep when he was dead. A shiver went through her that had nothing to do with the chilly dampness.

"You're cold. Get in." Still protecting her from the rain with the umbrella, Nic gave her a gentle shove. She went down without a fight. He leaned in and kissed her forehead. "Buckle up."

Bemused and too tired and concerned to argue with a man who would win anyway, Cassidy snapped her safety belt while Nic jogged around the car and climbed into the driver's seat. Holding the umbrella outside, he gave the handle a shake, popped it closed and tossed it into the backseat with a flourish.

As he cranked the car engine, Cassidy made one more feeble attempt. "You really don't have to go with me."

He didn't have to kiss her on the forehead, either. She was still contemplating that.

"Humor me. Alex is my little buddy. I need to."

She needed him, too, a fact that was becoming uncomfortably clear. In that moment with rain sluicing off the windshield and her life in a mess, Cassidy looked across at the man easing her Camry out of the parking lot and forgot all about Nic's occupation, forgot about his reputation and saw him for who he was.

And knew she loved him.

Notorious Nic, who owned more hearts than Alex had diapers, had stolen yet another—hers.

Nic sat beside Cassidy on pale-purple upholstered chairs in the surprisingly quiet and tidy waiting room of Dr. Margaret Fisher, waiting for Alex's name to be called. His stomach hollow and eyes gritty from lack of sleep, he wondered what he was doing here. Even the guys at the station had noticed his preoccupation with his neighbor and her new son. But one look at Cassidy and Alex through his front window this morning and he'd had no choice. They drew him with more power than an electromagnet.

Half a dozen other parents, mostly women, alternately wrestled small children and murmured reassurances. At a child-size table, two toddlers played with brightly colored toys and made car noises. Occasionally, a nurse appeared through a door to the left and all eyes turned in her direction as she called the next patient.

Alex was awake again, whimpering, his chubby face flushed. Nic's gut twisted at the sight of the little dude in discomfort.

"Want me to hold him awhile?"

Cassidy shook her head to decline, as he knew she would, but Nic took Alex anyway and laid the unresisting child lengthwise along his thighs. Alex's usual happy smile and vibrant energy were nowhere to be seen today.

"What do you suppose is wrong?" Cassidy murmured, her cornflower-blue eyes worried.

He lifted a shoulder. "We'll find out. Stop worrying. Babies get sick. They get well."

"Oh, great and wise baby expert." At least he'd roused a smile. "I visited your mother yesterday."

"Yeah?" That made him happy. He reached for her hand, happier still when she didn't resist. "How was she?"

"Strong as usual and ready to get the surgery over with."

The idea of his mother going under the knife shook him. "I scheduled Friday off duty to be there."

For some reason, he'd feel better if Cassidy was there, too, but he wouldn't ask. She had missed enough work already. He knew how much that bothered her, how important her career was.

"Do you mind if I come with you?" she asked, surprising him.

"Don't you have work that day?"

"No." Her chest rose and fell in a deep sigh. "I don't. This morning I joined the ranks of the unemployed."

He blinked at her, stunned. "Whoa, what happened?"

"My boss pressured me to come in to the office today and threatened to fire me if I didn't, so I quit."

"I thought your career was everything."

"Was." She stroked her index finger down Alex's cheek, the look in her eyes so full of love Nic's chest tightened with emotion. "Not anymore."

"What are you going to do?"

"I'll find something. Right now, we're fine. Janna and Brad had insurance. Alex and I inherited their estate. I'd intended to save the money for Alex's future so hopefully I can find work soon."

The nurse appeared at the door, holding a chart. Cassidy glanced her way but the name called wasn't Alex's.

"Won't you have the same problem with any company?" he asked. "I mean, with Alex."

He didn't add that she was overprotective, which could cause an issue with any boss. But she was still getting her parenting legs under her. The company should have been more understanding.

"Probably, but I'm sure something will work out. God didn't bring Alex and me this far to let us fall on our faces." She pressed a hand to Alex's cheek. Nic noticed her acrylic nails were missing. "We're a family now. We'll manage."

For all her brave talk, Cassidy was worried. Nic saw the truth in her troubled eyes, in the tightness around her mouth. She loved graphic design. She even created websites and other designs for friends simply because she loved the work.

An idea jiggled his consciousness. "Why not start your own business?"

She shook her head, blond hair whispering against her shoulders, but Nic saw a light go on behind her eyes.

He pressed. "Don't discard the idea too fast. You could work at home and take care of Alex without day care."

"Oh, that sounds good. Even the day care would love the idea. I drive them crazy calling every hour."

"You already have the contacts. You have the skills." He squeezed her fingers. "And you have a computer."

"I never thought I'd say this, Nic, but you're a good influence."

He laughed. She could say the cutest things. "And don't you forget it, either." Taking care not to disturb Alex, he leaned close to her ear and murmured, "Now, if I can only get you to come down and look at my etchings."

She patted the top of his head and gave it a little push. "I never did know what those were."

"Me, either," he admitted with a grin. "But I still want to show them to you."

The nurse appeared again and this time Alex was called. Feeling more domestic than he thought possible, Nic gently brought Alex to his shoulder and followed Cassidy and the nurse down a short hall lined with posters. A few depicted scenes of child development or calls for immunization. One was a poster about an upcoming blood drive. Yet another announced a Run for the Cure, a race to raise money for breast cancer research. That was something he and his siblings could sink their teeth into.

Lord, if a cure is possible, bring it on.

He could hardly believe how much he'd prayed since his mother went into the hospital. Something had changed inside of him, something that felt good and right. God was the answer, whether he knew all the questions or not. Funny how it took something bad to bring him around to the goodness of God.

"This way, please. Room three." The curly-haired nurse smiled and showed them into a room. Nic dragged his eyes away from the pink-ribboned poster and went inside.

He and Cassidy sat side by side in hard, straight-backed chairs, their knees touching. Nic couldn't help himself. Even with Alex snuggled against his shoulder he pulled Cassidy's hand into his.

The nurse asked a bunch of questions, jotted notes and took Alex's vital signs. Then she patted the paper-lined cradle of a scale.

"If Daddy will just lay the baby in here for a minute."

Cassidy's startled gaze flew to his. She flushed. Nic's heart did a strange lurch that slammed into his rib cage before settling again.

"He's not—I mean, we're not—" Cassidy stuttered, getting nowhere.

Nic winked at her and rose to do the nurse's bidding. The woman's mistake was a natural one. No use getting embarrassed.

Especially since the idea of being Alex's dad didn't bother him all that much. He was nuts about the little dude. Since meeting Alex and Cassidy, a strange kind of yearning had moved in with him. Watching his brothers and sisters with their families increased the urge.

Beside him, Cassidy patted Alex in reassurance. She brushed against Nic's side, a beautiful, motherly princess, a woman of faith and strength that occupied his every waking thought. And sometimes his sleeping ones.

A new reality punched him in the gut. One that he wasn't ready for.

He might be nuts about Cassidy, too.

The idea shook him more than a five-alarm fire in a fifty-story building.

Chapter Twelve

"Are you sure this isn't too much for you?"

Nic knelt on one knee next to a blue-striped lawn chair stationed on the sidewalk parallel to Broadway Avenue, the official start and finish line of the Run for the Cure. His mother, dressed in a pink shirt and cap, although she claimed the color did nothing for her, had insisted on watching the race even though she was still recovering from surgery.

"Don't worry, son." The aluminum legs of his dad's lawn chair clattered as he unfolded it next to Rosalie's. Other members of the Carano clan formed a watchful semicircle around Mom. "With all of us here, your mama doesn't stand a chance. One tired look and she's going home."

Rosalie patted her husband's weathered hand, a simple gesture Nic had seen hundreds of times over the years. Now, the depth and strength of their love and care for each other brought a lump to his throat. He saw the importance of what they shared…and wanted that same thing in his own life someday.

Of its own volition, his mind shot straight to Cassidy. He gazed around at the hoard of people crowding the streets and lining the race route, but didn't see her. She was here somewhere, preparing for the race. Earlier she'd dropped Alex off with Mia who had stayed home to look after the little ones. Although the little dude had recovered from his viral infection, Cassidy hadn't wanted to bring him out into a crowd, especially when she would be racing.

He spotted his sister's husband, Collin, dressed in police uniform as part of security. Seeing him reminded Nic of his own job here as one of many volunteer paramedics.

"I'm on my cell if you need me." He patted the instrument at his waist as he pushed to his feet.

"Those runners will need you more," his mother said.

"Yeah," Adam piped up from his spot just behind Mama. "Keep an eye on that pretty blond girl especially. You know the one. Big blue eyes. Dynamite smile. Looks great in running shorts."

He jabbed an elbow into his brother Gabe who added his two cents. "I heard she has a thing for firefighters."

Nic laughed off the teasing comments, waving as he headed for his assigned station.

The brothers were wrong. Cassidy didn't have a thing for firefighters. She might like him but she didn't like his profession. She'd told him as much.

He liked her, too. Good thing he wasn't going to be a fireman forever. He turned the situation over in his mind, thinking about exactly where he wanted the relationship to go. He didn't quite know yet, but he wanted to find out.

He wove his way through the spectators, thinking. His MCAT results would be back soon. With all the hard work he'd put in, he felt good this time about his chances for a top score. Yet, whenever he thought about the future, about leaving the fire department, his stomach tied into a hundred knots.

"Nic! Nic!"

Tottering on heeled sandals that Nic found ridiculous given the outdoor sporting event, several girls of his acquaintance rushed toward him. He was outside a small tent near the finish line, administering first aid to those runners with cramps, dehydration and plain old fatigue. Most of the entrants were holding up well today in this relatively short race.

He smiled at the girls, but his usual zip was missing. He had an eye on the race and was waiting for Cassidy to come into sight.

"What's up, ladies?" he asked. "Why aren't you running for the cure?"

Mandy made a face. "And get all sweaty? No thanks."

"But we donated to the cause, Nic," Lacey hurried to add.

"I appreciate that." When word of his mother's cancer diagnosis spread, most of his friends had bonded together to either form running teams or to raise money. The gestures blessed him.

Mandy fanned her face with one hand, blocking his view. "Hot out here."

Nic stretched around her to watch the race. Where was Cassidy? He'd expected her to be in with the early finishers.

"Earth to Nic. Hello."

He refocused on the speaker. "What?"

"Got any cold drinks in that tent? I'm parched."

"Only for the runners."

"Well, pooh." Mandy pushed her bangs back. "A bunch of us are going to the dance and fireworks after the awards ceremony. Want to come along?"

Before she finished, he was already shaking his head. "Can't. But thanks for asking."

"Why not? You never want to do anything fun anymore." She pulled a pretty pout that would have worked on him in the past. He didn't understand why it didn't now, but it didn't. "What's the deal?"

Just then, he spotted a shiny platinum blond ponytail bobbing up and down in a group of about six runners. His heart lurched. Cassidy. Finally.

He reached for a bottle of water. She'd need this. His focus on that bounce of blonde, he stepped around his friends in order to better observe.

Cassidy broke loose from the pack. He could see her arms moving, still relaxed as she powered for the finish line. Man, she was something.

Rachel followed the direction of his gaze. "She's the one, isn't she?" Rachel accused, one hand to her hip in disbelief. "That blonde who lives upstairs from you. The one with the baby. She's the reason you never want to have fun anymore."

Cassidy, running at a steady pace, perspiration giving her face a glow, spotted him and smiled. When she saw the girls gathered around him, the smile faltered and she glanced away.

The action struck him as meaningful. Suddenly, he was feeling really good.

"Yes," he said, never taking his eyes off the race. "It's her."

Without further explanation, he moved away from the gaping girls and toward the oncoming runner.

As she crossed the finish line, he stepped into her path. Startled, she pulled up but stumbled, falling against him. Down they went onto the hard street. Nic could feel Cassidy's heart pounding wildly against her rib cage. She was damp with perspiration and her breath came in deep drags.

Cassidy pushed away and sat up, arms over her knees to draw in deep drafts of fresh air.

"Good race," Nic said.

She grinned into his eyes, breathing hard but not struggling. Nic felt the strongest need to kiss her. Instead, he handed her the water bottle.

She took the bottle gratefully, uncapped and gulped down most of the contents. As she tilted back her head, Nic noticed her T-shirt. The same bright pink his mother wore, Cassidy's T-shirt displayed something special—a huge screen-printed photo of his mother with the words, "In honor of my hero, Rosalie Carano."

Nic's throat clogged with emotion. He draped an arm around the woman at his side and gently kissed her hair.

No doubt about it. If he hadn't been in love with Cassidy Willis before, he was now.

After the successful race Cassidy was stoked, so much so that she let Nic talk her into leaving Alex with Mia again that evening while they attended the race day finale, live entertainment and a dance. The idea of spending a romantic evening with Nic was both exhilarating and nerve-racking but she wouldn't have missed it for the world. In spite of her best intentions, she'd fallen in love with him.

"Your sister is a doll for babysitting Alex," she said as they entered the ballroom and started to weave their way through the crowd.

As a runner, she and her date were allotted a table close to the bandstand. Her date. Nic Carano. Her heart danced a happy jig. Would wonders never cease?

Somehow she'd convinced herself that once Nic left his dangerous job and entered medical school everything would be all right. The flock of females fluttering around him at the race should have stopped her in her tracks, but they hadn't.

Rosalie's words played in her head. If Nic wanted to be with those other girls, he would be. He'd chosen her, not only tonight but over and over again in recent weeks.

The reasonable portion of her brain said she was asking for a broken heart, and yet in the last few months she'd done a lot of unreasonable things. Just ask Grandmother.

"Can't argue that," Nic was saying, a hand at the small of her back as he guided her through the crush. "Mia's a jewel."

She turned her head to look at him, her stomach dipping at the look in his eyes. "We'll have to babysit for her and Collin some night and let them go out alone."

"Sounds good. You and me snuggled on the couch listening to romantic music while the rug rats play." They'd reached their table and Nic pulled out a chair, waiting for her to sit. As she did, he leaned down to nuzzle her hair, jump-starting her pulse.

Her heart as light as a helium balloon, she touched the side of his face, wishing she could hold him near this way forever. His clean, masculine smell lingered after he broke contact and took his own seat.

"If I know you," she said, not about to let him know how affected she was by his nearness, "you'll be on the floor playing with the rug rats."

"Mmm, maybe not. None of them smell as good as you." He scraped his chair closer and leaned in.

Cassidy smiled on the inside. Hadn't she just been thinking the same about him? "You couldn't have said that earlier today."

"Sure, I could have. It wouldn't have been true, but I could have said it."

She whacked his arm. "Flatterer."

"All for a good cause. When I saw your T-shirt— wow." His fisted hand thudded once against his chest. "Got me right there."

"Your mom's a special woman."

"Yeah." Some of his ebullience faded.

Hurting for him, Cassidy touched his arm. "She's going to beat the cancer, Nic. I believe that with all my heart."

His nostrils flared. "We're trying to stay optimistic."

"You're the king of optimism. That's one of the things I—" About to blurt that she loved him, Cassidy stopped the flow of words in the nick of time and fiddled with the small napkin under her soft drink.

Nic was different tonight. He felt much more like a date and far less like her goofy neighbor. But she wasn't complaining. She felt different, too, and had since he'd met her at the end of the race. Nonetheless, she had to be careful. Spilling her heart would be easy to do. A mistake perhaps, but easy.

Nic pushed a bowl of pretzels toward her. "Have I told you how pretty you look?"

She'd spent an inordinate amount of time trying to decide what to wear tonight, which was silly. Nic had seen her at her worst during the days of Alex's colic.

Finally, she'd settled on a white and turquoise polka-dot sundress with matching bracelets, a white belt that cinched her waist and white sandals. The expression on Nic's face when she'd opened her door told her she'd chosen well.

"You look pretty good yourself, mister." His snow-white polo shirt set off his dark skin and black hair to perfection.

They smiled into each other's eyes and Cassidy

felt the effects of either runner's high or Nic Carano. Maybe both.

A five-piece band kicked off with a well-known country tune. They listened for a while, talking in between tunes and sipping cold sodas. Nic's lighthearted banter, his funny comments about the band, the music and the dancers relaxed them both. He was so easy to be with.

When the band eased into a slow song Nic leaned in, dark eyes mesmerizing. "Want to dance?"

She shook her head. "I'm not much of a dancer."

"That's okay." A grin played around his mouth. "Dancing's just an excuse to hold you anyway. No expertise required."

"You're silly."

"Serious. Come on." He scraped back his chair and stood, holding out a hand. "We'll stand on the dance floor and hold each other while the band plays. No one will know we don't dance."

His sense of the ridiculous never failed to get to her. He was joking, teasing, being his usual funny self. But she had to admit, the idea of being in Nic's arms sounded good.

Feeling almost giddy, Cassidy placed her palm against Nic's and let him lead her to the dance floor. Dozens of festivity-goers crowded the long, narrow ballroom, many of whom spoke to Nic as they passed. A mix and mingle of voices and cologne and music swirled around them, heady and rich.

Cassidy thought she should be tired after today's race, but she wasn't. She was exhilarated, partly because of her good race time and the successful fund-raiser, but more because of the man at her side.

Instead of joining the crowd as she'd expected him to do, Nic worked his way to the perimeter of the room. Any farther away and they'd be out on the wide porch.

"Here we go." He slid an arm around her waist, pulling her near but not so close as to breach respectability. She appreciated that.

They swayed in time to the music, talking most of the time, though Cassidy was acutely conscious of everywhere Nic touched her.

"Any new business ventures?" he asked, gazing down with the most enthralling, heart-stopping expression. What, she wondered, was he thinking?

"You're not going to believe this, but my grandmother sent some work my way. She actually likes the idea of me being my own boss."

"I'm shocked speechless."

Cassidy laughed. "You've never been speechless in your life."

"True." He cocked his head to one side. "Well, maybe once."

"When?" she asked in disbelief, sure he was still teasing.

By now, Nic had guided them smoothly out onto the porch and into the cooler evening air. The night pulsed around them; light flowed from the interior like butter melted across the concrete. Cars passed on the street and doors slammed; people came and went in nearby restaurants.

Nic's expression grew serious.

"The first time ever I saw your face," he said, quoting the old song.

Though the sentiment touched her, Cassidy refused to let him see. "Because I looked so awful?"

Instead of the witty rejoinder she expected, Nic's voice dropped low and Cassidy could see the pulse beating in the hollow of his throat.

"Not even close," he murmured, drawing her slowly nearer until they were heart to heart, his gaze holding hers with stunning intensity. Her own pulse fluttered, with the scariest, most amazing feeling she'd ever had.

"Why then?"

"Because," he said, dark eyes liquid with something she couldn't fully read. "You stopped me in my tracks."

Cassidy fought the surge of tenderness, fought the melting of her resistance. "You probably say that to all the girls."

"No," he said, voice laced with frustration. "I don't. Come on, Cass, throw me a bone here. I'm trying to be romantic."

"Am I crushing your ego?" she asked, more for self-preservation than to get an answer. She was sinking fast.

His jaw tightened. "Is that what you want? To crush my ego?"

Stunned to think she could, Cassidy was suddenly contrite. She touched a palm to his smooth-shaven jaw and echoed his words in a whisper, "Not even close."

The tension left his body as he exhaled a long breath and rested his face in her hair.

"Something's going on between us, Cass," he murmured, the words warm against her scalp. "Don't you feel it, too?"

Oh, yes, she felt it. As powerful and overwhelming as a tsunami. Throat filled with inexpressible emotion, she nodded.

Nic tilted her head, strong hands bracketing her face with such tenderness. His fingertips made soothing circles at her hairline, his handsome face so near she could see the rims of brown iris circling black pupils.

"I care for you, Cassidy. A lot."

"More than your entourage?"

"My what?"

"Mandy and Candy or whoever all those girls are." If she sounded like a jealous woman, so be it. She needed to know.

"Way more. More than any woman I've ever known."

His heart beat against hers and she could feel the *thud-thud* inside his chest. He was telling her the truth.

Gulping back the fear, Cassidy admitted, "I care for you, too, Nic. More than I can say."

As if he'd been uncertain of her response, Nic pressed his forehead to hers and sighed. Music filtered out from the dance and they swayed in time, oblivious to everything else around them.

"So what are we going to do about it?" he murmured, his warm lips brushing her hairline as he spoke.

The possibilities were both wonderful and fearful.

"I don't know," she whispered. They were moving toward something that would either bring heartache or joy. Did she dare to take the risk with a man like Nic?

He lifted his head to melt her with a look. "Me, either. But how about this for starters?"

His lips touched hers in a kiss so shatteringly sweet, Cassidy forgot her reservations as she returned the gentle pressure. Only when a thin siren's wail broke above the other sounds, did she remember.

It required all her strength, all her resolve, to step away from Nic's embrace.

Nic reached for her, caught her arm and tugged. "Don't do that, Cassidy. Don't pull away out of fear."

"I can't help it, Nic. Please understand."

"I do understand. I know what you've been through. I know why fire terrifies you. After all the people you've lost, I'd be an idiot not to understand."

Desperately wanting things to be different and hating herself for spoiling their romantic evening, she stepped toward him. With the flat of her hand against his chest, she said, "Don't give up on me, Nic."

His arms went around her, drawing her back to him. Softly he said, "I couldn't if I wanted to."

Hope returned. Maybe, just maybe, she and Nic could make this work. Tiptoeing, she kissed the dimple in his chin. "Once you leave the fire department everything will be fine."

A muscle beneath his eye twitched. His gaze slid away to stare into the dark evening.

"Sure," he said finally. "Everything will be great."

But as Cassidy's cheek rested against the thudding of Nic's heart, she couldn't help wondering about that moment of hesitation.

Chapter Thirteen

Cassidy hit the Send key on her computer and rolled back in the desk chair with a satisfied smile. One of Grandmother's business contacts had just accepted her bid for a full website redesign, mail-out brochures and a logo update.

She stretched her arms high over her head to release the tension in her shoulders. Old-time rock and roll issued from her computer speakers. She stood to jitterbug around Alex's playpen located next to her desk.

Life was good.

The thought caught her up short. She pulled it back like a curtain and considered it again. A few months ago, she could not have said such a thing.

"Thank you, sweet Lord," she murmured. God had been faithful. He'd given her strength to face Janna's death. He'd given her more joy than she ever imagined possible in Alex. Even when she'd lost her dream job, God had sent a better replacement.

Granted she wasn't making as much money yet, but she was far happier running her own business.

Nic Carano's idea had been positively inspired.

She smiled. Nic. Something really beautiful was growing there, too. She had even begun dreaming of a future with him once he left the fire department.

"Which makes both of us happy, doesn't it, lambkin?" Cassidy leaned over the playpen rail to caress Alex's sweet face. The baby had loved Nic first and had become the magnet that drew them together until fantasies of a real family played through her mind like a sweet melody. She, Nic and Alex.

Her baby nephew was such a precious boy. He deserved a mother *and* a father. Nic would be a wonderful father. She was certain of it. He loved this child, and though motherhood had changed her drastically, Cassidy was thrilled to be Alex's mommy.

She swept him into her arms.

"You are getting so big," she said. He cackled as if she'd said the funniest thing. Cassidy laughed, too, full of love for her nephew.

She sat Alex on the carpet and eased down in front of him to play. Lately she had to watch him every minute he was out of the playpen. He could roll from one side of the living room to the other faster than she could turn off a light switch. She'd discovered this the hard way one evening when she'd gone into the kitchen to snap off the light only to turn around and find him under her feet.

"Little stinker." She wiggled his favorite squeaky toy. "Come get your bunny."

Alex blew a sloppy, wet raspberry. Cassidy laughed, her mind drifting to Nic again. He and Alex exchanged raspberries on a daily basis. Nic's were normally administered to Alex's pudgy belly, an action that caused gales of delight from the baby.

From Cassidy, too. Watching Nic with Alex blessed her all the way to her bones.

Since the dance, they'd seen each other every day that Nic wasn't on duty. Sometimes he jogged up the steps just to kiss her good-night. On those occasions she went to sleep with a smile.

Today, he'd spent the morning with his mother, but he'd invited her down to his place for lunch at noon. Cassidy glanced up at the sunburst clock. Soon.

She'd thought and thought about his odd reaction to her comment the night of the dance. Surely she must have imagined the doubt in his eyes.

Lord, don't let me be wrong.

Nic wanted to be a doctor. Med school was his dream. Now it was hers.

Once he resigned from the fire department she could breathe a sigh of relief, knowing he was safe. All her doubts and fears and anxieties would disappear then. They could be together without worry, without fear, without the deadly danger of losing someone else she loved.

Yes, as soon as he left firefighting, everything would be perfect.

At five minutes before noon, Cassidy swung happily down the stairs with Alex on her hip. She passed the postman and intercepted her mail, saving him a jog up to her apartment.

"Nothing but junk anyway," she said, not caring one iota.

The carrier probably heard the complaint on a daily basis because he only smiled and moved on down the sidewalk. The rise and fall of metal mailbox lids clanked in an irregular rhythm as he distributed his load.

Cassidy pounded on Nic's door as the carrier dropped several envelopes into the slot on the exterior wall.

Nic whipped the door open with a flourish.

"Soup's on," he declared, taking Alex from her grasp and giving her a peck on the nose during the exchange.

"Mail's here," she shot back, reaching under the lid to extract three envelopes and a sale insert. "Home Depot has chain saws on sale. Want one?"

"Don't tempt me. Every man wants a chain saw." He swung Alex in a circle. "Power tools rule."

"I'll remember that on your birthday."

He looked pleased.

"What else did I get? Bills?" he asked, indicating the mail in her hand.

She'd been so engrossed in looking at him with Alex and enjoying that rush of pleasure at the bond between them, her mind had strayed.

She turned the envelopes upright. "Looks like the electric bill, cable and—" she frowned down at the return address. "—I don't know what this one is."

"Let me see." Coming to her side, he leaned over her shoulder.

As if the sun had gone behind a cloud, his countenance changed. His smile faded. His stared at the envelope long enough for Cassidy to know something was wrong. Before she could ask, he took the missive from her fingertips, dropped it on the end table and headed for the kitchen.

"What is that, Nic?"

"Nothing much." But he didn't look at her.

"Then why are you acting so weird?"

"Is it okay if I put Alex on the floor while I dish up the grub?" he asked, clearly changing the subject. He knew she didn't mind if Alex played on the little mat. That's what it was there for. He even kept a basket of toys next to the couch.

Baffled by Nic's behavior, she picked up the troubling piece of mail and reread the return address. Realization crept in like a thief, stealing her pleasure. "These are your MCAT scores, aren't they?"

She stared at him across the divide of living and dining room. His reluctant expression terrified her.

"Nic?" What in the world was going through his head?

His chest rose and fell in a great huff of air. "Yeah, I think so."

"What's wrong?" She started toward him, heart thudding heavily. "Are you worried about the results?"

Surely that was it. Surely he was afraid of failing again.

"You could say that." But his gaze slid away from hers. "Put them over there. I'll look at them later."

"Nic, you passed. I know you did. You studied so hard. There's no way you didn't do well." She tapped his shoulder with the letter. "Come on, let's open this so we can celebrate."

"Leave it, Cassidy." He yanked the envelope from her hands.

Stung, she could only stare at him, reading the truth behind his behavior.

Instantly contrite, he reached for her hands and pulled her to him. "Hey, I'm sorry. Didn't mean to take a bite out of you."

"When were you going to tell me?"

He couldn't look her in the eyes. "Leave it alone, Cassidy. This is something I have to deal with."

"I thought you wanted to go to medical school," she said softly, longing for him to say he still did.

He pulled away to lean both hands against the divider bar. Head down, he said, "I thought so, too."

"But you changed your mind?"

A long beat passed while she waited for an answer. Alex slammed a toy against the floor. Cars roared past on the street. And Cassidy's heart broke.

"I know how much this means to you, Cassidy."

Did he? Did he have any idea of the terror she felt every time he went to work? Did he know of the hopes and dreams she'd let seep into a guarded heart that knew the dangers of loving?

"You don't want to leave the fire department," she

mumbled, almost to herself. One of them had to speak the words.

"I thought I could. I wanted to. For you. For my family…"

His voice drifted away on a tide of bewildered sadness.

"But it's not what you want." Tears gathered, threatening. "Is it?"

Please say I'm mistaken. Please say this is one of your silly jokes.

But she knew he was telling the truth. He had tried to be something he wasn't for her and his family. In the process, he'd lied to them all, even himself.

"I'm sorry, Cass."

"So am I, Nic. More sorry than I can ever say." Sorry that there could be no future for them now.

"This doesn't change us," he said, pushing off the counter, his palms upright, beseeching. "We can work this out."

As much as she longed to fall into his arms, Cassidy backed away, heart shattering like glass on tile. "There's nothing to work out, Nic. I can't ask you to give up the work you love any more than you can ask me to give up Alex."

She bent to gather the baby into her arms. Lunch held no appeal for her now.

"I'd never do that."

"Exactly. I won't ask you to give up your career. But I can't be a part of it, either. I can't live like that, in constant fear for your safety, terrified every time you leave the house that you won't come back. I can't.

Please understand," she pleaded. "I can't take a chance on losing anyone else."

She had started to shake, afraid of letting him go but more afraid of staying.

He noticed and moved toward her. She held out a hand, freezing him in his tracks. If he touched her, if he held her, she might crumble, and then this scene would have to play again. Because she couldn't, wouldn't, take this kind of chance. She and Alex needed a man who would always be there for them. They couldn't bear another loss.

"So where do we go from here?" he asked quietly.

Back to being alone. Back to struggling through each day, hoping the next will be better. Back to safety.

But she only said, "I'm sorry, Nic."

So terribly, brokenly sorry. So sorry that if she didn't leave now she would fall into a heap and beg to stay.

His throat worked as her words soaked in. "So this is it, huh? Goodbye, adios, farewell?"

She could read the hurt and bewilderment in his eyes, see that he felt betrayed.

In that moment, she hated herself as much as she hated the tragedies that had taken her family.

With all the self-preserving strength she could muster, she reached back to open the door. Her fingers trembled against the cold knob. She gripped it hard, holding on.

"I think that's best." The words rasped from her tight, aching throat.

Face like flint, Nic nodded.

Alex reached for him and the stony expression cracked. With a tenderness that nearly killed her, Nic kissed Alex's outstretched fingers and then touched her cheek. She fought not to close her eyes and lean into him. Instead, she kept her gaze trained on Alex. Looking at Nic would destroy her.

"I'm sorry, Nic," she whispered.

"So am I, Cass. So am I."

Blinded by a swarm of tears pushing to break free, she whirled away and rushed toward the steps leading to her apartment.

Breaking things off now was for the best. Wasn't it?

But as she stumbled into her living room, the sobs came and didn't stop for the longest time.

Nic kicked the door shut and stood, hands on hips, staring at the white paint. His knees trembled and his mouth was drier than the Sahara. A knot the size of Philadelphia rested just beneath his breastbone.

Stupid. He was stupid to have ever gotten involved with Cassidy in the first place. But he couldn't leave well enough alone. He'd pushed and charmed and forced his way into her life. She hadn't wanted him from the start. Why hadn't he gotten the message?

Her fire phobia should have been a red alert.

Dumb Nic thought he could cure her, thought if she loved him she would trust him, and the fear would go away.

"So much for the knight in shining turnout gear." The words meant to be sarcastic burned in his mouth as bitter as gall.

He kicked the leg of the couch. Pain shot up his foot, grimly satisfying and far less painful than a massacred heart.

He flopped into his recliner. Something shoved into his back. He reached around and withdrew a teddy bear. The anger went out of him like air from a punctured tire. He pressed the plush toy to his lips.

"I love her," he said to the sweet-faced bear. "I know you didn't think it was possible for a guy like me to get serious about one girl. I didn't, either. But there you have it. I love her. I thought she felt the same. Dumb, huh?"

The teddy bear stared back at him with shiny black eyes and a red smile. Nic pressed the toy to his chest in much the same way he sometimes held Alex.

For the longest time he sat there, clutching the bear, wishing he could be what others needed him to be and wondering how he was going to laugh his way through this.

The painful truth ripped at his insides. He couldn't. Getting over Cassidy and Alex was going to take a lot more than that.

With a heart heavier than a fire engine, he tossed the teddy bear into the basket next to his couch. As soon as the toy landed he got up and retrieved it, holding it on his lap as he'd done with Alex.

"Me and you, buddy," he said, a depressing statement that got him thinking.

He needed friends and fun around him. That was the only cure he knew for the blues. If Cassidy didn't want him, there were those who did, regardless of his career choice. He pulled out his cell phone and dialed.

By nightfall his apartment was rocking, packed with as many friends as he could round up on short notice. They crowded every room, talking, playing video games and jiving around to the music pumping from his stereo.

Slim Jim and Ty, another of his firefighter buddies, manned the grill, scorching burgers and dogs for the gang. Rachel, Mandy, Lacey and his other lady friends handed out chips and drinks, flirting with and teasing every guy in the place. Laughter abounded. Party Central was in full swing. Everyone was having a blast.

Everyone but the host.

"Great party, Nic." Someone slapped him on the shoulder.

"Thanks." He tried to smile but the action was too much work. Excusing himself, he rotated through the rooms, hoping something would snap him out of his lousy mood.

Instead, the revelry only depressed him more.

After an hour of forcing smiles he didn't feel and telling jokes that annoyed him, Nic grabbed a Coke from an ice chest and escaped outside. He stood on the sidewalk for a minute before venturing over to the stairs leading up to Cassidy's apartment. He stared up at the closed door. She was in there. She had to know he was having a party. She probably thought he was down here having the time of his life.

With a heavy sigh, Nic sat on the bottom step and sipped his soda. The carbonated fizz burned his throat, adding to the hot ache in his chest. Few things got him down. He was the life of the party, the fun guy.

Tonight he was dying. And he didn't even care. The party held no charm for him. Here in the dark with cars zipping past and music floating out of his apartment, he felt more alone than he could remember. And it was his own fault.

He should have told Cassidy from the start that he didn't want to leave the fire department. But he hadn't known for sure until the day he'd taken the MCAT. As he'd answered question after question with surprising knowledge and insight, he'd known he was doing well. Instead of triumph, his gut had knotted with dread.

When he'd begun praying about the choice, the dread got worse.

Maybe he should go ahead with the plan anyway and become a doctor. Then everyone would be happy. His family, Cassidy, everyone. Except him.

"You're messed up, dude," he said to the darkness. Messed up because he loved a woman he couldn't have and remain true to himself. Messed up because he wanted to make his parents proud, especially now that Mama was sick. She needed to know her baby boy was going to be something besides a goof-off.

He stared up into the night sky, wishing he could see the stars, but knowing they were obliterated by the city lights. God was up there somewhere. He was here, too, according to everything Nic believed, though tonight God felt far away.

"I could use some advice, Lord," he murmured.

He downed the rest of the cola and crushed the

empty can in one hand. After a minute, he rose, balanced the crooked can on a window ledge and then jogged toward the parking lot.

"You love her." His mother's words were a statement of fact, not a question. As always, Mama had suspected the truth, probably before he had.

"Yeah." The admission was a lead weight.

Like he'd done as a boy when trouble came, Nic sat at the table in his parents' terra-cotta kitchen, surrounded by the familiar trappings of his family. See-through jars of pasta lined the counter. Copper pots hung over the center island, shiny in the artificial light. The smell of chocolate chip cookies, warm from the oven, and freshly perked coffee filled the place.

When he'd asked God for advice, this had been his answer.

Just being here gave him hope that he'd get through this in one piece.

His mother and dad sat together, a united force as they'd always been, facing him. The dark circles beneath Mama's eyes made him feel a little guilty.

"Maybe I shouldn't have come. Mom's not up to this." He started to rise.

"Sit." Dad didn't say a lot, but he meant what he said. "Tell us what happened."

Nic sat and let the words tumble out. When he got to the part about retaking the MCAT, his mother gasped. "And you didn't tell us? Oh, Nicky, why?"

Before Nic could answer, his father spoke. "Rosalie, listen to what the boy is not saying."

With a quizzical expression his mother studied his father and then him. She nodded. "I see. Yes, I see. You didn't fail this time, but you're not happy about it."

More miserable than he could say, he dropped his face into his hands. "I don't know what to do."

"What do you want?"

There was the million-dollar question. "I want the people I love to be happy, but I can't be something I'm not. I thought I could, for you, for Cassidy—"

His mother placed a soft hand over his. "Stop. Look at me, Nic, and listen good."

Nic raised his face and saw the deep love glimmering in her Sicilian eyes.

"God gave you a special gift. You bring joy just by being alive. When you arrive, the room lights up, people laugh and feel happy."

"Nothing special about being a goof-off."

"You see it as a goof-off, but we know better." She patted him. "Oh, don't misunderstand, we've had our concerns, but no more with you than with the other children. We've watched you struggle and grow and come out stronger. Under that handsome smile is the heart of a lion. Your dad and I are proud of the man you've become."

Unaccustomed moisture sprang to Nic's eyes. His parents thought that? He looked at his father and saw his mother's remarks echoed there. "But Gabe and Adam are lawyers. I thought—" He shook his head. "I don't know. That being a doctor would make us even."

"We're proud of your brothers, but what you do is just as important. Law and medicine are noble careers, but so is firefighting. If not for you, baby Alex would never have made it into the hands of a physician. You saved him first."

He'd never looked at it that way.

"So you aren't going to disown me if I withdraw my medical school application?" he asked, only half joking.

His dad pushed the plate of cookies toward him. "My father was a baker and his father before him was a baker. I chose to be a baker, too, not because Papa expected it, but because I wanted to. I like the smell of yeast and the feel of the dough. I like making people smile with an extra donut in the bag. I'm a happy man, fulfilling the destiny God gave me. All I ever wanted for my children was the same—to be fulfilled and content in their lives. You don't have to be a baker or a doctor or a lawyer. You just have to be Nic, the man God intended you to be." Leo sat back and breathed in through his nose, his barrel chest expanding. "And I will be proud."

The speech was one of the longest he'd ever heard from his father. Nic took a cookie, thinking of the love his parents put into everything they baked at Carano's Bakery. He understood that kind of passion because he felt it every time he donned his uniform.

A weight seemed to lift from his shoulders.

"Thanks, Dad. Mom." He bit into the buttery cookie and savored the semisweet chocolate on his tongue, but savored more the knowledge that his family was behind him. "You always know what to say."

"What about your relationship with Cassidy?"

His mother's gentle question plummeted him back into the depths of despair.

"Unless I leave the fire department, there is no relationship."

"Your career is your calling. Turning your back on your life's work is not the answer to Cassidy's problem." Rosalie reached for the coffeepot, but Leo beat her to it. "Does she love you?"

"I thought so. Apparently not enough."

"I saw her looking at you the way Mama looks at me." Pouring more coffee into each cup, Leo winked at Rosalie, who winked back. "She loves you. But fear rules her life."

"She has reason to be afraid, Dad." He'd told them about the tragedy in the Philippines. "She was buried alive, her parents dead, smoke circling like a vulture. Now her sister's dead."

Rosalie spooned creamer into her cup and stirred but didn't drink. "These are all tragic circumstances, but the Lord never intended any of us to be a slave to fear."

"There's nothing I can do to change her mind, Mom. The decision is hers."

His mother got a look on her face that he'd seen dozens of times. He and his siblings called it the mother tiger look—protective, determined and full of fierce love.

"There *is* something we can do." She extended an upturned palm to each side, capturing his hand and his father's. "Let's pray."

Chapter Fourteen

Nic drove around for a while after leaving his parents' house. Sometimes he prayed. Sometimes he just drove and thought about what a great family he had. He was blessed beyond anything he deserved. Thankfully he'd wised up.

He'd wised up about a couple of other things, too. If he loved Cassidy the way his dad loved his mother, he wouldn't sit around moping. He would take action.

But his ego still smarted from her rejection. If she loved him, she'd try harder to overcome her fears.

The dilemma warred inside him like two gladiators, each as strong as the other.

The night was warm and humid. He kicked on the AC and then the CD player. Worship music flowed out.

The CD was Cassidy's. She must have forgotten it the night of the race.

Considering the CD as good an excuse as any, he turned his truck toward the apartment complex where he parked in a no-parking zone directly beneath the steps leading to Cassidy's apartment.

From his own home came the sounds of the party in progress. In the shadowy darkness, he made a wry face. His friends hadn't even missed him. He rubbed his chest with the flat of his hand. Today was an ego-crushing day and the ego at risk was his.

He took the CD, jogged up the steps and pounded on Cassidy's door. From inside he heard the television playing. Someone laughed. She was having a good time without him. His ego took another nosedive. Here he was moping and she wasn't.

Nic fidgeted, waiting only a few seconds before pounding again. If she didn't open the door quick, he might chicken out.

The door swung open. Backlit by pale lamplight, Cassidy looked as pretty as an angel, her hair glowing gold. Nic swallowed, more nervous than he could remember.

"Hey," he said.

"Nic."

"You forgot this." He held out the CD.

She took it. "Thanks."

He was hoping she'd invite him in. She didn't.

Okay, why had he come up here? To make a fool of himself?

"I thought you might want it back."

"I appreciate it."

"The music's good."

"I like it."

Talk about a sparkling conversation. This was not one.

Behind her, voices murmured. Nic's defenses rose. Was she with another guy?

A female voice called, "Cassidy, who's out there?"

His shoulders relaxed the tiniest bit.

Cassidy called over her shoulder. "It's Nic."

As she turned her head, the light illuminated her face. Nic saw what he hadn't seen in the shadow. Puffy, swollen eyes were redder than her nose. She'd been crying.

His heart dropped to the toes of his Nikes. Okay, that was it. No crying on his shift.

He grabbed her hand. "We need to talk. Let's take a drive."

She shook her head, pulling away. Pale hair swished softly against the shoulders of a shiny blue blouse. "I can't. I have company."

At that moment, two teenage girls appeared at her side. He recognized them from her Bible Study.

"We're not company," one of them said, eyeing Nic with interest. "Go."

Apparently, they'd overheard his invitation.

Still Cassidy hesitated, but something in the way she looked at him said she wanted to go.

"Come on, Cass. Just for a while. We need to talk."

"Talking won't do any good, Nic. Besides Alex is already in bed for the night."

Nic's hopes fell.

One of the girls gave Cassidy's back a little push. "Go on, Cassidy. Katie and I will watch Alex."

Nic held his breath while the love of his life tee-tered on the edge. Finally, when he was at the point of light-headedness, she capitulated.

Though her expression was grim and hopeless, she said, "Let me get my shoes."

Cassidy sat against the passenger door wondering why she'd agreed to this ride with Nic. Being this close to him again was nothing but torture.

"Aren't you missing your own party?" The question was almost an accusation. She'd seen the trail of people roaming in and out of the parking lot and heard the gaiety from below. The notion that he could throw a party only hours after their breakup hurt. For all his declarations of caring for her, the party spoke volumes about his sincerity.

He made a smooth turn onto the main highway. "I missed what wasn't there."

"Meaning what? Mandy or Brandy or Candy didn't show up?" She sounded every bit like a jealous woman. She shouldn't have come with him tonight, not while she was still so emotional. She was the one who couldn't move forward. She was the one who was stuck in fear. Why should she be upset if Nic wanted to move on with his life as soon as possible?

Because she loved him, that was why.

As they pulled into heavier traffic, he glanced her way. The dash lights cast him in gray shadow with only the focal points of his bone structure clear. Except for the dark coal of vividly alive eyes, he was like a sculpture, perfectly cast.

He never bothered to counter her foolish questions. Instead his words touched her to the core. "You've been crying."

She crossed her arms against a rush of longing to be in his arms again. "Is that what you wanted to talk about?"

"I want to discuss anything that makes you unhappy."

"Don't do this, Nic. Caring about each other is not enough. I know you care for me and Alex." Her voice choked. "We care for you, too."

"What about love? Is love enough?"

Was he saying he loved her? Even if he did, what good was it under the circumstances?

She closed her eyes against the rush of hopelessness. "Love can't enter into the equation. In some weird way, I feel that if I don't love you, I'm protecting you. People I love die."

"That's not rational, sweetheart." The baritone was gentle, but she heard his frustration. "You have to know that."

"Of course I know," she moaned, desperate for him to understand. This was for his good as well as her own. "But I can't help my feelings. Wonderful people I love die. That's a fact. You work in a dangerous profession. Your life is in jeopardy every time you go to work. I can't live with that kind of worry, Nic. I can't."

He was silent for a few seconds, attention focused on the road and traffic. An eighteen-wheeler passed, lights bright and blinding. Nic's truck wobbled in the powerful wake.

A sigh as soft as Alex's breath escaped him. Cassidy felt his heaviness and ached for all the things she couldn't change.

"We're praying for you," he said quietly. "That's the main thing I wanted to tell you. Mom, Dad, me. I went to their house tonight. We prayed together. We'll keep praying."

The revelation moved her to tears.

Cassidy pressed a hand to her forehead. What was wrong with her? She had faith for so many things. Why couldn't she have faith to conquer this?

Somewhere she'd heard that fear was the opposite of faith. The statement had hurt her terribly. She wanted to have more faith. She just didn't know how to get it.

"Take me home, Nic. This is only making things worse."

By now, they'd driven to the outskirts of town where the traffic thinned and a few stars could be seen above the city lights. Nic's shoulders slumped and she knew she'd hurt him yet again. She hated herself and wished a thousand times she'd followed her instincts the first time they'd met and stayed away.

But this man wasn't the Notorious Nic she'd wanted to avoid. This man was solid and strong and caring, and far more dangerous to her heart.

Without argument, Nic hit the signal light and turned, taking the side streets back to the apartment.

They'd driven several blocks, through one quiet neighborhood and into another when a frighteningly familiar scent invaded Cassidy's nostrils.

"Nic."

He glanced her way, eyes wary. "Yeah?"

"Do you smell that?" The blood began to pound in her temples. "It's smoke, Nic. I smell smoke."

The words were barely out of her mouth when Nic slammed on the brakes.

"There," he said. "That house."

The dash lights reflected off Nic's face, painting him yellow and red—the colors of fire. Slowly, she turned her head, mesmerized by the smoke billowing from one side of a sprawling brick house.

"Call 9-1-1." He popped the latch on his seat belt, reaching for the door handle at the same time.

Cassidy grabbed his arm. "What are you doing?"

"There may be people inside."

The knowledge of what he was about to do slammed into her with the force of a freight train. Rising panic clogged her lungs.

"No!" The scream was ripped from somewhere deep inside. She clawed at him. "You can't."

He placed a hand over hers, a light touch of reassurance.

Gently but firmly, he said, "I have to be sure no one is in there. Don't worry. It's only smoke."

She was not reassured. Flames could burst forth at any moment.

Frantically, she clung, desperate to hold him back. "No. I won't let you. Something bad will happen."

In a rush now, he peeled her fingers away. "What if that was Alex in there?"

What could she say to that? Stricken and terrified, her hands fell uselessly to her sides. Nic slid from the truck, his mind already leaving her behind as he focused on the burning house.

"Promise me you won't do anything stupid," she begged. "Promise me."

He had already moved a step away but he came back, shot her a cocky grin and saluted. "My middle name is careful. Now, call 9-1-1 and get me some help." He started to shut the door but leaned back in. "I love you."

Then he was gone, running full tilt toward the inferno.

With shaking fingers, Cassidy punched in the numbers, reported the blaze and then turned to press her face against the side window, hoping and praying to see Nic return.

The fire was young but growing. An eerie golden glow shone through a window on one side of the house.

She saw Nic running around the structure, pounding on windows and doors, his voice raised in alarm. He disappeared around back and then reappeared on the front porch, pounding and yelling. To her horror, he shouldered the front door open and disappeared inside. Smoke gushed out like fog beneath the streetlights.

To hold back the cries of despair, Cassidy's hands pressed against her mouth.

"Oh, God in Heaven," she begged. "Protect him."

A litany of prayers pouring from her lips and heart, she rolled down the passenger window and coughed when smoke seeped across the lawn and into her lungs. How much worse must conditions be for Nic inside the house? She shuddered and turned to stare down the street, but all she saw were darkened homes and a few cars moving parallel to the quiet neighborhood.

Where was that fire engine? Why weren't they here?

Most importantly, where was Nic?

Mouth dry as sandpaper, she watched in terror as the blaze grew in power, like a beast fueled by all it devoured. A windowpane popped. Glass shattered.

Cassidy gripped the door handle.

In the next moment, she was standing on the grass, outside the truck, the stench of smoke thick and acrid.

Nic was in there. Her Nic.

Suddenly, one side of the roof leaned. A crash echoed across the yard.

Cassidy jerked, her horrified gasp the only human sound in the empty, lonely darkness. A terrible certainty washed over her in waves that left her shaking. If the roof had caved, Nic could be trapped.

In her memory, she was transported back to two unspeakable days beneath bricks and dirt, waiting for the unseen flames to claim her. Dear Lord, please don't let that happen to Nic. Please don't take him, too.

The fire spread, glowing in several windows now, but the man she loved did not return. What if the blaze had already overtaken him?

"No!" she screamed. Galvanizing anger ripped through her. With strength she didn't know she possessed, Cassidy's wobbly legs began to churn. They propelled her across the grass and toward the inferno. She would not let Nic die. She would not let fire steal someone else she loved.

Her feet hit the porch and thick smoke boiled as she

charged through the door. A wall of heat slammed into her, scorching her lungs, sucking away her air.

In the distant night, sirens screamed, too far away. They wouldn't get here in time. She was the only one available to help Nic. She was the only one who could save him from the monster.

Please help me, Lord. Help me be brave. Help me find him.

Dozens of half-memorized scriptures flowed into her smoke-fogged mind. She grasped onto each one as if holding on to sanity.

Even in the shadow of death, I will fear no evil for He is with me. He is my fortress and strong tower. Even if I walk through a fire, the Lord God of Israel, the Holy One, is with me. God is with me. God is with me.

A beam crashed in front of her. She screamed and jumped back. Sparks shot out, burning her arms.

With a sob, she turned, trying to get her bearings. The gray smoke was everywhere and growing darker by the minute.

Where could Nic be?

A dog barked. She started in that direction. From somewhere she heard the crackle of fire but could see little other than thick, stinking smoke—just like in the Philippines.

She had charged into her worst nightmare.

"Nic! Where are you? Nic?" She screamed until the smoke stole her voice, refusing to be driven back by the crawling, clawing terror. Nic was in here somewhere. She wouldn't leave without him.

* * *

Nic jogged toward the curb to wait as Engine Four turned onto the street, lights and sirens in Code Three, and headed toward the burning house. The blast of noise brought people from their safe homes to gawk in curiosity. Nic paid them no mind.

From his cursory search, the blazing structure appeared empty, though for a minute there he'd been convinced he'd heard a voice.

The fire engine was still a couple of minutes away so he made his way to his truck to reassure Cassidy that all was well. Though she'd been terrified, he'd had no choice but to go against her wishes. With a heavy heart, he figured his decision was the final nail in the coffin of their relationship. He'd proven to her that he'd put himself in danger for someone else's benefit. This was who he was and what he did. He was finally proud of that, a pride Cassidy couldn't share. No amount of talking would change her mind now.

As he approached the vehicle, Nic slowed, squinting through the darkness. Then he froze. His heart ricocheted against his rib cage.

Cassidy was not inside the truck.

Whirling, he searched the area. Her pale hair would be easy to spot, even at night.

"Cassidy?" he called, pulse starting to race in an ominous manner. He looked toward the dwelling. No way. She wouldn't have gone in there. She was too afraid.

The truth slapped him in the face. When the roof

rumbled, he'd escaped through a side door. She hadn't seen him exit.

His knees went weak.

"Oh God," he breathed the prayer. Cassidy was in there. He knew that with a certainty he could not explain.

He started to run. From behind him shouts went up. "Stay back! Stay back!"

The fire truck was still a block away.

"There's a woman inside," he yelled as his feet clattered onto the porch.

Sirens screamed closer but not close enough.

Praying as he'd never prayed before, Nic flung himself into the inferno.

Chapter Fifteen

Cassidy was lost. Total blackness encompassed her. She gagged at the stench of smoke everywhere.

Tears streamed down her face. Her eyes burned so badly she could barely keep them open. Even with her shirtsleeve over her mouth, rasping gasps issued from her throat.

She was in big trouble.

Vague memories of elementary school programs flickered in her head.

Smoke rose. Get down low. She went to her knees and then lower, pressing her face to the cooler, hard-surfaced floor. Better, but not much. Her heart pounded hard and fast, pleading for air. Belly crawling, she felt around her for a landmark of some kind to guide her out.

Her lungs screamed.

"Nic!" she called again.

Her head hurt, spinning with a gray fog as thick as

the smoke. She couldn't be sure where the dizziness ended and the smoke began.

"Nic," she cried, though the effort cost her.

He was here somewhere, trapped and alone. She had to save him. No more deaths. The room faded. She struggled to keep moving, her limbs heavier and heavier.

God is with me. God is with me.

She pressed her cheek against the floor to rest. A momentary reprieve. Only for minute. A minute's rest.

Outward sound ceased. The sound inside her head roared loudly.

God is with me. I will not fear.

Peace flowed through her like cool water.

Then all went dark.

Nic wasn't worried about losing his life, but he thought he might lose his mind.

Cassidy, that crazy, brave, incredible woman, was in here somewhere, facing the beast because of him.

He yanked his shirt over his nose and mouth and hit the floor, crawling on all fours through the acrid smoke. For the moment, the flames appeared confined to the kitchen to his left, but smoke filled the residence. Whatever had started the blaze had smoldered for a while.

"Cassidy! Where are you? Talk to me, Cass."

He was certain he'd heard her calling his name from this direction. "Cass."

No answer.

Prickles of fear crawled over his skin. He fought them off. Panic used precious air.

Pray, Mama, he thought, *and this time I'll pray, too.*

God, you know where she is. Show me. Not for me. For her. For baby Alex.

She'd come in here to rescue him. He could barely wrap his mind around that precious, foolish act.

With rigid discipline that would impress his chief, he kept moving, searching along walls, sweeping his arms toward the center, praying every minute for contact.

Time was passing, seconds or minutes, he wasn't sure which. Little time remained before the smoke would be too much. Already tears streamed down his cheeks. His eyes burned ferociously.

One more pass, Lord. Give me strength.

"Cassidy!" he called, expecting nothing but hoping with all his being.

The sweetest sound echoed back, weak and raspy, a mere whimper, but close. "Nic."

From out of the smoke and darkness, Cassidy fell toward him. His heart surged. He gripped her arm. It was her. It was really her.

"Thank you, Lord," he croaked and felt Cassidy's answering nod. To her, he whispered, "Let's get out of here."

Upon entry, he'd mentally marked his escape route. Now, he began to backtrack, tugging Cassidy with him. Outside he could hear the calls of his fellow fire-fighters doing their jobs. A spray of water pummeled the side of the house.

A window popped. He heard glass shatter. Cassidy jerked. Her ragged breathing had worsened. She coughed.

Nic could take no more. Sucking in the thin air near the floor, he stood, pulling Cassidy up with him. Light beckoned to his right. Chest bursting, he swept her into his arms and raced toward what he hoped was a door.

Stumbling out onto the grass, Nic fell to his knees with Cassidy in his arms. Shouts went up from the bystanders. Footsteps pounded the grass. People ran toward them.

Sucking in great gulps of fresh night air, Nic tenderly cradled Cassidy against his chest. Gratitude welled inside him to the point of overflowing. They were safe. *She* was safe.

He gazed down at the woman he loved, the woman who'd faced death to save him. Emergency lights rotated like strobes, bathing Cassidy's soot-covered skin in alternates of red and blue and white. Nic thought she'd never been more beautiful.

Still fighting for breath, he stroked back her tangled hair and pressed his lips to her forehead. Her eyes fluttered open and then closed again. The knot below Nic's rib cage tightened.

Paramedics, rattling with gear, reached his side.

"I'm okay," Nic said, waving away the woman with a stethoscope. His smoke-scourged voice sounded rough but he'd live. Cassidy was the one who mattered. "Take care of Cassidy."

Cassidy's eyes flew open, wildly seeking his face. Her fingers clutched his shirt. "No. I'm fine, Nic."

She struggled weakly against him as though she wanted to stand. Knowing how impossible that was, Nic held tight. "Shh. It's okay now. You're safe. We're both safe."

The reassurance seemed to be what she needed because she went limp, unresisting.

"We got her, Carano." Strong arms lifted her from him. It was all Nic could do to let her go. He remained on his knees on the grass, watching with heartfelt thanks as the paramedics placed Cassidy on a gurney and administered oxygen.

His head reeled with what had occurred this night. Cassidy had almost died because she'd thought he was inside a collapsing house. She'd faced her greatest fear for his sake. The impact of that silent statement filled him with wonder. He closed his eyes and sucked in more of the precious clean air.

I love her, Lord. I don't want to lose her. Show me what to do now.

Someone clapped a hand on his back. He looked up into the sculpted face of Sam Ridge. "Good job, buddy."

Sam had no idea that this incident had been his fault. If not for him, Cassidy would never have gone inside that house.

Hands on his thighs, Nic kept his gaze trained on Cassidy. "She's the hero."

Sam, in bunker gear, pivoted toward the ambulance. His reflective stripes glowed in the half-light, giving him an eerie quality. "That your woman?"

Reality dropped down upon Nic heavier than a boulder. Cassidy would never be his woman. Not now. If he'd had any hope at all to see her free of fear, tonight had stolen the last chance once and forever.

As the ambulance pulled away with Cassidy and his heart inside, Nic dropped his head. "Not anymore, Sam. Not anymore."

Cassidy was treated and released from the hospital, anxiously insisting on getting home to Alex. The teenagers had been worried, certain something had happened, but her baby boy had slept through it all.

"Are you sure you're all right, Cassidy?" Angie asked, her thin face worried.

Cassidy swallowed, throat raw. "I will be, but thanks for spending the night."

The teen shrugged. "No problem. Is there anything I can do for you?"

Cassidy stood at Alex's crib, filthy and stinking of smoke. Her head hurt, but her heart hurt more. At the emergency room, she'd hoped for a chance to talk to Nic, but he'd never appeared.

She supposed he'd finally gotten the message that she didn't want him in her life.

"I'm such a coward," she whispered.

"Huh?" Angie shifted toward her, stirring the scent of her recent shower and Cassidy's borrowed shampoo.

"Nothing. Talking to myself."

"About Nic?"

She turned incredulous eyes on the fresh-scrubbed teen. "How did you know?"

Angie shrugged, a sly smile spreading over her lips.

"If I had a guy like that, I would talk to myself all the time."

The comment amused Cassidy. "I admit to being a blubbering idiot, but that wasn't what I meant."

"I know. I was kidding. What gives with you two anyway?"

"Nothing."

"Do you love him?"

Discussing Nic with a fifteen-year-old seemed ridiculous, but Angie and the other girls had poured their hearts out to her more times than she could count. "I do."

"So what's the issue?"

Teenagers saw everything in black and white. They thought love was the answer to everything. If you loved a guy, that was enough. Cassidy knew better.

"I messed everything up." Cassidy raised a hand to her forehead, rubbing the ache between her eyebrows. "The situation is too complicated."

Angie made a rude sound of disbelief. "Don't be a dill weed, Cassidy. The guy is a hunk. He's crazy in love with you. Do something about it."

"If only the solution was that easy."

Angie tilted her head as if certain Cassidy was off-center.

Maybe she was.

The mistakes had been hers. The problem was hers. Maybe the solution *was* that easy.

She spun toward Angie, headache suddenly unimportant. "Would you mind keeping an eye on Alex while I run downstairs?"

Angie pointed a hot-pink fingernail at the doorway. "Go. Now."

She was still grinning when Cassidy rushed out
the door.

Somebody was knocking.

Nic struggled up from sleep. A tune played in his
head. "Somebody's knocking, should I let 'em in?"

He chuckled and snuggled his face into the soft
leather. When he'd arrived home, he'd collapsed in the
recliner, too tired and distressed to undress. He must
have fallen asleep instantly.

The pounding came again.

With a growl, he struggled to sit up. The old recliner
squeaked into an upright position.

Somebody *was* knocking.

Curious but seriously dead-headed, he staggered to
the door and wrenched it open.

A gray-faced version of Cassidy spoke in a scratchy
whisper. "I was wrong."

He stared for two beats. Nah, couldn't be. He must
still be asleep. He closed the door and stumbled back
toward the recliner. Halfway there, he stopped. He
rubbed a hand down his face, shook the cobwebs out.
His hands stunk of smoke. Oh man. He wasn't asleep.

"Cassidy?" he said to the dark room.

His heart jump-started. Spinning so fast his head
swam, Nic yanked the door open again. She was still
there. He wilted against the jamb. "I thought you were
a dream."

"I know it's late. Maybe I should have waited until

tomorrow, but—" She stopped and bit down on that fascinating bottom lip.

Nic reached out and snagged her arm. "Get in here."

She obeyed. Fancy that.

"Did I wake you?"

"Nah." He tripped over his shoes. "Well, actually yes, but it's all good. What's up?"

He snapped on a lamp. A yellow cone of light flooded the floor, leaving the perimeter in shadows.

Cassidy fidgeted, twisting her hands in front of her. "I need to talk to you."

Right. Been there, done that. Still had the gaping wound in his chest. "We talked already. You gave me the boot."

Keep it light and breezy, Carano. One heart-stomping in twenty-four hours is enough for anyone.

"Can I take it back?"

He blinked, then scratched the back of his head. "Am I still asleep?"

"I hope not." She took a step. Approximately three feet separated them but she was definitely moving into his space. He didn't want to be happy about that but what could he do? He was a sucker for the woman upstairs.

"Nic." She twisted her hands again. "I love you."

Yeah, yeah, she'd said that before. "You said love wasn't enough."

"Maybe it's not."

"Right." He took a step away from her.

Cassidy moved forward. "Hear me out, please. I've only got so much throat left."

The raspy words reminded him of their night's work. Chastened, he said, "Are you all right? What did the doctors say?"

She waved him off. "Stop it, Nic. Let me say this. I love you. I love everything about you. Tonight when I thought you might die, I…"

Tears sprang to her eyes. She turned her head, trying to hide them.

That's all it took. Nic crossed the space between them in one second flat to cup her face. "You came in after me. Why? Why did you do such a foolish thing?"

Her hot tears fell onto his fingers. She lifted her chin. "Because I love you. I need you in my life. Alex needs you."

Though he'd kick himself tomorrow, Nic tilted her head and kissed the tears from her cheeks. "You are the most confusing woman but I love you anyway. I just wish…"

"What?" she whispered. "What do you wish?"

"I wish you weren't afraid. I wish you could accept me for the man I am. I wish we could be together." He dropped his hand, furious at the ache in his voice. She'd already made herself clear on the topic.

"Nic, that's what I'm trying to tell you." She grabbed his hand and held on tight. "Tonight something happened to me inside that house. I felt God's presence in a way I can't explain. And as I stumbled through the smoke, praying for you, begging God to spare your life, I realized something very important."

"What was it?"

"I'm not afraid anymore. Inside that house, the most

perfect peace settled over me. For the first time since I was a little girl, I knew I could trust God with my life. And with my love. He sent you along to teach me that and to set me free."

Nic was so stunned he couldn't speak.

Cassidy's beautiful, smudged face twisted in worry. "Can you forgive me? Can we start again? Please say I'm not too late."

All he could think of was, "This is a dream. I should lie down."

Cassidy moved closer. Sliding her arms around his waist, she stared up into his face. His heart chugged like a steam engine. Her blue, blue eyes melted him, boring into him, making promises he wanted her to keep. He knew then, knew without a shadow of a doubt, that Cassidy meant exactly what she said.

But he had to hear her say it. "You choose me? Fire helmet and all?"

She nodded. "I do, if you'll have me."

As if the weight of the earth had been lifted from his shoulders, Nic closed his eyes and rejoiced. "I love you, Cassidy."

Her eyes twinkled up at him. "More than Mandy and Rachel and all those others?"

He did his best to appear obtuse. "Who?"

She tiptoed up and bit his chin. "You heard me."

"Ouch. Wicked woman." Then all frivolity disappeared. "I've been looking for you all my life."

"Same here," she murmured. This time she kissed his chin.

"Much better." He smiled into her eyes. "But higher would be stupendously better."

Cassidy's beautiful mouth curved and moved closer. "I think," she whispered, "that's an excellent idea."

Epilogue

Fire Station One seemed unusually quiet as Cassidy pulled into the visitor's parking space, unharnessed Alex and went inside. She stopped in the doorway to listen. Cool air rushed at her, but the usual bustle and murmur of men at work was missing.

Rounding the small kitchen/living area, she headed down the hall past the offices and out toward the truck bay. Three trucks—the engine, the brush pumper and the air truck—were parked side by side as always, gleaming clean and ready to roll at the sound of an alarm. As she approached the double glass door leading out into the bay, a firefighter disappeared between the engine and brush pumper.

In the two months since the fire, Cassidy had found a new freedom as well as newfound happiness. Facing her fears head-on, she now visited the fire station to share lunch with Nic every time he was on duty. Though the other firefighters teased him about losing all his other girlfriends, Nic didn't seem to mind.

The more she learned about him and about his self-less work, the more she fell in love with Nic Carano. He was no longer Notorious Nic, the shallow ladies' man with no substance.

"Nic?" The heels of her sandals sounded hollow in the cavernous bay. "Sam?"

As if he'd been waiting for her voice, Sam Ridge appeared from the space between the two trucks. His expressionless face looked darker than usual. Was the man blushing? "Nic's over here. Come on around."

Those were more words than she'd ever heard the Kiowa say at once. Hoisting a babbling, bouncing Alex higher on one hip, Cassidy followed Sam's order.

As she rounded the front of the massive truck, the sight stopped her in her tracks. A dozen firefighters, a smattering of her and Nic's friends, the Carano family and even her grandmother stood around a white linen-covered table.

Bewildered, Cassidy looked at the grinning faces. "What's going on?"

Nic, looking crisp and handsome in dress blues, stepped from behind the gathering and strode toward her. The *tap-tap* of his black shoes matched the rhythm of her heart. Intensely dark eyes latched onto hers and wouldn't let go. She knew him well enough to see his nerves, though others wouldn't notice the rapid rise and fall of his chest or the way his nostrils flared the tiniest bit.

"Nic?" What was going on?

He took Alex from her arms, handing the baby off

to his sister. Then he shocked her silent when he took her hand and dropped to one knee.

"Cassidy Luanne Willis." He stopped and cleared his throat. Someone—Adam, she thought—chuckled. "When God brought you into my life, I was a mess. I didn't know it, but I was. I'd been running from God, running from my family." One shoulder rose and fell. "Just running in general, like a lost pup. Then you and Alex came along and suddenly the whole world took on new meaning."

Cassidy touched his cheek with trembling fingers. She smiled, felt her lips trembling, too, and her eyes growing moist. Was he about to propose? Here? In front of all these people?

She opened her mouth to speak but closed it again when Nic reached into his pocket and removed a black velvet ring box. When he flipped up the lid, Cassidy gasped at the stunning engagement ring inside.

"I love you, Cassidy. And I love that little boy over there. What I'm trying to say is this." His fingers shook as he removed the diamond solitaire. "Will you marry me? Will you do me the honor of being my wife?"

He slid the ring onto her third finger. Cassidy stared at her hand in stunned joy and then at the man she loved with everything inside her.

She didn't hesitate a second.

"Yes!" she screamed. "Yes!"

Her knees gave way then and she tumbled down, falling against Nic's sturdy form. His strong, firefighter arms circled around her, holding her safe. She could feel him trembling, too, and was humbled by the power and beauty of his love.

The tears she'd been holding back fell like rain. She buried her face in Nic's shoulder and sobbed.

In the next moment, they were surrounded by well-wishers. Voices rose and fell in laughter and congratulations. Cameras flashed.

With Nic's hand rubbing soothing circles on her back and his amused voice whispering sweet things in her ear, Cassidy finally hiccuped away the joyful sobs. Together they stood, Nic's arm firmly around her waist, snugging her to his side, right where she wanted to be.

He leaned to whisper against her hair. "I love you. Do you like my surprise?"

Through a watery smile she beamed up at him. "I love your surprise. But I love you more."

He patted his chest twice. "That's what I'm talking about right there. Come on. There's cake."

"From Carano's Bakery?"

"Where else? The best Italian cream cake on the planet."

Cassidy groaned in mock dismay. "I'll never fit into a wedding dress."

Her grandmother, dressed in pumps and a blue business suit, approached with her usual no-nonsense bossiness. "Cassidy, we need to talk."

Cassidy fought not to let the woman ruin her wonderful engagement party.

"Thank you for being here, Grandmother," she

said, hoping to circumvent any unpleasant remarks. "It means a lot to me."

"Of course I'd be here. You're my only granddaughter." Eleanor sniffed and Cassidy was astonished to see tears glistening in her eyes. "Apparently this young man loves you. He seems to be solvent, a man of character, and he's gone to a great deal of trouble to make this surprise engagement party work. You'll do well with him."

Cassidy was too stunned for words. Grandmother approved? She had never approved of anything Cassidy did. Cassidy turned her head the slightest bit to stare at Nic in wonder. Amusement twinkled from his eyes. He winked. Somehow he'd worked his charm on Eleanor Bassett.

"Now," Grandmother said, returning the attention to herself. "The two of you need to adopt Alex. A child needs two parents. I've already discussed the issue with my attorney. He'll take care of everything, paid in full. Just call him."

Though barely able to believe her ears, Cassidy was deeply touched. For once, Grandmother's bossiness did not offend. "Thank you, Grandmother. This means more than I can say."

"Well." Awkwardly, Eleanor patted her on the shoulder. "I think I'll have some punch."

With the regal posture of a queen, she moved toward the table where Captain Summers dipped golden punch into clear cups and Gabe Carano slid sandwiches onto paper plates. Next to him, his wife cut perfect slivers of Italian cream cake. Nic's father, Leo, captured all the proceedings on video, his balding head shiny with perspiration.

"I thought about pizza," Nic said.

"This is perfect. Perfect."

"Yeah," he said happily. "I think so, too."

He led her to the circle of folding chairs where several children, women and firefighters were gathered. He bent to kiss his mother on the cheek. "Doing okay?"

Although dark circles rimmed the eyes so like her son's, Rosalie touched Nic's cheek and beamed. "Happiest day I've had in months."

The words were true and a painful reminder that the Carano family faced struggles of their own. Yet, their faith and love sustained them. Cassidy vowed to remember and to continue that legacy in her own family. Hers and Nic's.

"Come on, you two, kiss for the camera." Nic's brother Adam pointed a digital in their direction.

Nic laughed and pumped his dark eyebrows. "I can handle that."

As he bent to kiss her, the fire alarm began to wail. Nic jerked upright. The other firefighters were already in motion, running toward the engine.

"Sorry, sweetheart. I gotta go." He kissed her nose.

"I know. It's fine. Go." And she told the truth. Fear no longer ruled her life. "I'll be here when you return."

He hesitated, fingers on her face. "You're really okay?"

She smiled, heart full. "I really am."

He stared at her for one more second. "I love you."

"And I love you with everything I am and all that I'll ever have. You are my hero."

"You're mine, too," he whispered, bending to press his lips to hers. Though the kiss was brief, she felt the love all the way to her toes.

As she watched her firefighter dive into the open door of the truck, heard the doors slam and watched the shiny red engine roll into traffic, horns and lights blaring, a beautiful, joyous peace flowed over her. God never promised that life would be without heartache but He'd promised to always be there to comfort, love and heal.

With His help, Cassidy had walked through the fire and come out stronger. She fully trusted that her hero would always do the same.

An arm went around her shoulders from the left, and then another from the right. She looked up to find herself bracketed by Adam and Gabe. In the next instant, she was surrounded by Caranos, stalwart and faithful and supportive.

Struck with awe, Cassidy could almost hear God whispering in her ear.

For as long as she could remember, she'd longed for a big loving family. Now, here they were, full of smiles and laughter and love, eager to welcome her into the fold.

* * * * *

Dear Reader,

Ideas for books come about in a variety of ways. Sometimes I get an idea from an incident in real life or from a song or a single turn of phrase that tickles my fancy. Sometimes an idea arrives like a gift. This is what happened to me with *The Baby Bond*. About the same time I began brainstorming ideas for my next Love Inspired, my grandson was born. A few days after Noah's birth, my son sent a photo of the new baby. Since my son, the baby's daddy, is a firefighter, the photographer had the brilliant notion to place the newborn inside my son's upturned helmet. The moment I saw that precious photo that spoke of the love of a firefighter for a baby boy, the wheels began to turn inside my head. What if a firefighter fell in love with an orphaned baby he rescued from a burning house? In a short time, the idea for *The Baby Bond* came to be.

I truly hope you've enjoyed the story. I love hearing from readers so feel free to write me c/o Steeple Hill, 233 Broadway, Suite 1001, New York, NY 10279 or through my website at www.lindagoodnight.com

Warmly,

Linda Goodnight

Questions for Discussion

1. Name the main characters. Who was your favorite? Why?

2. Could you relate to any of the characters in the book? How?

3. What incident drew Cassidy and Nic together?

4. Although a Christian, Cassidy was riddled with fear. What was she afraid of? Why?

5. Do you think Cassidy's fears were realistic? Is it possible to be so afraid that fear interferes with a person's life choices? Have you ever known anyone like that?

6. How can someone overcome great fear? Do you believe facing a fear will make it better or worse? How can faith help a person deal with fear?

7. Cassidy says someone told her that fear is the opposite of faith. Rather than helping, the statement hurt her. Why? Have you ever been told you didn't have enough faith? How did it make you feel?

8. Nic felt pressured by his family. In what way? Were his feelings justified? Explain.

9. Have you ever struggled under family expectations? In what way? How did you handle the issues?

10. Some people believe that everything happens for a reason. Do you? Can you find scripture to back up your opinion?

11. When Cassidy chose to raise her orphaned nephew, her grandmother fought against the decision. Why?

12. Nic's brothers claimed he slid by on his parents' prayers. What does that mean? Is such a thing scripturally possible? What does the Bible say about the power of a praying parent?

13. Scripture says that love will cast out fear. How does this relate to what Cassidy did at the end of the book?

SPECIAL EXCERPT FROM

Love Inspired

A new job has brought Heath Monroe to Whisper Falls
Cassie Blackwell might just convince him to stay. Read o
for a preview of THE LAWMAN'S HONOR
by Linda Goodnight, Book #4 in the
WHISPER FALLS *series.*

As he left the garage and started down Easy Street,
jaywalker caught his attention.

He whipped the car into a U-turn and parked at an ang
in front of Evie's Sweets and Eats. He pressed the windo
button and watched as Cassie stepped up on the curb.

"Morning," he said.

"How are you?"

Better now.

"Healing." He touched the bruise over his left cheekbor
"How's it look?"

"Awful." But her smile softened the word.

Cassie had something that appealed to him. A kind of cl
wholesomeness mixed with Southern friendly and a dash
real pretty.

He hitched his chin toward the bakery. "Were you goi
in there?"

"Lunch. Want to come?"

"Best invitation I've had all day." The ankle screamed
the first step, causing an involuntary hiss that infuriated Hea

Cassie paused, watching him. "You're still in pain."

"No, I'm fine."

She made a disbelieving noise in the back of her thro
"You remind me so much of my brother."

"Must be a great guy."

"The best. You should meet him."

"I'd like that."

"Come to church Sunday and you will."

With his ankle throbbing, he somehow held the door open [fo]r Cassie and limped inside a small business. The smells of [fre]sh breads and fruit Danish mingled with a showcase of pies [an]d homemade candies.

"A cop's dream," he muttered, only half joking.

A middle-aged woman—Evie, he supposed—created their [or]ders while maintaining a stream of small talk with Cassie. [Ca]ssie took the lunch tray before he could and led the way to [a t]able.

"So how bad is your leg? I mean really. No bluffing. Any [ot]her injuries besides that?"

"Just the ankle. Sprained. And a couple of bruises here and [the]re." Bruises that ripped the air out of his lungs.

"When do you want your mani-pedi?"

Heath choked, grabbed for the tea glass and managed to [sw]allow. "My what?"

The thought of Cassie touching him again gave him a [fu]nny tingle. A nice tingle, come to think of it. Did she have [an]y idea the thoughts that went through a man's head at the [mo]st inappropriate times?

"You don't remember our conversation?" she asked. "Is [the] concussion still bothering you?"

"Slight headache if I get tired. Nothing to worry about." [Th]en why did he suddenly have all these thoughts about a [wo]man he'd only just met?

Is it possible Heath's found something besides work to
focus on? Find out in award-winning author
Linda Goodnight's THE LAWMAN'S HONOR,
on sale in March 2014,
wherever Love Inspired® books are sold!

Cowboy, wanderer… Father?

Nate Lyster and Mia Verbeek are in perfect agreement—that letting someone new into your heart is much too risky. Left on her own with four kids, Mia can't let just anyone get close, while wandering cowboy Nate learned young that love now means heartbreak later.

But when a fire turns Mia's life upside down, Nate is the only one who can get through to her traumatized son—and her hea If Nate and Mia can forget the hurts of their pasts, they might g everything they want. But if they let fear win, a perfect love cou pass them by….

A Father in the Making
by
Carolyn Aarsen

Available April 2014 wherever
Love Inspired books and ebooks are sold.

LI8

SUSPENSE

RIVETING INSPIRATIONAL ROMANCE

FOR THE CHILD

Foster mother Noelle Whitman adores the little girl she's caring for. Noelle has terrible memories of her own foster care experience and vows to do right by this child. But when the girl's father, fresh out of jail for murdering his estranged wife, arrives for his daughter, Noelle is worried. The former SWAT team member insists he was framed. But moments later, someone shoots at Caleb, and the three are forced on the run. Protective and kind, Caleb is nothing like the embittered ex-con she expected. And learning to trust him may be the only way to survive.

TOP
COPS

WRONGLY ACCUSED

by
LAURA SCOTT

Available April 2014 wherever
Love Inspired books and ebooks are sold.

LIS44591R

OPEN TO LOVE?

After refusing to give in to an unwanted engagement,
Alice Hawthorne is determined to stake her own claim durir
the Oklahoma Land Rush. But when she meets Elijah Thornto
can the preacher convince her to open her heart?

BRIDEGROOM
BROTHERS

The Preacher's Bride Claim

by

LAURIE KINGERY

Available April 2014 wherever
Love Inspired books and ebooks are sold.

LIH2

Love Inspired

WITH HIS BLESSING

When Rick Salinger became a Christian, his entire life changed. Now a pastor in remote northern Canada, Rick focuses on his congregation and working with the kids at a center for troubled boys. But when the center's new nurse arrives with her own struggling son, Rick fears getting too close. Widowed mom Cassie Crockett lost most everything because of him. How can he share his past when she's struggling with faith? With the Lord's guidance, Rick will help the sweet family build a new life…one that just might include him.

North Country Family
by Lois Richer

Northern Lights

LI87872

A COWBOY WITHOUT A NAME

The only thing Brand Duggan's outlaw kin ever gave him was a
undeserved reputation. Once he's through breaking horses, he'
leave Eden Valley. Staying means risk—and heartache. And he h
no business falling for someone like Sybil Bannerman.

The rugged cowboy who rescues her from a stampede is just th
kind of man Sybil Bannerman's editor wants her to write about
Yet she has no idea how big a secret Brand Duggan carries, unti
her life is threatened. Despite the evidence against him, Sybil ca
walk away from the man who lassoed her heart….

COWBOYS
OF
Eden Valley

Winning Over the Wrangler

by

LINDA FORD

*Available March 2014 wherever Love Inspired Historica
books and ebooks are sold.*

Find us on Facebook at
www.Facebook.com/LoveInspiredBooks